MW00882632

Coast Range Mountains

Sacramento River

Sacramento Valley

Sierra Nevada Mountains

North Fork

Auburn

Middle Fork

American River

South Fork

L. Tahoe

Carson City

NEVADA

Folsom Lake

**Sutter's Mill**

★ **SACRAMENTO**

 Mockingbird Valley Ranch

Rancho Las Posas del Sierra

Wakamatsu Colony

● **Berkeley**

San Francisco

© 2013 by John A. O'Connor All rights reserved.

SCALE OF MILES

0  10  20  30  40  50  60

State Capitals  ★

The
**American River**
in
# CALIFORNIA

SACRAMENTO
AND
VICINITY

Auburn ○

Roseville ○

American River

Folsom ○
Fair Oaks

★ **Sacramento**

# American River: Tributaries

## BOOK ONE OF THE AMERICAN RIVER TRILOGY

To Reilly —
Here's to your career!

## Mallory M. O'Connor

**ARCHWAY** PUBLISHING

Copyright © 2017 Mallory M. O'Connor.

All rights reserved. No part of this book may be used or reproduced by any means, graphic, electronic, or mechanical, including photocopying, recording, taping or by any information storage retrieval system without the written permission of the author except in the case of brief quotations embodied in critical articles and reviews.

This is a work of fiction. All of the characters, names, incidents, organizations, and dialogue in this novel are either the products of the author's imagination or are used fictitiously.

Scripture taken from the King James Version of the Bible.

Archway Publishing books may be ordered through booksellers or by contacting:

Archway Publishing
1663 Liberty Drive
Bloomington, IN 47403
www.archwaypublishing.com
1 (888) 242-5904

Because of the dynamic nature of the Internet, any web addresses or links contained in this book may have changed since publication and may no longer be valid. The views expressed in this work are solely those of the author and do not necessarily reflect the views of the publisher, and the publisher hereby disclaims any responsibility for them.

Any people depicted in stock imagery provided by Thinkstock are models, and such images are being used for illustrative purposes only. Certain stock imagery © Thinkstock.

ISBN: 978-1-4808-4867-2 (sc)
ISBN: 978-1-4808-4868-9 (e)

Library of Congress Control Number: 2017909280

Print information available on the last page.

Archway Publishing rev. date: 6/27/2017

*For my son Chris,*
*a native of California.*

# ACKNOWLEDGEMENTS

Where to begin. My mother, a librarian, surrounded me with books from the beginning, and encouraged me to read them all. My father believed in me, and told me I could do anything provided I worked hard enough. Thanks as well to my husband John and my son Chris who cheered me on and provided criticism and suggestions. Their support has been invaluable.

In 1976 I attended a writer's conference in Gainesville, Florida, where I met John Knowles, author of *A Separate Peace*. Knowles critiqued the partial manuscript that I submitted for the conference and encouraged me to keep writing. He subsequently asked me to send him the complete manuscript and helped me secure an agent. Although I was ultimately unsuccessful in finding a publisher for my work, I never forgot his encouragement and his faith in my ability as a writer.

And I would be remiss if I didn't also thank my friends who have read my work over many years and offered criticism and advice: Diana Kurz, Elizabeth Barakah Hodges, Charlotte Porter, Michael Johnson, Raphael Haftka, Patience Mason, the members of my Book Club, and my good friends and Pod-mates in the Writer's Alliance of Gainesville. I owe you all a debt of gratitude.

# CAST OF CHARACTERS

### The Ancestors

Cormac Everette McPhalan—Irish immigrant who arrives in California in 1849 to seek his fortune. He is the original owner/founder of Mockingbird Valley Ranch on the American River.

Juan Dominguez Morales—Son of a Californio rancher, he inherits Rancho Las Posas on the American River, only to lose everything after California becomes a state. He moves his family to Mexico and tries to re-build his life.

Frank Yoshinobu—Orphaned son of a samurai warrior, Frank comes to California in 1869 to start a new life at a Japanese colony on the American River.

### The Inheritors
### The McPhalan Family

Owen McPhalan—Cormac's grandson and patriarch of the McPhalan family

Marian Archer McPhalan—Owen's wife who leaves Mockingbird to follow her dream of becoming a professional artist

The three McPhalan children:
Mary Katharine McPhalan (Kate)
Alexandria Archer McPhalan (Alex)
Julian Francis McPhalan

## The Morales Family

Jorge Morales—Mexican immigrant and self-made successful businessman

Rose Fitzgerald Morales—Jorge's wife

The three Morales children:
Carlos Estevan Morales (Carl Steven Fitzgerald)
Silvio Morales
Allison Morales (Ali)

## The Ashida Family

David Ashida—First generation Japanese American (Issei)
Connie Yoshinobu Ashida—David's wife
Tommy Ashida-David and Connie's only child

## Others

Willie Ashida—David's brother
Pearl Ashida—his wife
Ben Ashida—Tommy's cousin
Stefan Molnar–Hungarian émigré and classical piano superstar
Jerry McClosky—Carl's music agent
Armand Becker—Santa Barbara doctor and patron of the arts
Veronique Becker—Armand's wife
Chris Malacchi—Kate's best friend
Gwen Archer—Marian's aunt
Trevor Martin—British ex-pat and Marian's lover
Alan Townsend—Wealthy member of San Francisco's gay community who becomes Julian's mentor and lover
Dan Papadakis—Owen McPhalan's attorney and campaign manager
Helen Papadakis—Dan's wife

# PROLOGUE

"Everything flows, and is formed as a fleeting image.
Time itself, also, glides, in its continual motion, no
differently than a river. . . For what was before is
left behind: and what was not comes to be: and each
moment is renewed."

—Ovid, *The Metamorphoses*

The American River is born in the Sierra Nevada mountains just west of Lake Tahoe in Northern California. Fed by melting snow, rivulets of water trickle from the crevices of giant granite boulders and begin their journey westward toward the distant sea. Joining, they grow stronger—become stream—become creek, flowing through arroyos shaded by thickets of manzanita and groves of sugar pine. By the time they reach the foothills of the Sierra, the three main tributaries of the river have formed one exuberant artery that carries the lifeblood of water to the Sacramento Valley below.

The North Fork of the river is the wildest of the three—a whitewater torrent that is seldom still, and those who test its treacherous currents do so at their peril.

The Middle Fork rushes through rocky canyons and slides around glacier-gouged boulders, a powerful flood of liquid crystal bent on getting home.

The South Fork is the most sanguine, a welcoming stream that meanders through low hills and past meadows filled with wild oats and golden poppies. The three branches—North, Middle and South—come together east of the Capitol city of Sacramento before making confluence with the Sacramento River.

In January, 1848, James Marshall found several flakes of gold scattered in the gravel near a sawmill owned by the pioneer developer, John Sutter. Sutter's mill, on the South Fork of the American River near Coloma, California, became the axis of the biggest gold rush in U.S. history. Between 1848 and 1855, more than 300,000 people came to California to seek their fortuness. Among them was Cormac Everette McPhalan.

# PART I

# The Ancestors

# 1

## Mockingbird Valley Ranch
## Near Auburn, California
## June 1859

C ormac McPhalan paused at the top of the bluff and stood for a moment admiring the view. To the east he could see the peaks of the High Sierra that John Muir would later call the "Range of Light," lonely granite spires capped even in summer with a mantle of snow. Cormac studied the mountains, his spirits, as always, lifted by their grandeur.

Turning, he looked toward the west where the Central Valley of California spread out wide and flat, a violet lake bordered by the Coast Range, a wavy blue line on the far western horizon.

A hawk swept past, screaming its warning, and Cormac's eyes followed it into the still dark canyon where the North Fork of the American River had carved a rock-strewn channel. Although he couldn't see the river, he could hear its wild, cascading song, a husky roar fueled by snowmelt from the spring thaw. The river had been like that—high and wild—when he first laid eyes on the land that would become Mockingbird Valley Ranch.

Thursday, June 5, 1851 began, as usual, with Cormac climbing out of his bedroll, and pulling on his boots. He stood and stretched, trying to loosen up the tight muscles that ached with the daily work of searching for the elusive metal. He ducked out of the tent, and gazed up at a dark blue sky. The outline of the mountain tops were just visible in the muted, pre-dawn light. He stirred the embers of the campfire, and took a bucket to the creek to dip up water for some coffee. While the coffee boiled, he cut off a chunk of sourdough bread and sat down on a log to enjoy his breakfast.

Sometimes it seemed like forever since he'd left his parent's cottage in County Tyrone, Ireland, and made his way to the port of Sligo where he boarded a ship bound for Canada, one of 1.5 million Irish who left their homeland between 1845 and 1855.

After working for awhile at a lumber mill in Canada, he moved south into the U.S., where he found employment at a textile mill in southern Maine. It was here that he became acquainted with Maude Cahill, a schoolteacher and daughter of a local businessman. He hired Maude to tutor him in reading and writing, and after six months, their feelings for each other had grown serious. Determined to win Maude's hand, Cormac wanted desperately to make a name for himself.

Then Cormac read about John Marshall's discovery in a local newspaper. This was the opportunity he had been waiting for. He headed for California.

It was a grueling four-month trip across the continent. First by wagon, and later on horseback, he followed a diagonal route that led through the Wasatch Mountains of Utah and across the Great Salt Lake Desert, reaching California in May of 1849. Life in the mining camps was a rough affair, but Cormac soon met two "old miners," seasoned veterans who took him under their wing.

In Illinoistown, a bustling center that had become the distribution point of supplies for all the mining camps in the area, they helped him get the equipment he needed—pick, shovel, pan, tent. And they let him come with them to their "diggins" to learn the rudiments of his new trade.

At first, he wandered here and there, full of hope and expectations that were repeatedly dashed against the hard gravel of the streambeds. Unlike some of the miners, Cormac was reluctant to collaborate with other prospectors. Such ventures, he noted, often led to disagreements, or worse. So he continued doggedly to follow his own solitary path, using only the most primitive equipment. Finally, Cormac had filed a premptive claim on what he thought might be a potentially productive area, and had been working this stretch of the river for almost a year.

He thought several times about giving up. Came close when, after a year of back-breaking work, he had little to show but a handful of flakes and a heel full of blisters. But one of his miner friends pointed toward the river and said, "Look there, lad. You see them fish aswimmin' out there?"

Cormac followed the man's pointing finger, and saw a flash of silver as a salmon lept from the water's surface, arched through the air and slid back into the current.

"Why's he goin' upstream?" Cormac asked.

The miner grinned. "He's goin' home, lad. And he won't quit til he gets there." The man looked at Cormac. "If you want somethin' bad enough, you keep fightin' til you get it."

Cormac drank the last of his coffee and looked up at the towering Ponderosa pines that surrounded his little camp. The light from the rising sun was barely touching the tree tops a hundred feet above him. The pine needles glittered in the golden light, making Cormac smile. Maybe today . . . He gathered up his tools and headed for the creek.

On this Thursday morning, he focused on a stretch of the stream just before it flowed into the North Fork of the American River. The water there was shallow enough to mine, but flowed fast enough to sweep away any silt or other debris from his pan. He used his shovel to loosen the gravel just upstream of the site before dipping his pan into the water. There was quite a bit of clay and moss to extricate before he could begin to gently shake the pan so that the heavier material would sink to the bottom, while the lighter sludge would be swept from the pan and float away. He continued tilting and swirling for several minutes until only a layer of heavy black sand was left. Cormac squinted into the pan, tilting it slightly to see what remained.

A few rays of sunlight were filtering through the branches of a large bush on Cormac's left. He shifted the pan just slightly to catch the light and inhaled sharply. Were his eyes playing tricks on him? He set the pan down and rubbed his eyes with the cuff of his shirt. Then once more picked up the pan and tilted it toward the light.

Gold flecks like gilded raindrops glowed up at him from the black sand. He quickly added a bit more water and gave the pan a vigorous swirl. Pulling a small bottle from his pack, he picked out the larger nuggets and transferred them to the bottle. Holding the sample up to the light, he let out a small yelp of joy. If the strike was as good as it looked to be, maybe he could begin to search for a piece of land that he could call his own.

A bird's song interrupted his thoughts. He followed the sound to the top of a bluff that rose up behind the streambed. There, in the morning light, silhouetted against the azure sky, was a mockingbird. Perched on the branch of a gnarled live oak, the bird was hailing the morning with an incoherent string of calls, as if trying to find the right sound to salute the rising sun.

Cormac set down his pan. Grabbing at tree roots and sliding in the gravely sand, he made his way up the face of the bluff toward the tree. When he managed to reach the top, he pulled himself up and stood looking around.

What a view! He could see all the way from the summit of the Sierra to the far expanse of the Central Valley. Nestled between the river bluff and a low ridge of hills was a pristine little glen. Groves of live oaks sat like dark- green clouds on the surrounding hillsides, contrasting with the pale-gold of the wild oats. In the middle of the glen was an oval form like a dish of emeralds. Likely a spring, Cormac thought. Here it was. Exactly what he was looking for. And the bird had summoned him to this spot.

The bird stopped its garbled soliloquy, and, for a moment, the man and the bird gazed at each other. Then the bird took flight, passing so close to Cormac's head that he could feel the brush of its wings. In the distance, like a whispering voice, he could hear the river singing.

―∘∘❦❧∘∘―

Now, eight years later, Cormac stood looking down at what he, with God's help, had created. After that first strike, Cormac had turned to more advanced technology to work his claim. He began using a sluice box, a long wooden trough with cleats in the bottom. Gravel was shoveled in at the top, and the natural flow of water from the creek washed the gravel through the sluice, catching the heavy particles of gold in the cleats. Within six months, with the help of two Indian laborers, he had mined enough gold to enable him to buy a sizeable piece of land. Next, he sent for Maude, and made the arrangements for her to travel from Maine to California. Together, they had built their future, brick by adobe brick, from the red clay and the river sand and the wild oat straw that grew on the surrounding hills.

The sprawling adobe house had started as a one-room shed, but as his family grew, he added a second floor and two wings surrounding a spacious courtyard. There was a new stone barn, and a wooden packing shed where the fruit from the orchard was processed for shipment. The two hundred acres of pear trees that he had planted with the help of his Indian crew were finally in full production, and were his biggest cash crop, bringing in enough to pay the taxes, buy a few head of cattle, and make improvements to the property.

A smile played over his lips as he gazed with pride and satisfaction on what God and hard work had given him: seven hundred acres of productive land, a gracious home, a wonderful wife, two fine, healthy, children and a third one on the way.

The ranch had sheltered his family for over a decade, and it would shelter his children and his children's children into a golden future anchored in the land and protected by the strength and bounty of a special place–a place called Mockingbird.

# CHAPTER

# 2

### Rancho Las Posas del Sierra
### On the American River
### Near Sacramento, California
### April 1855

J uan Morales sat at the desk in his study at Rancho Las Posas. Through the casement window above the desk he could see evidence of a beautiful spring day—a deep blue sky, new bright-green leaves appearing on the branches of the live oak trees, blue chicory and pink Indian rhubarb blooming in the meadow.

In the pasture across the gravel road leading to the rancho entrance, a small herd of Corriente cattle grazed in the tall grass. Interspersed with the cattle were several Andalusian horses that were Juan's pride and joy.

He sighed as he looked down at the ledger that sat open on the desk. "*Madre,*" he muttered, "*estamos acabados, arruinados.*" "We are finished, ruined." He shook his head and thought of his father, Jose Dario Morales y Arguello, a descendent of the Morales family that had originally arrived in the New World in 1596. What would Papa have said about the looming crisis?

Las Posas del Sierra, a four thousand acre spread on the South Fork of the American River, had been granted to Jose in return for his service in the Mexican army. Juan Dominguez Morales, the eldest of Jose's four sons, had inherited the ranch when Don Jose died in 1840. He took up residence on the property, married Josepha Antonia Lopez, made numerous improvements, built a sturdy adobe hacienda, and set to work raising cattle and horses.

But in 1846 the United States declared war on Mexico. Mexican resistance ended with the Treaty of Guadalupe Hidalgo in 1848, the same year that gold was discovered at Sutter's Mill, about thirty miles up-river from the Las Posas ranch.

In 1851, the United States Congress passed "An Act to Ascertain and Settle Private Land Claims in the State of California." The Act required all holders of Spanish and Mexican land grants to present their titles for confirmation before the Board of California Land Commissioners. Contrary to the Treaty of Guadalupe Hidalgo, this Act placed the burden of proof of title on landholders. While the Land Commission confirmed 604 of the 813 claims it reviewed, mostly those of Anglo land-holders, the claim presented by Juan Morales was denied. He appealed the decision, but the confirmation process required lawyers, translators, and surveyors. When it proved too expensive for him to defend the title through the court system, Juan Morales found himself in a desperate situation.

The cost of fighting to save his land was overwhelming. He would have to accept the offer of a neighboring rancher to buy him out. And at a miserable price! Barely enough to cover the expenses to move his family to Guadalajara where he would join his brother's business making furniture and running a small dry goods store. No longer landholders, the Morales family would become part of the working class for the first time in nearly 400 years.

"*Papa, que te pasa?*" "Papa, what's wrong?"

Juan glanced up to see his son, ten-year-old Diego, watching him from the doorway. With the ranch in bankruptcy, how would Diego, Juan's wife Josepha, and his four other children handle the move to Mexico?

He got to his feet and walked slowly to the doorway and put his hand on Diego's shoulder. "My son," he said, "we are going to be leaving Las Posas."

Diego looked up at him with troubled eyes. "But why, Papa?"

"Your Uncle Ricardo has invited us to come and visit him in Mexico. If everything works out, we will find a place to live nearby."

"But we will come back to Las Posas, won't we?"

Juan took a deep breath and tightened his hand on his son's shoulder. "No, Diego," he said. "The Morales family is returning to Mexico. We will not come back."

But he was wrong.

# CHAPTER

# 3

## Wakamatsu Tea and Silk Colony
## Near Gold Run, California
## June 1869

I n April 1869, John Henry Schnell commissioned a steam-powered clipper ship, the *SS China*, to transport his wife, Jou, and their first child, Francis, from Japan to San Francisco, California. Also on board the ship were twenty-two Japanese samurai who, because of their defense of the Tokugawa shogunate in the Battle of Aizu, were forced to flee Japan. They brought with them hundreds of mulberry trees, tea plant seeds, fruit tree saplings, bamboo and rice to establish the Wakamatsu Tea and Silk Colony, the first Japanese colony in America. In June 1869, the colonists purchased two hundred acres of land on the South Fork of the American River near Gold Run.

Among the refugees was Yoshinobu Takashi, the six-year-old nephew of Tokugawa Yoshinobu.

---·∞∙▷◁∙∞·---

## Sacramento, California
## June 1908

Almost forty years later, Frank Yoshinobu stood on the wooden platform of the Arcade Station, the impressive Gothic Revival railway station in Sacramento that was a busy hub for the Southern Pacific Railroad. It was a hot day, but Frank was dressed in a grey wool suit, a white shirt with a fashionable stand-up collar, and a black silk tie.

He wore a felt hat and a pair of wire-rimmed glasses that he hoped did not make him look older than his forty-six years.

Frank had lived most of his life in Sacramento. He was only six years old when he left Japan and came to America as a part of the Wakamatsu Tea and Silk Colony. The Colony had flourished at first, sustained by the tireless efforts of the members and the financial assistance of their former leader, Matsudaira Katamori.

But after 1872, financial support from Matsudaira ceased. The loss of sustainable income—combined with a two-year drought—proved to be too much for the fledgling community. The colonists dispersed, and the first Japanese colony in America ceased to exist.

Frank—whose birth name was Takashi—moved with his mother to Sacramento where she found work as a laundress and he worked in the fields, picking strawberries and other crops in the fertile tracts along the Sacramento River. To blend in more easily, he took the name "Frank" as his given name and retained the family surname, "Yoshinobu."

Frank's intelligence, curiosity, and creativity led him to learn all he could about the new technology of photography. By the time he was in his mid-twenties he had become an accomplished photographer and, with the help of his family, was able to open his own photographic studio in Sacramento, three blocks south of the Arcade Railroad Station. He had married a local woman of Indian and African-American descent, but she died in childbirth a few months before their third anniversary. The baby also died. Frank had not re-married.

But now, after fifteen lonely years, he had decided that he wanted a family. In addition to longing for the security of married life, he had another reason for exploring marriage possibilities: the rising tide of anti-Japanese prejudice.

The xenophobic, white-supremacist sentiment that had targeted the Chinese in the mid-nineteenth century, turned, by the 1890s, toward Japanese immigrants who had begun to arrive in large numbers and quickly demonstrated their agricultural skills. In the western states in general, and California in particular, Asian exclusionists claimed that the immigrants were overrunning the country and were a threat to American society. After the passage of the Alien Exclusion Act, the only way that a Japanese-born immigrant (Issei) could obtain title to property was through his American-born children (Nisei). Thus it was that Frank Yoshinobu had gone to the trouble of sending a photograph of himself to a family member in Japan who would try to find a suitable young woman—preferably one from a good family who was young, healthy, and who would bring assets to the marriage—to be his "picture bride."

Frank's cousin in Kyoto had selected a young woman named Motome Matsumura who, while not wealthy, came from a family of distinguished lineage. Frank had a photograph of Motome and, as the train came puffing into the station, he took out the photo and anxiously began to scan the passengers as they disembarked. His mouth was dry and sweat trickled down his back beneath the woolen coat. He bit his lip and adjusted his glasses, shading his eyes from the afternoon sun. He wondered if she would be able to recognize him from the photo he had sent—it was five years old and he wasn't wearing eyeglasses.

He was growing desperate when he spotted a small figure standing halfway down the platform. She was wearing a white, high-collared blouse, a long black skirt, a tan coat, and a simple straw hat with no feathers or ribbons. She carried a small suitcase and glanced around shyly. Frank felt a rush of sympathy for her—such a tiny little thing, so alone and so far from home. And she was pretty, with a round face, delicate features and glossy black hair.

He made his way through the crowd and stopped in front of her, smiled and tipped his hat. "Matsumura-san?" he inquired.

She stared at him for a moment, and then a look of recognition brightened her face. "A, anata wa koko ni iru!" she exclaimed, "Oh, you *are* here!" Then, obviously embarrassed by her informality, she bowed and murmured, "Hajimemashite, yoroshiku onegai shimasu, Yoshinobu-san." "I am very pleased to meet you, Mr. Yoshinobu."

He returned the bow, straightened up and smiled. *"Amerika e yōkoso,"* he said. "Welcome to America."

Seven years later, Frank and Motome sat on the porch of their little house on O Street in Sacramento. James, who had just turned three, sat on the floor playing with a pile of wooden blocks—arranging them in stacks and then knocking them over—while Sarah, aged two, crawled over to the porch railing and, hoisting herself up, used it to make her way to the edge of the steps that led down into the garden.

"Sarah," cautioned Motome, *"Ki o tsukete!"* "Be careful! Don't fall!"

Frank put down his newspaper and hurried to scoop up the little girl. She giggled and tried to grab his glasses, but he turned his head. *"Baka-chan,"* he scolded softly. "Such a little rascal."

Motome shifted her position, trying to accommodate her swollen belly. "Oh," she said, grimacing, "I'll be glad when this baby comes."

"Just one more month," Frank said. He smiled at his wife. Frank now owned his own shop, the Yoshinobu Photographic Studio, which included the cottage behind the shop where he was raising his growing family. He looked at his little son, who had once more constructed a tower of blocks from the jumbled pile.    Glancing at his wife, he asked, "What should we name the new baby?"

"I've been thinking," Motome replied, "that if it's a girl, we should name her Connie."

In 1935, just a few years before the forced incarceration of "Persons of Japanese ancestry residing on the West Coast," Connie Yoshinobu married David Ashida, a first-generation Japanese-American who was employed as a gardener at Sacramento's McKinley Park.

In 1942, David and Connie were sent to the internment camp at Tule Lake, California. Their property was confiscated, their extended family divided. It was at Tule Lake that Connie gave birth to their only child, Tommy. In 1946, eight months after their release from the camp, David was able to find employment–as a ranch foreman at Owen McPhalan's Mockingbird Valley Ranch on the American River near Auburn, California.

# PART II

# The Inheritors

# CHAPTER

# 4

## Mockingbird Valley Ranch
## Near Auburn, California
## June 1959

The mockingbird's singing woke her. The bird was perched on a branch of the acacia tree just outside the open window, going through its entire repertoire—a chorus of chirps, squeaks, and trills—and the bedroom was filled with the cotton-candy scent of acacia blossoms.

Fifteen-year-old Kate McPhalan rolled over on her side, and wondered sleepily where the bird had learned all of those sounds. And why it was that, with all those myriad songs, the mockingbird had none of its own. A bird with many songs, but no voice. The bird fell silent, and Kate could hear her parents' angry voices coming from the next room.

"I know *why* you're going, Marian. Just tell me when you're coming home." Owen McPhalan folded his arms and glared at his wife.

Marian continued to toss clothes into a suitcase.

"Well?"

She glanced up. "We've been over this a dozen times, Owen," she said. "I'll be back at the end of summer, as soon as Alex's classes are finished."

"Why can't she go to the music school in San Francisco?"

"For goodness sakes," Marian said, "this is a wonderful

opportunity for Alex to study with the best teachers, meet the most talented students, and she has a scholarship. Can't you see that—"

"What I *see*," he interrupted, "is that you're taking off right before the harvest."

Marian banged the lid of the suitcase shut. "The hell with the harvest! I'm talking about your daughter's *future!*"

"And I'm talking *ours!*"

They glared at each other, then she looked away. "I'll be back in August," she said.

There was a gentle knock on the bedroom door. "Mrs. McPhalan? The car is here for you," said Connie Ashida, the McPhalan family's housekeeper.

"Thank you, Connie. I'll be right down."

For a long moment, Marian and Owen stood glowering at each other. Then Marian picked up the suitcase and headed for the door.

Kate sat up in bed, clutched the covers around her, and looked out the window. Glimmers of delicate pink light touched the tops of the pear trees. The sky was a deep blue, and the last of the stars were still visible. From downstairs Kate heard her younger sister, Alex, cry, "Mom, hurry up. It's time to go!"

Kate got up and went to the window. Mom and Alex were dark figures hurrying across the patio. Dad behind them carrying suitcases. Car doors slammed and tires crunched on the gravel drive. That's that, Kate thought. She's gone. Dad came back through the gate. He paused for a moment, then shook his head and strode across the patio.

Kate padded across the cool tile floor to the closet, pulled on faded jeans and a blue turtleneck sweater. She ran a brush through her auburn hair and pulled it back into a ponytail. Wide set eyes the color of woodsmoke stared back at her from the mirror. She frowned at herself and stuck out her tongue. Why did Julian and Alex get all of Mom's good looks? Carrying her cowboy boots, she tiptoed into the hall and headed down the stairs.

Connie looked up from the sausage patties that she was frying. "Good morning, Katie," she said.

"I don't think so," Kate said.

Connie gave her a sympathetic smile. "I know it's hard to have your mother gone, but it's only for the summer. She and your sister will have a great time in Boston."

"I guess so," Kate said.

Connie handed Kate a cup of hot chocolate. "Maybe this will help. Then you'd better go and wake your brother. Mr. McPhalan will want to get started on today's chores."

Kate paused outside her brother's bedroom door.

"Julian?" she called. "Are you awake?"

A groan came from within. Kate opened the door. Julian lay spread-eagled on the bed wearing only a pair of sweatpants. The muted light from a bank of aquariums cast a slick blue glow across his bare skin. James Dean, straddling his motorcycle, glared down sullenly from a poster above the bed,.

"What time is it?" Julian mumbled.

"Almost six."

He flopped over on his back. "Jeeze. How come we can't ever sleep 'til a reasonable hour around here?"

"Because there's stuff to do." Kate tossed a pillow at him. He grabbed it and covered his head. "Julian, get up!"

"Mom left yet?" Julian asked, his voice muffled in the pillow.

"A few minutes ago," Kate said. "What's this?"

"What's what?" Julian muttered.

"This." Kate picked up a dog-eared sheet of paper from the bedside table and flapped it over his head.

Julian sat up and shoved his hair back. "A letter from great-grandad. I found it up in the attic. Want to read it?"

"Why don't you read it to me?" Kate said, handing him the paper. "That way I'll know for sure that you're awake."

"Okay, smart-ass." Julian smoothed the rumpled pages and read:

*Dear Maude, At last I've found our land. Seven hundred acres of the sweetest earth the Lord has ever made nestled in a valley between two rows of hills, just like your father's land in Maine. To the south a bluff overlooks a river. The land is positioned so that it is safe from the floods that seem to threaten from time to time when the river rises swiftly. The native people called it "The Long House River," a place where the spirits were good. And the Spanish called it Rio de los Americanos. Some of them still have ranches along the sream.*

*But we call it the American River, and to me that am a proper name, for we've come here from every corner on God's earth to find ourselves a home. A number are from Erin like myself. There's quite a few that come from Italy. There's even settlers here from Greece and Russia, and some from China as well. And, I'm told a gentleman of color from the West Indies owns a large tract of land along the river not ten miles distant. In fact, your father would be pleased to hear that there is a Negro settlement along the river where both freedmen and former slaves have found a living working the mines. He might wish to mention this at the next meeting of the Anti-Slavery Society. There's less sympathy for the Chinese workers, I'm sorry to say, and even less for the Indians who are treated very poorly indeed.*

*But you see, my dear, I think we all are the tributaries of a great stream of humanity, and here among these golden hills we've come together to make*

*a grand new confluence. For the first time I think I
understand what it means to be an American.*

*Maude darling, I would that you were here with
me tonight so I could see your merry eyes and hear
your sweet voice. I hope with all my heart that I'll be
sending for you soon. I took the rest of the nuggets to
the assayer's office today, and tomorrow he should be
able to tell me for sure if our strike is a good one. It
will take a bit of time to mine the gold, but I can hire
some help to make it move more quickly. I know I've
strained the very measure of your patience, Maude,
these past two years. But please wait for me, my
dearest . . .*

Julian paused.

"That's all?" Kate reached for the letter, but Julian moved back.

". . . *But please wait for me, my dearest,*" he continued, "*and I'm
certain that our prayers will be answered.*"

"Is that it?" Kate said.

"Everything but his signature."

Kate rested her head against the headboard and gazed up at the
blackened beams. "He really loved her, didn't he, Pooh?" she said.

"And she loved him. Enough to wait two years for him, and then
come three thousand miles to join him in the wilderness."

"It *was* a wilderness then, wasn't it? Oaks and manzanita and
Indians and the river running past. Hard to imagine this place
without the orchards and the pastures and the house. Seems like the
house has been here forever."

"A hundred years is practically forever," said Julian.

Kate closed her eyes and thought of the faded tintype of her
great-grandfather that hung on the wall above her desk. He looked
formidable despite the fact that he was almost ninety when the
photograph was made. He had a high forehead, a prominent nose,
and a bristling mustache. His eyes were narrowed in a challenging
stare.

Whenever she thought about Cormac Everette McPhalan, Kate felt a glow of pride. He had started something grand and now, a century later, she was part of what he had created.

She looked at her brother. "Julian?"

"Hmmm?"

"Listen to me, will you? Are you sorry you didn't go back east with Mom and Alex?"

Julian, who was re-reading the letter, looked up and frowned. "What would I have done in Boston?"

"But what if Mom decides to stay?"

"She won't."

"But what if she does?"

Angrily, Julian tossed the letter aside. "Look, Roo, I've only got one more year of high school, and then I'm out of here. I sure as hell don't intend to stick around and pick pears the rest of my life."

Kate was silent for a moment. Then she said, "I think Dad's worried that you—"

Julian snorted. "Worried about me? That's rich."

"Give him a chance, Pooh."

"What chance has he ever given me?" Their eyes met for a moment before he looked away. "What about you?" he said. "Mom asked you to go too."

Kate picked up the letter and ran her fingers over the yellowed pages, tracing the lines of sepia-colored script. "I couldn't leave Mockingbird. Not even for a summer."

"You can't stay here forever. Everybody's got to leave home someday," Julian said.

"Julian?" Their father's voice sounded from the base of the stairs. "Mary Katherine? Will you two get a move on? Connie's got breakfast on the table."

"Coming, Daddy," Kate called. "Hurry up," she told her brother as she headed for the door.

—∘∘◦❧◦∘∘—

"Chocolate or coffee, Julian?" Connie asked as Kate and Julian sat down at the breakfast table.

"Coffee," Julian muttered.

"Thank you, Connie. That will be all," said Owen as the woman set Julian's cup on the table. "Now then," he continued, "Julian, I want you to go into town this morning and pick up that fitting for the conveyer belt. You can get some horse feed while you're at it. On the way back, I want you to stop at Donovan's and get a new tire for the truck."

Julian sighed. "Yes, sir."

"Kate, I want you and Tommy to go take a look at the south fence. David saw a couple of heifers up on the ridge." Owen looked up from his plate. "And don't get sidetracked looking for arrowheads. You can treasure hunt some other time."

"Yes, sir," Kate said. Then she added, "I'm glad Connie and David are here to help keep things going now that Mom's gone."

"Japs or not," Owen said, "the Ashidas are hard workers and I trust 'em."

They finished breakfast in silence. "Well, I'm off," said Owen. "I'm headed into town for a while this afternoon so don't look for me 'til suppertime." He paused for a moment at the door. "Remember, I'm counting on you two now that your mother's not here."

Kate raised her chin a notch. "I know, Dad."

Julian stared at his plate and said nothing.

Owen strode from the house, slamming the door behind him.

"I don't think he even cares," Julian said. "I don't think it matters to him one bit that Mom and Alex have gone."

"You're wrong," said Kate. "It's just his way, Julian. You know how he is."

"Don't I ever." Julian got to his feet. "I suppose we'd better make tracks. Herr General's given his orders so the troops had better fall in."

"There *is* a lot to do," Kate said. "Mockingbird won't stand still just because Mom decided to leave."

Julian gave her a sideways glance. "I'm worried about you, Roo."

"Oh, yeah? Why?"

"You sound more like Dad every day."

She knew he wasn't really angry, though, because he gave her ponytail a playful tug as they headed for the door.

# CHAPTER

# 5

Tommy Ashida sat across the kitchen table from his father and watched as he drank miso soup from a small lacquered bowl. At fifteen, Tommy was already half a head taller than his father, but David was muscular and compact, while Tommy was slender and lighter-complexioned. Tommy's mother, Connie, told him he was handsome. Tommy wasn't certain what that meant. Rock Hudson was handsome, and Tommy didn't think he looked anything like Rock Hudson. He didn't think he looked like any of the American movie stars. He looked . . . foreign.

"We have a lot to do," David said, setting the bowl down and wiping his narrow black moustache. "Mr. McPhalan wants the ploughing finished by the end of the week, and the south orchard still needs staking."

"Guelita's coming this afternoon to help me pick beans," said Connie. "We can start canning on Saturday."

David grunted and held out his bowl for another helping.

"Dad," Tommy said, "if I get finished by noon Saturday, can I go into town?"

The creases in David's forehead deepened. "What for?"

"I need some books from the library."

"What kind of books?" David said.

"For a paper I'm doing."

"What is the subject of this paper?"

"Sacramento Nihonmachi."

David said nothing for a moment and the boy squirmed under his gaze. "I'd like to see this paper," David said, "before you give it to your teachers."

"Sure, Dad."

Connie ladled another helping of soup into her husband's bowl. "I'm glad you're interested in Sacramento Nihonmachi, Tommy," she said. "It was a nice place to live."

"Hmpf," David snorted. "Have you forgotten the smoke from the railroad yards? The drunken men in the alleys?"

"Our neighbors weren't like that," Connie protested. "They were family people, like us."

"It was an ugly place to live."

"But very rich in heritage," said Connie.

David took a drink of soup and gestured toward the door. "I don't need Sacramento Nihonmachi to remind me of my heritage. Here the air is clean and pure. The work is hard, but it is good work, out of doors. Besides," he gave his wife a flinty look, "there is no one here to remind us of less pleasant times."

David rarely mentioned the internment camp at Tule Lake where they had spent four long years during World War II, but when he did there was a special anger in his voice. Tommy remembered only the cold and his mother's tears.

And the fence. It stretched for what seemed like miles across the hills, a huge net that trapped the forlorn tar-paper shanties like a school of small, dark minnows. The guard towers still appeared in his dreams like windmills advancing across the barren hills, trailing barbed wire in their wake. "Childish thoughts," he told himself whenever he woke shaking and gasping from one of the dreams. "When I am a man, these dreams will go away."

"Hey, Tommy."

At the sound of Kate's voice outside the cabin, he jumped to his feet and threw open the door.

"We gotta go check the fence along the bluff," Kate said. "Dad thinks some cattle might have gotten out."

"Be right with you."

"Meet you at the barn."

"S'cuse me," he told his parents. "I gotta go."

Connie giggled, hiding her mouth behind a small, plump hand. "Such a rush to go and look for cattle."

"You must ask Tony Malacchi if he has seen any strays," David said.

"Sure, Dad."

"And don't forget to take your pliers in case you need to mend a break," he called after the boy.

As Connie began to clear the table, David said, "My son spends too much time with Mr. McPhalan's daughter."

Connie stopped and looked at her husband. "You didn't mind when they were children."

David frowned. "They are no longer children."

Kate and Tommy had to lead their horses along the path that wound down into the river canyon. The ponies—sturdy reliable Morgans whose ancestors had been brought to California during the Gold Rush—squatted on their haunches, sliding and floundering in the loose dirt and gravel. Joe, the family's German shepherd, followed, his tail wagging furiously.

Near the base of the cliff, surrounded by a small grove of oaks, was the McPhalan family graveyard. "Let's stop for a minute," Kate said.

They settled themselves on a fallen log while the horses nosed at the dead grass that lay like a thick gold pelt on the body of the earth. Joe flopped down at Kate's feet and rested his wolfish head on his paws. The light was dim, and the musky scent of blackberries filled the air.     In the center of the graveyard, an elaborate obelisk bore the name "McPhalan" engraved in the grey granite. On either side were two headstones—a large one that read "Cormac Everette McPhalan, a native of Ireland. B. March 7, 1825. D. January 27, 1922. *Suaimhneas síoraí dá h'anam.*" And a smaller one that was engraved "Maude Cahill McPhalan, B. February 27, 1832. D. August 21, 1859. My beloved wife." And beside that was an even smaller marker, "Mary Katharine McPhalan, B. August 15,1859. D. August 20, 1859. Our angel."

"What's that one say?" Tommy asked, pointing to Cormac's headstone.

"Timeless peace unto his soul."

"Irish, right?" said Tommy.

Kate nodded. "Dad says he was from County Tyrone."

"Boy, his wife sure was young when she died," Tommy said.

"Lots of women died in childbirth in those days." Kate glanced at Tommy. "Have you seen her picture? It's on the wall in my room."

Tommy shook his head.

"She was really beautiful, especially her eyes. But she looks so sad. I've got her violin. They say she played it on her deathbed. It's all busted up, but I still like to unwrap it. Just to look." She fell silent for a moment, then added, "Must have been hard to come all the way out here and live at Mockingbird when there was nothing else here. And she was so young . . ."

After a minute, Tommy said, "I wish I knew more about *my* family. We don't have a place like . . ." he gestured toward the gravestones, "like this where I can see their names and think about who they were."

"Don't your parents ever talk about their ancestors?" Kate said.

"Not much. I know Dad's brother, Uncle Willie, and the rest of his family are in Stockton. Dad's parents came to California from Hawaii. My grandmother lived with us for a few months before she passed away." He smiled, remembering. "She was a funny little lady. She called me 'Tummy.'"

"What about your mom's parents?" Kate asked.

Tommy shrugged. "My grandfather's name was Frank. Before the war he had a photo shop in Sacramento. That's about all I know. It's like . . ." He hesitated for a moment. "It's like when the war came, everything broke apart, you know? Like the past kind of evaporated."

Wind stirred in the tree branches, making the leaves glimmer in the light.

"Tommy?" Kate said.

"Yeah?"

"How would you feel if your mom decided to leave? I mean, if she went away and never came back?"

Tommy thought for a moment, then said, "Mom wouldn't do that."

Kate sighed. "I didn't think mine would either."

"But your mom's different," Tommy said. "She was always off somewhere—Sacramento or San Francisco. Or back east to visit her folks."

Kate didn't reply.

"Hey, Kate," he said, putting his arm around her shoulders. "Don't be sad."

She leaned against him. "I wish she hadn't left. I'm scared she won't come back."

Tommy closed his eyes and waited. It was enough that she was in his arms. He could feel her warmth and smell the sweet scent of her hair. He wanted that moment to last forever, but she straightened up and rubbed her eyes with the back of her wrist. "Sorry," she said.

"S'okay."

She stood up. "We better go."

Joe scrambled up and stood beside her, ears pricked, tail wagging. For a minute everything was very still. In the distance Tommy could hear the quiet rushing of the river, the muttering of doves. Then the wind moved in the branches, and a stripe of light fell across Kate's face. It happened just as she turned toward him, and the strange beauty of it made him catch his breath. Slowly, she put out her hand and touched his cheek. "Hey, Tommy," she said, "I'm really glad you're my friend."

"I'll always be your friend," he whispered.

"Promise?"

"Cross my heart."

## Sacramento, California

Owen McPhalan's rugged, sunburned face was tightening into a scowl. Dan Papadakis, a wiry, dark-haired man who had been Owen's attorney for more than a decade, knew the signals and silently prayed that Owen would hold his temper. Burt Hubble, who sat next to Owen on the far side of Dan's mahogany desk, was not without influence in certain circles, and Dan was not one to burn bridges.

"Mac, what I'm trying to tell you is this," Hubble was saying. "You can go ahead and sell that property to Ned Warren, and maybe you'll make a little profit. But the real money's in developing it yourself."

Owen puffed on the cigar that Dan had given him and squinted at Hubble. "All right, let's suppose I decide to do it your way. What would I be getting into?"

Hubble leaned forward eagerly. "All it would take is sufficient capital for the initial investment."

"Don't like borrowing," Owen said.

"Wouldn't be for long. Twenty or thirty thousand would be more than enough to get you started. Once the survey work is done and the road's in, you can sell off individual lots. Take a low down, string the payments out over ten, fifteen years at a good rate of interest. Well, hell, Owen, the long range profits would be tremendous."

Owen looked at Dan. "This was your idea, Danny. Still think it's a good one?"

"Sounds fine to me, Mac."

"Hmmm." Owen stretched his legs out in front of him and studied the distant toes of his boots. "Hate to see that land go out of production," he said. "Good piece of land. Always gave me a fine crop." He let out his breath. "But, I reckon it's too close to town to be worth much as farmland anymore. I expect Ned would just cut it up into lots anyway."

"That's right," Hubble agreed. "Of course he would."

"Hell, it's only forty acres, Mac," Dan said. "And times are changing fast out this way. You gotta keep pace, partner."

"Yeah, yeah," Owen said.

Dan sat back and crossed his arms. "Come on, Mac. You're too good a businessman not to see the opportunities. You own what—eight, maybe nine hundred acres along the river? And that doesn't include your ranch."

Owen's mouth hardened to a thin line. "Just leave Mockingbird out of this. That's family land."

"Okay, okay. Point is, you've been selling off a few acres at a time down by the bridge and making a little money, but I've got to agree with Burt that you'd make a helluva lot more if you developed the whole tract. Why let some other guy make all the big profits?"

Owen said nothing.

"Be a great tax shelter," Hubble said.

"And you need to do some planning on that level," Dan added.

"That's right, Mac."

Owen ignored Hubble and gave Dan a long, thoughtful look. "How long would it take to set all this up?"

"A few days."

Owen considered for a moment. "All right. You draw up the papers, and I'll take a good hard look."

Hubble popped to his feet like a wind-up toy and pumped Owen's hand. "Good decision, Mac. I've got to run, but you come on in Monday and we'll discuss that loan."

"Bankers," Owen scoffed after Hubble had gone. "Wouldn't give you a nickel for the lot of them."

"They have their uses," Dan said with an easy grin.

Owen got to his feet and headed for the door.

"You got a minute? How 'bout a drink?"

Owen gave Dan a hard look. "None for me. What's on your mind?"

Dan pulled a bottle from the desk drawer and poured a splash of whiskey into a water glass. "You thought any more about that discussion we had last week?"

Owen sat back down and re-lit the cigar. "Not a whole lot. I got a ranch to run, remember?"

The lawyer toyed with his glass. "Well, take your time. It's a while yet before the primary."

"Hell, Danny, I'm no politician. I'm just a farmer. You know that."

"Listen, old buddy," Dan said, "you may be able to get away with that poor-country-boy routine with Burt, but I know better. Call yourself a farmer if you want to, but you're a born gambler, Mac, and I've never yet seen you back away from a game if the stakes were right."

"I play the game if I know the rules, but this stuff is new to me. Never had much truck with politicians."

"That's exactly why we need you. Folks around here are tired of those Johnny-come-latelies in Sacramento telling them what to do. What do they know? You understand the grower's point of view. Even better, you understand business. That's a combination we can win with."

A glint of a smile sparkled in Owen's blue eyes.

"You and I both know that the days of the little farmer are numbered," the lawyer continued. "Agribusiness—that's the coming thing. The small growers are going to get squeezed out eventually. What do you think is going to happen if those spics ever get themselves organized and start pushing up labor costs? Where're you and your friends going to be then?"

Owen leaned back and studied Dan. "Why all this sudden concern for us growers?"

Dan grinned and spread his hands. "Hey, I come from modest stock. My granddaddy was a farmer. Lost everything he had in the Depression. I can understand the problems of the little guy."

"Then why don't you take a crack at public office?"

Dan shook his head. "Because you've got a better image."

"Me?"

"Don't laugh. You look liked a damned general with those steely blues and that silver hair. And people know you as an honest man. That's something nobody can buy. Yes, sir," the lawyer nodded, "we've got the basis for a campaign that could put you right in the

Assembly a year and a half from now. It's not too early to start planning if you want to make the run."

"Danny?" Owen turned to see Dan's wife, Helen, standing outside the open door. She hesitated when she recognized her husband's guest. "Oh, I'm sorry to interrupt. Please don't get up on my account."

But Owen was already on his feet. "You're not interrupting a thing, Helen," he said. "Please, come on in."

Helen's cheeks flushed. "I'm sorry," she said to Dan. "I needed to get some grocery money."

Owen's eyes took in the soft curves of Helen's torso. She was short and round, and the passing years had only made her more voluptuous, while her face had lost nothing of its sweetness. Funny, he thought, a woman built like that—you'd never think she couldn't have kids. And there's Marian, skinny as a racehorse, and she probably could have dropped a dozen by now if she'd been willing.

Helen glanced at Owen, and the color in her cheeks deepened when she found him looking at her. "I hear Marian's gone back east for a visit," she said.

"That's right," Owen said.

"Are the children here with you?"

"Kate and Julian stayed on at the ranch. Alex went with Marian to take lessons at some fancy music school in Boston."

Helen smiled at Owen. "You must come for dinner sometime soon. And do bring the children."

"Thank you, Helen. I appreciate the offer. Surely do." Owen watched her leave, then turned to Dan. "You're a lucky man, Danny, to have a wife like that."

"Yeah, she's a great little gal," Dan said. Then he looked up at Owen. "By the way, exactly when is Marian coming back?"

Owen shrugged. "End of summer, I reckon."

"She *is* coming back, isn't she?"

Owen scuffed at the carpet with the toe of his boot. "Christ, Danny, you know Marian. Ever since she got back from San Francisco last fall, she's been crazy as a colt on locoweed. Got it into her head that she wants to be a great *artiste*. Figured I'd let her have her little fling so she'd see how silly it was. We'll work things out when she gets back."

"I hope you're right," Dan said

# CHAPTER

# 6

## Interstate 80 near Auburn, California
## June 1959

M usic. It had been Carl's love, his dream, his all-consuming passion for as long as he could remember, the one unbroken line that stretched from his earliest childhood to this, the nineteenth summer of his life. Everything else had changed—places, people, the shape and substance of his body, the contours of his world, but the music had remained. It was as if there was a part of him that had never changed at all, a core, a space within that time had left untouched. Music was his soul.

Carl Fitzgerald Morales rested his head against the seatback. The Greyhound bus wasn't as cramped as he thought it might be, and his six-foot frame fit the seat easily. He closed his eyes and let his mind drift.

He could remember very clearly the first time he had gone with Gramps Fitzgerald to a concert, could see as though it were yesterday the dimly-lit hall, the great sweep of wine red velvet curtains that slowly parted to reveal the tiers of seats upon the stage. The musicians entered, took their places, tuned their instruments, adjusted the stands that held their scores. The concertmaster signaled for the principal oboist to sound the A, and strings and woodwinds squeaked and whined as their voices sought a common harmony. Then there was a hush, and the hall went dark.

They played Mozart that day. The Symphony in C Major, K 551. *The Jupiter*. The boy had heard this music many times on Gramps's record player, but to hear the sounds rushing out to him from the stage, to see the musicians bend and sway as they formed the music with their hands, their lips, bowing and blowing, now gently, now fiercely, to hear them coax from pieces of wood and metal such perfect sounds—this was a magic beyond all imagining.

Throughout the years that followed, he had never once doubted his self-appointed mission—to be the best musician that he could be. By the age of seven, he had mastered the violin and the piano. At nine, he had written his first serious composition, a symphonic suite based on his favorite book, *The Secret Garden*. "Incredible," Gramps had said, reading over the score. "Incredible."

But three days later Gramps was dead. It had happened so fast— the accident, the funeral, the move to California to "start a new life," but not one that Carl had chosen. He found himself in an unfamiliar world with a family he barely knew–his birth-mother Rose Fitzgerald Morales, a dark-haired Irish beauty with pretty hazel eyes. His birth-father Jorge, a gentle bear of a man with golden skin and a thick, dark moustache. And baby Silvio, a chubby toddler. They said Carl was their son, but Gramps and Nana had been taking care of him for as long as he could remember.

He saw himself at nine—a thin, dark-haired waif with huge brown eyes lugging a suitcase filled with music scores, all alone with his grief. *They* were the family; *he* was an outsider.

Carl looked out the dust-smeared window of the bus as it climbed into the foothills of the Sierra Nevada Range, following the course of the American River. A tattered shroud of clouds hung on the peaks ahead giving them a ghostly look that made him shiver. He shook his head to clear away sudden anxiety. From his windbreaker pocket, he pulled out a folded piece of paper, opened it, and read:

*April 20, 1959*
*Mr. Carl Steven Fitzgerald*
*1215 35ᵗʰ Street*
*Sacramento, California*

*Dear Mr. Fitzgerald:*

*Congratulations. Based on the evaluation of your recent audition, you have been selected as a Fellow at the Berkshire Music Center at Tanglewood in Lenox, Massachusetts, beginning July 1, 1959. You are expected to arrive by that date to undertake the course of study indicated in your letter of application.*

*Enclosed is a packet of materials to acquaint you with the Center's programs and procedures as well as the regulations and responsibilities to which Center Fellows are expected to adhere. Should you require additional information, please do not hesitate to contact me. I am, very truly yours . . .*

*Tanglewood.* The very name made the hair rise on the back of his neck. How many years had he dreamed of visiting this place? "I was there," Gramps had told him, "when the first concert was played in the Music Shed. It was Bach they played, the Cantata No. 80, and then Beethoven's Ninth, the D minor. Koussevitzky conducted. Oh, I tell you, Carl, I will never forget that night."

And now, after all the years of dreaming, of study and preparation, he was on his way. Crossing the continent, fleeing the past, composing a future. Forget about the clouds' brooding presence. In just three days, he would be at Tanglewood.

## Lenox, Massachusetts
## June 1959

Marian Archer McPhalan stood in the open doorway of her parents' summer cottage in Lennox, Massachusetts. For several long minutes, she stared at the dingy scene before her.

The image in her mind had been so clear—a bright, friendly room with a velvet sofa, her father's favorite wing chair by the window, her mother's knitting in the basket beside the hearth. The small windowpanes had sparkled in the afternoon light. A perfect summer room her mother Charlotte called it.

But now only a little light filtered in through the shabby drapes, and the room looked sad and lonely. Cobwebs had collected in the corners of the ceiling, and above the mantel the wallpaper had come loose and sagged back on itself.

Marian crossed the foyer and lifted the corner of the sheet that covered the sofa. The rose-colored velvet had faded to a grayish-mauve. Scraps of paper littered the floor beside the sofa's wooden claw-foot. Mice, she thought. They must have built a nest in the springs. Her mouth pinched with distaste at the thought. She let the sheet drop. Sinking down on the hearth, she squeezed her eyelids shut.

"Marian, you idiot," she said aloud. "What did you expect? The place has been closed up for five years."

*Nothing* had gone the way she had expected. Her plan had seemed perfect—Alex's summer scholarship to the music conservatory in Boston was a great opportunity for her daughter. And it was also an opportunity for Marian to get away from the mind-numbing routine of ranch life. She would have time to paint. For a whole summer! She and Alex would live in Boston in the house left to her when Papa died. How could she have guessed that the pipes were broken and the kitchen empty of fixtures? Those damned tenants.

She should have hired a real-estate firm. As it was, the lawyer had already charged her more than five hundred dollars to straighten out the mess with the tenants and cover the liens against the property.

Poor Papa, he never was very clever about money. Mother had always handled the finances.

So she had arrived in Boston and found she had no place to stay. Thank goodness Aunt Gwen, her mother's younger sister, had offered to take care of Alex over the summer. It meant that Marian was free to visit Lenox so she could work in peace and quiet for a change. Alex could come up for weekends.

But now . . . She straightened up and gazed around. What a mess. It was going to take at least a week to get the place cleaned up. But it was better than staying at Mockingbird for another summer of canning vegetables and arguing with Owen.

She hauled herself up and took a deep breath. Looking around once more, she shook her head. Mother would have had a fit if she'd ever seen the house in this condition. But then, Mother always wanted everything to be perfect—the house, the family, the daughter. "Sorry, Mother," she muttered as she headed for the truck to get her suitcase.

### The Taconic State Parkway, New York

The pain was bearable today. He was never sure what to expect. Sometimes it was almost gone, just a small, nagging ache. Other times it came ferociously alive, as though the fire that had seared nearly one half of his flesh had burned into his bones and continued to smolder beneath the angry scars. But today it was bearable. Perhaps in time . . .

Stefan Molnar glanced out the window at the passing landscape, watched leafy thickets and soft-green meadows rush past. The limousine ride was very smooth, thank God. Only a few little bumps to jar his bones. He had slept well the night before—without dreams or medication. He was getting stronger with each passing day.

His thin mouth twisted in an ironic smile. He was alive to count his losses, to grieve, to feel the crush of loneliness and guilt that had him in its grasp. He had survived, but for what?

Angrily, he shook his head, trying to brush away the gloomy thoughts. "You'll be sensational," Rube Marin, his East Coast agent, had said that very morning as he tucked Stefan into the limo. "It'll be the comeback story of the decade. Trust me, good buddy. Just say the word and I got 'em lined up and waiting in the wings."

"I need more time," Stefan had said. At age twenty-six he felt twice that age. He had already been playing concerts for twenty years. His only "vacation" had been the two years that it had taken for him to recover from the wounds he sustained in the Hungarian Revolution.

"Take all the time you want," Rube had soothed. "I told 'em at the BSO that you're still not a hundred percent, so don't let 'em talk you into anything, okay? We don't want any more relapses. Just do a couple of master classes. Harry and Marge will take good care of you, and Lenox should be great this time of year. Hell, Stefan, you're still young. You got your whole life ahead of you. Okay, you ready?" Rube was hanging onto the limo door, grinning, his glasses balanced at their usual precarious angle on the end of his nose. "Off you go, Maestro. Give me a call if you need anything. I'll see you in two weeks."

"Sure, Rube," Stefan said. "Thank you for taking care of the arrangements."

"Hey, that's what I'm here for."

"How long will it take to get there?" Stefan asked the driver as the limo pulled away from the curb and headed up Fifth Avenue.

The driver glanced in the rearview mirror. "Couple of hours, Maestro. We'll take the new Parkway."

"Good," Stefan said. "I should be able to handle that."

Handle that. He loved using American slang. It made him feel comfortable somehow. This was, after all, America. Here he would start a new life. It was over, *over,* and he had to put it all behind him.

He sighed and shifted his legs, anticipating the inevitable stiffness that came with sitting still for any period of time. What was it Rube had said? You're still young? "You're an old soul," his former teacher,

François, had once told him, "an old soul in a young body. How else can one explain your being a mature artist at age thirteen?"

Dear François. Stefan could picture the round, pink face, the dark mass of curls, the small, impudent black eyes. Trust François to always come up with something lively and amusing. What an exceptional teacher he had been. But he was gone. So many were gone.

Stefan shifted his weight again, searched the landscape for something, *anything*, to deflect his train of thought. Was that a hickory tree? Yes! A solitary giant of a tree silhouetted against a mottled sky. He remembered gathering hickory nuts with his brother Janos on the shores of Lake Balaton outside Budapest. Summer vacations with the family. How simple it had all seemed—the laughter, the joking, the good dinners around the table, lamplight glowing in the window at dusk. . .

This was no good. Were there no safe memories? He squeezed his eyes shut for a moment, opened them, stared at the back of the driver's head. "I should like for you to tell me when we reach the border of Massachusetts," Stefan said. The concept of borders distressed him. Staying safe. Getting across.

The driver's eyes met his in the rearview mirror. "Sure, Maestro," the driver said. "I'll let you know the minute we cross the line."

# CHAPTER

# 7

## Mockingbird Valley Ranch
## July 1959

A gentle breeze rolled across the valley and set the leaves of the pear trees dancing. The breeze felt good against Tommy Ashida's face. He had been working in the orchard since daybreak—hefting the long poles from the bed of the pickup truck and propping them under the branches to keep the boughs from snapping under the weight of the ripening fruit.

The sun was blazing hot this time of year, even in the foothills. Tommy paused to wipe the sweat from his forehead, pushing back his straight, black hair.

"Hey, Tommy."

At the sound of Kate's voice, his pulse quickened. Shading his eyes, he spotted her running toward him between the rows of pear trees. She wore a pair of khaki-colored shorts over her swimsuit and he couldn't help but note her long, elegant legs and the delicate curve of her breasts.

"Hi," she exclaimed, "are you busy?" Then she burst out laughing and added, "I mean, I can see you're busy, but can you take a break? Christy and Gina are here, and we're going to have a picnic down by the river. Want to come?"

He shook his head. "Can't. I gotta finish the back orchard before dark."

Kate's smile faded. "Darn. You always have to work."

"Pop can't do it all himself."

"Guess not," Kate said. "So, maybe next time."

She was already turning to go, and Tommy, desperate to stop her, blurted, "Hey, Kate, heard anything from your mom?" Blue-grey eyes met his, making his heart skip a beat.

"Got a letter from her yesterday," Kate said.

"So, how's she like Boston?"

"Okay, I guess."

Why was it suddenly so hard to talk to her? They'd been friends forever, since the first day he'd arrived at Mockingbird, age five, in the back seat of his parents' old Chevy. "Wanta see my pony?" Kate had asked, sticking her freckled face through the open window, and he knew right then it was going to be okay. But now, what had happened? Had he changed? Had she? Tongue-tied, he stared at her.

"Come on, Kate," came a shout from the edge of the orchard.

"Sorry," she said, "I gotta go."

"Right. See ya." His eyes followed her until she and her friends disappeared among the trees. As he bent once more to his task, he let out his breath in a long sigh and noted, not for the first time, that the iron-rich, red California earth was exactly the same color as Kate McPhalan's hair.

"I feel sorry for Tommy," Christy Malacchi said as she helped Kate spread a blanket on the sandy riverbank. Christy, the youngest of the four Malacchi girls, had been Kate's best friend since first grade. At fifteen she was round and plump with short dark hair, sparkling brown eyes, and a winning smile. "He always has to work."

"There's lots to do this time of year," said Kate.

"I think he's cute," Christy said, flopping down on the blanket and resting her chin in her hands. "Don't you?"

Kate shrugged. "I guess so."

"I think Chinese boys are exotic."

"He's not Chinese, silly. He's Japanese."

"Well, he's still exotic." Christy rolled over onto her back and put her arms under her head. "Would you go out with him, I mean if he asked you?"

"Why would he do that? We're pals, that all."

"I'd go. I think Tommy's nice. And he's really cute in —you know—a Japanese kind of way."

Kate played with a shoelace.

"His dad sure is mean though," Chris said.

"He's not really mean, just sort of . . . gruff."

"I wonder why he's like that?"

"Tommy says it's on account of the camp."

Christy flipped over onto her stomach and stared up at Kate. "What camp?"

"Like a prison camp, I guess."

Christy's dark eyes opened wide. "What'd he do?"

"I don't think he did *anything*. Tommy says they all had to go, everybody who was Japanese. They made them stay there the whole time during the war."

"Was Tommy's dad a spy?" Christy's voice lowered to an excited whisper.

Kate laughed. "No, dummy, he was a gardener at McKinley Park, but when the war started, he lost his job, and they made them all go to a camp."

"What was it like?"

Kate frowned. "Don't know exactly. Tommy doesn't like to talk about it. All he'll say is that he was a little kid and doesn't remember much."

"Must be awful to be put in prison when you haven't done anything wrong," Christy said.

Kate tugged harder at her shoelace. "I don't think it was fair."

"Hey, you guys." Gina, Christy's older sister, scrambled up the bank, ankle-deep in the soft sand. "I thought you were going to come in swimming. The water's wonderful." She tossed her bag down and collapsed on the blanket. Her one-piece black swimsuit showed off her already voluptuous figure. "We need some music," she said.

"How can we have music out here in the orchard?" asked Kate.

Gina smirked and reached into her bag. "Ta-Da," she said, pulling out a small green radio.

"What's that?" Kate asked.

"My new *transistor*," said Gina. "It's the latest thing." Carefully she turned the dial and Paul Anka began to croon, "I'm just a lonely boy . . ."

"That's really cool," said Kate.

Gina smiled and tossed her hair. "Chris, did you bring the smokes?"

"Right here."

"Salems?" cried Gina with disgust.

"What's wrong with Salems?" Chris said.

"None of the guys smoke them."

"That's 'cause they're for women. They taste like mint so they won't make your breath smell bad."

Gina looked dubious.

"Oh, heck," Chris said, "I forgot to bring matches."

"Honestly, Chris," Gina scolded, digging into her tote bag, "sometimes I don't know where your head is at."

As a grey haze enveloped the group, Kate coughed and fanned at the smoke. "Don't you know how to inhale?" Gina asked.

Kate squinted through burning eyes. "Inhale?"

"Like this." Gina demonstrated, blowing smoke out through her nose while Kate and Christy stared at her in awe. "See? It's easy once you know how."

The whine of a distant engine drowned out Ricky Nelson's "It's Late" and brought the girls to their feet.

"Oooh, Kate," breathed Gina, "it's your *brother*."

Kate took the opportunity to dispose of her cigarette as she jumped up to wave. "Hey, Julian!"

Red windbreaker billowing behind him, blond hair flattened by the wind, Julian waved back. As the motorcycle hit a mound of dirt, it bucked and shivered, wheels spinning in the air.

"Oooh," gasped Gina as the cycle once more connected with the earth before disappearing into a clump of trees. "Your brother's dreamy," Gina said, sinking down once more.

Chris nodded. "He has bedroom eyes."

"Has *what*?" said Kate.

"You know, all moody. Like James Dean," said Chris.

"Forget it, Chris," Gina said. "She's just too square. I'll bet she doesn't even know what French kissing is."

"Do too."

"Oh yeah? Well, what is it?" Chris and Gina waited.

Kate hesitated. "I'm not going to say."

"That's when you let a boy put his tongue in your mouth," Chris stated with a superior smile.

"Uck," Kate muttered. "That's disgusting."

"I knew you didn't know," Gina said.

"Did too. I just think it's yucky, that's all."

Gina puffed on her cigarette. "Motorcycles are so cool." She gave Kate a sideways glance. "Who's Julian going with this summer?"

Kate shrugged. "I don't know."

"I thought he was going with Lisa Reynolds," said Chris.

"They broke up."

"Really?" Gina looked thoughtful. "That didn't last long, did it?"

"Nope."

"So how come he doesn't have a new girl-friend?"

"How should I know?" said Kate

"Maybe he's just shy," offered Chris.

Gina fingered a lock of hair. "How come Julian hangs around with that creepy Ricky Bennett? Boy, what a little creep."

"Ricky wants to be an actor. Just like Julian," said Kate.

"Ricky's too ugly to be an actor," said Gina, "but I'll bet Julian could be a movie star."

"Yeah," Chris sighed, "and I love his motorcycle."

"I want to marry a man who rides a motorcycle," Gina announced.

"I want to marry the Royal Astronomer of England," said Chris.

Kate looked stricken. "I thought you wanted to *be* the Royal Astronomer of England."

"That was last year, silly."

"You mean you don't want to be an astronomer any more?"

Chris shook her head. "I probably couldn't be the Royal

Astronomer anyhow. He probably has to be a *man*. But if I was married to him, then I'd be famous too, only I wouldn't have to do all the work."

"But it wouldn't be like being it yourself," Kate said.

"Well," Gina said, "I want to marry a count and live in Paris. Frenchmen are the best lovers, you know."

Kate and Chris glanced at each other, then looked at Gina. "They are?"

"Of course."

Kate's eyes narrowed. "Well, I want to be a veterinarian and stay right here at Mockingbird. And I'm not going to get married at all."

"But then you'll be an old maid," gasped Chris.

"So what?" Kate glared defiantly at her friends.

"Oh, Katie," Gina laughed, "you'll change your mind when you're older. You'll see."

"Venus," sang Frankie Avalon, "Oh, Venus . . ."

# CHAPTER

# 8

## Lenox, Massachusetts
## July 1959

Marian had started smoking again. She wandered from window to window, looking out at the rain-drenched lawn.

The kitchen smelled of cinnamon, a scent fondly remembered from her childhood, but today those memories brought small comfort as she prowled through half-dark rooms.

In the living room, a white cat lay curled up on the sofa. The cat had arrived a few days after Marian had moved in and, after trying in vain to shoo it away, Marian had accepted the arrangement. She had always wanted a cat, but her mother was allergic to them, and Owen said they were parasites fit only for eating mice. Harboring a cat made Marian feel smugly rebellious.

She stubbed out the cigarette and looked desperately around the room. The clock chimed three. "Dammit," Marian muttered, pushing her fists together until her knuckles cracked, "another day shot to hell. I'm not going to get anything accomplished at this rate." Angrily, she stomped into the kitchen and grabbed a poncho from a hook beside the door.

The remnants of her mother's flower garden bordered the path that led down the hill toward the pond. Lavender and daisies nodded between the roses. Honeysuckle vines lay in tangled masses where peonies and irises once bloomed.

Halfway down the hill stood a barn, once painted red and now weathered to a dusty rose. She tugged open the heavy double doors and stepped inside.

The interior was in the first stages of renovation—sawhorses standing among the stacks of two-by-fours and plywood. Her heart sank as she looked around. Remodeling the old barn for a studio was going to be a lot harder than she'd thought. She didn't have any idea how she would ever get the ceiling up without help, but help cost money. And money was in short supply.

She needed to pour footings for the studs or they would rot out within a year, but the estimates for such a small job had been outrageous. She would have to do that herself as well. That meant another trip into Pittsfield to buy the cement and arrange to rent a mixer.

Discouraged, she sat down on a sawhorse and thought once more about hiring an assistant. But the materials themselves were running up a staggering bill and there was Alex to consider. She ought to send Gwen another check to cover Alex's meals and bus fare. "Don't worry about it," Gwen had said, but Marian did worry.

The hell with it! She wasn't about to go crawling back to Mockingbird to face Owen's smug "I told you so." She hoisted herself up and marched out into the rain. She would go and get the cement now, right away. Before she lost her nerve.

"Pittsfield," the driver called. "Passengers going on to Boston please stay on the bus. This is a short stop, folks."

"Well, I guess this is it." Carl jumped to his feet and grabbed his bags from the overhead rack. "So long, Ralph," he said to the portly man in the window seat. "And good luck on your selling trip."

"And good luck to you, young fella," Ralph replied. "I'll be looking for your name in the papers when I get back to California."

Carl grinned. "It may take awhile, but keep looking."

"How do I get to Lenox?" he asked the driver, who was busy pulling baggage from the Greyhound's grimy hold.

"Go up the hill to the town square and take a number twenty bus," the man said. "They come 'round every couple of hours."

Outside the bus station, the air was heavy and oppressive. A sour smell rose from the damp asphalt, and a milky sky hinted at more rain. Carl's shoulders drooped as he looked around. It wasn't at all what he had expected. A paradise, Grandfather had called it. Some paradise. He stood for another moment gazing at the sorry collection of weathered, aging buildings, then he squared his shoulders and started up the hill. Funny, the way things so often didn't turn out quite like you hoped they would, the way reality intruded on fantasy, the way expectations—

"Look out!"

The dolly veered sideways as he crashed into it, sending several bags of cement mix sliding into the gutter.          "Just look what you've done," cried an indignant voice. "Why don't you watch where you're going?"

"Sorry," Carl muttered. "I didn't see you." He sat down on his suitcase and began to massage his bruised shin. Glancing up, he found himself confronted by a slender woman dressed in jeans and a faded denim shirt. Hands on hips, she glared down at him.

"Do you always go around with your head in the clouds?" Turning on her heel, she began struggling with the heavy bags, trying to stack them back on the dolly.

Carl watched her for a moment, then got to his feet. "Here," he offered, "let me give you a hand."

"Never mind. I'll do it," she grunted. But even as she spoke, the edge of the bag tore open and a stream of grey powder poured onto the walk. "Damn it!" the woman cried.   Carl grabbed the bag and set it on the dolly. "Where are you going with this stuff?"

"My truck's over there." She pointed to a dilapidated pickup truck on the far side of the street.

"Put the tailgate down, and I'll load these for you," Carl said. The back of the truck began to sag under the weight of the cement. "Looks like you could use some new shocks," he said.

The woman gave him a hostile glance. "You're just full of good advice, aren't you?"

Anger flared. "You bet I am. And you're welcome for the help." He started to stalk away.

"Wait a minute," she called after him.

He pivoted and glared at her.

"I'm sorry," she said in a small voice. When he didn't answer, she shrugged helplessly and added, "I really am. It's not your fault I've had a lousy day."

"No ma'am, it isn't," Carl said.

"Anyway, thanks for the help." With an impatient gesture, she pulled the bandanna from her head and shook out her hair. It was long and golden, and Carl couldn't help staring. She really was very pretty. Even beautiful, with those high cheekbones, straight nose, and full lips. And oddly familiar. Could he have met her somewhere before?

"I guess I'll take this back," she said, reaching for the empty dolly.

"I'll get it," Carl said. "Would you keep an eye on my luggage?"

"Thanks again," she said when he came back.

"S'okay." He was still trying to figure out where he might have seen her. Then he thought of the bus and glanced at his watch. "Damn!"

"What's' the matter?"

He sighed in exasperation. "Aw jeeze, I think I've missed my bus."

"Where are you going?" she asked.

"Lenox." Now what the hell was he going to do?

She looked at the bags and the violin case that sat alongside the curb. "Headed for Tanglewood?"

"Yeah."

"Fiddle player, huh?"

He nodded, wondering if there were any taxis in town.

The woman hesitated for a moment, then said, "Well, I'm going in that direction. I guess I could give you a lift."

Carl gave her a grateful glance. "Wow," he said. "That would be great."

He followed her across the street, tossed the bags into the pickup bed, and climbed into the cab, his violin case in his lap. As they pulled away from the curb, she said, "By the way, I'm Marian Archer."

"Carl Fitzgerald."

"So," she said as they bounced along the brick-paved street, "ever been to Tanglewood before?"

"Nope. I've never been east of Arizona. Except for Austria."

"What were you doing in Austria?"

"Studying."

"Music?"

He shrugged and grinned. "Mostly." He glanced at her and saw she was smiling. Tiny lines crinkled at the corners of her eyes. He decided she must be around thirty. Funny, thirty had seemed so old when he first met Anya. Now it didn't sound very old at all.

"Any family in New England?" she was saying.

"My mom's folks were from somewhere around here. Connecticut, I think."

"What about your father's family?"

"No," he said, "they weren't from around here."

"You must be thrilled to be going to Tanglewood," Marian said.

"You bet," Carl replied. "Only this doesn't look the way I thought it would."

Marian laughed. "Pittsfield's an old mill-town. It's had a rough time economically since the factories closed. But Lenox is a different story. You'll see."

The road crossed a grey stone bridge and plunged into a forest of hemlock and maple. Beyond the trees he could see deep-green fields dotted with herds of black-and-white cattle.

"So, you're from Arizona." Marian's voice broke the silence.

"Actually," Carl took off his cap and ran his fingers through his hair, "I've been living in California for the past few years."

"Where in California?"

"Uh—San Francisco." It sounded so much more romantic than Sacramento.

"I used to live in San Francisco," Marian said.

"No kidding?"

"I went to art school there."

Carl looked at her with new interest. "Are you an artist?"

"Not yet," she said with a little laugh, "but I'm working on it."

He liked the way she held her head—proudly, but without seeming arrogant. "What do you paint?" he asked.

She was silent for a minute, then said, "Ghosts."

"Ghosts?"

She nodded.

He wondered what she meant, but decided not to ask. They were entering the outskirts of a village. Graceful maple trees lined the street, their newly unfurled leaves creating a canopy overhead. "Gee," Carl exclaimed, "this really *is* pretty." Maybe Gramps had been right after all.

They left the main part of the village behind and started down a hill past meadows thick with gold and purple wildflowers. To the west, a lake lay nestled in the lap of the hills.

At the bottom of the hill, Marian pulled into a gravel drive and stopped before a cluster of wood-frame buildings. "Here we are," she said.

Carl took in the winding drive, the rustic buildings, the flower-spattered meadow and deep-green woods. "It looks like a summer camp," he exclaimed.

Marian laughed. "But that's exactly what it is. A very special sort of summer camp."

"I can't believe I'm really here."

"Nervous?"

"It's a big step for me." He started to get out, then stopped and said, "What about the cement mix? Do you need help unloading?"

"I'll manage."

He was suddenly reluctant to say goodbye. "Say, do you ever come to the concerts here?"

"Sometimes."

"Then maybe I'll see you again?"

She shrugged. "Maybe."

"I'd like to. See you again, that is."

When she laughed and shook her head, her blond hair caught the light. Beautiful, that golden hair. "Go on now," she said. "I'm sure they're expecting you."

"I suppose so." Violin case in hand, he hopped down from the cab. "Thanks again for the ride," he said.

"And thank you for the help."

He gave her a wink and his most dazzling smile. "See ya."

She laughed and shook her head.

He started up the drive, whistling, and then he remembered where it was that he had seen her—Tucson. She looked amazingly like that picture of the Angel Gabriel that hung next to Nanna's bedroom door. The same sternly beautiful face surrounded by a halo of golden hair. "Got a date with an angel . . ." he sang softly, then laughed at the thought. He glanced back and saw the truck was still there. He set his suitcase down and waved. After a minute, she waved back.

# 9

## The Berkshire Music Center
## Lenox, Massachusetts

"Now, this is the Hawthorne cottage," the thin, grey-haired woman was saying. "Nathaniel Hawthorne lived here while he was writing *The House of Seven Gables.*"

"What's the cottage used for now?" Carl asked.

"Studios, rehearsal space. And this is the Lion Gate, the main entrance to the original estate. And there," she pointed toward an imposing turreted mansion that sat on the crest of a gentle hill, "is the Tappan house. Mr. Tappan built it in 1849. It has twenty rooms. We use them now as offices and classrooms."

Carl realized music was coming from every direction—the sound of strings and woodwinds, the whine and twang of violins being tuned, the sudden blare of trumpets. Musicians trooped across the lawn, singly or in groups, carrying instrument cases and wads of sheet music.

"Come along, and I'll show you The Shed."

"Why is it called a shed?" Carl asked.

The woman laughed. "When Eero Saarinen first designed it, there was a big to-do over costs. He told the founders that if they just wanted a shed, then they didn't need him as an architect. So, the trustees hired Joseph Franz of Stockbridge to modify the plans. Mr. Franz built us a shed, and so it has been called to this day."

Carl smiled. "I hear that it has pretty good acoustics, for a shed."

"Yes," said the woman. "It does."

Carl's looked at the huge, wedge-shaped hall with its exposed metal girders and unfinished wooden baffles. Suddenly, the dramatic opening of the Beethoven Piano Sonata No. 4 echoed from the distant stage. "Jeeze," Carl said, "who's playing?"

"Stefan Molnar," the woman replied.

Carl listened intently. God, what a beautiful, mellow sound. He stared at the thin, elegant figure seated at the piano, watched his fingers move over the keys.

"Have you heard him play before?" the woman whispered.

Carl shook his head. "Not in person, but I have three of his recordings, including the Liszt B Minor Sonata. I think it was made when he was twelve or thirteen. It's unbelievable." He listened for several minutes then said, "Do you think I could meet him?"

The woman frowned. "We've been asked not to disturb him," she said. "He's doing a master class for the advanced piano students this afternoon, but he's still recuperating."

But Carl was already heading down the aisle and, when the pianist paused to make a notation of the score, Carl called out, "Excuse me, Maestro Molnar?"

Stefan looked up. "Yes?"

Carl bounded up onto the stage and held out his hand. "Hi. I'm Carl Fitzgerald. Gosh, it's a real honor to meet you, sir. I didn't know you were going to be here."

Stefan rose slowly and shook Carl's hand. "Thank you. You are too kind."

"I'm a real fan."

"Hello, Maestro." The woman had followed Carl to the edge of the stage. "How are you feeling?"

"Quite well, thank you," Stefan said. "The master class, it is still scheduled for one o'clock?"

"Yes, if that's all right with you."

"That will be fine." He turned to Carl. "Are you a pianist, Mr. Fitzgerald?"

"Nope, fiddle player. But I'm crazy about your work. I've studied your interpretations of Liszt, in particular, and found them very innovative."

"Thank you." Stefan's mouth twitched with a half-smile.

"What I'd like to know—" Carl began.

"Mr. Fitzgerald," the woman interrupted, "excuse me, but I believe Maestro Molnar would like to practice."

"Oh," Carl said. "Sure. Sorry."

"Forgive me," Stefan said. "I am afraid that my time is rather limited, and I have much work to do."

"I understand." Carl held out his hand. "So long."

Stefan smiled as he shook Carl's hand. "So long, Mr. Fitzgerald."

"He was wounded in the revolution in Hungary, wasn't he?" Carl asked as he and the woman walked back up the aisle.

The woman nodded. "They didn't think he would survive. What a loss that would have been."

The music began again, and Carl turned for a final look. I'm here, he thought, I'm really here. Bless you, Anya. Bless you, Gramps. This is going to be one great summer!

"Another rainy day," Marian muttered as she looked out at the soggy, flattened flowers. For just a moment, she was actually homesick for Mockingbird—for the blazing California sun and the pale-blue sky spread above the snow-topped mountains.

"I'm going for a walk," she told the cat as she headed for the door.

The scent of wet earth rose to greet her, and the air was heavy against her face. She pushed her clenched fists deeper into her pockets. Maybe she should get away for a few days. Maybe a weekend in New York. She could go to a couple of plays. Visit the mid-town galleries. The image of blistering asphalt, of sweating bodies crushed together in the subway banished the idea from her mind.

The gates of Tanglewood were suddenly before her. She remembered the first summer of the music festival. How excited Papa Philip had been. "It's the beginning of something truly wonderful, Charlie," he had said to Mama. "They're talking of making it an annual event. We must give them a small donation, don't you agree, my dear?"

Marian stared past the gates and wondered how young Carl was doing. How lucky musicians were. They had a sort of built-in family, a group of like-minded companions to talk to.

But as though her thoughts had conjured him, she spotted Carl coming toward her across the lawn. "Hi there," he called. "I thought it was you." He looked so charming, his dark hair spattered with drops, cheeks slightly flushed from the rain-cooled air.

For a moment they stood smiling at each other, then she lowered her eyes and began to walk along the drive. He fell in beside her. "So," he said, "how've you been?"

"Fine. What about you?"

"Fantastic. I love it here. I've been meeting the most incredible people—Stefan Molnar, Charles Munch. It's the coolest place I've ever been."

Marian laughed. "I knew you'd like it."

"So, how's the new studio going?"

"Fine."

"That's great."

She stopped and looked at him. "Actually," she said, "I haven't gotten a damned thing done on it."

His eyes widened. "Why not?"

"I think I'm in over my head," she admitted. "I'm just not sure I can do it all myself."

"Maybe I could help."

"Heavens no. I wouldn't dream of interrupting your studies. Besides," she glanced at his hands, "you shouldn't be doing carpentry. What if you hurt yourself?" She thought of her son Julian, and a twinge of pain shot through her.

"I really like building things," Carl said. "I used to help Gramps in his wood-shop."

Marian hesitated. "I couldn't pay you anything."

"That's all right. You could teach me about art. Maybe we could go into Boston. You know, to a museum. I've always wanted to know more about painting."

She studied the sky. The clouds had cracked open along the

horizon, and the fir trees were waving their arms. "Wind's shifted," she said. "Might clear off by tomorrow." She looked back at Carl. "I suppose if you have any spare time over the weekend, you could drop by. Here, I'll give you my address." She scribbled the number on the inside of a matchbook and handed it to him.

For a moment their eyes met, then she looked away, confused by the sudden rush of warmth.

"I have to go," she said quickly. "Come over on Saturday if you have the time. If not, I'll understand. Goodbye."

She started to walk away, but his voice followed her.

"Marian?"

She glanced back. How dear he looked standing there smiling that shy smile, his hands in his pockets, the wind toying with the dark cloud of his hair. "Munch's conducting the *Jupiter* tomorrow night," he said. "Would you like to come hear it with me?"

She felt a little flutter of delight, but shook her head. "I'm busy."

A look of disappointment swept across his face.

"Sorry," she added.

He nodded and stood watching as she walked quickly away.

She lay in bed that night, watching the moonlight flicker through the trees. The storm had cleared, and the night air was unbearably soft against her skin. She thought about Andrew—his hazel eyes, his bright-red beard. It had been such a crazy time, that summer in San Francisco—taking art classes at the Institute, meeting Andrew. How daring she had felt. How independent.

But then came the move back to Mockingbird, the nagging guilt, Owen's caustic dismissal of her work. "It's not a hobby!" she remembered telling him. "It's a calling."

"You call this stuff art?" he shot back. "At least the things you used to paint were pretty. This is trash."

She sat up and lit a cigarette and stared out at the black shapes of the trees. The old rules no longer applied, and she had not yet faced the necessity of finding new ones. "Oh brave new world," she said with a shaky laugh.

Crushing out the cigarette, she lay down again, eyes open in the darkness. When at last she fell asleep, she dreamed she was a fish that was climbing a ladder—jumping up again and again, trying to make it to the next rung, but flopping back each time into the same pool, trying to get up the strength to try again.

# 10

## The Berkshire Music Center
## July 1959

"I got a speeding ticket last night," Zev Zabrisky announced.

"On a Vespa?" snorted Dave Maddox, flipping open his instrument case and dusting the rosewood finish of his cello with a small piece of felt.

"Zev could get a speeding ticket for walking," Carl said, rubbing resin on his bow.

"Us New Yorkers march to a different drummer," laughed Zev.

"How do you mean, different drummer?" asked the second violinist, an Indian boy, small and dark-complexioned. Then his eyes brightened. "Oh, it is like a metaphor, yes? That's very clever, Zev."

Zabrisky bowed. "Thank you, Jamali, but alas it's not an original."

Carl tapped his bow on the music stand. "Come on, gentlemen. Let's get to work. We have to get this ready for class by Monday."

"Cool it, Maestro," Zev retorted, settling his large frame into the folding chair. "You're supposed to be our mellow Californian."

Carl raised his bow and, at his signal, the four musicians began to play the first movement of Mozart's String Quartet in B Flat Major, "Hunt".

"Wait a minute." Carl lowered his bow. "Something's wrong." The music dissolved into dissonance. "Can we do that whole statement again from nine to the forte at twenty-six?"

Dave threw his arms around his cello and rested his chin on its shoulder. Zev tossed back unruly dark-blond hair and winked at Jamali.

"When I go up at twelve," Carl said, "I'm going up high and you're going down low, Dave. Could you possibly be a little flat?"

Dave played a descending line. Stopped. Repeated it.

"That's better," said Carl. "But it's still not quite right."

"It's because there's such a long space here," said Jamali, pointing to the score with his bow.

"Maybe that's it," said Carl. "Who's got a pencil?"

"Right 'ere, gov'ner," said Zabrisky. The musicians took turns making notations on their scores.

"Okay," said Carl, "let's start from nine. And three, and four . . ."

For several minutes the music flowed smoothly, four voices in perfect unison. Then Zev broke off, waving his bow. "Wait a minute. I'm getting lost. I always get lost at that same place."

"What place is that, Zev?" Carl asked.

"The complicated place. Where there's too many notes."

Jamali and Dave laughed. Carl had to smile. A little comic relief could be a welcome break from the rigid concentration.

"Let's start from fifty-five," he said, once more raising his bow.

They were together now, each voice fitting perfectly into the larger pattern of the composition. This was what made it all worthwhile—those moments when some magical barrier dissolved and the music floated effortlessly from his hands, the way it was meant to be.

"Bravo," Carl said as they finished the movement and lowered their instruments. "That was first-rate."

"Hear, hear," chorused Zev. "I think we're going to have to take you seriously, Maestro."

"Get off it, Zabrisky," Carl said, flushing with pleasure. "Let's get back together after the one o'clock seminar. We need more work on the third movement."

"Count me out," said Zev, dusting off his viola and putting it to rest in its velvet-lined case. "Vicky and I are going on a picnic."

"Pleasure before business?" Carl chided, shaking his head. "I don't know about you, Zev."

"Hey," said Dave, "you know what they say about all work and no play, right, Jamali? Why don't you take some time off, Carl? We're going into town to see *Ben Hur*. Rachel and those two friends of hers from Germany are going to join us. Shall we make it a triple date?"

Carl hesitated. "I have . . . other plans."

"Do we know her?" Dave asked.

"Perhaps it is the beautiful blond lady I saw you talking to outside the gate last Thursday?" hinted Jamali.

Carl glanced up.

"What blond lady?" Dave asked.

"Oh," Jamali sighed, "she is truly lovely. Beautiful face. Beautiful hair that hangs like this around her shoulders." His hands caressed imaginary tresses.

"Name," Dave cried. "I want a name."

"Forget it, Maddox." Carl snapped shut his instrument case. "See you guys later."

"Just a minute," Marian called, wrapping her wet hair in a towel. She opened the door. "Oh," she said, "it's you."

"Yes," said Carl. "Me. Am I interrupting—something?"

Marian's neck prickled with embarrassment. "No. I'm . . . just surprised to see you."

"I had some spare time so I thought . . ."

"Right," she said. "Well, come on in."

"Nice place," he said, glancing around.

"It was my parents' summer house."

"Where did they live in the winter?"

"Boston," she said. Suddenly nervous, she looked away. "Would you care for some lemonade?"

"Sure."

Uncomfortably aware of her nakedness beneath the robe, Marian ducked into the back porch and pulled on jeans and sweatshirt.

"What's the cat's name?" Carl called from the living room.

"Cass," she called back.

"Like in Cassandra?"

She handed him a glass. "Like in Cassatt. Mary Cassatt."

"Thanks. Who's Mary Cassat?"

"An artist." She sat down on the sofa, and the cat jumped up beside her. "Cassatt was born in Philadelphia, but went to Paris to study with Degas."

"I've heard of Degas," Carl said. "Ballet dancers, right?"

"Among other things."

Looking around at the bare white walls, he asked, "Where are your paintings?"

"Most of them are in storage."

"Oh."

"I'm only going to be here for the summer."

"Then why are you building a studio?"

Marian shrugged. "Good question. I need a place to work and . . . I didn't think it would be such a big job."

Carl sat down on the floor next to the coffee table. "Will you be moving into Boston for the winter?"

"I expect so, if my daughter gets a scholarship to the Conservatory there."

He set down his glass and stared at her. "I didn't know you were married."

She looked down at her hands and realized that she wasn't wearing a ring. She'd taken it off the day she left California. "My husband and I are . . . separated." It was the first time she'd said it aloud.

He watched her for a minute, then leaned back against the sofa. "How old is your daughter?"

"Twelve."

Again, he gave her that disarming smile. "You don't look old enough to have a twelve-year-old daughter."

"Thank you, I think." And I won't mention my seventeen- year-old son, she added silently.

"What instrument?" Carl asked.

"What?"

"Your daughter. What instrument does she play?"

"Piano. She's quite accomplished," she added.

He sipped his drink. Presently, he glanced up and said, "Marian, what did you mean when you said you painted ghosts?"

Surprised that he remembered, she thought for a minute, then said, "Have you ever seen a soul-catcher?"

"A what?"

"A soul-catcher. Indian shamans used them in healing ceremonies. They're supposed to swallow up the sick person's soul so the shaman can heal it."

"Actually," he said, "I remember hearing about that in Arizona."

"Well, I think artists are sort of like soul-catchers," Marian said. "They gobble up the spirit of a thing and make an image of it so that everyone else can see it. Maybe it's a kind of exorcism. You bring the spirit out in the open and then you can deal with it."

He was watching her so intently that she felt shy and added quickly, "Anyway, I guess that's what I'm trying to do—take my ghosts and make them visible."

She said it half in jest, but he didn't laugh. Instead, he said, "I think I know exactly what you mean. Did you ever write invisible letters? You know, you write the words in lemon juice and then you hold the paper over a candle and the words appear?"

"I used to love to do that," she said.

"Well, that's sort of how I feel when I'm playing music. Like I'm revealing a secret message." He sat up and his hands, which were long and slim and very finely structured, circled restlessly. "I want everything that's not perfect to burn away," he continued. "That way, I can reveal the core, the very essence of the music. And when that happens, you can hear it."

"Yes, that's true," Marian exclaimed. "You can always tell when you've gotten to the very heart of it."

"When it's exactly right." Carl's eyes were shining. They sat smiling at each other.

Overwhelmed by an almost irresistible urge to put her arms around him, she jumped to her feet and began to gather up the empty glasses and damp napkins from the coffee table. The cat, annoyed at being disturbed, hopped down from the sofa and trotted toward the kitchen, tail waving like a warning flag.

"What's wrong?" Carl said.

"Nothing," she said. "It's just . . . it's been a while since I had someone to talk to about . . . anything." She hurried to the kitchen and rinsed the glasses, then stood at the sink for several minutes staring out at the garden. When she came back, he glanced up and said, "Can I take a look at the studio?"

She shrugged. "I'm just getting started, but what the heck."

He followed her down the path to the barn. When they stepped inside, he stood for a moment looking around at the interior. "Quite a project," he said, glancing at her.

She nodded. "I know."

He walked slowly around the room, stopping here and there to look at the renovation materials. "You're trying to do all this by yourself?"

She bristled. "I know something about carpentry."

"Yeah, but some of this is going to take two people. You can't hold up a piece of wallboard and nail it at the same time."

She didn't answer.

"You've got nice light," he said. "Those clerestory windows are on the north side, aren't they?"

She wondered how he knew that north light was important in a studio. "Yes," she said. "That's the best light for making art."

"I saw this really interesting documentary on a French artist." He paused. "Started with a D. Not Degas. Uh—*Delacroix*," he exclaimed. "They filmed part of it in the studio that he had in Paris and made a big deal out of the windows on the north side."

Marian smiled. "I visited that studio last time I was in Paris."

"Have you been to France often?" he said.

"Twice. I went with my aunt both times. We like to travel together."

He glanced around at the room once more and said, "I think that, together, we could make this a great studio for you."

She tried to imagine them working together, holding up panels, nailing boards, plastering, painting. She felt confused and excited and frightened at the same time. But it was likely the only way she would get her studio. "Well," she said, "I've got pretty much everything I need, so if you're serious, we can start on it whenever you have some time."

As they walked back to the house, she wondered if she was making a huge mistake. It wasn't like her to be so indecisive. Confused, she shook her head.

"What?" he asked.

"I didn't realize it was getting so late," she said. "You'd better get going."

He stopped and studied her. "I thought we might go into town. Get something to eat?"

"I really can't. I've got things to do. Letters to write. You understand." It sounded so lame.

He nodded. "Then I suppose I should go. I'll try to come earlier next time."

"If you're too busy, I'll understand."

"I really want to help."

"Well, if you're sure. Maybe I'll see you next week then." She glanced at him and felt warmth rise in her face.

"Yes," he said with a little smile. "I expect you will."

# CHAPTER

# 11

"Is it lined up down at your end?" Marian asked.

Carl squinted along the edge of the board. "A-okay. Hang on 'til I can get a nail in it."

From the top rung of the stepladder, Marian surveyed her domain. "We're making real progress. The floor and the ceiling were the hard parts."

"Here," Carl held out his hand, "let me help you down."

Standing next to him at the bottom of the ladder, she realized for the first time how tall he was. Her head was barely even with his chin. "Thank you," she said, straightening her shirt. "Shall we call it a day and have some tea?"

He settled himself in a wicker chair on the veranda. She watched him through the kitchen window. It seemed indulgent to stand there gazing at him, but she couldn't seem to stop. He had put his shirt back on, cuffs rolled up, but the collar left unbuttoned so she could still see his bare chest down to the line of his jeans. "For God's sake," she told herself, slamming the plates around and dropping the napkins. "You've got to quit this nonsense."

"I made cookies." She set the plate down next to him. "Peanut butter."

He'd finished two before he spoke. "I got a book on Mary Cassatt at the library."

"Oh?"

"Why did she paint so many pictures of children?"

Marian sat down beside him. "Maybe it was because she didn't have any of her own."

"She wasn't married?"

"She was married to her art."

Carl was silent for a minute, then said, "I guess it would be hard to be an artist and have a family, too."

"Very hard," Marian said.

"Maybe artists shouldn't get married."

She frowned. "It's different for men."

"Is that why you left your husband?" When she didn't answer, he studied her for a minute, then said, "So why do you think Cassat painted children?"

"Maybe because they were there," she replied. "They were beautiful, and she loved to look at them so she painted them. Maybe it's as simple as that."

"Maybe sometimes things are a lot simpler than we think."

The garden basked in the sun, filling the air with the heady scent of lilacs and poppies. He got up and leaned against the corner post, watching her silently until she glanced at him. "I'd really like to see your work," he said. "Don't you have anything you could show me?"

She didn't reply.

"I'm serious, Marian."

"I know."

"Well?"

"I suppose I do have a few drawings . . ."

Her arms felt heavy as lead as she dragged the portfolio from the closet and propped it up against the sofa. "These were done last spring," she said. "Right before I left San Francisco."

"They don't look like drawings," he said. "At least not like the drawings I've seen."

"I was using oil pastel. I guess some people might call them paintings."

"The colors are wonderful. I feel like," he struggled for a moment, "like I can almost *taste* them."

Marian's scalp tingled with pleasure.

"Who's that?" he asked, pointing.

"My daughter."

"She's very beautiful." He turned to her and added, "Just like you."

She felt as though she was falling very fast down a long shaft. His shoulder was nearly touching hers, and she could feel the warmth coming from his body. She felt flushed and soft and helpless and couldn't bear for another minute to be so close to him. "Well, that's it," she said as she gathered up the drawings and closed the portfolio.

"That's all you're going to show me?"

"Yes."

"I guess I said the wrong thing?"

She stared at him. "No. I liked what you said. It's just . . ." She felt trapped by his eyes. He was too damned beautiful. He terrified her completely. "It's late," she muttered. "I have some things to do, so please leave."

He got up slowly, crossed the room, and stopped before her. "What did I do?"

"Nothing. I just want to be alone." She couldn't look at him. If he touched her, if he so much as brushed against her . . .

For a moment he hesitated, then he stepped past her and was gone without another word.

"I've been trying to call you all week," Carl shouted over the phone. "Where have you been?"

"Out of town," she said.

"You could have told me."

"I hardly think I have to explain my plans to—"

"I want to see you."

"I'm really very busy."

"I'm coming over anyway."

In the porch light's yellow glare, his face looked hollow and forlorn. "What did I do?" he said. "Why are you angry with me?"

"I just felt that we'd been seeing too much of each other."

"I don't understand."

She lit a cigarette and noticed that her hands were shaking. "Look, Carl," she said, "we're both trying to get something accomplished this summer. I want to get the studio finished and get to work on a new series of paintings, and you're supposed to be studying your music."

"But that's what we're doing, isn't it? I've never worked so hard in my life."

She took a deep drag on the cigarette and said, "You were spending too much time with me."

"I can't spend all my time studying."

"I'm distracting you."

"No, you're not."

"Yes, I am."

Suddenly, he grinned, like a child who's been caught doing something naughty and doesn't mind a bit admitting it. "All right, you're distracting me. I like being distracted by you, okay?"

"It is not okay."

"Why not?"

She shook her head. "I don't want you to get the wrong impression."

"And what would that be?"

Damn. This wasn't going at all the way she had intended.

"Marian," he said, "why don't you just relax?"

She sank down into a chair, took another drag on her cigarette. The cat padded noiselessly across the room, hopped up on the sofa, and settled down next to Carl. For several minutes he sat stroking the soft white fur, then he raised his head. "I just like talking to you, okay? It means a lot to me."

They were both silent. She could hear the cat purring.

"I've been trying to . . . decide some things," he said. "And talking to you has been a big help."

"What do you mean?"

"Like when we were talking about Hermann Hesse the other day, and I said I admired Hesse because he understood Mozart, and then you said that you always remembered the line he wrote—you know, 'The most important thing in life is to find out who you are—and what you do determines what you are. To do anything else is to back up into the grave.' Remember?"

She nodded.

"Well, the next day I was sitting in the cafeteria, thinking about what you'd said, and all of a sudden I knew what I needed to do with my life. Isn't that fantastic?"

Marian smiled. "Fantastic. And lucky."

"I'll say. Imagine if you never found out what you were meant to do."

"Or if you found out too late."

"Of course, I always knew it would be music," Carl continued. "Gramps started giving me lessons when I was four, and I played my first recital when I was seven." He laughed, tossing back his hair with a little jerk of his head. "After we moved to California I started working with Werner Krantz. That was Rose's idea. Not that Krantz isn't good, he's just sort of . . . limited."

"Who's Rose?" Marian asked.

"My mother."

"You call her Rose?"

"That *is* her name," he said.

She nodded.

"Anyway," he continued, "then I got a scholarship to the Conservatory in San Francisco, so twice a week Rose would drive me down to the City. And then, when I was sixteen . . ." He stopped. "God, I don't know why I'm telling you all this."

"Go on," she said.

"I remember when I was maybe five or six, I used to stand on a hassock in Gramps's living room and practice conducting. I knew a few scores by heart even then. One day Nanna came in and said, 'How cute. He's pretending to be the maestro.' 'No, Ellie,' Gramps said, 'he's not pretending.'"

Carl was silent for a moment, then said, "I hadn't thought about that for years. It's funny that he knew, isn't it? He knew so many things." He paused. "I really miss him. He's been dead for ten years, but I still . . ."

"You must have been very close," Marian said.

"We were. I lived with him and Nanna until I was nine. Gramps taught music at the university in Tucson. He used to take me with him to rehearsals and master classes. Introduced me to his friends."

"Didn't you ever play with kids your own age?"

Carl shrugged. "Sometimes, but they were boring."

"Weren't you lonely?"

His eyes met hers and held them. "Isn't everybody?"

She took a drag on the cigarette. After a minute she said, "So when did you leave Tucson?"

He stared straight ahead. "When Gramps and Nanna died."

"Oh," she said. "I'm sorry."

"They were killed in an accident. Some bastard ran a stop sign. Rose sold their house, and I had to move to California."

"So your family still lives in California?"

"In Sacramento."

"What does your father do?"

"He's in the restaurant business." Carl jumped to his feet. "I'm going now, okay?" He stopped at the door and looked back at her. "You're not still angry with me, are you?"

"Of course not," she said.

"I'm free on Tuesday. Okay if I come over?"

"All right."

"Maybe we could go into Boston. Visit a museum. If you're not too busy, that is . . ." He looked at her hopefully from beneath long, coffee-colored lashes.

"Why not."

"Terrific. See you Tuesday."

"Tuesday it is."

It rained that Tuesday, and the street outside the Boston Museum of Fine Arts was dotted with puddles. Puffed white clouds sailed past overhead, racing inland from the bay.

"I liked the Turners best," Carl said as they walked along the sidewalk. "They looked like they're on fire, like the light was coming from inside. I never thought of light that way. You know, as color. Great golden washes of color. And the way everything disappears into the light. Everybody's always saying that light reveals, you know? But here it was, fracturing everything: boats, houses . . . everything exploding into particles of light. Wow. That is so cool!"

Marian laughed. "I guess it was worth the drive?"

"Absolutely. You know, I never realized how similar painting and music are. Like Monet and Debussy, for example. I was thinking about Debussy while we were looking at that Monet, the one with the river and the row of trees? That painting had a lot to say about Debussy's music. Now, whenever I see a Debussy score, I'll remember that painting—the way the light breaks up on the water, the way the water reflects the sky, forms breaking apart . . . This is great!"

She loved the way he gestured when he talked, his fine, slender hands circling and swooping.

They were passing through a park—raindrops glinting on bright-green leaves, small white flowers spreading like stars across the lawn.

"I'm hungry," Carl announced.

"Me too," she said.

"Where's a good place?"

"There's a little café a couple of blocks from here."

They found the café and settled in at a small table in the garden. "I'll have Campari and soda with a twist of orange," she told the waiter.

"The same for me," Carl said.

"You like Italian aperitifs?"

"I guess I'm about to find out."

They both laughed, then sat smiling at each other. The waiter brought their drinks. She sipped her Campari and studied him. Such an interesting face—the arched brows, the straight nose, the full mouth, the slightly cleft chin. For someone so young, the lines were surprisingly firm and strong. And yet there was a softness to him, a wistfulness that made him seem vulnerable and endearing. Maybe it was his hair. . . .

"What are you thinking?" he asked.

"How much I like your hair. I'm glad you don't wear it all slicked back in one of those awful DAs."

"I had a crew cut in junior high."

"Oh no. I can't even imagine that," she exclaimed.

He chuckled. "I looked like a sheared sheep. Made my ears stick out too."

"How ghastly."

"It didn't last long. As soon as I started high school I got into my romantic-poet phase and let my hair grow. Everybody thought I was weird, but what the hell. I like hair."

They ordered veal marsala and shared a bottle of wine. After dinner, they drove west into the remnants of a resplendent sunset. The trees soon turned to flat-black shadows and a full moon rose from behind low hills.

When they reached the gates of Tanglewood, Marian pulled off the road and stopped, but Carl made no move to leave. He turned toward her, and in the pale silver light his face was very mysterious and grave. "It's been a special day."

She nodded, not trusting herself to speak. He bent forward. She turned away.

"Why are you running away from me?" he asked.

"I don't know. I . . . I need time to sort things out."

"I understand."

"Do you?"

"I think so." He took her hand, which was clenched into a fist, and held it for a moment, carefully opening the curled fingers one by one. Gently, he drew it to his mouth and pressed his lips to her palm. Then he got out of the truck, closed the door, and crossed the meadow without a backward glance.

# CHAPTER

# 12

## Sacramento, California
## August 1959

For days Tommy had agonized over his decision, but he finally convinced himself that he had to try. Kate had said he was her friend. Perhaps she too was shy, waiting for a sign from him, something to let her know how he really felt. So it was up to him. But how? And where?

It was ferociously hot on this, the first day of the California State Fair. Owen had dropped them off at the fairgrounds on his way into town and now, Kate, Tommy, and Julian had taken refuge in the Hall of Flowers. Ponds and pools and streams and waterfalls glistened and gleamed in the mysteriously muted light. The earthy scent of moss mixed with the spicy smell of chrysanthemums and the delicate fragrance of roses.

Tommy and Kate paused before a waterfall, the rocky ledges covered with white orchids, while Julian moved on to the next display. "It's so beautiful," Kate whispered.

Tommy gazed at her. The mist from the waterfall was chill against his face. Very quickly, before his courage could abandon him, he brushed his lips against her cheek and took her hand in his.

The gesture was so gravely proprietary that for a moment she simply stood there staring at him. Then she snatched her hand away and stepped back. "What did you do that for?"

He didn't know what to say, so he stood there, looking at her hopelessly.

"Tommy," she repeated, "why did you do that?"

His face began to tingle as the blood rose from collarbone to neck to temple. "Forget it," he said. How could he have made such a disastrous mistake?

"Why are you looking at me like that?" she said.

"I said forget it." Please, please forget it. I take it back. It never happened. His face burned.

"I don't get it," she said.

"No," he said, "I guess you don't. Or maybe you just don't want to be seen holding hands with a Jap."

Kate's mouth flew open. "Are you crazy or what?"

At that moment, Tommy wasn't sure. He only knew that he had humiliated himself completely. He shoved his hands into the pockets of his jeans and strode away.

Kate trotted after him. "What's the matter with you?"

He didn't answer. A small red exit sign loomed, and he made a very sudden ninety-degree turn toward it.

"Tommy," Kate cried as he stalked out the door. "Tommy, wait."

"Where's he going?" Julian had hurried to catch up.

"Tommy!" she called. Just as he was disappearing into the crowd that surged along the wide, baked-clay path in front of the Hall of Flowers, she yelled after him, "We'll be at the Golden Bears at six o'clock." She couldn't tell if he'd heard her or not.

For the next five minutes Tommy ran, pushing through the blur of bodies, stumbling on curbs. He ran all the way to the amusement park—a jumble of gaudy awnings, tacky booths, and erector-set rides. The noon sun was dazzling and dust burned in his nose. Stopping under a blue-striped awning to escape the heat, he saw a hand-lettered sign: "Madame Zoya will read your future in your palm. 75 cents." Tommy stared at the sign for a moment, wondering. "What the hell," he muttered as he ducked inside.

Madame Zoya was very plump. Her frizzy blond hair, bisected by a strip of unbleached roots, was plastered by perspiration to her temples. When she looked up at him, her dangling plastic earrings caught the light. "Come in, young man. Sit down and give me your hands," she said, affecting a vaguely Eastern European accent.

Spare me the bullshit, thought Tommy, but he did as he was told.

For a moment, she sat holding his outstretched hands, turning them back and forth, looking at them with a vacant, dissociated gaze. "Move closer," she directed in hushed tones. "Rest the backs of your hands on the top of the table."

He looked anxiously at her rouged and wrinkled face.

"I see that you work hard for a living," she said. "Your hands are very strong and capable."

"Am I supposed to say anything?" Tommy asked.

Her little eyes flickered. "Only if you want to ask a question."

She once more turned her attention to his hands. "You are very creative," she continued, "but there are many obstacles before you. It will be a long time before your efforts find true fruition." She nodded slowly. "Your road of work will not be an easy one, but eventually you will find great happiness and success in your occupation."

Her fingers moved across his palm. "Your life will be a long one, but it will not be happy. Not for many years. Do you see these little cross-lines?"

Tommy peered at the spot along the base of his thumb where her stubby fingers were making little chopping motions. "I guess so."

"Each of these represents a major setback. Here, here, and here. You will meet with many frustrations. But do you see that past this point the cross-lines cease? If you do not succumb to desperation, you will at length have the sort of life you long for." Her fingers ceased to move, and she caught her breath.

"What?" Tommy said.

"There is danger here," she whispered. "A crisis. Something terrible. Do you see?"

He didn't, but he said, "I guess so."

"But your heart line . . ." She frowned and shook her head. "It is worst of all."

"Really?"

"I see many disappointments. You have much love in you, but it can easily be misdirected."

"It can?"

"You will marry twice," she said with flat finality. "The first will be disastrous. The second may succeed if you are not too hurt to try again."

She sat back abruptly and looked up at him. "Questions?"

Tommy's hands remained turned upward on the table. "There's this girl . . ." he said.

"Yes?"

"I love her. Do you think I have a chance?"

She smiled a tarnished, melancholy smile. "Oh," she whispered, "there is always a chance. Hope is what gives us the courage to continue."

He got up quickly, wiping his hands along his jeans as though to obliterate the evidence. "Thank you," he said.

Madame Zoya picked up the three quarters that lay before her on the table. "Any time, kid."

Heat snakes rippled upward from the dust as Tommy wandered aimlessly among the ferris wheels and cotton-candy booths. He squinted up at the sun. It was barely past noon, and he had six hours to kill.

Maybe he'd catch a bus downtown. Go and take a look at Sacramento Nihonmachi where his parents had lived before the war. "Can I get back in if I leave for awhile?" he asked the gate attendant.

"I'll give you a rain check," the man told him.

Tommy had to ask three drivers before he got the right bus, but soon the golden dome of the Capitol loomed above the trees. He got off and walked through the shady grounds, pausing for a moment to watch a group of tourists who were taking pictures of each other on the steps of the Capitol building.

"Young man. Hello there." One of the women was waving to him. "Could I take your picture with my sister? You know, for local color?"

Tommy sucked in his breath and hurried away. Was yellow the local color? "Maybe he doesn't speak English," he heard the woman say. *Shitshitshit* he shouted inside his head. Shoulders hunched, fists jammed into his pockets, he headed west toward the river.

Four blocks past the Capitol, he found himself surrounded by bulldozed lots and chain link fences with signs announcing redevelopment in progress. The storefronts had shop signs bearing Japanese names—Hayashi Dry Goods and Kobayashi Fish Market—but they were empty or boarded up.

Further toward the river he found grime-coated brick and abandoned alleyways bordered by waist-high clumps of milkweed. Stubble-faced men in tattered woolen overcoats slumped in recessed doorways, clutching brown paper bags.

Two more blocks and the Tower Bridge confronted him, its metallic pillars blazing in the sunlight. Beneath the bridge, the Sacramento River made a lazy curve and headed for the sea.

Tommy turned south and wandered along the river. Here and there the sagging facades were decorated with wrought- iron balconies and rows of ceramic tile—remnants of the Spanish architecture that had once graced the waterfront. How beautiful it must have been. What a joy it would be to restore this crumbling ruin to its former glory.

Music and cheering interrupted his thoughts. Peering through a half-open doorway into the smoky darkness of what had once been a movie theater, Tommy spotted a fleshy blond woman gyrating across the stage with her back to the noisy audience. As he watched, she whisked off her red bolero and spun around revealing enormous, bouncing breasts. Tommy, his neck hot with embarrassment, gawked. The men whooped their approval.

"Hey, kid." He found himself face to face with a burly, crew-cut man. "You wanna look, you gotta pay."

"No, I don't. I mean, I'd really rather not."

"Then get going. Go on, vamoose, you horny little Nip."

Tommy ducked past the man and hurried down the street. The next doorway held a hand-printed sign: *Good Food Cafe*, and some Japanese characters that he couldn't read. It had been a long time since breakfast.

The stairs creaked and the walls were dingy, but something smelled wonderful. Stopping at the landing, he looked into a room filled with low tables and tatami mats. A young Japanese woman wearing a tight black skirt, a red sweater, and a little blue scarf around her neck glided toward him.

"*Konnichiwa*," she said. "You want lunch?"

Lunch sounded more like *runch*, and it took him a moment to respond. "Yeah. Lunch."

She bowed. He bowed back. Travel posters of Japan decorated the walls, and white paper-lanterns muted the light. Vaguely, he could hear the bump-and-grind music from the theater next door. "Shoes, please?" she said.

"What? Oh." He took off his shoes and followed her to a low table next to the window.

"Here menu," she said, gravely handing him a dog-eared sheet of paper covered with Japanese characters.

"You have *hiyashi somen*?" Tommy asked, remembering a dish his grandmother had prepared on hot summer days.

The girl looked doubtful. "Please?"

"*Hiyashi somen?*"

"Ah, right away. What you want drink?"

"Uh, tea?"

She smiled and bowed. Was he supposed to bow back? Had she understood anything he said?

A few minutes later she returned with a large bowl of noodles, shrimp, and mushrooms, tea, and a small dish of salted plums. "That one dollar," she said. All this for a dollar? He pulled out a dollar and added a quarter for good measure.

"What's your name?" he asked.

"Name of Kiko," she replied with a little giggle. "I no see you here before."

"I don't get into town much."

She smiled, nodded, and said something in Japanese. Connie

had taught him a little of the language, but David didn't approve, and there was no one to practice with. Tommy shrugged and laughed.

The girl giggled again. "You Korean?"

Tommy shook his head. "Just dumb."

She gave him a puzzled look, then smiled and pointed to the bowl. "Food good. Please to eat?"

"Okay."

She retreated to the doorway and stood whispering with another waitress, watching him as he ate. Whenever he looked at her, she giggled and hid behind her hand. As he left the cafe he bowed and said, "*Arigato*, Kiko-san."

Her black eyes sparkled. "Bai-bai," she murmured as she inclined her head. "Please to come again."

Outside the heat was overpowering, but the sour smell of garbage mixed with the sharp odors of salted fish and spiced meat seemed more exotic than obnoxious. Tommy ambled along the street, stopping to examine the displays in shop windows and to look at the people who hurried past. There were as many Mexicans as Japanese among the crowd. The offices of the farm-labor contractors were in the area, and migrant workers, mostly braceros, hung around waiting for the opportunity to hire on.

South of Capitol Avenue, the harshness of brick commercial buildings gave way to clusters of wooden homes perched on stilts to accommodate the Sacramento River which had periodically flooded the lower floors. Long-necked palm trees flanked the streets, and orange trees and camellia bushes flourished in the tiny yards.

Connie had told him that they had lived on N Street, and he walked up and down N Street for a long time, trying to guess which house his parents had occupied before their removal to Tule Lake.

It was after five when he caught a bus back to the fairgrounds. Kate was waiting anxiously beside one of the life-sized golden grizzly bears that flanked the entrance to the Counties Building.

"Boy, you had us worried," she cried. "Where'd you go?"

"Nihonmachi," he said. "I just went . . . home to have a look around."

# CHAPTER

# 13

## Lenox, Massachusetts

The finished studio smelled of wood shavings and fresh paint. A newly stretched canvas stood on the easel, its pristine surface taunting her. It was so hard to draw that first line, make that new commitment. She might make all the wrong decisions, end up with a hopeless muddle, have to scrape it off and start again.

Marian lit a cigarette and picked up a recent copy of *ARTnews.* Thumbing through it, she was conscious of the small patch of sunlight slowly crawling across the concrete floor, of the dryness in her throat, the steady beating of her heart.

She tossed the magazine aside and ground out the cigarette on the clean floor. It left a stain of umber and a black splotch that pleased her very much. For another minute, she stood glowering at the blank expanse of canvas.

Then she picked up a stick of charcoal and walked rapidly to the easel. "Okay, you bastard," she growled at the canvas, "we'll see who wins this one." With large, determined strokes, she began to draw a portrait of her mother.

An hour later she halted in frustration. Muttering to herself, she hurried up the path to the cottage and rummaged through the bureau, trying to find a photograph that she remembered, a picture of her mother taken when she graduated from Wellesley. There it was. Class of '17. That was the year that her brother David was born. Had he survived the war, he would have been what, forty-two? She remembered the day he left to go to France, standing in the kitchen doorway, so handsome in his uniform. She stared for a moment at the faded photo. What beautiful, sad eyes her mother had. Then she rushed out of the house and ran down the path to the studio.

Her breath hurt in her chest as she pinned the photo to the top of the easel and stood back. Okay. That was what she was after—that light across the face, the flat black shape of the robe, the pale roll of hair above the thin, handsome face, that small, strange smile. She loaded the brush with sepia-tinted stain and began blocking in the patterns of shadow and light.

It was after dark when she left the studio and dragged herself up the hillside to the kitchen door. The cat wound itself around her ankles. "Why do people think it's fun to paint?" she asked the cat as she opened a can of tuna. "It isn't fun. It's damned hard work." She smiled a little as she added, "I wouldn't like it half so much if it was fun." She looked down at the cat. "Do you think I'm crazy for talking to you like this?"

The cat looked back with patient, half-closed eyes.

"Never mind," sighed Marian. "Don't answer that." The cat purred louder. "I was just thinking, Cass, how much fun it would be to paint our friend Carl. Such beautiful features. Especially his eyes." The little flush of warmth across her thighs surprised her. "Better keep an eye on me, Cassy. Next thing you know I'll be out molesting the neighborhood children, and they'll burn me as a witch."

So, she thought, here I am. A lonely, neurotic, middle- aged woman who's run away from home to become an artist. Who would have thought it would come to this?

After a supper of canned soup, she started up the stairs to collapse into bed, but stopped and headed for the door instead. The night outside was huge—blue-black and filled with stars. She sniffed the air and caught the lingering scent of honeysuckle, then ambled down the path and heaved open the heavy studio door.

She peered critically at her mother's portrait. The colors were subtle—earthy ochres, silvery grays, muted greens. Against the somber palette, the flesh seemed to glow with a blush of light, and the tendrils of blond hair that framed Mother's face were shot through with a strange radiance. Beneath the strong, firm line of the nose, the mouth hinted at a contradiction—the upper lip thin and tight, the lower one full and voluptuous. The smile was more implied than actual—a slight softening at the corners of the mouth, mysterious, inscrutable.

That was Mother, all right, thought Marian. Always an enigma. Satisfied, she turned off the lights and headed once more up the hill.

A strange dream woke her before dawn. She thought Carl was with her, but the bed was the one she had shared with Owen at Mockingbird—a ponderous antique that had been in his family for a century.

Then it seemed that Julian was in the room, sitting in the corner, watching them. She began searching for her robe. She could hear Kate and Alex arguing. What were the children doing here?

Dogs began to bark, and she ran to the window and looked out, but the yard was dark and she couldn't see who was there. When she looked around, Carl was gone, and it was Julian who was in the bed. His skin was pale blue. He must be dead, she thought, and began to scream his name—"Julian, Julian!"

For a minute she had no idea where she was. Then she saw the open window, the white lace curtains stirring in the gentle pre-dawn breeze. Shivering, she lay back down and stared at the shadows that flickered on the ceiling. Time to call Owen, she thought. I can't put it off any longer.

She waited until ten the next morning. He would be up by seven California time—probably much earlier. It was one of the things she had always disliked in their twenty years of marriage—only when she was ill had she been allowed to sleep past six o'clock.

"Operator," she said, "I'd like to put through a call to California." She waited, sipping tea, as the phone buzzed and clicked and began to ring.

"Hello?"

"Owen?" she said.

"No, it's Julian. Is that you, Mom?"

The dream came back along with a flood of memories, and tears welled up in her eyes. "Good heavens, sweetheart, you sounded just like your father."

"Oh yeah?" He didn't sound exactly pleased.

"How are you, Muggins?" It had been her pet name for him since he was a baby.

"Pretty good, I guess." He paused. "I miss you, Mom."

She was drawing little flowers on the napkin next to her teacup. "I miss you too, sweetheart," she said, wadding up the napkin to wipe her eyes. "How's Katie?"

"Fine. Mom, when are you coming home?"

She swallowed and said nothing.

After a minute he said quietly, "You're not coming back, are you?"

"Not right away, sweetheart. There's a chance that Alex will get a scholarship at the conservatory, and I don't think she should stay here by herself."

"She could stay with Aunt Gwen, couldn't she?"

"Gwen works, honey. I can't ask her to look after Alex for a whole year. And besides, I think twelve is too young for her to be on her own. Is your father there? I need to talk to him."

"I don't know. I just got up. Hang on a minute."

She waited, daubing at her eyes.

"Marian?"

"Hello, Owen."

"Well," he said, "how are you?"

"Fine. And you?"

"Fine." After a minute's silence he asked, "How's Alex?"

"Oh, she's doing very well. That's what I wanted to talk to you about." I can't tell him yet, she thought. I just can't face it. "It looks as though we may be staying here for the year. Alex might get a scholarship, and I'd hate to see her turn it down."

"Oh."

Was that real disappointment in his voice? Could he actually be missing her? "Miss Romanova has told me that she thinks Alex has unusual potential. Extraordinary talent was what she said."

"Uh-huh."

"So, I hope you'll agree that if her scholarship's approved, it will be best to continue her education here." She waited for a reply. "Owen?"

"Well," he said, "if you really think it's that important."

"Of course it's that important. Her whole future's at stake."

She heard him sigh. Alex's future was the best weapon in her arsenal, the one he couldn't defend against. "Well, I'm sure you know what's best." He paused. "Can I send you anything?"

"We're comfortable enough."

"Sure you don't need some extra cash?"

"I recall you saying that if I was going to embark on such a harebrained scheme, I'd have to do it by myself."

"All right, all right." After a moment he said, "Well, take care of yourself, Marian."

"I am, thank you." She instantly regretted the curtness in her voice. "It sounds like Kate and Julian are doing pretty well," she added.

"They could use a mother."

"You're the one who kept telling me they were old enough to take care of themselves," she shot back. "You were always criticizing me for being too soft with Julian."

"You spoiled him rotten when he was a baby."

"Not half as much as the way you spoiled Alex—giving in to her and letting her wrap you around her little finger."

"I didn't spoil her, you did. Putting all those big ideas in her head."

"It always seemed unfair to me, the way you had one set of rules for Julian and Kate and then let Alex—"

"All right!" he said. "Do we have to have a god-damned argument over the god-damned phone?"

She loathed herself for feeling smug. "Of course not. I apologize."

"That's more like it."

She gritted her teeth and crushed the soggy napkin into a tight little ball. "Well, I'm running up an enormous bill."

"You could call collect next time," he said.

"Thank you, but I don't want to cost you any extra money. That was our deal."

"Whatever you say."

The wires crackled in the silence. "Well," she said, "I guess I'll say goodbye."

"So long."

"Take care of the kids and tell them I . . . miss them."

"Okay."

"Owen?" She hesitated.

"What?"

She took a deep breath. "Thank you for understanding," she said. "I appreciate it." She squeezed her eyes shut and waited, but he didn't say anything. "Goodbye," she said through the lump in her throat.

"Goodbye, Marian," Owen said with cold finality.

# CHAPTER

# 14

## Lenox, Massachusetts

L ocusts buzzed in the thickets, and the air was heavy and still.
"Carl," Marian said, "if you don't sit still, I can promise you this
will take a terribly long time."

"It's already taken a long time," he said.

She was squatting at the edge of the pond, a sketchpad resting
on her knees, a stick of charcoal poised above the page. This was
the fourth time in a week she'd asked him to sit for her. A dozen
drawings lay crumpled in the trash can—the results of her struggle
to find the perfect lines to express that combination of elegance and
strength she saw in his lean, young body.

"Mannerist garbage," she muttered as she erased and tried again.
It had to be fluid without being soft, sensuous without becoming
effeminate. She held the charcoal stick at arm's length and squinted,
checking the relationship of ear to anklebone.

"Dammit," she said, erasing and re-drawing the line. "Stop
fidgeting," she cried. "How can I get this right if you won't sit still?"

"Sorry." Carl resumed the pose, one knee drawn up, his forearm
resting on the railing of the weathered dock.

"Marian?"

"Hmmm?"

"Let's go somewhere tonight."

"I can't."

"Why not?"

"I have to work."

"You always have to work.

"My work's important to me."

"I'm taking time off from my work to be with you," he said.

A wave of guilt spilled over her. "Maybe you shouldn't come by so often. I certainly don't want to interfere with your studies."

He lowered his head a little, the bottom lip becoming petulant.

"Dammit," she said aloud, erasing the line of his hip and struggling to re-draw the diagonal slice of bathing suit across his thigh. Damned swim-trunks, she thought. They interrupt the flow of that wonderful transition from hip to thigh. Wish we could do away with them. Her neck tingled at the thought, and a flush of color spread across her cheeks. But then I probably couldn't draw the . . . rest of him, she thought, and burst out laughing.

"What's so funny?"

"Me. What a sorry excuse for an artist I am."

"You'll get it right. I know you will."

For several minutes he remained completely still, posing beautifully. And for several minutes Marian struggled to render the elegant line that ran from ear to collarbone. The charcoal broke.

Angrily she erased the line and began again, more and more conscious of the heat that poured down from the summer sky. Her ankles itched, and the straps of her bathing suit chaffed her neck. She longed to strip off her clothes and dive into the cool, bottle-green water.

"Marian?"

"What?"

"Why do you draw figures?"

She stopped mid-stroke and looked at him. He remained unflinchingly committed to the pose. After a minute she said, "I suppose it's because I'm interested in people."

"But so much modern art is abstract—Pollack, de Kooning, all that stuff that's popular right now."

"Ab Ex is the major movement of the decade," she said without conviction. "The great new direction of our time."

"Then why do you do figures?"

She began to draw again. "Because, dear boy, I could give a fig for what's in fashion. I put in my time with the drip-and-dribble school, the glorification of the brushstroke, the tyranny of the spontaneous gesture. All very well and good for those guys on Fifty-seventh Street, but not for me." He had broken the pose, and impetuously she cried, "Carl, would you please stop moving your head."

"I can't help it. My neck's stiff."

She tossed the pad aside and walked out onto the dock. Kneeling down beside him, she began to knead his shoulders. His skin burned beneath her fingers. She tried to ignore the rough warmth of the wooden planks against her knees, the trickle of sweat that was inching its way down the small of her back. A few strands of her hair worked loose and fell across Carl's shoulder. She paused to stare at them—flaxen threads against the darkness of his skin.

"Marian?" His voice was tight and thin.

"What?" Her own voice was barely a whisper.

"I think I'm in love with you."

The stab of warmth across her pelvis and down the inside of her thighs made her wince. "Don't say that," she said.

"Why not?" He turned his head toward her, and suddenly the splendid tautness of his neck, the glow of light along his shoulder terrified her. He tried to take her hand, but she pulled away and scrambled to her feet.

"Marian!" He sprang up and caught her in his arms. "Please don't keep running away."

"Carl, I . . ." Her head was spinning, heat and light poured down. Her body felt heavy as lead, incapable of resistance.

"What are you afraid of?" he asked.

Of myself, she thought as his mouth closed on hers.

Marian arrived home a few days later to find Carl sprawled on the living room sofa reading a letter. "Hi," she said.

"Hello, beautiful." He gave her a quick smile and continued reading.

Half-annoyed, half-amused, she watched him for a moment,

then sat down across from him and poured herself a glass of sherry from the decanter on the coffee table. An opened envelope lay next to the decanter. "Silvio Morales," she read aloud, picking up the envelope. "A friend of yours?"

"My brother," Carl said.

"Morales?" She re-examined the envelope. "Is he your half-brother?"

Carl looked up sharply, and color spread like a stain across his face. "Morales is my father's name," he said shortly. "My grandfather's name was Fitzgerald."

"Oh." After a moment she asked, "Why do you use your grandfather's name?"

"Why shouldn't I? He was more a father to me than my own father ever was," he said, tossing the letter aside.

"I was just curious."

He got up and stomped across the room. A moment later she heard the back door slam.

Unperturbed, the cat sat purring on the sofa, contemplating the world with knowing, half-closed eyes. "Leave it to me," Marian said to the cat, "to get involved with an egotistical, temperamental, overbearing—I ought to have my head examined. Again."

It was dark when she heard him come in.

"Marian?"

"I'm in the kitchen."

He stood in the doorway and stared at her unhappily. She continued washing dishes and said nothing. After a minute he slumped down in a chair and watched his hands build a steeple. "I'm sorry," he said.

She didn't reply, but glanced at him out of the corner of her eye.

"I didn't mean to be . . . rude."

Sometimes the resolution of an argument is best delayed. "Want some dinner?" she asked.

"I'm not hungry."

"Make yourself a sandwich." She took a loaf from the breadbox and set it on the counter. Got out peanut butter and jelly. Watched him silently as he put a sandwhich together. Presently, she said, "What is it about your family, Carl? Why are you so angry?"

"Nothing important," he said between bites.

"I think it is."

The chin was stubborn, the eyes opaque. "Jorge and I just don't get along very well."

"So your father's Spanish?"

"Mexican."

"And I guess your mother's Irish. With a name like Fitzgerald—"

He put the sandwich down. "Look, Marian, do we have to have this dumb conversation? I really don't want to talk about it."

She studied him for a moment. "I'm just trying to understand. I thought maybe I could help."

"Well, you can't."

She sighed and looked away.

He got abruptly to his feet. "I'll come by on Saturday."

"I'm going to Boston for the weekend," Marian said shortly. She had just decided this.

He sat back down and gave her a reproachful look. "Did you forget about the recital?"

"I'll try to get back in time." She said this rather harshly, and to avoid his look she got up and made herself a cup of tea. Carl sat at the table drawing little circles in the water left by his glass. "Actually," Marian said, "maybe Alex would like to come up for the day. I could take her back to Boston Sunday night after the recital."

Carl's face lit up. "That would be super. I've been wanting to meet her."

# CHAPTER

# 15

"I didn't see your uh . . . lady friend out front," said Zev. "Don't tell me she's going to miss our little debut."

"She'll be here," said Carl, pulling nervously at his collar. "Is my tie straight?"

"You're perfection personified," laughed Zev. "Not that she cares about your tie."

"Stuff it, will you, Zabrisky?"

"It's time," hissed Dave. "Let's go." Gripping their instruments, the quartet strode onto the stage.

An hour later the audience gave the young musicians a round of applause. Flushed and smiling, Carl and his three companions bowed and smiled and bowed again. As the lights went up, Carl searched the audience, still hoping that Marian might be there. When he caught a glimpse of golden hair, his heart leapt with delight. "Marian," he called, pushing his way through the milling crowd. She saw him and waved and, as she did, the girl beside her stopped and turned toward him. Carl caught his breath.

With her exquisite, flawless features, Alexandria was a younger, more perfect version of her mother. Wisps of honey-colored hair framed a perfect oval face. Her eyes, which were the deep blue of lupine, stared back at him with an intensely curious but guarded gaze.

"Congratulations," Marian said. "You were fantastic."

He managed to pull his eyes away from Alex's face. "Thank you. We worked awfully hard." He looked back at the girl. "You must be Alex."

She nodded.

"So what did you think of our little recital?"

She tossed her head, blond curls shimmering in the light. "The Mozart was passable. I don't like Ives, but the Schubert was okay."

Carl covered his confusion with an awkward laugh. "You're a pretty tough critic."

"I try to tell the truth," Alex returned, fixing him with her gaze.

"Your mother tells me you're quite a pianist."

"That's right."

"Who are you studying with?"

"Sonya Romanova," she said.

"Really?" He had recovered enough composure to give her his most dazzling smile. "You must be quite advanced. I hear she doesn't take on many students."

"She made an exception for Alex," Marian said.

"That's because I'm exceptional," Alex said.

Carl laughed. "Tell me, is she as much an old bear as they say?"

"It depends. I found her to be quite impossible early in the day, but I changed my class time from eleven to three, and now we get on famously."

"A shrewd political move."

"I'm nearly thirteen," Alex said. "It's not as though I'm completely inexperienced."

Carl found himself once more at a loss for words.

Marian came to his rescue. "Come on, sweetheart," she said. "I think we'd better get going. I have a lot to do."

"Do you have to leave so soon?" Carl asked.

"I'm afraid so," Marian said. "I have some errands to run, and it's a long drive back to Boston, even with the new turnpike."

"But I want to stay and hear Bernstein conduct the Mahler," Alex cried. "Can't I, Mummy? Please?"

"Absolutely not. I don't want you running around Tanglewood by yourself."

"I could keep an eye on her," Carl offered.

"There, you see?" Alex said. "I can go to the concert with Carl." She turned to him. "You *are* going, aren't you?"

"I wouldn't miss it."

Marian raised her eyebrows and looked at Carl across the top of Alex's head. "Well, I suppose . . ."

"Smashing!" Alex clapped her hands.

"You're sure it's all right?" Marian said to Carl.

"Of course. You can pick her up at the gate at ten o'clock."

They stepped from the hall into the rose-tinted light of late afternoon. "Thank you," Marian said to Carl. "I know this means a lot to her."

"My pleasure," said Carl.

"I hate that," Alex said as she watched her mother walk away.

"What?"

"The way parents talk about their children in front of them as though they weren't there. It's as though I'm not a real person."

"I'm sure she knows that you're real."

Alex favored him with a precociously coy glance. "Well, what are you going to do with me for the next four hours, Mr. Fitzgerald?"

I've been wondering the same thing, he thought with mild panic. "Do you have something in mind?"

She studied the sky, then looked at him and said, "I'm hungry."

He felt a wave of relief. "Fine. Let's go into the village and get some dinner. Okay?"

"Okay."

They gorged themselves on hamburgers and French fries at a local diner, then ordered hot fudge sundaes for dessert. She told him about her studies. He told her about his. They sauntered along the sidewalk, enjoying the balmy evening, stopping to look in the windows of closed shops.

"Oooo, look at that," Alex cried, pointing. "I'd love to have a purple cape like that one."

"It would look terrific on you," Carl said.

"Would it?" She turned to look at him. "Do you think I'm pretty?"

He laughed to cover sudden confusion. "Of course. You're very pretty."

"I don't think you mean it," she said with a pout.

He cocked his head to one side and studied her. "You really are, Alex. Very pretty." Beautiful, in fact, he thought, but I can't tell you that. "Come on," he said, "we're going to miss the Mahler."

She was quiet during the concert, glancing at him now and then. He wanted to stare at her but stopped himself. He wondered about taking her backstage after the program to introduce her to his friends, but decided against it. He could almost hear Zev whispering, "What's this, robbing the cradle?" The idea made his face go warm. It's not as though this is a real date, he told himself. I'm just doing Marian a favor.

When they reached the front gate, he was both disappointed and relieved to see that Marian's car was already there. She got out and waved. "Hello there. How was the concert?"

"Wonderful!" they both exclaimed, then looked at each other and laughed.

"Consensus," Marian said. "It must have been good. Did you have fun, sweetheart?"

Alex nodded. She was looking at Carl very directly, which made him feel strangely unsettled. This is crazy, he thought. She's just a little girl.

"Come on, darling," Marian was saying. "We'd better get going." She turned to Carl. "I really appreciate this."

"No problem. I enjoyed it."

"*Au revoir, Monsieur*," Alex said, holding out her hand.

With a gesture both formal and familiar, he swept her hand to his lips and bowed. "*Enchanté, Mademoiselle.*"

"*Oui*," she whispered, "*enchanté.*"

"See you Monday," Marian called to him as she slid into the driver's seat.

"Oh, Carl, that's wonderful." Marian exclaimed. "I'm so happy for you."

"The best thing is they're going to let me sit in on the conducting seminar even though it's more than halfway through the term. Marian, there are people in that class—well, they're so talented. I can't tell you how much I'll learn just by being with them."

The waiter brought their food. She sat admiring him as he attacked his dinner. So young, she thought again. Not much older than my Julian. Involuntarily, she shuddered.

Carl looked up. "Are you cold? We could go inside."

"Just a chill. I love it out here on the patio."

"You're sure?"

She nodded. "By the way," she said, "you never did tell me if you have a girlfriend back in California."

"I don't." It was a matter-of-fact, almost careless reply.

"Really? A good-looking young man like you?"

"I haven't gone out much with girls."

"Carl," she said, "I'm certainly not the first woman you've made love to."

He put down his fork and gave her a reproachful look. "No," he said, "but I wouldn't exactly call Anya a girlfriend."

"Anya?"

"Anya Wilhelm. I studied violin with her, and after we'd been working together for several weeks she—I guess you could say she seduced me." He smiled. "Not that I minded. She took me with her to Vienna. It was my first experience inside the real music world, and I fell in love with it that summer."

After a minute he added, "She taught me things, Marian—about music, about love. Now and then I send her little gifts—things I know she'll appreciate. But I don't go to visit her anymore. It wouldn't be the same."

"Everything has an appropriate ending."

He looked up. "What's that supposed to mean?"

She was picking at the remnants of her dinner, eyes lowered, avoiding his look. "Summer won't last forever."

"I've been thinking, Marian," he said. "What if I were to transfer to the Conservatory in Boston instead of going back to San Francisco? I might be able to get a scholarship. I've done well here this summer. I could get good recommendations. Or maybe—"

"Don't," she whispered.

"I could get a job in Boston. I could give lessons. Maybe—"

"Carl, please."

"Listen to me." he said. "A lot of things have changed for me this summer. And you're one of them." He hesitated for a moment, then said, "I don't want to lose you, Marian."

She had closed her eyes, but now she opened them and forced herself to look directly at him. "I'll always treasure the time we've spent together, Carl. But what we have can't last."

"How can you be so sure?" he said. "Why won't you give us a chance?"

"I'm trying to build a new life for myself and my daughter here. Darling, you're only a few years older than Alex. Can you imagine how she'd feel? What it might do to her?"

"What would it do?"

She reached across the table and took his hand. "Carl," she said, "we only have two more weeks to be together. Let's not spoil them, please?"

# CHAPTER

# 16

Marian stripped off her bathing suit and draped it across the porch rail. The light was like honey, and every leaf glimmered, washed by the rain and polished by the light. But the leaves were already tinged with gold, the flowers shaking off their petals. She leaned for a moment on the rail, savoring the smell of the late-summer garden, feeling the sunlight on her bare skin.

California, Owen, even the children—everything that had come before seemed so far away. But ahead lay the cold reality of winter, the real test of her resolve. Chilled, she hugged her arms around her and hurried into the kitchen.

Carl, dressed only in swim trunks, stood at the sink stirring a pitcher of lemonade. "*Pour toi, Madame*," he said, offering a glass. "Well, well," he said, raising his eyebrows. "What have we here? *The Birth of Venus?* Or are you Eve emerging from the garden?"

"I'm going to be Eve on ice if I don't get some clothes on," laughed Marian.

"Cold?"

"It was the wind."

He took her in his arms. "I can provide a remedy."

"Can you now?" she teased. "And exactly what do you propose?"

"I have a terrific imagination." Drawing her close, he kissed her neck.

"Carl," she protested, "I really should get some clothes on."

"I have a better idea," he said. "I'll take mine off."

She tried to push him away, but he held her even tighter, pressing her to him, covering her with kisses. "I want you," he whispered.

"Not now, darling. We only just—"

"Mama? Where are you, Mama? Guess what. I got—"

Marian spun around. Alex stood frozen in the doorway clutching a white envelope. Her eyes moved from Marian to Carl and back to Marian, and the color drained from her face.

"Alex!" Marian exclaimed. "Sweetheart. I didn't expect you so early."

"I can see that," Alex replied.

"Uh, I'll go and get my robe." Marian ducked into the bathroom and grabbed her dressing gown. "Damn," she muttered under her breath as she hurried back into the kitchen.

Neither Carl nor Alex had moved. Like two cats poised for battle, they stood appraising each other with narrowed eyes.

"Where's Mrs. Crowther and Kitty?" Marian asked, fastening the robe around her.

Alex gave Marian a withering glance. "In the car, thank goodness. It would have been a bit of a shock, don't you agree, if they'd walked in and found you cavorting in the buff with—"

"That's enough, young lady. You might have knocked."

Alex straightened her shoulders and said, "I thought you said this was my home too."

"Of course it is, sweetheart. I only meant—"

"Here." Alex threw the envelope down on the table.

"What's that?" asked Marian.

"My scholarship papers. I'm in."

"Sweetheart, that's wonderful!"

"You don't care at all about my scholarship," Alex shouted, her face once more flushing red. "You *never* cared."

"That's not true. I'm delighted for you, darling. Why—"

"You are not. You never gave a *damn* about me. It was just an excuse to stay here with your . . . your *boy*." She turned her fierce gaze on Carl. "You're not the first, you know."

"Alex. That's enough." Grabbing the girl's arm, Marian pulled her into the living room and slammed the door behind them.

For several minutes, Carl stood frozen, fists clenched, heart pounding. Through the door he could hear their angry voices. He fought to get his breath, anger and humiliation rising in this chest. He spun around, bolted out the back door, across the terrace, and down the hill to the edge of the pond. Flinging himself down on the dock, he confronted his own distorted reflection in the grey-green water. The hell with her, he thought. I'll go back to California and never see her again.

He started to get up, then sat back down and glowered at the pond. He couldn't rid himself of Alex's contemptuous stare—those ice-blue eyes boring into him. He'd wanted so much for her to like him, but now . . . .

For many minutes, he continued to sit by the water's edge, brooding. The cool pressure of Marian's hand on his shoulder startled him.

"I'm sorry," she said.

He didn't reply. After a minute she sighed and sat down next to him. The pond was livid now—a saucer of burnt orange like the crater of a volcano. He squinted at it, trying to ease the burning in his eyes. After several minutes, the color began to fade, leaving small embers among the ripples. "What did she mean, 'You're not the first?'" he said.

"It's not like it sounds."

He gave her a flat, hard stare. "Then how is it?"

"She was angry," Marian said. "Alex will say almost anything when she's angry."

"Then she was lying?" he persisted.

"Dammit," Marian cried, "she's twelve years old and too precocious for her own good. And she's angry with me. More than I ever realized." She took a deep breath. "The summer I was in San Francisco I had an affair with my painting instructor. Alex knew something was going on." She lowered her head. "I guess I've let her down."

For a moment, she was silent. Then she added in a low voice, "She says I'm using her."

"Are you?" Carl asked bluntly.

"No! Well . . ." she hesitated, "maybe I have been. I don't know."

The wind stirred the grass. Carl plucked roughly at a few wisps and let the breeze take them from his fingers. "It hurt me, what she said," he said in a thin, low voice.

Marian wiped her eyes and nodded. "Alex has a way of knowing how to hurt."

The final concert of the summer was over, and the concert hall was almost empty. Abandoned programs skittered along the floor, driven by a rising wind. In the artist's room behind the auditorium, a stream of admirers sought out the evening's soloist. "Bravo." A tall man with a silver moustache pumped Carl's hand. "Extraordinary performance, my boy. We'll be hearing great things of you in the years to come."

"Thank you, sir."

"You were unbelievable, young man." A woman swathed in pink linen crushed him to her bosom. "Mendelssohn will never be the same for me again."

"Could you sign this program for me, Mr. Fitzgerald? It's for my little boy."

"Thank you. Of course. Certainly."

Marian stood watching him from across the room. Smiling, he took the hand of an elderly matron, then bent to kiss her cheek. A man thumped his shoulder, beaming. Look at him, Marian thought with a mixture of pride and envy, he's on his way and how he loves it.

"God, I thought they'd never let me go," he told Marian as they finally escaped the crowd.

"Are you sure you're ready to leave? There must be at least two dozen ladies back there who'd love to take you home with them."

He caught her arm and turned her face toward his. "There's only one lady I'm interested in going home with," he said. His lips brushed her forehead, making her shiver. "It's our last night together. I know how I want to spend it."

"Tired?" she asked as they sat across the table from each other in the dining room of the Avaloch Inn across the street from Tanglewood.

He shook his head. "No. I'm really wired. It takes a while to wind down."

She took his hands and studied them. They were almost too beautiful, too perfectly formed. The reality of his leaving came to her with the thought that she would never again hold those beautiful hands.

They ordered champagne. The stars walked down the sky and fell into the lake. From behind the trees, the moon came up—a giant golden globe marbled with violet. "Come on," he said. "Let's go home."

The bedroom window was open to the garden and the air filled with the scent of roses. Grave as an acolyte, Carl lit the candles on the bedside table. Shadows rippled on the wall. "Let me," he said, and crossed the room to undo the strand of pearls she wore around her neck. Gently, he lowered the zipper in the back of her beige silk dress, the dress she'd bought especially for this evening. The silk brushed against her thighs as the dress fell to the floor. His hand was firm on her shoulder as they turned to kiss, his mouth cool against hers. He slipped the straps from her shoulders.

She leaned against him, tempting him to kiss the soft nape of her neck, but he ran his hands along her sides and gently pulled the slip down to her waist. She started to reach back to unhook her bra, but he caught her hands. "No," he said, "I want to. Let me, please?"

"Carl—" She tried to trap his hands between her own.

"No, no," he protested, pulling away. "Everything. I want to do everything." One by one he plucked the pins from her hair and brushed the curls around her shoulder. "Beautiful," he murmured. "Have I ever told you how much I love your hair?"

"Yes." She could scarcely speak.

"I'll tell you once more. I love your hair." He ran his fingers through the mass of golden curls. "You've been my angel. My guardian angel."

His hands were moving down her sides, tugging gently at her garter belt. He sank to his knees and quickly slipped off her panties and hose. She felt his breath against her inner thigh as her fingers tangled in his hair. A low moan escaped from her throat. He teased her with his mouth, his hands, until she moaned again.

"Please," she whispered urgently. "Please, now."

Lifting her in his arms, he carried her to the bed. "Hurry," she pleaded as he stripped off his clothes and lowered his strong young body down upon her.

Hours later they lay amid the rumpled sheets. "I'll be back someday," he told her.

"I don't think so," she said.

"Yes, I will."

"Maybe," she laughed, "when you come back to conduct the Boston Symphony." Tears threatened, and she stared up at the ceiling. "Put out the light," she said.

He leaned across her to blow out the sputtering candle. She could smell the slightly salty, slightly musky scent of his sweat and was filled at once with an empty, desperate longing. With a little groan, she turned away and took refuge in her pillow.

"Look at me," he whispered, touching her bare shoulder.

With great effort, she turned. His face was silver in the moonlight. "I'll never forget you, Marian," he said softly.

"Damned right you won't." Roughly she pulled him to her and kissed his cheek, then let him go. "Now be still, my love. Just be still."

But his fine, knowing hands were moving over her once again, drawing her to him. Fighting the tears that welled up along with her desire, she clung to him in the darkness.

The cornfields of Kansas slipped past under a somber, late-summer sky. Through the bus window, Carl watched jagged bolts of lightning stab at the distant horizon. Blackbirds rose, swarmed like insects, and dropped once more into a stubbled field. A white farmhouse appeared, silver lightning rods atop the roof, a huge red barn, a single elm tree in the yard.

Beneath the tree a blond young girl played with a puppy. As the bus sped past she straightened up and waved. Carl waved back, knowing she probably couldn't see him. Then, resting his head on the back of the seat, he closed his eyes.

Images began to blur and slide. He was sitting beneath an apple tree. Small green fruit dangled above his head. Alex skipped past. Between her bright pink lips he noticed sharp little teeth. She smiled at him and tossed her curls. He started toward her, but she had grown wings and flew off laughing into a hazy sky.

Two ladies went past speaking German. The older one leaned on the younger one's arm. He saw her face. It was Anya, his former teacher, but she'd grown so old! Suddenly, his father was there, asking the women questions, but he was speaking Spanish, and they couldn't understand him. Carl hid in the tree. Jorge had taken Anya by the arm and pulled her along. He heard Jorge calling his name, "Carlos? Carlos? *Donde está?*" Carl huddled among the branches. Anya looked up and saw him. He was afraid she'd tell his father where he was.

Jorge began to cry. Carl wanted to call out to him, but the branches had grown thick, and he couldn't move. He was underwater, caught in a tangle of seaweed. Above he could see distant, muted light. He floundered upward, gasping for air.

Rain was pelting down, smearing the glass. Carl rubbed his eyes and found them wet with tears. Reaching into his duffel bag, he brought out the score of Haydn's Symphony No. 104. Beyond the window, rain thundered down on the endless, grey plain.

# CHAPTER

# 17

## Mockingbird Valley Ranch
## September 1959

The first storm of the season had blown in from the Pacific—a ferocious gale that rushed through the mouth of the Golden Gate, thundered up the Delta, and plowed into the Valley, flattening trees and ripping power lines from their moorings. But the McPhalan house sat solidly in the midst of the storm, its massive adobe walls impervious to the lashing rain.

Inside, the dinner table was an oasis of light in the darkened house, but anxiety pinched the back of Kate's neck as she glanced from her brother's face to her father's and back again. "D?" Owen said, "How the hell could you get a D?"

"I dunno."

"For Christ's sake, Julian," Owen said, "chemistry's not a difficult subject. You're just not concentrating."

Picking up his fork, Julian began stirring his mashed potatoes into a spiral.

"Stop messing with your food and look at me."

Julian lowered the fork but didn't raise his eyes.

"How much time did you spend studying for this test?"

"A couple of hours, I guess."

"I said look at me."

Julian continued to stare at his plate.

Owen threw down his napkin. "Just get the hell out of here, will you? I swear," he continued as Julian fled toward the stairs, "I don't know what's wrong with that kid."

Rain spattered roughly against the window, sharp, staccato taps.

Kate took a few more bites, then got up and began to clear away the dishes.

"Let Connie do that," Owen said. "That's what we pay her for."

"Yes, sir. May I be excused, too?" she said.

Owen took a bite of bread, chewed furiously, and waved the crust at her. "Why not? Then maybe I can finish my dinner in peace."

She paused outside her brother's room and listened. "Julian?" she called. "Are you all right?"

"Go away," came a muffled voice.

"Are you all right?"

"I just want to be alone, okay?" he said.

For a long time she sat in her room, listening to the wind moan in the eaves. The branches of the oak tree creaked and groaned like the timbers of an ancient sailing ship. There was comfort in the sound, something that made her feel peaceful in spite of the storm.

She pulled open the desk drawer and got out her diary.

*Dear Great-grandfather,*

*Well, Daddy and Julian are at it again. Now that Mom's not here, they fight more than ever. But I guess that pretty soon Julian will be going away to school. I'll miss him a lot, but maybe it will be good for him. I sure miss Mom. I even miss Alex. It's going to be strange with just Dad and me here. And Tommy's been acting weird.*

Standing up and cupping her hands around her eyes, she pressed her face against the window. Through the branches of the oak tree she could barely make out the faint, distant glimmer of the lights from the cabin where Tommy and his parents lived.

She started to go downstairs to say goodnight to Owen, but as she passed Julian's door she heard the sound of retching. For a minute she hesitated, then she opened the door. He was huddled on the bed, his face buried in a pillow. "Julian," she said sternly, "you are *not* all right."

"What?" He sat up and stared at her.

"I said, you are not all right. If you were, you wouldn't keep getting sick."

He fell back on the bed. In the muted light, she could see his eyes were swollen from crying. "What's wrong with you?" she said.

"I don't know. I keep having these dreams and then I get sick."

"What kind of dreams?"

"Just dreams." He turned away from her.

"Tell me."

"No."

"Tell me or I'll tell Dad that you throw up all the time."

He was silent. She waited. After a minute he said, "They're always different, but they all end up the same. Sometimes I'm falling and I start going around and around. It gets darker and darker, and I feel like my head weighs twenty tons. Then other times I'm caught in the tide. A big whirlpool pulls me down, round and round and round. There are always people shouting at me and I'm trying to tell them something, but they won't listen. And then sometimes I'm with—with Ray or Donny or Mr. Marley . . ." His voice trailed off.

"The English teacher?" said Kate. "What about him?"

"Nothing." Julian turned away again and hugged his pillow.

Kate waited. Finally he looked at her and said, "Everybody's always wanting something from me. Why can't they just leave me alone?"

"Who wants something?"

"Everybody! Dad's always at me, bugging me to study, And Mom wanted me to be a musician. But I screwed that up. Boy, did I screw that up."

"It was an accident," said Kate.

"Was it?" Julian asked. "Maybe I fell off that tractor on purpose. Maybe I knew I'd never be good enough. Maybe—"

"Stop it, Pooh."

"And Ray. I didn't even catch on about Ray until after he'd moved to LA, and I went to visit him and found out he'd moved in with Gary and Dale and they . . . and now Mr. Marley . . ."

"I thought you liked him," said Kate.

"Right," Julian said with a snort. "My big hero. But when it came right down to it, all he cared about was saving his own skin and keeping his precious job. He never cared about me. All he . . ." Julian gave Kate a hard stare. "You don't know what I'm talking about, do you, Roo?"

She shook her head. "Are you in some kind of trouble?"

He looked away. "Forget it."

"What did Mr. Marley do to you?"

Julian began to laugh. "Like I'm going to tell you, little sister. That's rich."

"I'm just trying to figure out what's wrong."

"Me! That's what's wrong. Can't you tell? I never do anything right. And I'm stupid. God, I'm stupid. I'm just— I'm . . ." Suddenly he was crying again. His voice muffled by the pillow. "He hurt me, Roo. I trusted him, and I never should have."

For a long time Kate sat next to him, listening to the wind sighing in the trees. "Julian?" she said, wondering if he was asleep.

"Hmmm?" His voice was drowsy.

"If you keep getting sick, shouldn't we tell somebody? Shouldn't you go to a doctor or something?"

"I'll be okay."

"Are you sure?"

He smiled up at her sadly. "Go on to bed, Roo. Everything's going to be fine."

---

### Sacramento, California

"So Marian's staying on in Boston for the year. That's a hell of an inconvenience." Dan was standing in front of his office window, frowning at the gloomy, rain-soaked landscape.

Owen slumped in the leather chair and sipped a water glass of un-iced bourbon. "I think we should forget this whole fandango," he said. "My life's private."

Dan crossed the room and settled on the edge of his desk, arms folded across his chest. "Don't be too hasty," he said. "Maybe she won't ask for a divorce."

"Goddammit," Owen said, "this whole business makes me sick. Let's just call it off."

"Come on, Mac," Dan said. "I'm just thinking strategy, that's all. You've got too much support from both the growers and the business community to back out now." When Owen continued to frown into his half-empty glass, Dan added, "Just have lunch with those guys tomorrow. After that, if you don't want to go on with it, I'll shut up. But at least join us for lunch."

"All right," Owen said. "I'll be there."

The next day, during the drive into Sacramento, Owen grew more uncertain. He'd never been comfortable in social gatherings. When he arrived, the others were already at their table in the far corner of the steakhouse. Dan introduced the two men, members of the Republican Party's Central Committee. Uneasy at first, Owen soon warmed to the conversation that had to do with farming and the recent figures on fruit production, subjects familiar to him.

Toward the end of the meal, one of the men, a small, dapper-looking fellow with a soft voice and slicked-back hair, turned to Owen and said, "What do you think of the proposed new zoning laws that would put a lid on development in the river basin?"

Owen realized that the question was not an idle one, and he hesitated for a moment before saying, "I think it's a smart idea."

"Why is that?" inquired the white-haired man who sat opposite him across the round table.

"That flood plain's a natural part of the river," said Owen. "Why build on land that nature intended to be flooded half the time?"

"But since the dam's gone in at Folsom, the flooding can be controlled," said the white-haired man.

Owen shrugged. "A lot of things can happen to a dam. Earthquake, heavy snow-pack. That channel could still flood."

"Then you're in favor of re-zoning to stop development?" the small man said.

"I didn't say that," Owen replied. "There's plenty of high land along the river for residential or commercial purposes. The issue is common sense."

The two men exchanged glances. "Well," the small one said, "I'm glad to hear your position, Mr. McPhalan"

"You can call me Owen."

The man smiled. "Very well, Owen." He sipped his drink, his eyes still on Owen's face.

The discussion continued for a while with Owen doing more listening than talking. They were cordial when he got up to leave, and he wondered as he walked out into the gloomy afternoon what they really wanted.

"All right," Dan said after Owen had left. "What do you think? Charlie? Bob?"

After a pause, the small man said, "Dan, I think you've found us a candidate."

"I can live with that," said the white-haired man.

Dan smiled and sipped his drink.

# CHAPTER

# 18

## Sacramento, California
## September 1959

"I'll miss you," Silvio said.

Carl turned to look at the small, dark-eyed figure sitting on the edge of the bed. "I'll miss you too, sport." He continued removing shirts and socks from the dresser and piling them into the suitcase.

"I wish you weren't going."

"Hey," Carl said, "you can always come and visit me in San Francisco."

"Won't be the same," said Silvio, rubbing the toe of his tennis shoe against the carpet. "I won't have anybody to talk to."

"Sure you will," Carl said. "You've got lots of friends at school, don't you? And there's Rose and Jorge. And if all else fails," Carl cuffed his brother lightly on the arm, "you can always try talking to Ali. If you can understand all those big words she uses."

Silvio smiled. "That's our sister.     The walking dictionary." The smile dissolved. "But really, big brother, I wish you could just stay here with us."

Carl sat down on the bed and put his arm around Silvio's thin shoulders. "Hey, little brother, I'll tell you what. When I get famous, I'll dedicate my first recording to you. Okay? 'Carl Fitzgerald plays Silvio's favorites.' What do you think? What would I have to play?"

"I dunno."

"Come on," Carl insisted. "What would it be? 'Jingle Bells'?"

"No," cried Silvio, wrinkling his nose.

"No? Then what about the 'Purple People-Eater'?"

Silvio punched Carl's shoulder. "You don't play that kind of stuff."

"Ouch. A furious fan. Now I'm in trouble. Come on then, name the program."

"Okay. You'd have to do that Tchaikovsky piece. The one with the real high notes."

"The D Major Concerto," Carl said. "Okay. What else?"

"And the Mendelssohn Concerto."

"Yes?"

"And the Brahms Concerto."

"Good God, what a program." Carl wiped his brow.

"And . . ." Silvio paused. "And all of Vivaldi's *Four Seasons*."

"Whew. I'm exhausted."

"And then on the other side . . ."

"No. Mercy. I beg you." Carl fell to the floor and covered his ears with his hands.

"Beethoven's Ninth Symphony," Silvio cried. "With you playing all the parts."

"Aagh." Carl collapsed, arms outstretched.

"Ah-ha," Silvio cried, jumping down and straddling his brother. "You see? You can't take the competition, so you'd better stay right here in Sacramento."

"A fate worse than death. Let me out of here." Carl made a break for the door, but Silvio tackled him from behind and they crashed to the floor, laughing and grappling.

"Me, too!"

The boys stopped and looked up as six-year-old Allison stomped into the room. "I want to play too."

"We're not playing," Silvio said. "We're wrestling."

"I want to wrestle too."

"You can't," said Silvio.

She stamped her foot. "Why not?"

"'Cause you're a girl."

"Misogynist!" Ali cried. "Misanthrope!"

"What?" chorused Silvio and Carl together. Ali used the opportunity to jump on Silvio's back and pin him with a chokehold.

"Help!" cried Silvio. "Get her off me."

"Stop it, Ali," Carl laughed, prying her loose and holding her squirming in the air.

"Let me down!" She grabbed his hair in her fists. "Let me down, Carlo!"

"Children." Rose's voice floated up the stairway. "Stop that racket and get ready for dinner."

"Saved by the bell," said Carl. "Come on, pipsqueak," he said, ruffling his sister's hair, "go get your hands washed."

"Last one downstairs is a rotten egg," cried Silvio.

Rose stood at the sink peeling an avocado. Her grey-streaked dark brown hair was piled atop her head, and she wore a flowered apron over her dress. She looked up and smiled as her three children trooped into the kitchen. "Ali, would you put the napkins on, please? And Silvio, you get the plates."

"And I," said Carl, opening the refrigerator door with a flourish, "will get the wine."

"Jorge," Rose called. "Dinner's ready."

"What a feast you have for us, Rosita," Jorge exclaimed as he seated himself at the table. "Roast chicken, avocado salad—a beautiful dinner."

"Some wine, Jorge?" Carl asked

"Sure, I'll have a little."

"A Chateaux Javernand 'Fifty-seven," Carl said.

"Carl picked it out himself," Rose said.

"Ah yes. Very nice I'm sure."

"Not a bad year," Carl said.

"Have you found an apartment, Carl?" Rose said.

"I have."

"Tell us about it."

"It's just a big room, actually. But the front window overlooks Nineteenth Street, and I can see the top of the Golden Gate Bridge."

"Oooh," squealed Ali. "Can you see Chinatown too?"

"Afraid not, sweetness," said Carl. "That's on the other side of Nob Hill."

"I want to live at the Top of the Mark," Ali announced. "I would have a superlative view."

"You can't live there, silly. It's a bar," Silvio said.

"Can too."

"She can't, can she, Mom?"

"Hush, darlings," said Rose. "I want Carl to tell us about his new apartment."

"Does it have a kitchen?" asked Jorge.

"Yeah, but I don't plan to spend much time cooking," Carl said between bites.

"Of course not," said Jorge.

"What will you be studying this term?" asked Rose.

"Conducting, mostly. But they've agreed to let me take advanced classes in transposition, and I may even get a chance to conduct the student chamber orchestra."

Rose beamed. "Gramps would have been so proud of you, Carl."

"Would you like for me to help you take your things down to the City?" asked Jorge.

"No, thanks. I've made my own arrangements."

"I could take the day off from work—"

"I said I've taken care of it."

"Okay," said Jorge. "Sure."

Rose held her breath for a moment. There had been enough arguments at the Sunday dinner table over the years. This would not be another. "I'll do the rest of the laundry after dinner," she said, "then everything will be clean for you to pack."

"Thanks, Rose," said Carl, then glancing at his watch he added, "Wow. Look at the time. Sil, if you and Ali still want me to take you to see *Fantasia,* you'd better eat up. We've got to make tracks or we'll miss the beginning."

—••o◖◗o••—

After the children had gone, Rose began to clear away the dishes. "Let me do that, Rosita," Jorge said. Gratefully, she sat down at the kitchen table and watched him as he worked. He'd grown stout over the years, but he'd never lost that special gracefulness that had always fascinated her. He had moved with that same easy economy the first time she had seen him, harvesting lettuce in a dusty Arizona field.

At seventeen, she had taken her assignment to do an article on migrant farm-workers for the local paper very seriously. She remembered standing at the edge of the field, clutching her notepad, her hat flapping in the desert wind. Jorge was the only one of the workers who spoke a little English—the formal, stilted English he had learned in school before his father had died.

"Young mistress," he had said to Rose, bowing. His face registered his confusion when she giggled.

"Is not right?" he asked.

"It's fine," she said. "I've just never been called a young mistress before."

"Then I will call you *señorita*, is *permiso?*"

They sat on the running board of the car she had borrowed from her father, and Jorge told her about the conditions of the worker's camp—the meager food, the lack of facilities.

"If you don't believe me," he said, seeing her shocked expression, "then come to the camp. I will show you."

She followed him around the pathetic collection of shanties, scribbling in her notebook, then sat up all night writing her story. Triumphantly, she took the published article to the camp to show to him, but he was not there and no one would tell her where he was.

For days she searched the town and then, miraculously, she spotted him standing in the line where foremen came to pick up their crews. He greeted her with a tired smile and eagerly scanned the story. "Would you read it to me please, *señorita?*" He listened silently as she read. When she had finished, he smiled and nodded. "Thank you," he said. "Now, I will show you something else." Gravely he unbuttoned his shirt and revealed the bruises across his ribs.

"What happened to you?" Rose asked, her face registering her concern.

"The overseer came to my cabin after you left. This was my punishment for telling you about the conditions in the camp."

Tears sprang into her eyes. "He did that because you talked to me? Oh, Jorge, I'm so sorry. Please forgive me."

"Oh no," he protested, "I show you this so that you will write another story. I can show you other things that have been done to the workers. Please, *Señorita* Fitzgerald. You must help us. Everyone must know how we are being treated." His eyes, so gentle and so full of sadness, melted her heart completely.

When six months later Rose became pregnant with Jorge's child, her father, Andrew, had threatened to have him deported. "That wetback bastard's ruined your life," he shouted.

"But Daddy," she cried, "I love him. We want to get married. Please, Daddy, give him a chance."

But forgiveness was not one of Andrew Fitzgerald's stronger virtues. He hated Jorge until the day he died. It was the one regret Rose had about her marriage—that and the fact that her son Carl had spent so much time with Gramps Fitzgerald that he too had been blinded to those qualities of gentleness and strength that she had seen so clearly through the Arizona dust.

Jorge whistled as he moved about the kitchen. After twenty years, he still limped from the wounds that had brought him home to her from the South Pacific. "Really something, our Carlo, eh, Rosita?" he said as he wiped the counter. "Maybe one day he will conduct a big orchestra, no?"

"He's very talented."

"You bet he is. Your papa was right about him. He will make us all proud."

"Just as long as he's happy."

Jorge stopped scrubbing and looked at her. "You don't think he's happy?"

"Sometimes I wonder if Papa didn't push him too hard when he was little. He never had a chance to enjoy himself."

"Don't you believe it," Jorge said. "There is nothing our Carlo enjoys so much as making music."

"I guess you're right."

"Now, Silvio," Jorge said, returning to the counter, "he will be a scientist, I think. Chemistry, that's what he likes. Did you see how he loves the set I buy for him? And our Ali, what a live wire she is. So clever." He put the sponge away and sat down next to his wife. "Life is very good to us, Rosita. Look what we have—three fine children and such a pretty home. And the business goes well, too. Just today I found a lady to make tortillas for us at the restaurant. She is Maria Gonzales. Her husband was killed in Korea, and she has a little boy to care for. You see? I knew we would find just the right person. She can help oversee the kitchen. Good idea, no?"

"If you don't stop opening new restaurants, I'm going to have to hire someone to help me with the books," Rose said with a laugh.

"Then hire. We can afford, no? Four locations we got now for Casa Morales. And to think we started with a tortilla shop in the back of my cousin's drugstore. I tell you, Rosita, America is still a land for the opportunity."

# CHAPTER

# 19

## Auburn, California
## October 1959

The social life at Sierra Vista High revolved around two poles: the Starlite Drive-In Theater and the after-the-game dances held each Friday night in the boys' gymnasium. If you were going steady, you went to both the dances and the drive-in. If you were still among the unattached, you went to the dance with a group of friends and hoped that your status might take a turn for the better.

Tommy Ashida was one of only two non-Caucasians in a student body of nearly twelve hundred. He also had the dubious distinction of being a straight-A student. This might have proved to be his undoing, had it not been that he could also run the hundred in 9.9 and throw a curve ball that was generally conceded to be un-hitable. The coaches had courted him, but the only team that Tommy's father would permit him to join was the California Scholarship Federation, a prestigious little group of college-prep students who were already filling out applications for Berkeley, Stanford, or one of the Ivy League schools back east.

Nancy Chen was the other non-Caucasian. Her father owned a pharmacy in town and Nancy, who was a senior, drove a white Thunderbird convertible. She was pretty, popular, a cheerleader, and had dated most of the "cute guys" at Sierra Vista High. Everyone agreed it was romantically appropriate when, at the first of the school year, Nancy and Tommy were suddenly seen everywhere together. (Weren't they just the perfect couple?)

Kate had decided that she hated Nancy Chen. "She's just all

wrong for Tommy," she told Christy Malacchi over root-beer floats at the local A&W. "She's such a phony."

"I don't suppose you're jealous?" Christy said.

"Are you kidding?" Kate snorted. "Tommy's like my brother. I just don't want to see him hurt, that's all."

"You gotta admit they look divine together. And you can tell she has a terrible crush on him, even if he is a junior. They've been together like glue for ten weeks now, and Nancy has never gone steady that long with *anyone*."

"I don't care. I think she's just a hussy," sniffed Kate.

"You *are* jealous," Christy exclaimed.

"Am not."

"Well," Christy said, "everyone says they're made for each other."

Kate sucked furiously on her straw. Nancy simply wasn't right for Tommy. And why had he been so different since the start of the school year? He'd hardly talked to her since they'd gone to the State Fair. The week after that he'd started going out with Nancy.

Kate hadn't wanted to go to the dance that rainy Friday night after the Del Norte-Sierra Vista game. It was Christy who talked her into it. Now she sat on the sidelines, listening as her companions scrutinized the action on the floor.

"There's Gina with Bruce Fowler," Kathy Sommers said to Christy. "Isn't he just the dreamiest thing you ever saw?"

Christy feigned indifference (why couldn't she be popular like her sister?). "He's not so great."

"He's captain of the football team."

"Who cares? He's dull. *Dull.* I don't know what Gina sees in him."

"With eyes like that, who cares if he can read," sighed Susie Warner. "Oh, look. There's Patty Adams. Who's that gorgeous thing she's with?"

"I think he goes to Sac State."

"Oooh, a college man. I wonder how Patty does it? She isn't even all that pretty."

"Guess," said someone cattily, and the girls giggled and glanced at one another.

"Well, well, well," Christy murmured, bumping Kate with her elbow. "Look who just wandered in."

But Kate had already spotted Tommy standing in the doorway, glancing around with that distant, reserved look of his that Kate's friends had labeled "cool."

"Where's Nancy?" whispered Susie.

"Haven't you heard?" said Kathy smugly. "They broke up."

"Nooo."

"Yes. It was all over the cafeteria at lunch."

"Poor Tommy," Susie said with a sigh.

Kathy shook her head. "Oh, no. Stephanie Williams told me that *he* broke up with *her*."

"A first!" said Christy. "Nooobody drops Nancy Chen."

"Well, Tommy Ashida did. White Thunderbird and all."

Kate stared across the dimly lit gym, past loops of wilted crepe paper hanging from trestled rafters, past clinging couples barely swaying to a Johnny Mathis ballad. She simply couldn't stop staring at Tommy, and as though her eyes had shouted to him, he started toward her through the forest of bodies.

Why had she never noticed before how beautiful his hair was—dark and straight and smooth as a blackbird's wing? Or the way he walked—that easy, graceful stride. Then he was standing right in front of her, smiling a little smile, looking down at her with his impenetrable eyes. "Hey, Kate."

"Hey, Tommy." The words barely squeezed from her throat.

"You want to dance?" he said.

Somehow, she got to her feet and took his outstretched hand and followed him into the "Twelfth of Never."

The girls stared after them. One of them murmured, "Did you see the way he looked at her?"

"I was afraid of this," Christy said.

"The ranch-hand's son," tsked Kathy. "Shades of *Lady Chatterley*."

"I wonder what poor Nancy will do now?" said Susie.

But after that night, none of them saw Kate and Tommy together again. Neither, however, did they see either of them with anybody else.

# CHAPTER

# 20

**Boston, Massachusetts
January 1960**

B right sunlight streamed through the windows, contrasting sharply with the blanket of snow that covered the city streets. Alex sat at the piano. Head high, chin thrust forward, she ignored the ringing phone. Marian hurried from her studio and grabbed the phone.

"Hello?"

"Marian?"

"Wait a minute. Alex, please, darling. I can't hear a thing."

Alex slammed her fists down on the keyboard, jumped to her feet, and stalked out of the room.

Marian shook her head in exasperation. "Yes? Owen? Is that you?"

"You haven't—uh—heard from Julian, have you?" Owen asked.

"What do you mean? Isn't he there with you?" Marian said.

There was an audible sigh. "I thought he might have gotten in touch with you."

"Oh no," she cried. "What's happened?"

"He and I had a little disagreement New Year's Day. He took off on his motorcycle, and I haven't heard from him since."

"New Year's Day. My God, Owen, that's over a week ago." She sank into a chair.

"Now don't get yourself all stirred up. He's almost eighteen. He can take care of himself."

"Oh Lord," she moaned. "I was afraid something like this was going to happen."

"Don't start blaming me. I've done my damnedest to keep that kid in line."

"Do you have any idea where he went?"

"Kate thinks he may have gone down to the City."

"Oh, Owen, he could be in trouble. He could be—"

"Simmer down," Owen said. "He'll come back once he runs out of money."

"Do you think I ought to come out there?" Marian asked. "Maybe I could find him."

"Don't be silly," Owen said. "You can't come running out here every time some little thing—"

"This is hardly some little thing!"

"I'll be back in touch in a few days. Just sit tight, and let me know if you hear from him, okay?"

"Call me, won't you? The minute you know anything?"

"Sure."

She dropped the receiver into its cradle and stared at the blinding glint of snow outside the window. Alex stomped back into the room, glaring. "Who was that?"

"Your father," Marian said. "Julian's run away from home."

"I wondered how long he could survive without you there to cover for him."

"Cover for him?" Marian stared at Alex in surprise. "What makes you say that?"

"Julian never stands up for himself. He's too chicken," Alex said.

"Some people just weren't cut out to be fighters."

"Well," said Alex, "now that he's on his own, Julian had better figure out how to stick up for himself. Or he won't last long."

God, Marian thought. Out of the mouths of babes. . .

Four days later, a letter post-marked San Francisco arrived.

*Dear Mom,*

*I guess you probably know by now that I've decided to make a go of it on my own. Seems I wasn't much better at getting along with Dad than you were. Anyway, life in the Big City (SF) seems to agree with me. I've got a job at the Blackhawk. I remember you telling me you'd been to the Hawk to hear Miles Davis the summer you lived in San Francisco. Bet you never thought I'd be working here.*

*I've gotten to know some really cool people in North Beach. Last week I heard Lawrence Ferlinghetti. Mom, you've got to read* A Coney Island of the Mind. *If you can't get a copy, I'll send you one from City Lights bookstore. Also, I met a wonderful man named Larry. I stayed with him and his girlfriend for awhile, and they helped me find an apartment and a job.*

*So you see, everything is going very well. Don't worry about school. I'm going to save up some money and go to City College.*

*Well, that's about all for now. Just wanted to let you know that I'm okay. If you talk to Dad, please don't give him my address. I don't want to see him. I'll write again soon.*

*Love and hugs,*
*Julian*

She read the letter a second time as she climbed the stairs. Then she tucked it into her purse and put through a call to California.

Larry Flagstaad referred to himself as a poet, and that allowed him a certain status among the North Beach literati. He frequented the coffee houses on Columbus, Broadway, and Upper Grant, and the apartment that he shared with a gaunt, forlorn-looking woman named Frankie was the center of a non-stop mélange of free spirits and runaways, dropouts, and drifters.

Larry's primary contribution to the cultural life of the community was measured in actions, not words. He supplied. Just about everything. Owen would have called him a gutter-variety hood, but to Julian, eighteen years old, broke, hungry, and homesick, Larry Flagstaad was a gift from the gods—a bearded, sandaled Bohemian angel.

Over cups of cappuccino at the Cafe Trieste, Larry sympathized with Julian's plight and offered sanctuary. Did Julian need a job? Larry would ask around. The next week he advanced Julian enough money to cover the first month's rent on a one-room flat on Vallejo Street, and landed him a job sweeping up after hours at the Blackhawk. Julian became one of the many visitors who drifted in and out of Larry's flat. In time, Julian came to think of Larry's pad as a sort of underground railway station, a hospice on the road to beatific self-fulfillment.

"It's only the Beat in us that counts," Larry said, sitting cross-legged on the dirty mattress that served as a sofa, "for Beat is Truth. You dig, Julie?" From the hi-fi, John Coltrane's "Giant Steps" seemed to mirror the sentiment.

"You gotta be cool, man. That is the first and primal law. Be cool."

Reverently, Larry shared the Mysteries of the Holy Magic Weed with his convert—a new communion. And Larry encouraged his protégé to write, provided criticism and advice. When one evening, a month later, Larry asked Julian to do him a big favor and deliver a little package to a friend, Julian was only too happy to oblige.

The next day Larry asked him to make another delivery. By the time Julian figured out what the little packages contained, he had delivered quite a few of them. Julian kept his mouth shut. He was cool.

But, he was also homesick. One night, alone in his shabby little room, he wrote to Kate—a long, emotional letter telling her how much he missed her, how good it would be to hear from her, and please, please not to tell Dad that he had written.

She answered at once. Yes, she missed him too. And yes, so good to hear that he was alive and well and living in San Francisco, how exciting. It was awful that Dad had been so mean.

Then one April afternoon he answered a knock on the door, and there she was, dressed in a white blouse and a blue gingham skirt, her hair loose and beautiful around her shoulders. He stared at her for a minute, and she stared back.

"Julian?" she said.

"Roo," he cried and gave her a crushing hug.

"You look different!" she exclaimed.

"Maybe it's the beard," he said, rubbing his chin.

"Must be."

"You look great," he told her and gave her another hug.

"Can I come in?"

"Sure. Of course."

She walked past him through the door. He followed and watched as she glanced around at the barren little apartment—a scuffed wood floor, dingy wallpaper, a curtain-less window that overlooked an alley. Two piles of bricks and a wooden plank provided a shelf for books and a small aquarium. Beyond a curtain of beads, a narrow mattress lay atop a tatami mat. The scent of incense hung in the air.

"Well," said Julian with a tight little laugh, "it ain't much, but it's home."

"It's really . . . nice."

"I was just on my way to the beach," said Julian. "Want to come along?"

They took the trolley out Geary Street and walked south along an ocean swathed in fog. A few couples and a half dozen children were plodding along the sand south of the Cliff House. Kate left her shoes next to the concrete retaining wall and followed Julian onto the beach. He strode along, head down, a cigarette dangling from his lower lip. He looked so much older, and the black turtleneck sweater made his blond hair seem paler than ever. "So," he said, "how's everything?"

"Okay."

He nodded, squinting through the smoke. "How's Dad?"

"Same as always. He's decided to run for the State Assembly," Kate said.

"No shit?" A thin, tight smile. "I figured Danny'd talk him into that."

"He's worried about you, Julian."

"Oh? He has a funny way of showing it."

"Come on," Kate protested. "You're both being stubborn. Why don't you call him?"

"Why doesn't he write?"

"You want me to give him your address?"

"No."

"Then how can he—"

His look stopped her. They walked in silence for several minutes. "How's Tommy?" Julian asked.

Kate hid a smile. "Fine."

Julian gave her a sideways glance. "Sounds from your letters like you two have been having fun together."

"It's supposed to be a secret."

"Why's that?" asked Julian.

"Guess," said Kate.

Julian laughed. "Because our august father would have a royal fit if he caught you going out with the help? Especially if the help is a Jap?"

Kate sighed. "It isn't fair. I told Tommy that I didn't care what Daddy says, but Tommy thinks we shouldn't push it."

"Kid's no dummy," Julian said. "I'm sure he'd like to keep his head connected to his body."

"Be serious, Julian. I don't see why it should matter. People are just people. What difference does it make if they're Irish or Polish or Japanese or—or Martian, for that matter?"

"Very egalitarian, dear Roo. But that's not the way it works in this imperfect world. I should know."

"S'not fair," grumbled Kate, kicking at the sand.

"A fair is a place where they judge pickles," said Julian. "And speaking of tarts, how are the Malacchis?"

Kate gave him a disapproving glance, but said, "They're okay. Well, sort of okay. Actually, Gina's pregnant. She had to get married over Christmas vacation."

"Oh yeah?" Julian smirked. "Who'd she marry?"

"Some jerk who works at Aerojet."

"Figures. How 'bout Chris?"

"She's fine. She wants me to room with her if we both get into Berkeley." She shrugged her shoulders against the cold. "How 'bout you, Julian? When are you going back to school?"

Julian shoved his hands deeper into his pockets and blew a puff of smoke into the wind. "I'm not. They don't teach you anything in school except a pile of crap."

"You really believe that?"

"You bet I do. I'm through with that bourgeoisie shit."

"Don't you still want to be an actor?"

He threw the cigarette down on the sand and buried it with his toe. "Look, Roo," he said, "I'm not making a lot of plans just now. One day at a time, okay?"

She nodded. Cormorants skittered before them like dry leaves along the surf line. "Julian?"

"What?"

"I think I figured something out, but you gotta tell me if I'm wrong."

"Oh?"

"It's about you and Mr. Marley . . ." She stopped and looked at him hard.

He looked away. "I don't want to talk about it."

"He shouldn't have been able to do what he did."

"It was my fault," muttered Julian. "I was dumb. Naive."

"But that's why he shouldn't—"

He glared at her. "Drop it, will you?"

"Sorry. I just wanted you to know I don't think what happened was your fault."

The deepness of the hurt came back to him—that and the

memory of Kate's unswerving loyalty. It was only with her that he felt accepted. Carefully, he brushed a lock of hair back from her forehead and gave it a gentle tug. "You're all right, Roo. You know that?" he said.

# 21

## Boston, Massachusetts
## April 1960

Marian was in the Boston Museum of Fine Arts examining a Constable landscape when, stepping back to get a better view, she planted her heel directly on Trevor Martin's sandaled toe.

After listening to her apologies, he said that he would forgive her only if she would allow him to buy her a cup of coffee. She studied his grey-streaked, collar-length hair, his salt-and-pepper-beard, his tweed coat with leather patches on the elbows, his quizzical grey-blue eyes, and decided to accept the invitation.

"Where are you from?" she asked as he helped her out of her coat and pulled out the chair for her.

"Recently or originally?"

She laughed. "I'm wondering about your accent."

"Oh, that. A dead-on giveaway that I'm not to the colonies born."

"I don't think you're Canadian or Australian, so you must be English, right?"

"Astonishing deduction, dear lady. And you, I perceive, are not a native of these parts."

"Ah, there you're wrong. I was born right here in Boston. But I guess any accent dissipated after my years in California."

"So much for my perceptiveness. What part of California?"

"The northern part."

"I've always wanted to go to San Francisco. Is it true that the buildings there are only a few stories tall to guard against the likelihood of their tumbling down in an earthquake?"

"Not anymore. Skyscrapers are popping up all over the city."

"What a shame. I always seem to arrive a bit too late. Tell me, are you married?"

"I used to be."

"Ah. Perhaps my luck is changing."

She found out a month later that Trevor Martin was married, but by then she had already spent a weekend with him at his cabin in Vermont. Married or not, he was amusing company, and Marian was grateful for that. When she told him she would be spending the coming summer in Lenox, he was delighted.

"Splendid," he said. "I'm teaching a poetry workshop in Stockbridge whilst my wife takes the kids to the Cape. I'll be able to pop 'round and see you every few days. Think of it, Marian. Six weeks without elaborate fabrications to explain my forays, of suspicious glances over the morning paper. My god, Marian, that woman will be the death of me one day."

Secretly Marian believed that Trevor reveled in his martyrdom. He adored having things to complain about—his colleagues at the college where he taught English literature, the lack of sensitivity in the publishing world resulting in his rejection slips, his children's taste in friends, his wife's taste in everything.

"Of course," he said, "she can't really help it, poor thing. Her family was well-to-do in money, but poverty-stricken where culture was concerned. I don't think she'd ever been to the theater until she went with me. As far as I know, she'd spent most of her childhood playing team sports and going to parties."

"Then why'd you marry her?"

He paused. "I think it was because she seemed so *American*, so wonderfully secure. It was right after the war, and I was desperate for stability, for the company of anyone who wasn't terror-stricken at the sound of an aeroplane. It took me a while to realize that her tranquility came not from strength of spirit but simply because she completely lacked the smallest twinge of imagination. She is absolutely incapable of conceiving a life without station wagons, clam- bakes, and the PTA."

"Then why don't you leave her?"

He paused and gave Marian one of his *meaningful looks*. "I told myself for years that when the time was right, I would. Perhaps that time has come."

But then, poor darling, Marian thought, what excuse would you have for all your discontents?

—••o❯❰❪❬o•—

## Sacramento, California

Dan Papadakis stood smiling behind the podium, waiting for the applause to subside. Then he said, "And so, without further introduction, I give you the next State Assemblyman of the Thirteenth District, Owen McPhalan."

Owen made his way to the podium, shaking outstretched hands along the way. Through the roar of applause, he heard Dan whisper, "Give 'em hell, Mac."

Owen looked out at the ballroom filled with glittering women and well-tailored men. His new grey suit felt tight around his shoulders. Nodding acknowledgement, he raised his hand to ask for silence, and a sea of faces gazed up at his expectantly. He cleared his throat and looked down at the sheaf of papers that lay before him on the podium.

"I want to thank you all for being here tonight to eat a five-dollar dinner that cost you five hundred," he began. Through the ripple of laughter, he continued, "And I want to thank my staff for putting together this fine speech that I'm supposed to read to you. I'm sure it's a dandy speech and says all the right things, but . . ." he pushed the papers aside and rested his arms on the podium, "I'm not going to read this speech to you folks tonight. I've got something to say, and I aim to say it straight from the heart. So if you'll just bear with me, I'll tell you what's on my mind."

He shifted his tall frame and glanced at Dan whose face was a study in repressed panic. Owen smiled inwardly. "My grandfather came to this valley in 1849 to look for gold," he began, "and he found what he was looking for. Some folks might have taken that gold and gambled it away or spent it on fancy clothes or bought a big house in the city, but my granddad wanted just one thing from that gold—he wanted a piece of land to call his own. And that's what he got.

"You know, down in Texas they talk about black gold. But I'm telling you, here we've got brown gold. We've got land." The hall was silent, attentive. Owen was surprised at the sense of purpose that gripped him.

"This valley has some of the most productive agricultural land in the world. You can grow anything here and more of it than you can most anywhere else. You've all seen how this area has grown just since the end of the war. And I think we're only seeing the beginning of a land boom that'll make the gold rush look like small potatoes."

For the next twenty minutes, Owen spoke about his deep concerns for the future of the region and outlined his plan for a bi-partisan coalition to resolve the conflicts that were blocking meaningful progress.

"If we have a plan for growth," he said, "if we take it upon ourselves to control development, then businessmen and growers alike can work together to make this valley a showcase for the whole state. Whether we're Republicans or Democrats, we've got to go beyond partisan issues and personal gain to look at the larger picture. If you love this valley the way I do, if you think of it as home, then I hope you'll join with me and help to make it the kind of place where our children and our grandchildren will still want to live and work ten or twenty or fifty years from now. I'm asking for your help. I'm asking for a bipartisan group to give me the backing I need to represent the best interests of all of the people in this valley. Thank you."

Owen sat down to a crash of applause. At Dan's urging, he twice more got to his feet to acknowledge the crowd. As he sat back down, Helen Papadakis leaned toward him, her eyes glowing, and said, "What a good speech, Owen."

"Was it?" Owen said. "I wouldn't know. Never come out much to this kind of shindig."

"Danny's right," said Helen. "You're just the man to bring these people together."

"Well, if I can do that I'll have earned my keep and more," said Owen.

"You will, Owen," she said.

He started to reply, but Dan rushed up, followed by a small, plump, red-faced man. "Walter Devin, Mr. McPhalan," he said, not waiting for Dan's introduction. "I congratulate you on your speech. I'm sure you know that many of us hereabouts are Democrats by tradition, but what you said made a lot of sense to me. If you'll have lunch with me tomorrow, I'd like to talk to you about starting a Democrats for McPhalan organization. I think we can help out quite a bit."

"Mr. Devin, I surely do appreciate that," Owen said, getting to his feet and towering over the smaller man. "I'll be happy to join you for lunch."

"One o'clock at the Manzanita Room? I'll bring some friends."

"Who was that guy, Danny?" Owen asked as Devin scurried away.

"Owns a walnut ranch down the river a-piece. He's a real honcho with the local Democrats." Dan winked at Owen. "I'm glad you tossed in that business about bipartisan support. Hell, we need to bring a few stray sheep into our fold if we're going to win in this district."

Owen nodded. "Well, I don't mind working with Democrats if that's what it takes. There's going to be some new alignments in this state."

"You know what they say about politics making strange bed-fellows," said Dan.

Owen gave Dan a sharp look. "I said I'd work with them, Danny. I sure as hell know where to draw the line."

# CHAPTER

# 22

## Auburn, California
## June 1960

M iss Blye was the counselor for the college-prep students, and her last official duty in this, the final week of school, was to call in each of her charges to query them about their college plans. The early-summer sun that streamed through the window reminded her that next week she would be in Santa Cruz, enjoying the luxury of the Pacific surf. She couldn't wait. And her patience was being challenged by the polite intransigence of the Japanese boy who sat across from her at her cluttered desk.

"Agriculture?" she exclaimed. "Tommy! You *can't* be serious."

His dark eyes fixed her with an impenetrable gaze. "Why not?"

"Well, I mean—farming? You shouldn't waste your talent on that."

He gave a mirthless little laugh. "That's what my father says. He gave me a choice—medicine or architecture."

"Well, either would be appropriate." She studied the sheath of records that lay before her. "You've got excellent grades in math and science. And the art teacher says you have a natural talent for design. With grades like these, I'm sure we can get you placed at any one of a number of outstanding colleges."

But Tommy didn't want to be placed at an outstanding college. The only place he wanted to be was at Mockingbird Valley Ranch. With Kate. Forever. "But I like farming," he said.

Miss Blye sighed. "What about landscape architecture? It can be very lucrative, and with your horticultural experience it should come to you quite naturally."

Tommy was silent.

"I'll tell you what, I'll find some catalogues that will give you info on programs at several different schools. You'll have the whole summer to think about it. Okay?"

"Okay." His smile was mechanical.

"You know, Tommy," she said as he got up to leave, "people as talented as you really do have an obligation to their families and to society to fulfill their potential. Farming is a perfectly noble occupation for people who— well, who have no other abilities. But intelligence like yours is a gift. It's your duty to use that gift wisely."

"Yes, ma'am," he said.

"I'll leave the catalogues with Linda at the front desk. You can pick them up on your way home. Have a nice summer."

"Thank you, Miss Blye."

He walked home from the bus stop, kicking a clod of rust-red clay and wondering how his life had gotten so screwed up. He'd lived at Mockingbird for more than twelve years—more than two-thirds of his life. He knew every tree and bush, every boulder and bird's nest of the seven hundred and fifty acres that comprised his personal kingdom.

It was only lately that he had realized that Mockingbird wasn't actually *his*, and that his time there might be drawing to a close. Kate had always been there, too, as much a part of the ranch as the river or the orchards. But what if she no longer lived there? What if she went off to Berkeley and decided that she wanted something else? Or someone else? What if his father insisted, and Tommy got that degree in architecture? How then could he live at Mockingbird?

And Tommy's Uncle Willie was pressing David to move to Stockton where, with the help of Willie's four children, he ran a thriving produce business. Connie, in her gentle way, had mentioned several times how nice it would be to live close to the family and a Japanese community.

At first it hadn't seemed so impossible. A love so strong, so right, so destined, couldn't fail. But how could you get other people to see the rightness? If you were afraid to explain the situation to your own parents, how could you expect an unsympathetic world to understand?

Whenever he was with Kate, he felt certain that they would find an answer. Nearly every day, as soon as his chores were finished, he hurried to meet her in their secret place—a small grove of willows at the bend of the river. In former years it had been, depending on their mood and age, a cavalry fort, an outlaw hideaway, a council lodge, a pirate ship. And now it had become their secret hideaway. She would be waiting for him by the river. . . . As he turned into the long driveway he began to jog.

The list of chores, printed in his father's small, neat script, looked endless and, although he worked as fast as he could, the light was already beginning to turn from yellow to gold by the time he finished and set out along the road that led up the hill to the bluff. The dark scent of the river filled his nostrils as he scrambled down the face of the cliff, sliding in the loose shale. A coolness rose up from the tangle of blackberry vines and ferns. He could hear the river, still high with snowmelt, rushing over the stones.

In the three months they'd been meeting in their secret space, he'd never been this late. What if she'd gone? It had been two days since they'd been alone. At school, they carefully avoided being seen together. A rarefied torture that—seeing each other and pretending indifference. Trying not to watch each other across the cafeteria.

Kate thought he was being silly to keep their relationship a secret. Tommy thought otherwise. People would talk, he said. And then her father would find out. And Tommy dreaded what might happen if he did.

He trotted along a sandy path through a thick clump of live oaks. Not much further now. He could see the rushing water, gold and copper glimmering among the ripples. Like her hair, he thought. Her beautiful, copper-colored hair.

Over the past six months, they had explored more and more

deeply into those forbidden territories neither of them had explored before. With Nancy there had been a lot of making out but never anything serious. Physical sensations, tentative groping. And kissing. Lots of kissing.

But with Kate, it was as if his whole body was catching fire and she was like the sweet cool water of the river. Their kisses left him giddy and weak. His hands shook as they moved over her, feeling the warm, round forms of her breasts beneath her cotton shirt, his mouth tasting the coolness of her throat, each breath drinking in her sweet scent. Her skin was soft. So soft. How could any creature be so soft? He longed to drown in her, melt into her. But always he had stopped. So far.

At night he lay on his narrow cot and ached for her. The consummations that took place in his dreams made their absence in reality even more unbearable, and yet he hesitated to ruin the perfection of such an extended and exquisite anguish. And he was afraid. Of what, he wasn't altogether sure. Breathlessly, he parted the willow branches.

"Hi," she said. "You're late."

"You waited." He dropped down beside her on the blanket. "I was afraid you'd be gone." His lips brushed her cheek as she threw her arms around his shoulders. "I love you."

"I love you, too," she whispered.

For a long time they lay in each other's arms, whispering, kissing. His hands slid beneath her blouse and fumbled desperately with her bra. She twisted away, and he pushed himself up on his elbows and stared at her in the shadowy light. "You want to stop?" he asked.

She shook her head.

"Then what?" His heart was hammering against his ribs.

"I want *not* to stop."

He felt exultant. And terrified. "Maybe we shouldn't, Katie. I wouldn't want—"

"I want to."

"Truly?"

"I love you," she whispered.

His throat was dry. He rested his hand against her cheek, then let his fingers again move slowly down her neck and beneath the collar of her blouse.

"Wait a minute," she said. She unbuttoned her blouse, reached back to unhook her bra. She half-turned away from him with a sudden modesty that made him ache. Slowly she undid her shorts and slipped them off along with her panties.

"Now you," she said.

"What?"

"I want to see you."

He couldn't take his eyes from her. Besides his mother, he had never seen an undressed woman before, and he stared at her, stunned by the iridescent paleness of her flesh, the dark pink of her nipples, the fleecy, red-gold nest of pubic hair.

She watched him as he stripped off his jeans. When he stood naked before her, she gave a small, shy smile and held out her arms.

She whimpered softly as he pushed into the secret tightness of her body. Afraid that he was hurting her, he started to pull away. But her hands pressed urgently against his hips. "Don't stop," she pleaded, rising and falling beneath him like a wave. "Please don't stop!"

Lost in her warmth, he rose and fell with her, drowning in her, the sound of the river roaring in his ears. Gasping her name, he felt himself exploding, melting, becoming one with her in the darkness of her secret inner space. Caught up in a mindless sort of joy, he continued to thrust until he felt her twist and shudder beneath him.

"Tommy," she was crying, "Tommy." For a long moment they lay still. When very slowly he raised his head and looked down, he saw her face was wet with tears. Remorse rushed over him.

"Did I hurt you? God, I'm . . ."

But she was laughing through her tears. "No. It's all right. Truly it is. I love you."

Carefully, he moved back. She was slick with sweat, her body steaming like a newborn foal. Gently he touched her breasts, the curve of her hip, the tiny smear of blood along her thigh. Lowering his body down to her once again, he kissed her forehead, her eyelids, the warm, moist hollow of her neck. Her hair smelled of balsam, but her skin gave off a heady, earthy scent, like musk, like dry grass, like the rust-red earth itself. "You are forever," he whispered, knowing and not knowing what he meant.

It was nearly dark when they started back to the ranch. They helped each other up the path and, reaching the top, they paused and clung to each other. Behind them, the bluff dropped away into the gathering dusk. Ahead, the road was a silver ribbon between the trees. To the west, the Sacramento Valley stretched out like a pastel sea, lights glittering in the violet mist. And to the east, the last reflections of the sun still lingered on the tallest slopes of the Sierras, turning them pink with alpine glow.

"This is the most beautiful place in the world," Kate said. "I'll never leave Mockingbird. Never."

"Neither will I," Tommy said.

She leaned against him. "Someday, we'll build our house right here, on top of this ridge. And every morning we'll watch the sun come up . . ."

". . . out of the Range of Light," he said. He pulled her into his arms and kissed her. For just an instant, he believed her completely.

# CHAPTER

# 23

## Boston, Massachusetts
## July 1960

In the summer of 1960, thousands of teenage girls were swooning at the gyrations of Elvis and screaming in ecstasy over the Everly Brothers. A few were already twisting to Chubby Checkers. But for Alexandria Archer McPhalan, there was, that summer, only one idol worth worshipping: the legendary classical pianist, Stefan Molnar.

Since his much-publicized escape from Hungary in 1956, critics had hailed Maestro Molnar as the concert genius of the decade, comparing his technique with that of Horowitz and Rubenstein. For over a year, Alex had been collecting his recordings. Posters of the artist covered her bedroom walls, his hooded eyes staring mournfully from his gaunt face.

She had begged Marian to take her to a concert given by her idol in Carnegie Hall, but an unexpected snowstorm had forced a cancellation of the pilgrimage. Despondent, Alex had refused food the entire weekend, coaxed from her room only by the scent of baking brownies late on Sunday night.

"The next time he is anywhere within a hundred miles," Alex told Marian, munching her fourth brownie, "promise me, *promise me*, Mother, that you'll take me to hear him play. No matter what."

She was ecstatic when the summer's program for the Tanglewood Festival arrived announcing that Stefan Molnar would be appearing as soloist for the final concert in July. He would play Rachmaninoff's Second Piano Concerto. Alex was delirious with joy.

It had been raining, and the air inside the Shed at Tanglewood was warm and damp. Mist clung to the lake, and a bronzed moon peered through the pines. Next to Alex, an large woman dressed in peach-toned polyester complained that her feet were wet. Marian and Trevor were talking about art galleries in the Berkshires. Oblivious, Alex pored over the program notes.

*Sergei Vasilievich Rachmaninoff was born April 1, 1873, in either Oneg or Semyonovo, Russia, and died March 28, 1943, in Beverly Hills, California. He composed his* Second Piano Concerto *in 1900-01: the second and third movements in 1900, drawing on material written up to a decade earlier, and the first movement in 1901, completed on May 4. It was also premiered piecemeal: the second and third movements on December 15, 1900, in Moscow, the complete three-movement concerto on November 9, 1901, also in Moscow. Alexander Siloti conducted, and the composer was the soloist on both occasions.*

The audience shuffled and buzzed as the orchestra tuned. A wave of applause greeted the conductor and the soloist. Alex bolted upright and put the program aside, craning her neck to see past the forest of heads. As the tall, elegant figure strode across the stage, shook the conductor's outstretched hand, inclined his head toward the audience, and seated himself at the Steinway, Alex clasped her hands in an attitude of prayer and surrendered herself completely to the music.

For the next sixty minutes, she scarcely remembered to breathe. From the mysterious opening chords of the first movement through the haunting reverie of the second and the boldly passionate third, she sat transfixed, following the score in her mind, but feeling as though she was hearing the composition for the first time.

As the final notes of the third movement died away, there was an awed silence. Then, bravos resounded as audience members rose to their feet, clapping deliriously. Maestro Molnar, smiling that melancholy smile, acknowledged the ovation. Members of the orchestra beamed and applauded, stomping their feet. The conductor grasped the pianist's hand and held it skyward in a victorious salute.

Alex's own hands remained clasped before her, tears stinging her eyes. Through the roaring of the crowd, she watched the soloist leave the stage, return, bow, leave, return again and again. Then he was gone, and Alex sat frozen in her chair.

The lights came up and the crowd began to shuffle from the Shed, heading for the cold drink stands, the gift shop, the restrooms. Still she didn't budge.

"Darling?" Marian's voice came to her from a great distance. "Honey, are you okay?"

With an effort, Alex turned toward her mother.      "What?"

Concern gave way to amusement. "I take it you were duly impressed?"

Alex nodded and got slowly to her feet.

"Where are you going, sweetheart?"

"Backstage," said Alex, "I must offer my congratulations."

"What a nice idea. You'll be back, won't you, by the end of the intermission?"

"Probably," Alex murmured as she started to make her way through the crowd.

Trevor shook his head and said to Marian, "Are you sure she should go back there?"

"I'm not sure I can stop her," Marian replied.

"Hmmm. Headstrong, isn't she?"

Marian rolled her eyes. "That's a bit of an understatement, luv."

The scene backstage was chaotic. The line of well-wishers stretched around the reception room and out the door. Alex took her place in line, standing on tiptoe as she neared the door, hoping to catch a glimpse of her idol. She wasn't sure that she was supposed to be backstage, but no one seemed to notice her.

Then she saw him amidst the crush of admirers, his tall form looming above the swirl of bodies. He was smiling, nodding, shaking hands, bending down to autograph a program. From that moment on, she didn't take her eyes from him as the line moved, like a slow tide advancing up a beach.

The lady in front of her stood on tiptoe and planted a kiss on the

Maestro's hollowed cheek. "You were divine, *mon cher*," the woman cried, "*Brilliante. Merveilleux.* When will you be coming to Boston?"

Stefan's smile was polite. "Next April, I believe."

The woman pressed his large hand between her small ones and sighed, "Until next time, *adieu.*"

Stefan's eyes followed her with mild amusement, then he turned and looked down at Alex. "Good evening," he said.

She had rehearsed a little speech, but the words flew from her head as she looked up at him. For the first time in her life, Alexandria Archer McPhalan could think of absolutely nothing to say.

"Would you like for me to sign your program?" His voice was rich and deep with a lilting accent that she found mesmerizing.

She nodded.

"There you are," he said, handing the program back to her.

"Thank you," she murmured.

"Not at all." What a curious smile he had. It seemed more sad than happy.

Then the man behind her was pumping Stefan's hand and Stefan was saying, "Thank you. So glad you enjoyed it," and there was nothing to do but to move away through the jostling crowd.

The bell that signaled the end of intermission was ringing as Alex, clutching the wrinkled program to her chest, made her way back into the Shed. Marian was standing up, gazing around. Relief flooded her face as Alex approached. "Thank goodness, sweetheart. We were getting worried." She smiled. "Did you get to meet the Maestro?"

Still dazed, Alex merely nodded. When she didn't take her seat Marian asked, "What's wrong, darling? Where are you going?"

"To the car," Alex whispered. "I want to be alone."

"You don't want to hear the Wagner?"

"I don't want to hear anything else. Ever. Perfection cannot be duplicated."

Marian nodded. "Are you sure you'll be all right out in the parking lot all by yourself?"

Alex gazed at her mother with patient compassion. "I won't be alone, Mother. Stefan's music will be with me."

"Do you think she's okay?" Trevor asked as they watched the girl move slowly up the aisle. "She seems quite terribly infatuated with this fellow Molnar."

Marian raised her eyebrows. "As heroes go, I guess she could do worse."

# 24

**Mockingbird Valley Ranch**
**August 1960**

A relentless sun scorched the river's rock-strewn bank. A few weeds struggled up between the rocks, prickly strong-smelling stalks topped with fluffy, yellow tufts. In a sandy swale beneath a clump of willows, Kate and Tommy had taken refuge from the heat. They had been swimming and despite the noontime sun, Kate was shivering. "Oooh, my fingers are frozen," she laughed, rubbing her hands together.

Tommy took her hands in his. "This will warm them up."

She lay back, naked and golden, little drops of water clinging to her lashes and dappling her breasts. He leaned over her, nuzzling her hair, and eased his body down on top of hers.

"Again?"

"Why not?" His hands slid along her inner thighs. "God, I love you," he whispered. "No matter how often we do it, it doesn't seem to be enough."

"I know," she murmured, drawing him to her. "I know."

Sam Hunter had been doing odd jobs at Mockingbird since before the Ashidas arrived, and Owen called on him now and then to do some extra work. On this particular summer morning, Sam had been mending fences and, soaked with sweat, was ready to take a break. A grove of willows by the water's edge beckoned.

But when he pulled aside the branches, he gasped. "Ohmygod," he mumbled. "I'm—I'm sorry." Then he recognized the girl's startled face. "I can't believe it," he said to himself as he hurried toward the bluff. "Mr. McPhalan's daughter out here makin' it with that Ashida kid. Just wait 'til her father hears about this!"

"Oh, Christ," Tommy said as they watched Sam vanish from sight.

"Do . . . do you think he'll tell?" Kate said.

"I don't know. I hope not. But maybe he will." Tommy jumped to his feet and pulled on his jeans. "Come on. Let's go!"

As they neared the McPhalan house, they saw Owen waiting for them at the courtyard gate. "Uh-oh," Kate said.

Tommy squeezed her hand. "We might as well tell him the truth. Maybe if he knows we're going to get married—"

"Mary Katherine!" Owen roared. "Get in here. And Tommy, your father wants to see you right away."

"Yes, sir. But we'd like to talk to you, Mr. McPhalan," Tommy stammered. "Please, we want you to understand—"

"Shut up!"

"But, sir—" Tommy said.

Owen grabbed Kate's arm. "I said get the hell in here."

"Daddy, don't! You're hurting me."

Tommy took a step forward but withered under Owen's look.

"I can't believe it," Owen said as he dragged Kate toward the house. "My God, I can't believe it."

"Let me explain!" she wailed.

"Tell me Sam was wrong," Owen said, pushing her roughly into the living room. "Was he wrong?"

She stood facing her father. "Not . . . exactly . . ."

"What the hell is that supposed to mean? Were you screwing him or not?"

"Don't say that, Daddy," she begged. "We love each other. We want to get married. We—"

"Married?" Owen shouted. "Are you out of your mind? Do you think for one minute that I'd let you marry a stinking, slant-eyed Jap? Do you think I'd ever let some god-damned Jap have my land?"

Stunned, she stared at him. "How can you say—"

For a moment he struggled, arm raised while she cowered, terrified, before him. Then his arm fell stiffly to his side. "Go to your room," he said. "And stay there, or, so help me God, I'll beat the living daylights out of you."

"You have disgraced us!" David cried, his face livid. "You have brought dishonor upon your family."

"But, Dad—"

Slamming his fist down on the table, David shouted, "Are you merely dumb, or did you suppose that Mr. McPhalan would accept you as husband to his daughter? Did you think to inherit his property through this means? Did you suppose that such a plan would succeed?"

"It—it isn't like that, Dad." Tommy's eyes filled with tears. "I love her. I've loved her for years. We just want to be together."

"Then you are merely a fool," said David. "A stupid, ignorant fool. Mr. McPhalan trusted me, and you have betrayed that trust. You have violated more than his daughter. You have destroyed all that I tried to build for us here. I must offer my resignation at once."

"But why, Dad? I don't understand."

David wheeled to face his wife. "You will take our son and go to my brother's house in Stockton. I will stay here until Mr. McPhalan can find someone to replace me."

"Dad, listen," Tommy pleaded. "You don't have to do that. There must be some way—"

"Do as I say." David stalked from the room.

"Mom," Tommy cried, "can't you stop him?"

Connie's lips were pressed together in a thin, tight line. "I tried to tell him," she said, "but he wouldn't listen."

"Tell him what?"

"Living out here with no suitable girls for you to meet. What did he expect?"

Tommy gave her a blank stare. "Suitable girls?"

"*Japanese* girls," she said.

"But he doesn't have to resign. Couldn't we just—" The words died on his lips as a flash of understanding struck him with the impact of a remembered dream. Suitable girls? An abyss opened beneath his feet. If even his own mother. . . .

"Go pack your things," she said. "We must leave at once."

Kate opened the door to the patio and strained to catch the words.

". . . hate to lose you," she heard her father say, "But it's best if you leave. You're sure you can move in with your brother?"

"He has asked me many times to join him in Stockton," David said.

"You've done a good job here, Ashida. I'd be happy to give you a recommendation and some severance pay as well."

"Thank you. Very kind."

"Can I count on you to stay through the harvest?" Owen asked.

"Of course. My wife will take our son and leave at once, but I will remain until you can arrange for a replacement."

From beyond the gate came the crunch of tires on gravel. Kate threw open the door and sprinted across the courtyard.

"Mary Katherine!" Owen shouted, "Get back inside."

Tommy jumped from the car. He and Kate tumbled into each other's arms.

"Don't go!" she sobbed. "Don't let them do this to us."

"I'll get word to you somehow. I love you, Kate. I love you!"

"I love you, too," she cried as Owen pulled her from Tommy's embrace and shoved her toward the house.

# CHAPTER

# 25

## Boston, Massachusetts
## September 1960

"But my dear Marian," Trevor exclaimed, "these are wonderful. Simply smashing. Why on earth do you persist in hiding them in closets, squirreling them away beneath your bed as though you were ashamed of them? They ought to be out where they can be seen."

Marian sat twisting a button on her sweater. "I don't know. I'm not sure they're good enough to be seen."

"Nonsense," Trevor said. "They are . . . exquisite. Sublime. They must be shown at a proper gallery."

"I did have a little show of drawings at a frame-shop but nothing sold, so I—"

"Frame-shop!" Trevor cried. "Dear lady, you must have the courage of your convictions. I insist that you take these remarkable paintings straight to New York and put yourself in the hands of a reputable agent."

"I wouldn't know where to start," Marian said. "There must be hundreds of artists in New York who are trying to get their work into galleries."

"Of course there are, but most of them are lamentable hacks who possess only the very rudiments of style and technique, fakes and fabricators slobbering on the heels of fashion." He tugged furiously at his beard.

"Oh, Trevor," Marian laughed, "you do get carried away." Her eyes once more settled on the half dozen pastels lined up against the wall of the studio. "You really think they're that good?"

Trevor folded his arms and squinted. "Indeed. They are spectacular, unprecedented, completely original."

"Maybe I should hire you as my agent."

"And I would gladly accept the job and take credit for your discovery myself, but alas I am merely an aging college professor with only minimal credibility in the world of La Bella Arte. No, my dear, you must approach a professional and convince him to handle your work."

"But I don't know any agents," sighed Marian. "Most galleries are not handling the sort of thing I'm doing."

Trevor raised his eyebrows. "They ought to be."

"Well, they're not. If it's not Ab Ex, forget it."

"That's bound to change eventually," Trevor said. "Why just the other day I was reading about a new style of art that's been developing in England—recognizable figures, totally new subject matter."

"There are a few artists in California painting figures. But . . ." She spread her hands before her in dismay, "how on earth would I find a New York dealer who'd be interested in figurative work?"

Trevor tugged more gently on his beard. "You know," he said, "I might actually be of some assistance after all. Have you heard of the Rocklin Gallery?"

"Of course. It's one of the best in Manhattan."

"Well," Trevor said, "it happens that I know Lloyd Rocklin."

"You do?"

"Not all that well, mind you, but I met him in London back before the war. He was studying at the School of Economics, but he used to come 'round slumming at the Royal Academy. We did a lot of serious drinking together. I'd be more than willing to drop him a line and recommend you to his attention."

"Oh, Trevor, would you?"

"Delighted to be of service, dear lady," Trevor replied, beaming as she planted a kiss on his cheek.

---

## New York, New York

The Rocklin Gallery was on the sixth floor of a large office building on West Fifty-seventh Street. Inside the foyer, a young woman, dressed in black, sat behind a sleek white desk filing her fingernails. The polished hardwood floor glinted, reflecting pools of illumination from the overhead spotlights.

Clutching her portfolio beneath her arm, Marian approached the desk. "Excuse me," she said, "I'd like to see Mr. Rocklin?"

The girl glanced up. Her carefully outlined eyes looked Marian over with vaguely disguised contempt. "Do you have an appointment?"

"Not exactly. But a friend of mine, Trevor Martin? He wrote to Mr. Rocklin on my behalf. And I wrote too. About three weeks ago. I said I'd be in New York and that—"

"I'm afraid that Mr. Rocklin's terribly busy," the girl said, "but I'd be happy to take your name. If he wants to see you, I'm sure he'll be in touch."

Marian took a deep breath and put her portfolio down beside the desk. "I'd like to see him today," she said. "I'm an artist. I've come down here from Boston. It's difficult for me to get into New York. If you'd be good enough to ask Mr. Rocklin if—"

"I'm sorry," the girl interrupted, "Mr. Rocklin only interviews artists on Tuesdays between two and four."

"But surely, if he's read Trevor's letter he'll know who I am."

The young woman stood up. "I really must ask you to leave," she said. "Mr. Rocklin is not in the habit of—"

"Leslie, whatever is going on out there?" A frail-looking man with thinning hair and melancholy eyes stepped through the doorway from the inner office. "What is all the shouting about?"

"I'm sorry, Mr. Rocklin. This woman has been arguing about a letter from a Trevor Martin."

"From who?" Rocklin said, staring at Marian across the receptionist's desk.

"Mr. Rocklin." Marian thrust out her hand, "I'm Marian Archer, Trevor Martin's friend from Boston."

"Oh," Rocklin gave her hand a limp shake. "Oh, yes. That's right. Trevor Martin's friend. Well, how do you do, Miss Arthur?"

"Archer. Marian Archer."

"Yes. Of course." He blinked and gave her a tight smile. "So, how's—uh, Trevor doing these days?"

"Very well indeed."

"Good. Good. Wonderful fellow, Trev."

"Oh, yes."

"A writer, isn't he?"

"Well," said Marian, "actually he's teaching English literature."

"That's right. At a college in the Boston area?"

"Yes."

There was an awkward pause, then Rocklin said, "Well, it was very nice meeting you, Miss Arthur. Do tell Trevor hello for me and please, feel free to look around." He waved a long, thin arm toward the gallery.

"I brought some of my work with me," Marian said, picking up her portfolio. "I'm an artist, and I was hoping you'd have time to take a look. I wrote to you, don't you remember?"

Rocklin consulted his watch. "Well . . . I do recall something about someone from Boston, but—"

"About a dozen pastels," said Marian, holding up the portfolio. "It won't take long."

His pale blue eyes surveyed her unhappily. "All right. I suppose I can give you a couple of minutes."

"Thank you, Mr. Rocklin." As she started past him into the white-walled office, she heard him say, "Leslie, I'm expecting Mrs. Rosenthal at ten-thirty. Be sure to tell me the minute she comes in."

Heart pounding, Marian set the portfolio against the mahogany desk. Rocklin's thin lips twisted in something resembling a smile, "Well, let's see what you have there."

She flipped slowly through the sheets of paper while Rocklin stood, one hand resting against his hollow cheek, face expressionless.

Marian finished and sat back on her heels, glancing up at Rocklin's inscrutable face.

He took a cigarette from a small cloisonné case, lit it, and squinted at her through the smoke. "Your work's quite competent," he said at last. "Quite—professional."

"Thank you."

Rocklin nodded, drawing hard on the cigarette. "You have a strong personal vision." He paused to flick ashes into the black-lacquer bowl. "But these are not the sort of thing I'm handling these days."

"Trevor thought that you might be moving in a new direction," Marian said. "Looking for some different talent."

Rocklin laughed. "Did he? Well, that's perceptive of him." He took another drag on the cigarette. "It's true that I am taking on a few new people."

"Trevor felt that since my work is figurative, you might—"

"It *is* true that Ab Ex is past its prime. But I'm predicting that the next major movement will be along the lines of what Hockney and Hamilton are doing." He paused and raised an eyebrow at her. "You *are* familiar with their work, aren't you?"

Marian's face grew warm. "Of course. A sort of satire on commercial art."

"Something along those lines. Certainly the imagery is drawn from popular culture."

"I guess I've never been very interested in commercial art."

Rocklin shrugged. "Well, I find your work far too romantic. The sensibility is too feminine."

"I *am* a woman."

"Yes," he agreed, "but it's a shame that it shows up so clearly in your art. It's simply not . . ." he cocked his head to one side. ". . . tough enough."

Marian looked at the portrait of Carl, his face touched by the light of late afternoon, dark hair spilling across his forehead. "I suppose," she said, "that my feelings are not best described as *tough*."

He was silent for a minute, looking at the drawings, then glanced at her, and his thin lips once more parted in a waxy smile. "Well," he said, "I'm sure you know what you do best."

There was a knock at the door. "Mr. Rocklin?"

"Yes, Leslie?"

"Mrs. Rosenthal is here."

"Thank you, Leslie dear." He opened the office door and extended his hand. "So nice meeting you," he said to Marian.

"Maybe if I were to show you some of my paintings."

"I'm sorry. I really must ask you to excuse me," Rocklin said. "Good luck, Miss Arthur, and do say hello to Trevor for me."

"That's Archer," Marian muttered as she gathered up the drawings and shook Rocklin's unresponsive hand. The receptionist didn't look up as Marian trudged past her.

Outside, the wind had grown colder. Marian looked around at the bleak buildings, the skeletal trees, bits of paper swirling along the gutter. "Well," she muttered to herself, "Rocklin's isn't the only gallery in Manhattan." Chin up, she set out along the street, portfolio clutched firmly beneath her arm.

Four hours later, she sat slumped on a green plastic chair in the outer office of a gallery on Forty-seventh Street. Her feet ached, her throat was sore, and the buzz of the fluorescent light was boring its way into her temples. The receptionist, still another coldly attractive young woman indistinguishable from the seven or eight others Marian had confronted over the course of the afternoon, scurried out from the inner sanctum to answer the phone. Finally, she looked up at Marian and said, "Sorry to keep you waiting so long. What was it you wanted?"

"I'd like to see Miss Jefferson."

"I'm afraid she's busy."

"I've been waiting half an hour," Marian said. "I can wait a little longer."

"Was it about buying a painting?" The girl looked at her expectantly.

"No, I'm an artist. I want her to look at my portfolio."

"I'm afraid she's tied up with a client."

"Perhaps I could come back tomorrow."

"She's leaving for Paris this evening and won't be back for three weeks."

Marian's head throbbed, and she realized that she had not had lunch. "Then would you please go and ask her if I can have five minutes of her time?"

The girl returned a moment later. "If you'd step right this way?"

Marian jumped up, grabbed her portfolio, and followed the girl through a side door.

"Just take the second door on your left," said the girl, pointing. "Someone will be with you in a minute."

The corridor was badly lit, grey and unpromising, but Marian marched down the hall and opened the door. A blast of cold air stung her face, and she found herself looking out into an alley. Crouched on the freezing pavement, a scruffy orange cat stared up at her with terrified eyes.

"Bastards," Marian muttered. For a moment she stood still, unable to decide whether or not to storm back into Marilyn Jefferson's office and scream at the receptionist. Then, shoulders hunched, she stepped out into the alley. "Good luck," she told the cat as she headed toward the lights of Fifth Avenue.

# CHAPTER

# 26

## Boston, Massachusetts

"So Lloyd wasn't interested," Trevor said, toying with his glass of sherry. "Well, at least he found the work professional."

"For all the good that did me."

"Don't be too hard on yourself. I'm sure if you just keep after it, someone will give you a show."

"It was humiliating, Trevor, dragging my work from one snotty gallery to another, getting doors slammed in my face."

"You don't have to tell me," exclaimed Trevor. "I've encountered enough rejections to last for several lifetimes. Why, the walls of my study are virtually papered with rejection letters."

"Maybe it's easier to get rejected by mail," Marian said.

"It is *never* easy, dear lady," said Trevor, his voice taking on the self-consciously tragic quality that she was beginning to find irritating.

"Do you know what one SOB actually had the audacity to tell me?" Marian said. "If I'd change my style, modify my palette, and paint only children, he thought I might be marketable. *Marketable!*" Nearly choking on her indignation, she quickly downed half her scotch and soda. "Bastards."

Trevor nodded sympathetically. "Yes, well, it is tough to get oneself established."

"I hate being treated like shit," Marian cried. "It's bad enough that I have to work 'til I'm ready to drop, have no money, live like a hermit. I can't stand being humiliated by a bunch of sanctimonious, superficial idiots. The hell with them."

"There, there," Trevor said, taking her hand. "Don't cry."

She snatched her hand away. "I'm not crying, damn it."

"At least you gave it a go."

For several minutes they were silent. Marian stared blankly out the window. Trevor glanced aimlessly around the lounge. Squinting, he examined his watch. "Blast. I'd better get going."

Marian glanced up. "So soon?"

"Loretta will throw a bloody fit if I'm late again." He reached for his muffler.

Marian watched him glumly. "Will I see you next Sunday?"

"I think not. My wife is being quite the beast these days."

"Do you think she knows about us?"

"Maybe. It's so bloody tiring. All this sneaking about, the pretense, the excuses."

"I'm not so keen on it myself," Marian replied. "Maybe we should just call it quits."

She glanced up to find him staring at her, his pale eyes blinking as though he'd just been awakened from a nap.

"You really are upset, aren't you?" he said, sitting back down beside her.

"I suppose I am."

He pursed his lips. "I know you've been feeling neglected. I say, Malcolm's giving a reading at Boston College on Thursday night. Why don't you meet me there? We could go back to your apartment and—"

"You forget I have a daughter. What am I supposed to do with her? Tie her up in a closet while we screw?"

"Don't be crude, Marian. This is just as difficult for me as it is for you."

"Oh sure," she cried. "It must be dreadful to go home after our furtive little encounters. All you have to look forward to is a big comfortable house, a hot meal, and a wife who waits on you hand and foot. Oh, I feel awfully sorry for you, Trevor." She really was crying now.

"Let's not have a scene. You know how I detest scenes."

"Oh, the hell with you, too," she cried, struggling to her feet.

Trevor grabbed her arm and pulled her back down beside him. "Will you behave?" he hissed.

She hid behind her hands, trying to quell the tears of frustration that rolled down her cheeks.

"I was only trying to help," he said.

She dug at her eyes. "I'm not blaming you. It's just so damn—stupid and I don't know what to do next." She pulled some wadded Kleenex from her pocket and blew her nose. "I guess I'm just depressed about . . . everything."

"Poor luv," he said. "I understand. You've had a rotten time. Sorry I can't be of more assistance, but you can see how complicated everything is for me, can't you?"

She nodded, wiping her eyes.

"I really must be going, but I'll ring you up on Thursday. We'll get together for a drink at least. What do you say?"

"Okay," she said.

He patted her cheek. "That's my girl." He got to his feet and handed her his most understanding smile. "Take care of yourself, luv. And mind the roads on the way home."

"'That's my girl,'" she muttered as he walked away. "Forty years old and I'm still being treated like a child."

"You're late," Alex said as Marian closed the door and set the heavy portfolio and a bag of groceries down beside the sofa.

"Sorry, sweetheart. I had to stop at the store."

"You weren't here when I got home."

Marian met her daughter's flat, hard stare. "I'm sorry," she said. "I didn't mean to worry you.

"Oh," said Alex, tossing her head, "I wasn't worried. Not in the least. I just thought that you'd be home, that's all." She spun around on the piano stool and began to play the last movement of Bach's *Italian Concerto*. Very fast.

Perplexed, Marian stood gazing at the girl's ramrod- straight back, barely aware of the music that burst angrily from the keys.

"By the way," said Alex, breaking off in mid-phrase and spinning back around to face her mother, "you got a letter from that boy."

"What boy?" said Marian, taking off her coat and tossing it down on the sofa.

Alex's mouth tightened. "You know, the one that you were skinny-dipping with the day I—"

"Carl?" asked Marian hopefully. She hadn't heard from him for several months. One of his amusing, enthusiastic letters was just what she needed after a long and disappointing day.

"Was that his name?"

"Where is it?"

"Oh, do contain yourself, Mother," grumbled Alex. "I put it on the mantel beside the clock."

Eagerly, Marian tore open the envelope and sank down in the leather easy chair beside the window, oblivious to Alex's hostile stare.

*Dear Marian,*

*Sorry to be so slow in responding to your last good missive and thank you for the sound advice regarding my hassles with the administrative bureaucracy here at the Conservatory. Thanks to you I was able to work out an excellent program for the summer semester and now have finished most of my requirements ahead of schedule. My work with the student ensemble has gone especially well. Just last week we gave a little recital for the faculty and a few distinguished visitors, and I'm pleased to report that the response was extremely enthusiastic."*

"What does he say?" asked Alex.

Marian looked up. "What? Oh, just some things about his schoolwork. I'll let you read it in a minute if you like."

"Why would I want to do that?" muttered Alex.

*In closing, I had to let you know that I finally bought some furniture for my apartment, so I'm no longer eating on the kitchen counter nor sleeping on the floor. As I told you, I wanted to wait until I could afford a few nice pieces of good quality rather than cluttering the place up with junk. I intend to keep it very simple—necessarily so, considering my income—but it will be quite elegant I assure you. I still haven't figured out how to solve the problem of having that wonderful Ukrainian bakery downstairs. If I don't stop succumbing to temptation pretty soon, I'll no doubt be the fattest conductor on record.*

*Write, right?*

*And take care of yourself, ma cherie.*

*Fond thoughts,*

*Your Carl*

"Well?" said Alex.

Marian folded the letter and laid it aside. "He's doing fine."

"Did he mention me?"

"No," said Marian. "Why?"

With a shrug, Alex turned back to the piano and resumed playing.

Still tired, but less depressed, Marian got up and carried the groceries into the closet-sized kitchen. She began to put away the food, smiling a little, thinking about Carl's letter.

Alex again broke off her practice and called, "What are we having for dinner?"

"I got some tuna fish," Marian called back. "I thought I'd make a casserole."

Alex appeared in the kitchen doorway and wrinkled her nose. "Tuna casserole again? Why can't we go out to dinner?"

On her knees before the refrigerator, Marian paused and looked up at the girl. "We just did."

"That was almost a week ago," Alex protested. "Four or five days at least. Besides, you said we could go shopping for a dress for my recital. Oh, I forgot to tell you. Trevor called."

"When?"

"Just before you got here. He asked if you'd gotten home all right, and I said no."

"Oh, Alex."

Alex scowled. "Well, you hadn't."

"Oh dear. Now I suppose he'll worry."

"He said he'd call you at work tomorrow. So he can't be all *that* worried."

Marian watched the girl for a moment, then said, "You don't care much for Trevor, do you, sweetheart?"

"He's all right. Sort of boring, but his accent's nice. At least he's about your age."

Marian laughed.

Alex chewed her lower lip and regarded Marian with a look of patient contempt. "What about dinner?" she said. "What about my dress?"

Marian looked around at the scattered groceries. "I wasn't in much of a mood for cooking anyway."

"Whoopee! I'll go get my cape."

"But we'll have to do Italian or Chinese," Marian called after her. "I can't afford to indulge your taste for filet mignon and champagne." Shaking her head, she hurried to put away the groceries.

"I saw the most gorgeous purple dress at Saks," Alex said, rushing back into the kitchen, her wool cape swirling around her shoulders.

Marian got to her feet. "And I'm sure it had a perfectly gorgeous price tag. Besides, white would be more appropriate for a girl your age."

"White," snorted Alex, "that's for brides and first communions. I'd rather be dangerous than demure."

"You're dangerous enough already," muttered Marian as she struggled into her coat and picked up her purse. "We don't need to advertise the fact."

Alex laughed and showed her pretty teeth. "Come on, Mummy," she said gaily. "I'm completely famished. We can discuss my wardrobe over dinner."

Thinking that the question of a suitable dress was a great subject for an argument, Marian followed her daughter down the stairs.

# CHAPTER

# 27

## Roseville, California
## October 1960

K ate closed her eyes and hugged her knees. Outside, the autumn wind was shaking the bare trees and buffeting the window with a spatter of rain. She shivered, sniffling. Tommy sat up and wrapped a blanket around her. For a moment he held her silently, his cheek against her hair.

"Sorry," she muttered. "It's just so awful having to meet like this. This stupid motel makes me feel dirty."

"What else can we do?" said Tommy.

"Maybe we should quit using those . . .those *things*. If I got pregnant they'd have to let us get married."

Tommy sighed. "Don't count on it. You're still not eighteen. Your dad could make it plenty rough for us. Besides," he glanced at her, "what would we do for money? I couldn't support you and a baby on what I make at Uncle Willie's store." He shook his head. "Come on, Kate. We've got to be reasonable."

"It's now or never . . ." Elvis crooned from the radio.

Kate collapsed on the bed. "But, I love you. What are we going to do?"

"We're going to wait," Tommy replied. "We're going to finish high school, and then we're both going to go on to college. I've applied at Berkeley and Stanford and San Francisco State, and you'll get into Berkeley or Mills. After I make some money, we can get married and buy a ranch of our own." He leaned over and kissed the back of her neck. "It'll work out, Katie. I know it will."

"But what if you don't get a scholarship? What if your dad makes you go to Oregon? What if I don't get into Berkeley?"

"Shhh." He stroked her hair. "We'll be all right. You'll see." He crawled under the blanket and they hugged each other in the thin, grey light.

After a minute she said, "I can't see you next week."

Tommy sat up and looked at her. "Why not?"

Kate lowered her head, inspecting the ragged seam of the blanket. "Election week. Dad wants me there with him."

Tommy checked the rising wave of jealousy with a counterweight of logic. "Yeah, I guess you have to do that." Even in this paltry light, in this grey and dismal place, he thought she looked remarkably beautiful.

"There've been a bunch of reporters hanging around the ranch," she said. "I was scared that one of them might follow me."

Tommy nodded. "We've got to be careful."

"I hate having all those strangers around, asking questions, taking pictures. Dad's trying to be really nice to me. I think he's scared that I might run away. Like Julian."

Tommy leaned back on his elbows. "How is Julian?"

Kate shrugged. "Okay, I guess. He said in his last letter that he's moving to a nicer apartment. And he's got a new job."

"Doing what?"

"Waiting on tables at the Blue Fox. You know, that swanky restaurant in San Francisco." She smiled. "Can't you just picture Julian dressed up in a tux, gliding around with a silver tray in his hand?"

Tommy laughed. "I'm glad he's doing okay. He was always nice to me."

"Dad won't even talk about him or write or anything. So naturally Julian won't either. Boy, I wish they'd make up."

"Maybe someday . . ."

"It's sad when people who ought to love each other end up hating each other instead. Like Mom and Dad, you know?" She twisted around to look up at him. "We'll never be like that, will we? I'll always love you. Always and always."

"I'll always love you, too," he promised, kissing her soft, cool cheek. For several minutes they were silent, holding each other. Then Tommy stirred and said, "We better go. It's getting dark, and it'll take you awhile to get home in this rain."

"I don't care." Her voice was muffled against his chest. "I just want to stay here with you."

"We can't," Tommy said. "We've got to be careful."

Angrily, she pulled away from him. "For how long, Tommy?"

"For as long as it takes."

"Why can't we just tell everybody? Why do we have to keep hiding and hiding?"

"Listen to me." he said sharply. "You think your dad's the only bigot in the world? You think he's the only guy around who'd like to string me up for being with a white girl?"

"But that's crazy, Tommy. What's the difference as long as we—"

"You're not listening to me," he cried. "Why the hell do you think I spent the first three years of my life in a prison camp?" He grabbed her hand and held it next to his. "See that? I'm yellow and you're white and there's a lot of people who don't like that combination."

She pulled her hand away. "Maybe it's different now."

"You want me to spell it out for you?" he demanded. "I'm a Jap. *JAP*. You got that? What do you think your father's fancy friends would say about his fancy daughter marrying a Jap, huh?"

Kate bit her lip and looked away. "They're stupid." Then she looked back at him. "Oh, Tommy, why did everything have to change?"

He shook his head. "Katie, Katie. We were living in a dream. Mockingbird was our Fantasyland, but . . ." His voice slowed, the words becoming very deliberate, ". . . we don't live there anymore. We can *never* live there again."

She turned away silently, her shoulders shaking. He rested his hand on her arm and said, "We've got to face the facts, Kate, and the fact is, we've got a real problem. We can't just pretend we don't."

With a little sob, she threw her arms around him. "I don't care what anybody thinks. I love you, and I want to marry you."

"We'll find a way," he promised. He tried to smile as he kissed the tip of her nose. "Come on. Let's get out of this dump before we freeze."

---

## Sacramento, California

The air in the room at the Senator Hotel in Sacramento was close with smoke and tension, and a nasty headache had settled itself in the center of Owen's forehead. Scowling, he stared at the flickering television set and wished mightily that he was back at Mockingbird breathing fresh, cool air and watching the hawks dip and skim above the pear trees.

"We're getting there, partner," Dan murmured.

Owen glanced at the lawyer who was hunched forward, tie loosened and sleeves rolled up, watching the TV screen with the zeal of a cat intent on its prey. "We're inching up," Dan said, giving Owen a grin. He drew deeply on his cigarette, exhaled and waved his hand at the screen. "Rural vote's starting to come in. That's where we'll make some hay."

Owen grunted a response. His eyes wandered to Helen, who sat in a chair beside the window, her chin resting on her hand. From her pensive, dreamy expression, she might have been gazing at a peaceful landscape rather than watching the returns of a hard-fought election. She glanced at Owen and smiled encouragingly. His pulse quickened as he smiled back.

"Dad?" He looked down at Kate who had settled herself on the floor beside his chair. "If you win, does that mean you're going to have to live in Sacramento?"

"If I win," Owen said, "I expect I'll get something here in town. Someplace to park myself during the legislative session. Nothing permanent."

"I'll look after the ranch when you're away," Kate said.

"I appreciate that, sugar," he said, patting her hand. Too bad she wasn't a boy.

"Placer County rancher Owen McPhalan is widening his lead over incumbent Ralph Starks," the announcer said.        " W i t h sixty-two percent of the precincts reporting, McPhalan has pulled ahead by nearly six hundred votes in this hard-fought race."

"Wahoo!" Dan cried. Beaming, he slapped Owen's shoulder. "Look at that, partner. What'd I tell you?"

Dan's secretary and two campaign aides stood up and hovered before the television, as though physical proximity could somehow affect the election results. Dan ground out his cigarette and lit another. Owen glowered at the screen and chewed on his lower lip, thinking that he would not enjoy having to live even part-time in Sacramento. Sighing, he shifted his position and squeezed his daughter's hand.

"Aren't you excited, Daddy?" she said, grinning up at him.

"Ummm," he murmured absently.

"Additional returns have just come in," the announcer stated. "Results from four more precincts show McPhalan widening his lead by close to a thousand votes over his opponent. McPhalan was expected to do well in the rural areas, where results have been much slower to come in." The announcer paused, then said, "We take you now to Stark campaign headquarters where Joe Rixie is standing by. Joe, what's the situation there?"

"Fred, we understand that Ralph Starks is on his way down to address his followers here at the El Rancho Hotel. . . ."

"Sucker's going to concede," Dan shouted, leaping to his feet.

Owen got to his feet as well, his arm around his daughter. "I want to read a statement," Starks was saying in muted tones.

Owen strained to hear what his opponent was saying but Dan, Helen, the secretary, the aides and Kate were all laughing and pounding his back and saying, "Congratulations." Well, thought Owen, that's that. He felt neither elation nor surprise, but rather a sense of resignation and a kind of philosophical acceptance. I wonder, he pondered silently, what Pa would have thought of all this?

A crowd of well-wishers jostled Owen happily as Dan guided him toward the podium. Kate stood beside her father on the raised platform, watching as he addressed the frenzied crowd. She was proud, proud that he had won the election, proud that he was her father. He was familiar—the father she'd always known—and yet different now in his tailored suit and his white shirt and his red-and-blue- striped tie.

She realized that he had talked more in the past six months than she could remember in all the years before— speeches, press conferences, meetings with Dan and other party regulars, long planning sessions in the living room at Mockingbird, telephone conversations late at night. He spoke well, forcefully and with conviction. She had never thought about him that way—a tall, well-dressed man, slightly reserved but obviously sincere, speaking to the jostling, beaming crowd. She studied him with wonder, and a little awe.

"Too bad your mother isn't here," Helen whispered, pressing Kate's hand.

"Not her kind of thing," Kate said.

"I suppose not." Helen looked at Owen, her eyes glowing with admiration. "You must be so proud of your father."

"Yes, I am," Kate said.

Owen's final words were drowned in cheers and music. He turned and smiled at Kate. In a rush of emotion, she threw her arms around him and hugged him hard. "Congratulations, Daddy!"

"Enjoy yourself, sugar," Owen said to her as Dan guided them down the steps and into the press of admirers. "Just don't drink too much champagne."

An hour later Owen pushed his way through the celebrants to reach Helen's side. "Where's Katie?"

"I left her in the custody of three charming young men who were all bent on impressing her with their diverse exploits. Don't worry," she added, seeing his expression, "I'm keeping track of her whereabouts."

"Thanks. You and Danny have been swell. I couldn't have done it without you. Incidentally," he smiled at her,"that was one heck of a fine dinner we had at your house last week. Kate couldn't stop raving over the apricot pie."

"I'll send her the recipe. It was my grandmother's favorite."

"And what'd you do to the salad?"

"I make sure everything's fresh. If I can't pick the lettuce an hour before dinner, I forgo the salad course."

"You have a beautiful garden, Helen."

"Why, thank you, Owen."

"I don't think I've ever seen prettier roses." It occurred to him that she was like a rose herself—all curves, with not a single angle to break the softness.

"Mac," Dan was threading his way toward them. "Here's somebody I want you to meet."

"Clayton Russell's my name, Congressman," said the tall, balding man. "I own the Springtree Ranch over in Winters. Danny here's been telling me about your plans to organize a group of growers to look into the farm-labor problem."

"Helen," said Dan, "will you excuse us?"

"Of course. The Hubbles have offered to take me home, so I'll be leaving shortly."

"But it's still early," Owen protested. "Can't you stay awhile?"

She smiled at him. "I'd better not. I'm hosting a luncheon for the Sutter Club wives tomorrow, and I have to be up early. Don't worry about Katie. I've made arrangements for her to come along with us. I'll see that she gets home."

"Thanks, Helen," Owen said.

The dimples deepened at the corners of her mouth. "Good night, Mr. Assemblyman," she said.

The crowd had thinned, and the caterers were gathering up the empty champagne glasses as Dan ushered Owen out the door. "I got one last somebody for you to meet," Dan said as they crossed the lobby and entered a paneled lounge.

"Lord, Danny," Owen groaned, "when the hell do I get to sleep?"

"You can bed down in just a few minutes, partner. This is our final appointment of the evening."

Two young women were sitting in the booth at the far end of the lounge. One of them raised her hand in a coy, fluttering wave as they approached.

"Who are they?" Owen asked.

Dan winked. "Couple of friends of mine. You know, the best thing about this business is you get to meet the most interesting people. Come on. They're dying to meet you."

"I'll bet," Owen grumbled.

"This is Sherry and Cindy," Dan said as the girls slid over to make room. "Girls, meet Assemblyman McPhalan."

"Hi," Cindy said, eyeing Owen. "I've been a fan of yours since way back in the spring."

"Sure you're old enough to vote?" said Owen.

She laughed, tiny teeth flashing between her dark red lips. "Well, there are many ways to provide support."

"I suppose."

The girls ordered daiquiris. Owen toyed with a double shot of bourbon.

"Will you excuse us?" Dan said, ushering Sherry from the booth. He nodded to Owen, grinning. "I'll see you tomorrow, old buddy. Have a real good evening."

"We could go up to my room," Cindy suggested. "We'd be a lot more comfortable."

"Young lady," Owen said, putting his glass down hard, "I have a daughter not much younger than you. Now maybe my friend Danny approves of this sort of thing, but I find it disgusting, and I don't mind telling you so."

The girl's brittle smile shattered. "Listen, Mr. Big Shot, I don't make judgments about what you do for a living."

"I think you'd better leave," said Owen.

"With pleasure," the girl said, jumping to her feet. Angrily she snatched up the fur coat that lay beside her on the seat.

For several minutes Owen sat staring into the empty space where the girl had been sitting. Then he shook his head, drained his glass, and got heavily to his feet. Glancing down at the glass-topped table, he caught sight of his own reflection amidst the ashes and the cloudy rings of water.

# CHAPTER

# 28

## San Francisco, California
## January 1961

"Michael?" Julian poked his head into the alcove off the foyer—
the parlor, Michael insisted on calling it—and squinted
into the darkness. The streetlight outside the window provided just
enough illumination for Julian to see the scattered newspapers, the
empty glasses on the coffee table, everything just the way he'd left it
six hours before. The apartment was dark, the doors locked. Maybe
Michael had gone out, too.

The argument had been intense. But silly, Julian thought with
tired regret, so silly. Who cared where they went for dinner? Was that
important enough to shout about? Why were they fighting over every
minuscule decision? Dejected, he lowered himself onto the sofa and
stared into the darkened fireplace.

Michael Saunders had been conspicuously out of place among
the bearded, sad-eyed bohemians when he first started showing
up at Larry's infamous parties. Tall, blond, tan, he had just arrived
from Los Angeles where he had spent a number of years in what he
laughingly referred to as "post-graduate study in oceanography." More
specifically, surfing. His father was involved in some mysterious way
with the movie industry, though in what capacity Julian had never
managed to discover. It had been mid-summer when Julian moved
into Michael's opulent Pacific Heights apartment. Fascinated by
Michael's energy, his frenetic pace, his excesses, Julian was enthralled
by the "Gospel according to Michael"—try anything, do everything.
The ultimate consumer of experience.

When had it started going wrong? Was it the party at Wally's when Michael had gotten smashed and called Julian a silly cunt in front of everyone? Was it that night at Finnochios when Michael had laughingly suggested that Julian would look great on stage. "We could shave your legs, put a basket of fruit on your head. Why, you'd put Carmen Miranda to shame." Julian hadn't thought it was very funny.

Listlessly, Julian's hand dropped to the floor next to the sofa. His fingers encountered a mass of something cool and smooth. It wasn't a sofa pillow. Or a blanket. Curious, Julian got up and switched on the lamp.

It was a leather jacket—black and decorated with metal studs. Michael didn't have a jacket like that.

Overhead, a floorboard creaked and Julian looked up. What the hell was going on? Anger grew with every step as he mounted the stairs. He reached the landing and started for the bedroom door when it opened and Michael stepped out, wrapping a velour bathrobe around him. "Oh, you're back," said Michael.

"Who's been here?" Julian asked, his anger mollified a little by the relief at seeing his lover.

"What do you mean?" said Michael, taking a cigarette from the pocket of his robe and putting it between his well-formed lips.

Julian gestured with his head. "Somebody left his jacket downstairs, and unless you've decided to go in for the Hells Angels look, it wasn't you."

"Really?" said Michael. "My, my. I wonder whose it could be."

There was a slight scuffing sound from behind the door. Julian tensed. "Who's in there?"

"Where?" said Michael, flicking his lighter.

"God-dammit." Julian clenched his teeth. "You've brought somebody here, haven't you?"

With deliberate disdain, Michael blew a puff of smoke into Julian's flushed face. "So what?"

Julian furiously slammed open the door. The man who sat on the bed was large and powerfully muscled. The light from the hall gave his copper-colored skin the sheen of polished marble. "He's got a dick like a bull elephant," Michael murmured in Julian's ear.

Rage bit into Julian's stomach. He wheeled around and glared into Michael's smugly smiling face. "You creep," he hissed. "Why'd you have to bring him here? Why'd you have to use our bed?" Choked with rage, he grabbed the cigarette and wrenched it from Michael's mouth.

"Ouch. You stupid little cunt!" Michael shrieked. Grabbing Julian by the throat, he flung him against the wall. Startled by the force of the attack, Julian froze.

"Get out!" Michael screamed, his face contorting with rage. "Get your goddamned ass out of my apartment."

"But you asked me here," Julian said inanely. "You said I could stay."

Michael's face twisted in a sardonic smile. "Did I? I really don't recall." The smile was transformed into a sneer. "I've had it with you, Julian. Just get out."

"I thought we—"

"I'm sick of you," Michael hissed. "I'm bored silly with your nagging and your endless, endless scribbling. Now get your stuff and leave, will you?"

"Tonight?" Julian asked in disbelief. "But I don't have any money. What am I supposed to do?"

"Frankly, my dear," Michael said with a vicious laugh. "Well, you know the rest. Get rid of him, will you, Vern?" he said to the man.

"Hey, wait a minute—" Julian protested, but the hulking giant was already on him, twisting his arm in a vice-like grip. "Michael!"

The first blow caught him in the jaw and knocked him to the floor. Dazed, he tried to struggle to his feet, but a second blow glanced off the side of his head and sent him reeling through the open door. He tried to grab the banister to break his fall, but a huge hand clamped on his wrist and wrenched his fingers free. Then a fist caught him full in the face and his mouth filled with the taste of salt and iron as the banister wheeled past. He landed at the base of the stairs, his head swimming, his breath coming in gasps.

As he staggered to his feet and limped toward the foyer, Julian wondered if indeed Hell might not be preferable to San Francisco.

"Yeah, yeah. Cool it, will you? I'm coming." Larry's voice sounded through the bolted door. "Yeah? Who is it?" he growled, squinting into the dim hallway.

"Can I come in?" Julian mumbled through swollen lips.

"Julie?"

"Please, Larry. Let me in?"

Larry opened the door wider and gaped at Julian's bruised and swollen face. "Jesus, Julie, you look like shit. What the hell happened to you, man?"

"I got beat up."

"No shit? Here, come on in," said Larry. Carefully, he guided Julian through the clutter of empty beer cans, overflowing ashtrays, and assorted comatose bodies. "Come on. Let's have a look."

Frankie was sprawled naked on a dirty mattress, a yellowed pillow pulled over her head.

"In here," said Larry, pushing Julian gently into the bathroom. In the light of a swaying bulb, he carefully examined Julian's battered face.

"Ow." Julian winced as the fingers probed the inch-long gash where Vern's fist had connected with his cheekbone.

"Whooee," whistled Larry. "Somebody sure worked you over good. Who was it, man?"

"Some guy at Michael's," Julian muttered.

"Hey, I tried to tell you about that Michael, didn't I?"

"Yeah."

"Damn right I did. Look at you now, pretty face all busted up. Should have listened to me, little buddy."

Julian nodded miserably.

"Look, man, sit down." Larry gestured toward the toilet seat. "Let me get something for those cuts." He rummaged in the medicine chest. "Hold still now. This is gonna sting."

Julian tried to shrug, but he grimaced at the jagged pain that coursed through his cheek.

"So what's the plan, man?" Larry enquired.

"Don't have one."

Larry shook his head sadly. "You forget everything I told you? Julie, you gotta have a plan."

"I screwed up."

"Not too bright, Julie baby," Larry said.

Julian looked up hopefully. "I thought maybe I could stay here for a couple of days? Just 'til I can—can think of something to do?"

Larry folded his arms across his chest and leaned against the sink. "Didn't like the way you walked out on me, little buddy," he said.

Julian lowered his head. "I know. I'm sorry I left like that, but Michael said—"

"And look where it got you? Now you got no place to live." He shook his head and sighed. "I don't mind helping you out, Julie, but it's gotta work both ways, you dig?"

Julian nodded mutely.

Larry brightened. "Well, like they say, tomorrow's another day. You just relax now, little buddy. Ole Larry's got just the thing to fix you up." He disappeared into the bedroom and returned a moment later with a small plastic syrette. Holding it up, he grinned at Julian. "Guaranteed to cure what ails you."

"What is it?"

"Something to make you feel a whole lot better. Come on now, roll up your sleeve," he added when Julian hesitated.

"I don't like needles," muttered Julian.

"Hey, man, don't you trust me?"

"Sure I do."

"Then just do what I say. Come on now, roll up your sleeve." Larry quickly applied a tourniquet and selected a vein.

"What is it?" Julian repeated, flinching as the needle jabbed into his arm.

"High-grade shit," Larry replied. "I don't handle nothin' but the best. There now." He tossed the used syrette away and helped Julian to his feet. "I told Frankie to get her ass outta here so you can have some peace and quiet."

Gently, he lowered Julian onto the mattress. "You just take it easy, little buddy. You'll be feeling a whole lot better in no time."

Gingerly, Julian raised his fingers to his face. The gash in his cheek throbbed at his touch, and the skin around his mouth was puckered and squishy. I should have listened to Larry, he thought once more.

But the mattress was becoming a luxurious raft adrift on a summer sea, and the thought melted away along with the pain. A blissful warmth spread outward from his shoulders and eased down the backs of his legs. A wonderful, drowsy, warmth, like curling up before a friendly fire, like stretching out in a hammock on a lazy, golden afternoon.        Somewhere just outside the range of his vision, Julian felt something moving—an amorphous, frightening form—but he was too serene to care. He was sinking slowly, so slowly, into a warm cloud of comforting fuzziness. From somewhere far away, Miles Davis was playing softly. Something smokey and slow. So good to be home.

He woke with a start a couple of hours later, his stomach churning, and staggered to the bathroom. Vomit came up in a series of strangled heaves. Then, feeling slightly better, he crawled back to the mattress and fell asleep once more.

"Hey, Julie." Julian squinted up into Larry's benevolently smiling face. "Hey, man, how you doing?"

"Better, I guess," Julian said vaguely, rubbing his head. There was an astonishing pain inside his skull.

"We got to clean you up, little buddy," Larry said. "Here, let me give you a hand."

"You should have been a nurse," Julian said as Larry bandaged the cut beneath his eye.

"Hey, man, it's the least I could do for an old friend. Like, I feel terrible, Julie. That Michael's such a shit."

"He is that," agreed Julian.

"Tell you what, I'm gonna go over there and pick up your stuff for you, okay?"

Julian stared at Larry with simple gratitude. "Gosh, Larry, would you?"

"Sure, man. Glad to." Larry dug in his pocket. "Look, Julie, I'm gonna leave a couple of these right here on the sink for you, dig?"

Julian swallowed and looked at the two plastic cartridges. "That's okay. I really don't . . ."

"Hey, no sweat. Just use one if you want to. Takes the edge off, know what I mean?"

Julian sat staring at the syrettes. His head ached relentlessly, and his cheek had begun to throb once more. He remembered so vividly the delicious warmth, a feeling of peace so complete that it blotted out every care. What could it hurt to use just one? Tomorrow he'd be feeling better. Tomorrow he'd figure out what to do. Slowly, he rolled up his sleeve.

# CHAPTER

# 29

## San Francisco, California
## January 1961

"I know it's terribly short notice, Carl," the manager of the San Francisco Philharmonic said hesitantly, "but if you think you can handle it, we'd be most grateful. We're really in a bind. And, of course, it's a great opportunity for you."

"I can do it."

"You're certain? What about the program? It's too late to change it."

"I know the program backwards and forwards," Carl said. "Upside down if you like. Seriously, there is no problem with the program."

There was a pause at the other end of the phone. "All right, then. We'll see you Monday for rehearsal. Ten o'clock sharp."

"Monday. Ten o'clock." Carl dropped the receiver into its cradle and let out an exuberant whoop. Clapping a hand over his mouth, he tried to restrain himself. Monday. Rehearsal. As guest conductor of the San Francisco Philharmonic.

The program. He ran frenzied fingers through his thick, dark hair. My God, he'd just said that he knew everything on the program. You arrogant bastard, he told himself, then burst out laughing.

He dashed to the piano and shuffled through a stack of scores. Ah, here it was. The Brahms Symphony No. 2. No problem there. He'd just conducted it in Sacramento.

And the Liszt Piano Concerto No. 1. Where the hell was it? There. Chewing furiously on his thumbnail, he scanned the score. Okay. The manager had said that the soloist was Austrian—some wunderkind that Carl had never heard of. Wonder if the guy speaks English, he thought. Not to worry, I can practice my German. He rolled his eyes heavenward—thank you, Anya, for teaching me German.

But then there was Mussorgsky's *Pictures at an Exhibition*. Carl sank down on the piano bench and stared at the stacks of music. I don't even have a copy of the score, he thought with dismay. He would have to know it start-to- finish by Monday. And it was already Friday. Jumping to his feet, he grabbed his coat and raced out of the apartment.

*Pictures at an Exhibition consists of ten programmatic pieces, prefaced by a* Promenade *that recurs four times during the progression of the work and serves as a connecting device,* Carl read. *The work was composed in 1874, but not published until 1886, five years after Mussorgsky's death.*

He pushed aside the sheath of notes and returned to the score that lay open on the table. Munching absently on a sandwich, he scanned the pages, humming to himself. After two days of continual study, *Pictures at an Exhibition* was firmly planted in his brain.

Nevertheless, on Monday when Carl walked on-stage and set the score down unopened on the podium, there was a whisper of skepticism among the members of the orchestra.

"The Mussorgsky, please, ladies and gentlemen," Carl said crisply. He signaled the oboe player to sound another A. The musicians fine-tuned their instruments. Taking a deep breath, Carl raised his arms.

It took only a few minutes for the nervousness to subside. He could feel the growing response, the doubts fading away. When he stopped the musicians to make suggestions, they listened attentively, exchanging bemused glances with one another. He might be just a kid, but damned if he didn't understand Mussorgsky.

His confidence growing, Carl grew more demanding, stopping again and again to try to convey the exact coloration that he could hear so plainly inside his head. The orchestra responded ever more strongly to his carefully phrased suggestions, beginning to share the electric excitement that throbbed in his veins. He drew them out, eased the tension with little asides, asked searching questions. He was molding them to his wishes, forcing them to experience the music as though they had never heard it before.

When he finally said, "Let's take a short break, ladies and gentlemen," he heard an audible sigh, as though the musicians had been holding their breath and had just realized it. He smiled as several players crowded around him.

"Why haven't we seen you here before?" the first violinist said.

Carl shrugged. "Nobody asked me," he said with an easy grin.

By the end of that week, the San Francisco music community was buzzing with rumors. A few devotees had heard of Carl's recent success with the Sacramento Symphony, but that was Sacramento. This was *San Francisco*. Ticket sales escalated as patrons decided to see for themselves.

The late January evening was unusually warm, and the War Memorial Opera House was bathed in a diffuse lavender glow. Limousines hovered next to the curb, discharging mink-draped ladies. A willowy blond dressed in silver lamé shimmered amidst a sea of dark suits and coffee-brown furs.

As eight o'clock approached, the red-plush seats of the concert hall filled with eager patrons. Programs fluttered, voices chattered, feet shuffled. There was a slithering of silk, the scent of expensive perfume. Musicians trailed onto the stage, arranging music stands, fingering instruments, grinning like conspirators.

Alone in his dressing room, Carl sat staring at the grey-green wall. Through a week of rehearsals he had been as calm and assured as the most seasoned professional. Why was it that he was sitting here now staring at this ghastly-tinted wall, his hands cold as ice, his back dripping in sweat, his stomach clenched like a desperate fist?

He swallowed, trying to ease the ripples of nausea that were making the wall quiver like moldy jelly. A knock at the door interrupted his tangled thoughts.

"Yes?" he managed.

"We're ready."

"Just a minute," he answered, bounding up and dashing for the bathroom as the taste of bile rose in his throat. He clung to the tank, retching blindly. Struggling upright, he gazed glassy-eyed into the mirror, rinsed his mouth with water from the tap.

"Carl?" The voice from beyond the door was urgent. "We're ready."

"All right. I'll be right there." Sucking in his breath, he flushed the toilet and headed for the door.

From the wings he could hear the grind and squeak of instruments being brought into tune. The concertmaster patted his shoulder and gave him a little salute before walking out onto the stage.

Carl leaned forward, trying to force air into his constricted lungs. Coward, he sneered at himself, get out there and get to work. Head up, chin thrust forward, he strode decisively toward the podium.

It never failed. As soon as the music began, he forgot the audience, forgot the weakness in his knees, the churning in his stomach, the trickle of sweat inching its way down his back. There was only the music, the sound, the magic. He was sailing now on familiar seas, and Brahms was his first mate. Together they guided the work through the lyrical meadows and turbulent seas of the piece, culminating in a triumphant blaze of brass. The burst of applause at the end of the final movement surprised him. He took three modest bows and headed for the wings.

A few moments later, he followed the Austrian pianist onto the stage, acknowledged the audience without really seeing them, spun to face the orchestra, tossed back his dark mane of hair with an impatient jerk of his head and raised his arms. The soloist nodded, and the concert resumed with the triumphant opening theme of Liszt's First Piano Concerto. Carl and the soloist were completely together on the nuances of interpretation demanded by the score.

"What contrast. What audacity," Carl had exclaimed, sharing a late-night brandy with the Austrian the night before the performance. "What liveliness. What urgency," the Austrian cried, raising his glass. *"Das versteht ihr alle nicht!"* "None of you understands this."

As the final notes of the exultant presto finale died away, the audience rose, applauding wildly as Carl and the soloist reached to share a triumphant handshake.

But if the first half of the program had been dazzling, it was Carl's brilliant and innovative reading of Mussorgsky's *Pictures at an Exhibition* that was destined to establish him that night as the darling of the San Francisco music world.

From the beginning statement, Carl wove an ever-expanding net of visual poetry, molding the sounds like streaks of color on a canvas, adding measure after measure, like pieces of a puzzle, until the grand design took shape. Carl brought the audience to the edge of its seat, teasing them with hints of resolution, until the final, delirious grandeur of the theme rose to a crest of passion and crashed to the breath-taking conclusion.

After a moment of awed silence, the audience exploded, rising to its feet, roaring approval. Dazed, Carl turned and stared into the darkness of the concert hall. Forgetting to bow, he stepped from the podium and made his way across the stage. The applause was like a distant pounding in his head.

He would have gone straight to his dressing room, but the symphony manager grabbed him and turned him back toward the stage. "Go," urged the manager.

"What?" Carl murmured.

"Bow!" the manager cried.

"Oh. Right." Carl headed unsteadily toward the sound of cheering. The lights dazzled his eyes.    Bewildered, he looked out at the audience. The orchestra members were applauding too, stomping their feet. Mechanically, Carl motioned for the orchestra to stand, shook the concertmaster's hand, gestured toward the beaming musicians. Then he made his way toward the refuge of the wings.

"Go back again," prompted the manager's laughing voice.

"I can't."

"Oh, yes you can."

Carl felt like a sleepwalker as he returned to the glare of the lights. Once more he surveyed the cheering crowd, hesitated for a long moment, then bowed and bolted once more for the wings.

"And he's gorgeous, too," Wally sighed, pausing, comb aloft, eyes half-closed. "They say he's the most phenomenal conductor since Bernstein made his debut twenty years ago."

"Who's Bernstein?" sniffed Lillian Meridith Chambers, pouting at her reflection in the wall-sized salon mirror.

"Oh, Mrs. Chambers," giggled Wally, returning to the comb-out with concerted attention, "You know, Leonard Bernstein."

"Oh, I get them all confused."

"Now there's a gorgeous man," Wally continued. "Some of them are so grotesque—fat and little and bald—it's a wonder they can make such pretty music. But Bernstein, *quel homme,* my dear, *quel homme.*"

"Ow! Will you watch what you're doing?"

"I'm sorry, Mrs. C," Wally said contritely, "I'm still just all a-tingle from the concert last night. What a shame you had to miss it."

A shame indeed, thought Lillian as Wally finished swirling her long, dark hair into an elegant French twist. The one concert of the year that might have been exciting. How dreadful of Marcus to insist that she go with him to that boring Bar Association dinner. Glowering, she critically surveyed Wally's handiwork. "A little more fullness on the right," she decided, pointing.

"Yes, ma'am." Obediently, the hairdresser loosened a few strands, teased them with his comb, and pressed them back in place. "How's that, Mrs. C?"

She turned her head from side to side, vaguely annoyed by the boy's youthful, pink-cheeked face smiling at her from the mirror. "That will do, I guess."

Still nonplussed about missing the concert, she tipped the hairdresser, suffered his fawning good-byes, and waited impatiently at the curb for the doorman to bring her Mercedes around.

It wasn't that Lillian truly enjoyed good music. In fact, except for some Tchaikovsky and a little Beethoven, she had trouble distinguishing one composition from another. But it was expected that a woman of her position would support the cultural attractions of the community, so every year she dutifully purchased season tickets to the ballet, the opera, the symphony.

Her husband, Marcus, cared even less for classical music. He rarely showed up at performances, unless it was to entertain an important client or humor the senior partner of the prestigious law firm where he had risen to "Number Two." Marcus's lack of interest didn't bother Lillian. She had her own set of friends and, unless it was absolutely necessary, rarely crossed paths socially with her husband.

To amuse herself, Lillian had taken to collecting. First it was French antiques, then Chinese porcelains, then Italian statuary and English tapestries.

More recently, she had been collecting men. Marcus had long been engaged in various extramarital pursuits, so as long as Lillian was reasonably discreet, he was willing to overlook her affairs and continued to pay the enormous bills that arrived each month from high-end stores like The White House, Gumps, and I. Magnin.

As she settled in behind the wheel of the powder-blue Mercedes, Lillian's thoughts focused on the brilliant new conductor who was receiving rave reviews from every sector. Now there was a prize worth pursuing. She had seen his picture in the *Chronicle,* and Wally had confirmed her own observation—he was a gorgeous-looking boy.

She pictured the young maestro lying among the satin pillows in her pink-draped boudoir. Marcus would be out of town on one of his numerous business trips. She would give the servants the night off. Oh, how delicious. She would let word of the liaison drop to just a few of her closest friends. Wouldn't they be green with envy? Now, how to launch her conquest?

# CHAPTER

# 30

## San Francisco, California
## March 1961

*You are cordially invited to*
*a reception on*
*Saturday, March 17, 1961*
*at 8 p.m. at the home of*
*Mr. and Mrs. Marcus N. Chambers,*
*218 Brentwood Circle, Saint Francis Wood.*
*RSVP KL2-1122*

Carl smiled as he read the invitation. Another soirée at the Chambers'? That made three in the past five weeks, not counting the Valentine's Day gala to benefit the symphony retirement fund. Amazing, wasn't it, how Mrs. Chambers's patronage had blossomed in such a short period of time? Lifting the embossed card to his nose, he inhaled, and his smile widened. Was every guest's invitation doused in *Shalimar*?

He was holding a half-empty glass of champagne and admiring the two splendid Rose Famille vases that occupied the mantel when he caught sight of Lillian gliding toward him. Her white skin was dappled with drops of light from the crystal chandelier, the black crepe of her Dior gown clung deliciously to the curves of her well-proportioned body.

"Darling," she cried, brushing his cheek with a kiss, "how divine that you could join us."

"Mrs. Chambers," he replied, raising her delicate hand to his lips and letting his eyes linger on the soft curve of her bosom. "Delighted to be here."

"You naughty boy," she chided, "I told you to call me Lillian. Don't you remember?"

"Very well, Lillian," he returned, letting the name slide across his tongue.

"That's better." She took his arm and whispered confidentially, "Come along, darling. I have something to show you."

"Oh?" He allowed himself to be propelled into the small library adjacent to the hall.

"It's a little present," she said, cocking her head to one side and teasing him with her glance. "Close your eyes."

Smiling, he obliged. His skin tingled when he felt her hand brush his neck.

"And open."

He looked down to find a small gold medallion glinting on the front of his white shirt. "What's this?" he asked.

She moved close to him, fingering the medallion, her eyes downcast demurely. "It's a Saint Christopher medal," she said. "To protect you."

"And from what do I need protecting?" Carl asked, "You, perhaps?"

"Oh, darling," she laughed, "why would you need protection from me?"

"Because, Mrs. Chambers," he said, "you are too rich, too beautiful, and too spoiled to care about anyone but yourself. Good night," he added pleasantly, slipping the medallion over his head and handing it back to her.

End of round five, he thought, grinning as he stepped through the front door into the bracing San Francisco night.

A few days later, he received a package in the mail. Inside, he found a letter and a small cloisonné case. He opened the case first, and there was the medallion. Grinning, he tore open the envelope and read:

*My darling Carl,*

*I can't go on like this. Surely you must know that I can't stop thinking of you. I have tried in every way that I know to convey my feelings to you, and still you reject me. Am I so unworthy of your affection? Please, mon cher, tell me what I must do to please you. My anguish knows no bounds. I will be at the Saint Francis on Friday night following the concert. I must see you.*

*'Til Friday,*

*Lillian.*

"TKO in the sixth," he chuckled, raising the perfumed envelope to his nose.

He played the Tchaikovsky D Major Violin Concerto brilliantly that Friday evening as featured soloist with the visiting Los Angeles Philharmonic. The audience was thrilled with his performance, and the reception held at the Saint Francis Hotel was packed with admirers.

However, it wasn't until near the end of the evening that he spotted Lillian. She was dressed in a green velvet, Empire-style gown that set off her dark hair and porcelain complexion to perfection. She made her way through the crowd. He met her questioning gaze with a curt nod. "Mrs. Chambers."

"You were wonderful, Carl," she said.

"Thank you."

"Did you . . ." she hesitated, her cheeks coloring prettily, ". . . did you get my letter?"

"Yes." He let her stand there blushing for a full thirty seconds before he added gravely, "I had no idea, Lillian."

"But surely," she protested, "I've given every indication . . ."

"I thought it was a game," Carl said, giving her a reproachful look.

She turned her face a little to the side, eyes downcast. Anna Karinina, Carl thought with amusement. Camille. You could have played them all, couldn't you, my dear, delicious Mrs. Chambers.

"Ah," she sighed, "how little you know me."

"I would like to know you better," Carl responded, taking her slim hand and raising it to his lips.

"Oh," she sighed, resting her other hand against her cheek, "I feel dizzy. It's so warm in here." Her violet eyes gazed up at him. "Could you get me something cool to drink?"

"No," Carl said, "but I'll take you home with me if you like."

Her eyes widened momentarily, then a smile spread across her carefully painted lips. "I'll get my coat," she said.

"It's so austere," she remarked, looking around the apartment as he hung her mink on the mirrored Victorian hall tree. "But elegant," she added, her eyes sweeping approvingly over the Queen Anne sideboard and the pair of Windsor chairs.

"I live quite simply," Carl said as he guided her toward the sofa. "My music is my life."

"Such artistic devotion." She turned to look at him, and he stared back, intensely aware of the blood pounding in his ears, of the urgent tightening in his loins. Her eyelids half-closed as she lifted her arms. "Oh, Carl," she sighed, "darling Carl. Hold me. Please."

He took her in his arms and kissed her almost roughly, sliding his hands swiftly down her sides, loving the feel of velvet-covered flesh beneath his fingers. She smelled of roses, jasmine, lemon flowers. The skin of her neck was the color of cream.

"Want you so terribly," she whispered, her fingers prying at the gold studs on the front of his shirt.

For over a year he had been faithful to his music, avoiding nearly every physical pleasure, determined to devote every ounce of energy to his art. Repressed needs surfaced with the impact of a thunderclap. Frenzied, shaking, he struggled out of his coat and ripped loose the black-silk cummerbund.

She watched him wide-eyed, face flushed, pink lips parted in wonder as he ripped open his shirt and flung it to the floor. He grasped her shoulders and kissed her brutally on the mouth, his hands fumbling desperately with the tiny covered buttons on the back of her dress. He heard the fabric rip and she moaned, "Oh yes, yes, yes . . ." against his neck.

The velvet tore beneath his hands, and he pushed it down to her waist, exposing full, pink-nippled breasts. Falling to his knees, he pulled her down beside him and pushed aside the folds of velvet skirt. Inflamed still more to find her naked beneath the dress, he groaned and straddled her, thrusting himself immediately into her, letting his own exploding passion set the time.

"My god, you're an *animal*," she panted when he had finished. "You practically raped me."

He opened his eyes and stared down at her. "Did I?"

"I loved it."

He pushed away from her and sat back on his heels, trying to regain his composure.

She sat up slowly and looked down at the ruins of her dress.

"Sorry," Carl said, gazing at the shredded velvet in dismay.

"It's nothing," she said with a shaky laugh.

Untangling his legs from the muddle of trousers, shorts, and socks, he got to his feet and held out his hand to her. "Come on," he said.

"Where to?" she asked, taking his hand.

"The bedroom. I want to prove to you that I'm not just an animal."

"Look, Julie," Larry sighed, "it's not that I don't want to help you, man, but I can't afford to keep giving you high-grade shit for nothing, dig?"

Julian chewed his thumbnail, his eyes riveted to Larry's hounddog face.

"Like, I have to keep my accounts in order."

Julian examined his thumbnail intently and tried to swallow the dryness in his throat.

Larry shook his head sadly. "You know I'm a reasonable, guy, Julie, but you haven't even paid me for the last bag. It's not good business, man."

"Come on, Larry," Julian said. "You know I'll pay you when I get the money."

"I know that. But when? That's the question, isn't it?"

Julian licked his lips. His left knee began to quiver, and he put his hand on it to stop the involuntary movement. "Look," he said, "I can give you half now and the rest the first of the week. I'm working overtime this weekend and all day Saturday and Sunday. I'll have a check on Monday. I'll sign it over to you as soon as I get it," he added quickly when Larry failed to respond. "Come on, Larry, please?"

Larry's brow crinkled. "Shit, man," he groaned, flopping down on the mattress and stuffing a pillow behind his head, "I'm sorry, man, but I just can't go on making exceptions for you, Julie. My other clients don't like it, dig? I got my reputation to consider."

The muscles worked in Julian's jaw. He glanced at the little bag of white powder that lay on the floor next to the mattress. "One more time," he pleaded. "I'll never ask you again. Look," he continued when Larry remained silent, eyes closed, hands folded across his chest, "maybe I could do something else for you. Make some extra deliveries or something. What do you say, Larry?"

Larry opened one eye and glanced at Julian. "Naw, I don't think so, man."

"Come on," Julian exclaimed. "There must be *something*. Come on."

Larry propped himself up on his elbows and studied Julian's face.

He frowned. Scratched his head. Ran a finger over his nose. "Well..."
He squinted, considering.

"What?" Julian sat forward eagerly. "Tell me."

"Naw," Larry collapsed back onto the mattress. "You wouldn't
be interested."

Julian's stomach lurched. "Sure I would."

Larry sat up. "Well, I got this friend, see, Mr. Smith? He sets up a
few of his pals with good-looking young studs now and then, know
what I mean? For a fee, of course."

"You mean... tricks?" said Julian, feeling suddenly lightheaded.

"They provide... services, let's say. Depends on what the client's
willing to pay for." Larry leaned forward confidentially. "These are
rich guys, dig? The money's great. I hear you could pick up forty, fifty
easy in one evening. Maybe more."

Julian's palms began to sweat. "Gee..." he said, "I don't know."

"Well," Larry settled back on the mattress and paused to light a
joint, "I figured you wouldn't be interested."

Julian's eyes wandered to the little plastic bag. Forty or fifty
bucks in one evening? It would take him more than a week busing
dishes to make that. Maybe just this once....

"Uh, who's this Mr. Smith?" Julian asked.

Larry took several deep drags and passed the joint to Julian. "Just
a guy I know," he said tightly, holding the smoke. "Does me a lot of
favors. Keeps certain folks off my back, know what I mean?" He let
out his breath and continued. "I try to help him out now and then.
Show my appreciation, dig?"

Julian nodded, inhaled, and handed the joint back to Larry.

"Got a call from him this morning," Larry continued, searching
for a roach clip on the cluttered coffee table. "He's got a problem
with one of his boys for tomorrow night and wondered if I knew of
anybody. Course I didn't think of you right off, Julie. I mean, you
never done nothing like that, have you?"

Julian shook his head.

"Well," Larry studiously attached the clip to the joint, "I
don't suppose you'd want to." He sighed plaintively. "Sure do hate

to disappoint Mr. Smith, though. Haven't been able to find him anybody else."

"Well, maybe just this once," Julian heard himself say.

Larry looked surprised. "Hey, no shit? I appreciate that, man, but like I don't want you doing nothing you don't want to."

"No big deal," Julian said with a tight little laugh. "Going out with some rich guy, having a good time . . ."

"Only he'd be paying you," crowed Larry, sucking on the joint.

"Right," Julian agreed. "That's right."

Larry blew smoke rings, scratched his beard. He picked up the little bag and swung it back and forth slowly. "Naw." He tossed the bag down and crushed out the joint. "Don't want you involved in hustling. I'll find somebody else. Tell you what, Julie, I got some new stuff coming in the first of the week. Maybe I can make you a better deal on it. Why don't you drop by on, like Monday, and we'll talk. Maybe you can come up with some extra bread by then."

"No!" Julian cried, half-rising from the chair. "It's okay, Larry. Really it is."

Larry raised his eyebrows, pursed his lips. Then he shrugged and picked up the little bag. "Hey, tell you what, Julie. You do me a favor and help me out just this once and I'll let you take this stuff along home with you right now. Pay me later, dig? Here, catch."

Julian made a little lunge and caught the bag. Quickly, he stuffed it in his pocket and stood up. "How do I get in touch with Mr. Smith?" he asked.

"Here." Larry scribbled a number on the back of a matchbook. "Just give this a call. Ask for Sheila. She'll tell you what to do. Got that?"

Julian studied the number. "Got it," he said and started for the door.

"And hey, Julie," Larry's voice stopped him. "You be sure you clean up real good. This cat's got a classy clientele. I can't send him no hole, dig?"

"Right," said Julian. Again, he headed for the door.

"And, Julie?" Larry called after him.

"Yeah?" Julian turned, his hand on the knob.

"Thanks, man."

For a moment, Julian stared at the figure slumped on the sofa. Then his lips parted in a brittle smile. "No sweat," he said.

# CHAPTER

# 31

"Wilson Escort Service," a woman's voice said.

Julian swallowed. "Uh, is Sheila there?"

"One moment please."

Canned music flooded his ear, a Montovani rendition of *The Blue Danube Waltz*.

"This is Sheila. How can I help you?" The voice was somewhere between throatily sexy and briskly professional.

"This is Julian. Mr. Flagstaad told me to call you about tomorrow night."

"Oh, yes," Sheila said. "Larry said you'd be getting in touch."

"Well, here I am."

"Good. Look, Julian, usually we don't hire anyone without an interview, but we got in a bind. Still, I need to ask you some questions. Have you ever done this sort of work before?"

"No."

"How many partners have you had in the last six months?"

Julian flinched. "Just one."

"That's it?" Sheila said incredulously. "Umm, is it a serious relationship?"

"Not anymore."

"Good." Sheila sounded relieved. "We don't want any jealous lovers hanging around hassling clients. Now then, any health problems? Mental or physical disorders that we need to be aware of?"

"Healthy as a horse," said Julian, feeling very much as though a sharp-eyed trader was examining his teeth and fetlocks.

"Current employment?"

"I work the lunch shift at the Blue Fox."

"Oh, good. Then you probably have decent manners."

"I know which fork to use."

"We're a top-of-the-line organization, Julian," said Sheila. "We have a reputation to maintain."

"I understand."

"We expect our boys to dress well, to be courteous and punctual, and keep our customers happy. Do you do drugs?"

"Now and then," Julian lied.

"Ummm," she said. "Well, as long as it doesn't interfere with your work, we don't quibble about your personal habits. Just don't show up for an appointment stoned."

"No, ma'am."

"All right, take down this address. Your appointment is for seven o'clock. Drinks and dinner at a private club, light recreation afterwards. Think you can handle that?"

"Sure," said Julian, wondering exactly what *light recreation* meant.

"Be sure to be on time. Dress will be informal—a nice sport coat and slacks. Nothing flashy. Ever."

"Fine."

"One more thing," said Sheila. "Do all right this time, and we might be able to use you again. Keep that in mind. We're always on the lookout for new talent."

"How do I get paid?" asked Julian.

"An envelope will be waiting for you at the client's home."

"How much will I get for Friday night?"

"You've got a head for business, haven't you," Sheila said pleasantly.

"That's right."

"Forty this time. Maybe more next time, depending on your performance."

"Fair enough."

As the seven o'clock appointment approached, Julian's nervousness increased despite a carefully timed hit and a couple of glasses of wine.

He thought briefly about taking a cab to the posh Nob Hill address, but decided that he couldn't afford it and besides, the walk would do him good.

The spring evening was brisk, even by San Francisco standards, and catching sight of himself in the gilded mirror that hung in the foyer of the elegant apartment building, Julian smiled to see his rosy-cheeked, slightly wind-blown image. Like I've been out playing soccer, he thought. The very image of wholesomeness. He punched the elevator button. It was just this once, after all. Just a favor to a friend.

The man who opened the door to 1106 was medium height, balding, and dressed smartly in a navy-blue blazer and grey- flannel slacks. Gold cuff links glinted momentarily as he reached to take Julian's outstretched hand.

"Hello," said Julian. "I believe you're expecting me?"

"The young man from the escort service. Julian, isn't it?"

"Yes, that's right."

"Come right in," the man said. "My name is Richard. Why don't you take off your coat and make yourself at home. I thought we'd have a drink here before we go to the club. Will white wine be all right?"

"Fine," said Julian, taking off his London Fog and draping it over the back of a sleek Mies van der Rohe chair. "What a terrific view," he added, looking with admiration at the spectacular panorama outside the window

"That's what keeps me here," said Richard. "Have a seat. I'll be right back."

Julian made himself comfortable on the black-leather sofa and glanced around the room, noting with interest the Danish-Modern carpets and Art Deco-inspired lamps. Eclectic, but not bad, he thought. Stan Kenton's *Cuban Fire* played at a low volume on the hi-fi. Julian's eyes fell upon a small aquarium and he got up to take a closer look.

"Here you are," said Richard, handing him a crystal goblet. "A domestic Chenin blanc. One of my favorites."

Julian took a moment to savor the crisp, slightly perfumy wine. "Excellent," he said. Clearly this line of work had its compensations. "Nice angelfish," he continued, tilting the wineglass toward the aquarium.

"I have another aquarium in the bedroom," said Richard, obviously pleased. "Would you like to see it?"

Julian managed a bright, impersonal smile and said, "Sure."

In the dim, turquoise-colored light he watched the brightly striped fish circle and glide. There was something uncanny about the setting, the familiar glow of the aquarium combined with the thoroughly unfamiliar hands that began to stroke his shoulders, then his sides, and finally his thighs. "The service always sends me such lovely boys," Richard whispered as his fingers grazed Julian's crotch. "Such lovely boys."

"Would you like me to get undressed?" said Julian, hoping that his voice wouldn't betray his nervousness.

"Not now." said Richard. "I want to enjoy the anticipation." He stepped away and smiled at Julian through the gloom. "Let's finish our wine in the living room and go along to the club. We have plenty of time for . . . other things later on."

Two of Richard's friends were waiting for them in the dining room of the private supper club. They appraised Julian with considerable interest while Richard smirked with proprietary delight. Over an impeccably broiled lobster and several glasses of Meursault, Julian relaxed enough to enjoy the conversation that centered on the stock market and recent economic trends. Although he didn't know much about the subject, it seemed enough to simply sit there and smile pleasantly while Richard and his friends discussed the indicators. Now I know what a wife feels like, Julian thought.

However, when the discussion turned to music, Julian was able to join in.

"I haven't seen that new conductor that everyone's raving about," said Richard. "What was his name?"

"Fitzgerald," replied the man named Eric to Julian's left. "I was there for his debut. He was inspired. Absolutely inspired."

"I heard him play the Tchaikovsky concerto several weeks ago," Julian offered. "I thought his technique was superb."

"You enjoy the symphony?" asked Richard.

"Oh, yes," exclaimed Julian. "I go whenever I can."

Richard was obviously delighted with his new companion and, by the time they finished dessert, Julian was actually enjoying himself, feeling quite glamorous to be the center of so many lustful glances and envious asides.

"Shall we be going?" said Richard, standing up and placing a hand on Julian's shoulder.

"Of course," replied Julian, favoring Richard with his most ingratiating smile.

Back in the strangely familiar gloom of the apartment's bedroom, the feeling of *savoir-faire* nearly caved in as Richard's roving mouth and probing fingers explored Julian's naked body. But Julian managed to control his inclination to fight off the assault and bolt for the door. He even managed a convincingly exuberant orgasm and was rewarded, as he left, with Richard's slightly drunken compliments and an extra twenty-dollar bill pressed into his hand along with the envelope. "I hope we see each other again soon," said Richard as Julian stepped into the hall.

"Oh, yes," Julian responded, smiling brightly, "that would be lovely. Good night, Richard. Thank you for a delightful evening." Alone on the elevator, he closed his eyes and felt like throwing up.

# CHAPTER

# 32

"You make me divinely happy," Lillian sighed, "divinely happy." Obligingly, Carl kissed her flushed and slightly dampened forehead, each petal-soft cheek, each rosy-nippled breast. Fatigued and inexplicably depressed, he stared up at the pink-gauze canopy of Lillian's bed.

It looked like a child's room, a little girl's fantasy— the pink-swathed bed, the fussy, chintz-covered chairs. He hated it. I feel like a pampered house pet, he thought moodily, like a poodle or a Persian cat, being fed smoked salmon from a crystal dish, paraded about on a rhinestone leash, allowed to nap in the boudoir while the master is away. He smiled grimly at the image.

"Why are you smiling?"

Lillian's question interrupted his thoughts. Turning toward her, he let his eyes travel over the soft curves of her body, noting the lush fullness of her breasts, the satin texture of her skin, the waves of glossy, coffee-colored hair. Lovely, he thought, but her question sent a small flurry of annoyance through his mind.

"Why shouldn't I smile?" he said with forced sincerity. "After all, I just made love to the most beautiful woman in San Francisco."

"Only San Francisco?" she said, pouting.

"Northern California?" Carl suggested with growing irritation.

"That's better," she said. Closing her eyes, she fingered a lock of her hair. "You are so good to me," she whispered. "So very good."

But what now, Carl thought. We can't stay in bed forever. Suddenly restless, he got up and crossed the bedroom to the lace-draped window. The late-afternoon sun had broken through the layer of fog, and in the distance he could see the flat blue water of the Pacific. "Let's go for a walk," he said.

Lillian sat up, wrapping a jade-green kimono around her shoulders. "I don't think that's wise," she said. "What if the neighbors saw us?"

Carl stared at the blue strip of ocean visible through the eucalyptus trees. "I thought you didn't care what the neighbors thought."

"I said I didn't care what *people* thought," Lillian corrected. "People in general. But I don't want to start a scandal in the neighborhood. Marcus wouldn't like it."

"'Marcus wouldn't like it,'" Carl echoed mockingly. "Why should I care what Marcus likes?"

"Oh, Carly," Lillian scolded, "don't be angry with me, precious. I do have my reputation to consider."

"Really?" said Carl. "What reputation is that, Mrs. Chambers?"

"Would you please come away from that window," Lillian snapped. "Someone's going to see you standing there naked."

Carl turned to face her. "I should think you'd find that titillating. Why don't you waltz over here and let me do rude things to your body in front of the glass. If we're going to cause a sensation, it might as well be a humdinger."

"Oh, Carly," she giggled, "you do say the most provocative things." She smiled at him coyly. "Now come away from there, you naughty boy."

Carl stared at her for a moment, then turned away from the window, giving the gauzy curtains an angry tug. "Why don't we go out for dinner," he suggested, throwing a borrowed dressing gown around himself and plucking a cigarette from the silver canister beside the bed. He rarely smoked, but this was an occasion that cried out for something fractious. "We could drive over to Stinson Beach and have dinner at the wharf. Surely, none of your chic society friends will spot you there." He exhaled forcibly, blowing smoke at the photograph of Lillian and Marcus that hung on the wall above the bureau.

"I'd love to, sweet," Lillian said, getting up and coming to him. He turned his back to her, and she hugged him, resting her face against his shoulder blade. "But you know perfectly well that Marcus will be getting in at eight. He's expecting me to be here. We're going to Rome next week, and we have to finalize the details. Please don't be angry, precious. You know I'd rather be here with you, but we've been planning this vacation for months. It wouldn't look right for me to decide to stay home at the last minute. You can understand that, can't you?"

"Of course," Carl muttered. "I understand quite well."

"I thought we'd have some dinner here," Lillian continued. "We could send out for something yummy from the deli, have a little champagne, think of something even better for dessert." She nuzzled his shoulder. "Come on, darling, what do you say?"

Carl turned around and folded her in his arms. He kissed her deeply, letting his hands stray down her sides to grasp the flesh of her buttocks, firm and round beneath the filmy kimono. Then, gazing into her upturned eyes, he said, "Thanks, but maybe another time."

"Beast," she muttered, pouting, as he pulled on his trousers and began to button his shirt.

You have no right to feel like this, Carl chided himself as he trudged along the beach, head down, hands deep in the pockets of his corduroy pants. You've just finished a spectacular season, your debut was a fantastic success, you're playing as well or better than you ever did, and you're having an affair with a glamorous, wealthy woman who adores you. What the hell is wrong with you, for Christ's sake?

All right, he continued, pausing to pick up a piece of driftwood and toss it angrily into the cold Pacific surf, so she's a little empty-headed. What's wrong with that? She doesn't have to be a genius to be terrific in bed, does she? Of course not. He halted once more, considering just how terrific she was. Exquisite form, he thought, superb technique.

He began to walk again. Okay, so it would be nice to have a little more in common, to be able to talk to her about his work, but that really wasn't necessary, was it? He certainly enjoyed satisfying himself on her wonderfully insatiable body, didn't he? "So what's the big deal, Fitzgerald?" he asked himself aloud, squinting into an amber sun suspended above violet fog.

A gull circled above his head, mewing plaintively. He followed the bird until it disappeared into the sun-splashed waves, thought briefly, wistfully, of Marian, of their long conversations, their earnest arguments. Perhaps he should write to Marian. He hadn't written since his debut. But what was there to say? He'd allowed that friendship, along with too many others, to slip through his fingers.

Sighing, he turned and re-traced his footsteps, sitting down on the concrete retaining wall. The wind was colder now. It clawed at his hair and flung a burst of sand against his cheek. Hugging his coat around him, he headed up the hill toward the trolley line, but a low stonewall and a flood of pink azalea blossoms caught his eye.

He'd never noticed the pristine little park that sat like a jewel on the rugged cliffs above the beach. Sheltered by groves of cypress from the biting wind, he sauntered along a narrow path that led through camellias and rhododendrons. A green park bench was at the end of the path overlooking the sea. He sat down and gazed at the spreading colors of the sunset, savoring the lingering melancholy, the amethyst glow of light.

Maybe he should go to Sacramento for the weekend. He hadn't been home since before his much-heralded debut six months before. There hadn't been time. The sudden rush of invitations, guest appearances, interviews. The affair with Lillian. There didn't seem to be time for anything anymore.

It's what you wanted, isn't it? he thought with a trace of bitterness. You're a success. You might as well enjoy it.

Or was he? The critics said so. But they were local critics. What if they were wrong? The idea brought a cold sweat to his forehead. Maybe he wasn't as good as they thought. He had expected offers from major symphonies, guest conductor spots, perhaps even a principal position. So far, only a handful of smaller organizations had been courting him, and he had arrogantly brushed them aside. Perhaps that hadn't been wise.

He closed his eyes and pressed cold fingers against his eyelids. Getting slowly to his feet, he looked once more at the deepening hues of the western sky, then started slowly along the path through the park. If he'd made the wrong choices, it was too late to worry about it.

Two weeks later he got a letter from Lillian. Postmarked Rome, it contained an airline ticket and a note explaining that Marcus had been forced to return to San Francisco early because of business. "Italy is divine," Lillian wrote. "Why don't you join me, Maestro?" It took him just twenty minutes to find his passport and pack his bag.

# CHAPTER

# 33

## Boston, Massachusetts
## June 1961

Alex got off the bus at the corner of Massachusetts Avenue and Shawmut, and walked two blocks to the brownstone apartment that she shared with her mother and M.C., the cat. It was nearing the end of the school term, and people were just starting to leave town for the summer. Alex wondered if they would be able to go to Tanglewood again this year.

She'd gotten a copy of the summer schedule the minute it became available and pored over it, looking for one name in particular: Stefan Molnar. And there it was. August 25. The Shed. The Beethoven Piano Concerto No. 1. She *had* to be there, and decided to put the question to Marian at once.

She ran up the front steps and nearly dropped her key as she hurried to open the door. "Mother," she cried. "Where are you?"

The house was silent. No sound but the ticking of the clock. She toured the empty rooms with growing annoyance. Where could Marian be? It was almost five o'clock. She was usually home by this time. "Mother?"

Why was everything going wrong today? First, she and Marian had gotten into an argument about the lack of orange juice. "But I *always* have orange juice for breakfast," Alex had exploded. "How could you forget?"

"I actually have a few other things to do besides catering to your every demand, Missy."

"I can definitely see that." It had gone downhill from there.

Then there was another argument with Madame Romanova

about what she would play for the recital that was coming up in just two weeks. "But Madame, why can't I do the Liszt *Rhapsody Number Two*? It's wonderful!"

"You must walk before you can run, and run before you can fly, *lenoschka*. I want to hear perfect technique. You will play the Bach *Italian Concerto*. Now, do not argue with me further."

"Old bat," Alex muttered under her breath, and she grabbed her music book and headed for the door.

And now here she was, hot, hungry, and angry and no one was home. It wasn't fair.

She tossed her books on the piano, got a glass of chocolate milk, and went to her bedroom to sulk. She lay down on the bed and closed her eyes. She hated being alone. It made her feel small and insignificant. It made her feel . . . empty. And scared.

And there was something biting at her, a sort of buzzing inside her head. Suppose Mother never came home? Suppose she had been run over by a truck? Or kidnapped by some awful gangster? What would Alex do if Mother was gone? She pressed her fingers against her temples and groaned. Stop it. Just stop it.

For a few minutes, she dozed. Then she started up and looked around wildly. Where was she? Sitting up, she felt dizzy. The bed tilted and rocked like a boat on a rough sea. What was happening? Was it an earthquake? Fear clenched like a cold hand around her neck. She couldn't breathe and felt her face going numb. Stop it. Stop it!

Whimpering, she dropped to the floor and crawled toward the bedroom door. She was going to be ill. Where was she? *Who* was she? The world seemed to go blank one piece at a time—places and people blinking out like switched-off lights. She scratched at the carpet. Was this up? Down? Ceiling? Floor?

"I'm going out," she thought, "like the rest of the lights." A rough tide was sweeping over her. She was drowning and there was no one to turn to. "Help," she cried weakly. "Help me."

I don't exist, she thought. That's why no one can hear me. She had disappeared somehow, hollowed out entirely, enveloped in mist. Where was something solid? *Where?*

She felt the wooden planks of the hallway beneath her fingers and followed the hard path to the door of the bathroom. Cold tile felt more reassuring, more solid. But she had to bang her fists on it to make sure it was there. There was a metallic taste in her mouth. Was it blood?

She grabbed the edge of the sink and hauled herself upright. The face in the mirror confronted her—a twisted, splotched mask. Who is that? she thought. Surely that's not me. But who am I? Where am I?

"Liar," she shouted at the mirror. "Damned, stupid liar!" She flung open the medicine chest and scanned the bottles and flasks. Maybe she should take a pill. Maybe a lot of pills. But which ones? Prescription medicines? What would they do?

The scissors lay on the counter next to the sink. Scissors. That might do it. She picked them up. Barber's scissors. Nice and sharp.

Feeling stronger, she looked down at the back of her arm with curious detachment and carefully placed the point of the blade on the skin just above her wrist. Pushing the blade down, she made a three-inch-long slice. Ahhh. That was better. Now another, parallel to the first. And one more.

Now she could breathe. The world came back into focus. Reality was pain/pain was reality. I hurt, therefore I am. She watched with distant interest as the blood welled up into the cuts—little beads as red as rubies. She closed her eyes and smiled.

"Alex?"

Marian's voice made her jump. Guiltily, she grabbed a wad of toilet paper and wrapped it around her wrist. Blood leeched through so she added another layer of paper.

"Alex? Where are you honey?"

"In here, Mother," she cried. "I'll be right out."

She took time to wash her face and brush back her hair, then applied a new bandage of toilet paper and headed for the kitchen.

"Sorry I'm so late," Marian offered, her head in the refrigerator. "We had a rush job at the frame shop, and Jerry was off sick so I had to . . ." She turned and then stared at Alex. "What happened to your arm, sweetheart?"

"The cat," Alex said.

Marin scowled. "What did you do to the cat?"

"Oh, so it's my fault your stupid cat clawed me?"

"For goodness sakes, Alex. What happened? Here, let me see."

Alex pulled her arm away. "I took care of it."

"Honey, I'm sorry, but you know how kitty is. She doesn't like being teased."

"I didn't tease her!"

Marian sighed. "Well, be sure to put some peroxide on it. I don't want you to get an infection."

Alex turned away. "I'm fine, Mother. Just fine."

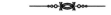

## New York, New York

The next day, Marian caught the commuter train from Boston to New York and took the bus to midtown. Carrying her portfolio, she made her way to the Fisher Gallery. Through Fisher's office door, she could see Jon seated at his desk, light beaming like a beacon from the slick dome of his bald head. He jabbed at the air with his cigar and shouted into the phone, "I don't give a goddamn what he thinks they're worth. I know what I can get for them, so you can tell him to make up his pea-brained mind. It's no skin off my nose one way or the other. These jackasses, fresh from the provinces, think they're going to be overnight stars. Gives me a royal pain in the butt." He paused to light the cigar. "You got that? Good. Just do what I tell you and deliver the message."

Puffing furiously, he slammed the phone down. Without turning, he called out, "And if you stand out there in the hall all day, you'll never get anywhere either."

Marian blanched. "I'm terribly sorry," she faltered. "I didn't want to interrupt. If you're busy, I could always come back another—"

He spun around and glared at her. "Look, sweetheart, if you've got something to show me, get your ass in here. I haven't got time to play games. You want to see me or not? You won't get a better opportunity."

Marian swallowed, set the portfolio down, and held out her hand. "I'm Marian Archer, Mr. Fisher. I wrote to you a couple of weeks ago. Perhaps you remember . . ."

He waved a plump pink hand in her direction. "You and a hundred others. Let's see what you got."

Marian fumbled with the zipper. The sheets of paper slithered this way and that, refusing to stand upright. Cursing under her breath, she managed to subdue them. The dealer leaned forward and peered at the large ink drawing of a girl seated at a piano. Marian studied his face, but it was impassive, the small porcine eyes alone seemed to glitter with life.

"Let's see another," he said.

She flipped through the drawings one by one. Fisher sat back in his chair and pursed his lips.

"Mr. Fisher?" the receptionist called from the adjacent office, "Mr. Castelli on line one."

He grabbed the phone, his eyes still on Marian's drawing.

"Leo? Yeah, I saw the show. Sure it's good. Kid's got a lot of know-how. He came by here four or five years ago. Showed me the biggest pile of shit you ever saw. I told him to go back to Peoria or wherever the hell he was from. Sure, Leo. We'll have lunch and talk about it. I've got a couple of other ideas you might be interested in. Right. Give me a call tomorrow." He jammed the phone down. "Okay, sweetheart," he said to Marian. "I've seen enough."

"I've brought some slides of my paintings. Maybe you'd care to take a look at—"

"Sorry. Got an appointment to get to. Now let me tell you something. You're living up in Boston, aren't you?"

"Why, yes," she said, surprised that he knew.

"You're doing some nice work, sweetheart. And it's different. I like the figurative stuff. Might even be able to sell it. But I won't be

able to do a damned thing for you unless you move to New York—
Manhattan, not Brooklyn, not Jersey."

"Why?"

"*Because.* I've gotta be able to send my clients to your friggin'
studio. You think we're selling paintings here? Wrong. We're selling
personalities. We're selling contacts. That's how this business operates."

Marian frowned and said, "But if my work's good, then surely—"

"If you're not in town, I can't do a thing for you."

"But Mr. Fisher, I have a house in Boston. I have a daughter in
school there. I have a job. I can't just pick up and move to New York!"

The dealer spread his hands. "Then there's not much I can do for
you, is there? Now, like I said, I got an appointment."

"But if you'd just let me leave a couple of drawings, maybe
somebody . . ." She realized she was kneeling at his feet. She didn't
like the feeling.

"Look, angel," he said, "you can walk your socks off visiting
dealers in this town, and maybe one of them will let you leave a few
drawings on consignment. Somebody might even give you a show.
But unless you're willing to live here and be a part of the scene,
you're not going to get to first base. You'll just be wasting your time."
His smile was not unkind. "I'm telling you this because your work
is good. Otherwise, I'd just tell you to get lost, all right? Now," he
jumped up and headed for the door, "if you decide to take my advice,
come see me. Otherwise, don't bother."

"I appreciate your candor," Marian began, but Jon Fisher was
already striding off down the hallway. Marian sat back on her heels
and looked glumly at the portrait of her daughter. Alex's haughty face
stared back at her accusingly.

## Boston, Massachusetts

The studio was cold, but she didn't bother to turn on the gas heater
below the north-facing windows. Instead, she wrapped herself in the

folds of an old patchwork quilt and huddled, shoulders hunched, in the tan director's chair near the easel. Time to review priorities, she told herself, staring at the blank canvas that was wedged between the easel's wooden crossbars. Where do we go from here?

The soft brush of the cat's tail against her ankles momentarily distracted her, and she bent to gather the small warm body in her arms. "What shall we do, old pussums?" she asked the cat as it settled into her lap, paws kneading gently on the folded edge of the quilt, eyes half-closed as if deep in meditation. "What would you do if you were me?

The cat purred as Marian stroked its silken fur, the tip of the plumed tail tapping a steady rhythm on her knee. "What do you think, old girl? You've watched me struggling away, bashing my head against the doors of the art establishment, painting canvas after canvas. Do you see any progress, or are you just waiting for me to come to my senses and give it all up?" She stared at the empty canvas.

"We could move back to the ranch," she said. "You'd love it in California—fat little rabbits to chase, plenty of sunshine, fresh catnip from the garden."

The words stuck in her throat. Give up? The hell I will, she thought angrily.

Okay, then tell me, said the voice inside her head. Are you still determined to be an artist?

Absolutely yes.

A serious artist?

Yes. I told you, yes.

Still think you're good enough?

Don't know, but I've got to keep trying.

You've never even had a one-man show.

True, but I've gotten into some pretty good group exhibits, the reviews have at least been . . . .

Jesus Christ, who do you think you're kidding? You might as well be using your damned canvases for landfill. Take them to the dump and bury them with the rest of the garbage. No one's ever going to take you seriously because you don't take *yourself* seriously.

She groaned and pressed her hands against her face. What the hell do I have to do? she shouted silently. I've given up my home, my family, traumatized my children, abandoned my husband, alienated my friends. What else do I have to do?

Take the man's advice, the voice suggested coyly. Move to New York.

I can't, she protested. It wouldn't be fair to Alex. She's been doing so well here.

Fair? the voice persisted. Since when has that bothered you? Have you been fair to Julian? To Kate? To Owen?

Exhausted, she slumped forward and buried her head in her arms. The cat hopped down, sat, and began to bathe. "Stick around, pussums," she muttered. "I've still got a bag full of questions and not a single answer on the horizon—"

"Mother!"

The scream came from the upstairs bedroom. Marian sprang to her feet, while the cat scurried to take refuge beneath the sofa. "I'm coming, darling," Marian called as she scrambled up the stairs. "What is it, sweetheart?" Heart pounding, she switched on the light.

Alex was sitting up in bed, eyes wide with terror, golden hair tumbling around her shoulders. She held out her arms and began to sob.

"Alex, angel, what's the matter?" Marian asked as she hugged her.

"Dream," Alex choked. "Terrible dream. I was lost. I kept running and running. I was trying to find you, but I couldn't. I kept calling and calling, but you didn't come. It was so dark, and it was raining. I couldn't find you anywhere!"

"It's all right, darling, I'm here. Mummy's here."

"Dark and raining, and I couldn't find you . . ." sobbed Alex.

"Shhh. It's all right. I'm here." Marian kissed the soft blond hair. "You've been working too hard, sweetheart," she said when the girl stopped shuddering. "You've been practicing too much."

Alex drew back and looked at her mother. "But I have to practice, Mummy. I want to be good. I want to be the best!"

"I know you do," said Marian, brushing damp curls back from

the thin, delicate face. "But you should take some time off, do other things now and then. Tomorrow we'll take the afternoon off. Go to a matinee and out to dinner. What do you say?"

Alex snuffled and blinked rapidly. "Can we go see *The Red Shoes* again? Can we go to Antoinette's for pastries?"

"Of course we can, sweetheart."

Alex lay down, hiding a yawn behind her hand. "Mummy?"

"Yes, darling?"

"Don't go. Stay here with me. Please?"

"All right, angel."

"Leave the light on, Mummy, okay?" Alex's voice had grown drowsy.

"All right, sweetheart."

"You won't leave me, will you?"

"Of course I won't."

That's it, thought Marian as she listened to her daughter's breaths grow slow and regular. I'm not going anywhere until this child is grown and on her own. New York, my career, the whole crazy business, will simply have to wait.

## Mockingbird Valley Ranch
### June 1961

" Daddy will be in LA until tomorrow night," Kate said as she pulled off the road and parked the car in the midst of a grove of willows, "so we'll have the whole house to ourselves."

"What about the new foreman and his family?" Tommy asked, his stomach tightening to a knot.

"Relax, will you?" Kate laughed, punching his shoulder. "We'll leave the car down here. After I take you back to Stockton, I'll drive in, and they'll think I'm just getting home. I told Consuelo that I'd be very late. After all," she leaned over to kiss his cheek, "it *is* graduation night."

Still uneasy, Tommy got slowly out of the car and stood looking at the distant lights of Mockingbird. It had been more than a year since he had left, a year of exile and of bitterness. A year of stolen moments and furtive lies.      He hated the clandestine meetings, the fabricated excuses, the dishonesty, but how else could they see each other? Soon, he promised himself, this will all come to an end. We'll get married. We'll get a place of our own. Just a while longer. Sighing, he took Kate's hand and walked beside her up the winding drive.

The sand was soft beneath his feet, and the dark shapes of the pear trees hid the rising moon. The wind stirred, and he caught the scent of dried wild oats, of damp earth, of . . . home. Not any more it isn't, he thought, and walked a little faster.

The house was dark and still. Beyond the leaded windows, the sky was a deep, ethereal blue. Kate opened the doors to the patio, and he stood looking out at the rose garden, watching the leaves turn silver in the moonlight.

"You want something to drink?" Kate asked. "There's some beer in the 'fridge."

Tommy shook his head. Then said, "Hey, you know what I would like?"

"What?"

"A drink of water."

"Sure," said Kate and went to find a glass.

"Thanks," he said when she returned from the kitchen. He took a sip and closed his eyes, savoring the coolness. "The water here always tasted so good."

They were silent for a moment, then Kate said, "So, when are you leaving?"

Tommy put the glass down and looked at her, barely able to make out her features in the muted light. "What?" he asked in dismay.

"You know, Oregon. When are you going?"

"How did you . . ."

"Christy Malacchi told me. She was visiting her aunt in Stockton and saw the article in the newspaper. *Honors student wins full scholarship to University of Oregon.*"

"Oh, great," groaned Tommy. "Some friend that Christy."

"Don't blame Chris. She thought I knew."

"I was going to tell you," Tommy said. "I started to say something earlier this evening, but I didn't want to spoil . . ."

"It's okay," Kate interrupted.

"I don't have to accept it," Tommy said. "I haven't signed the papers yet."

Kate took two steps toward him and looked into his eyes. "Nothing from Berkeley?" she asked.

He turned away and stared down at the floor. "Nope. And the partial I got to Stanford wouldn't even cover the tuition."

"Then you've got to go to Oregon."

He glanced up and met her look. "I could go to San Francisco

State. The tuition's really low, and I could get a part-time job to cover expenses."

Kate shook her head. "Are you crazy? Give up a full scholarship at a really good school like Oregon so you can scramble around trying to make enough money to go to a nothing school like SF State?" She gave him a lopsided grin. "You ought to have your head examined, Ashida."

He had to smile. Always, she had been able to make him smile.

"Go to Oregon," she said.

He put his arms around her and closed his eyes, his cheek resting against her hair. She smelled so good. That balsam fragrance of her hair. How he would miss that scent. His arms tightened around her. God, he couldn't leave her. Couldn't.

"I'm going to San Francisco," he said with flat finality.

She drew back and looked up at him. Even in the dim illumination of the moonlight, he could see the serious expression in her eyes. "Hey, Tommy," she said, resting her slender hand against his cheek, "you said we had to stick to the plan, didn't you?"

"Yes," he admitted, "but—"

"No buts. If you don't take that scholarship, you'll have to take out loans or only go to school part-time. It would put us way behind schedule, wouldn't it?"

He nodded slowly, unable to refute her logic.

"Let's try it for a year," she said. "We'll still get to see each other. You'll be back in town for Christmas, and I'll find some way to get to Oregon for spring break. It's not like we'll be a thousand miles apart."

"Even sixty miles is sixty too many," he muttered, thinking of the gulf that separated Stockton from Auburn, of the nights he'd lain awake thinking of the inches and feet and yards and miles that kept them so unjustly apart.

"Okay," she agreed, "but Oregon's not too far. It's not like you were going back east or something. And besides, we've been pretty good at getting together so far, haven't we? Well, haven't we?"

He nodded once more, smiling at her seriousness.

"So, see?" she said, planting a kiss on his cheek. "It'll work out."

His fingers twined in her long red hair, and he tilted her face toward his. "Of course it will," he said. "It'll take more than a few hundred miles to keep us apart." He kissed her deeply, exploring the sweet inner softness of her mouth, wanting to be with her, in her.

"Let's go to my room," she whispered.

His knees felt spongy as he followed her down the narrow hall. It had been years since he had been in Kate's room. They had played there together as children. One time they had made a tent of blankets and crawled into it. The light inside was thin and blue. "Let's take off our clothes," Kate had whispered, "and pretend we're mermaids and mermen that live under the sea."

Connie had come in just then and made them come out and put away the blankets. "Go out and play in the garden," she had said firmly.

A candle sat on Kate's desk. She lit it and pulled the curtains across the windows. Turning, she smiled at him, reaching back to unzip the pink and blue graduation dress that she wore. Unable to take his eyes from her, he undid the buttons of his shirt, kicked off his shoes, pulled off his socks. It seemed to take forever to undress. "Love you, Kate," he whispered shakily as they fell onto the bed.

But even as he entered her, became as much a part of her as any being could, he felt a terrible, desperate sense of loss, as though she was being swept away by the current, and he was powerless to stop her, as though she was floating away from him, growing ever fainter. "Don't leave me," he pleaded, covering her face, her throat, her shoulders with kisses.

"You know I won't," she said. But afterward, as he cradled her in his arms, their bodies still entwined, he felt desperate. All I ever wanted, he thought, was this place, this piece of land, this woman— was that too much to hope for? Dumb Jap, he answered himself coldly, you must have been crazy to even think it. "Don't leave me," he said again, hugging her even closer.

"Hey, Tommy," she whispered, "you know I won't . . ."

# CHAPTER

# 35

## Salzburg, Austria
## August 1961

Salzburg—the city of Mozart, the city where music is the undisputed queen. From the moment he set eyes on the resplendent domes and towers, the sinuous iridescence of the Salzach River, the majestic granite face of the Mönchsberg, the Monk's Mountain, Carl fell in love with Salzburg.

His whirlwind summer with Lillian had landed them in the city just in time for the Salzburg Festival. After ten days of attending three, even four, magnificent concerts, operas, or other special events each day, Carl was nearly delirious with joy. Major orchestras, distinguished conductors, renowned chamber groups, operatic divas—all had descended, a great confluence of talent, experience, and passion—on this beautiful city in its breathtaking mountain setting to bring the very stones alive with the most sublime music ever composed.

While Lillian browsed among the colorful shops that lined the avenues, Carl visited the city's many musical attractions, making a pilgrimage to the well-kept yellow house at Getreidegasse 9 where Anna Maria Mozart had given birth to her son, Wolfgang Amadeus, exploring the festival theater complex, pausing to talk with the musicians and composers who were practicing, rehearsing, conversing over endless cups of excellent cinnamon-flavored coffee.

He made a special visit to the Mozarteum to see the legendary "Magic Flute House," a tiny, worm-eaten wooden hut where Mozart reportedly wrote his final opera in 1791 during the last months of his life. Transported to Salzburg from Vienna in the late nineteenth century, the little house was installed in the Mozarteum garden. Carl spent over an hour sitting before the little hut, thinking of the composer who, lying on his death-bed had taken out his watch and followed the performance of *The Magic Flute* in his imagination, singing in his weak voice the passages as they were being performed in the distant theater. The work did not meet with immediate success. "The content and dialogue of the piece are utterly worthless," announced a critic of the day.

Walking back to his hotel along the incandescent waters of the Salzach, Carl brooded over the hard fate of his idol. Why did it happen that way so often—the great artist dying alone and penniless, leaving behind a legacy of sublime work that only later generations could appreciate? "It's for them we work," he thought, "for those Children of the Future who can understand what we have done."

And yet . . . He paused to stare up at the imposing Hohensalzburg Fortress, its grey stone turrets standing guard over the graceful city, ". . . I want to be successful *now*, to be recognized and acknowledged within my lifetime."

Then do something worthy of that recognition, he told himself and smiled at the thought. As a performer, he had won acceptance. As a conductor, he was on his way to fame. Perhaps someday he would also be acknowledged as a *composer*.

But that would have to wait. He wasn't ready yet to lay his compositions upon the altar of public scrutiny only to have them sacrificed by a critical priesthood who had been wrong so often in the past. He would wait, establish his credibility first, assure his place in the music world. There would be plenty of time then to unveil the work that he so far had kept almost entirely to himself.

"It looks Italian," Lillian said, standing at the window of the sumptuous hotel suite that overlooked the river and the Old Wall of the town.

"It ought to," Carl responded, looking over her shoulder at the lilac twilight-glow punctuated with the jewel-like myriad of lights. "A lot of the buildings were commissioned by Wolf Dietrich von Raitenau, one of the early archbishops who went to school in Rome, and was related to the Medicis. He wanted Salzburg to be as beautiful and graceful as the great cities of Italy."

Lillian turned to face him, tilting her head back and gazing at him through slightly narrowed eyes. "How do you know all these things?"

Carl grinned and playfully tweaked her nose. "I *read*, dear Lilly. You ought to try it sometime."

"Don't tease me, precious," she pouted. "I've tried, but I just find those guide-books that you haul around so dreadfully boring."

"I've read enough for both of us anyway," Carl said. "Now, why don't you go and put some clothes on, Mrs. Chambers. You'd cause a riot if you went to the opera like that."

Lillian made a face. "Do we have to go to another opera? Honestly, Carl, we've already been to three this week. I'm sick to death of warbling divas and howling tenors." She sidled up to him and rested her hands on his shoulders. "Can't we just stay here tonight and think of something else to do?"

Carl pressed her to him and kissed each cheek, her forehead, the tip of her nose. "Indulge me," he said. "I promise when we get back that I'll make it worth your while."

"Mmmm," Lillian purred, nuzzling his chest. "I guess that's worth the price."

He loved going out with her in the evening. She had a dozen different evening gowns, a sable stole, a silver-fox jacket. He loved the way heads turned and eyes swiveled whenever they walked into a room. "Isn't she that American heiress from Texas?" people whispered. "Isn't he that Italian movie star?" Someday, Carl thought, they won't have to guess about who I am.

To circumvent the society gossip columns, Lillian had insisted that they have separate suites at the hotel, and although tongues wagged and eyebrows lifted, there was only speculation about their relationship after the well-planned separate departures from the opera house, the cafe, the theater.

Carl found the clandestine nature of their midnight rendezvous and pre-dawn partings especially tantalizing. They reminded him of the games of hide-and-seek that he had played in Gramps's rustic adobe house in Tucson.

But by the end of August, he was beginning to tire of it. The familiar restlessness reminded him that it was time to get back to work. A new season would be starting soon, and he was anxious to begin rehearsals, to settle in to the satisfying discipline of his life in San Francisco. Although he loved Salzburg, and promised himself that he would often return, he was glad to be alone at last on the British Airways flight across the Atlantic. He slept for most of the twelve-hour crossing and woke to see the golden hills of California greeting him like a tawny lioness lying in a gentle semi-circle around the deep blue waters of San Francisco Bay.

—∞◦❄◦∞—

## San Francisco, California

For a middle-aged man, Brett Whittaker had a nice body— firm, well muscled, with only the slightest hint of a paunch beginning to form below his rib cage. Much nicer than most, Julian thought.

Propping himself up on his elbow, he squinted critically at Brett's well-formed back—he must work out a lot to keep that muscle tone. Of course, he could afford it— a split-level redwood palace in Sausalito, a black Lincoln Continental, a posh office in one of the high-rise buildings that had recently sprouted like giant stalks of asparagus in the rich soil of San Francisco's financial district. Some of these bastards really had it made.

Taking a deep drag on his cigarette, Julian practiced blowing smoke rings as he watched Brett pull on his slacks and button his shirt. "What time is it?" Brett asked, turning up his collar and snaking the paisley tie around his neck.

Julian glanced at the clock that stood on the bedside table. "Five forty-five. Leaving early?"

Brett fumbled with his tie. "I was late getting home last week, and Annie gave me the third degree."

"Afraid there's another woman in your life?" Julian said with a smirk.

Brett grinned. "Probably. God, if she knew the truth— Goddamn this fucking tie!"

"Here," Julian set down his cigarette, "let me do that for you." He moved aggressively close as he re-tied the knot, enjoying the slight shudder that he felt as he trailed a playful hand across Brett's buttocks. "There now," he said, "isn't that better?"

"Watch it," Brett warned. "You'll get me all worked up again."

Julian gave him a coy look. "Well, you've still got fifteen minutes of my time. Seems a shame to waste it."

Brett hesitated, then shook his head. "I'd better not. Don't want to press my luck." He picked up his sport coat and slung it over his shoulder. "Oh, I—uh—left the money on the hall tree. Thanks."

"My pleasure," Julian assured him, slipping into a robe. "Come on. I'll see you to the foyer." At the top of the landing, they paused to share a lingering kiss.

"Same time next week?" Brett said.

"That'll be fine. I'll tell Sheila to put you down for Friday afternoon."

Julian heard the street door open, but it didn't distract him from the business at hand. When he glanced down, however, he caught his breath.

"What's the matter?" Brett asked in alarm.

"Jesus Christ, it's my sister," muttered Julian.

"Your sister?"

"But there's no problem. Hi, Katie," he called. "What a nice surprise."

Kate looked up at him sheepishly. "I guess I should have called."

"Don't worry about it. This is my friend Stuart. He's just leaving."

Brett threw Julian an appreciative glance, mumbled a greeting to

Kate, and made a quick retreat down the stairs. "See you, Stu," Julian called after him. "Well," he met his sister's eyes with difficulty, "do you want to come in and have a drink or something?"

"Sure." She followed him into the apartment. "Gee, Julian, this is nice," she said, glancing around at the white walls and period furniture. "Where'd you get the nifty Victorian sofa?"

To calm his nerves, he switched on the radio. Bobby Darin's "Mack the Knife" was playing. "A lady in the Sunset district sold it to me. She was moving back east and didn't want to take all her stuff with her. If I'd had more cash, I could have gotten some terrific deals. Uh—'scuse me for a minute."

In the bedroom, he hastily straightened the bed-covers before pulling on faded jeans and a cashmere sweater.

"I didn't know you were interested in antiques," Kate called.

"My latest passion," he called back. He lit another cigarette and paused for a moment to stare at himself in the mirror before he hurried back to the living room. "So, what can I get you to drink?"

"Got a beer?"

He wagged his head. "Tut, tut. How plebian, my dear sister. What are they teaching you over there at that fancy university?"

"So, what are you drinking, big shot?"

"As a matter of fact, I've developed a certain fondness for domestic white wines. Want to sample some simply smashing Napa Valley pinot blanc?"

"Why not?"

"So, how's it going, Roo?" he asked gaily, handing her a glass and settling down on the velvet sofa.

She sat down next to him. "The dorm's kind of a drag. We're supposed to be in by ten every night. But what the hell. I don't have anything to do but study anyway."

He raised his eyebrows. "No social life?"

"It wouldn't be fair." Her chin jutted forward. "Tommy and I have plans."

"Still going to marry Tommy?"

She shot him a sideways glance. "I certainly am."

"Four years is a long time, Roo."

"I can handle it. So how's your social life these days?"

He was silent for a minute, running his finger around the edge of his wine glass, then looked up and cleared his throat. "Look, Katie, ummm—well, see, I've gone through a lot of changes since I've been living here in the City. I mean, I've learned some things about myself, about the way I want to live. I've decided there's nothing wrong with—well, with—"

"With liking boys instead of girls?" Kate prompted.

Relief swept over him. "You know about that?"

She leaned back and gave him a little smile. "Gee, Julian, I figured that out ages ago. What's the big deal?"

"You don't mind? I mean, some people . . . do."

She shrugged. "Why should I mind? I love you. Whatever you do is okay with me."

She made everything sound so simple. "You're terrific, Roo. You know that?"

"I hope I didn't embarrass your friend," she said.

Julian brushed the idea aside with a wave of his hand. "No damage done."

"Hey, have you got some more of this wine?" Kate said. "It's really good."

Julian laughed. "Coming right up, *ma cherie*." He poured the wine and held up his glass. "Here's looking at you, kid."

She grinned and sipped her wine.

# CHAPTER

# 36

## Mockingbird Valley Ranch
## September 1961

Owen picked Marian up at the Sacramento Airport, and they drove east in silence through the golden California hills. Now and then he glanced at her. She seemed so distant, like a stranger. The nearly twenty years they had shared as man and wife seemed eerily like something out of a dream.

He carried her suitcase into the house and set it at the door of the guest room. When she appeared in the living room a half-hour later, he got to his feet as though she were a visitor. "You're looking well," he said, fumbling with his glass of bourbon.

"Thank you. You're looking pretty good yourself. Very distinguished."

"My politician image." He laughed tightly.

She smiled. "You always did look nice in a suit, Owen. I often regretted that I rarely got to see you in one."

"That so?"

She walked to the open door and stood looking out at the garden. "How 'bout a drink," he said.

"Do you have any sherry?"

"I'll check." He came back with a glass.

"Could we sit on the patio? It looks so lovely."

Sunlight filtered through the oak trees, casting dusky shadows across the warm red stones. He studied her intently, trying to fix her image in his mind. Except for a sprinkling of grey in her golden hair she hadn't aged—her skin was still smooth and firm. Striped cotton slacks and a pale pink blouse had replaced her jacketed linen dress. She wasn't as thin as he remembered.

"What do you hear from Julian?" she asked.

Owen stiffened. "Not much. Kate sees him now and then. She seems to think he's doing okay."

"You haven't seen him?"

"No," he replied, avoiding her look.

"Don't you think you ought to make an effort to end this feud?"

Anger tightened the muscles in his neck, and he snapped, "I hope you're not going to start telling me how to do my job, because—"

"I'm sorry," she said quickly. "You're right. I didn't mean to criticize." After a moment, she added, "It's just that I worry about him living by himself and not having anyone he can turn to if he needs help."

"It was his decision to leave home. He knows where to reach me."

Marian studied her hands.

"Besides," Owen continued, "he writes to you, doesn't he?"

"Now and then." She seemed distracted and stared at the garden.

"Well, there you are," Owen said. "And, besides, Kate's down at Berkeley now. She keeps in touch with him."

Marian turned toward him. "When will she be home? I can't wait to see her. I was so disappointed to miss her graduation, but I just couldn't get away."

"She should be along any minute now. Said she'd leave after her last class." Owen smiled. "She looked so cute in her cap and gown. Played the organ for the ceremony. I had to take off right after the diplomas were handed out, but I guess she had a real big time with her friends. One of those all-night parties."

"How are the new employees working out?" said Marian. "I was surprised to hear the Ashidas had left."

Owen shifted uncomfortably. "David's brother needed him to help run the produce store down in Stockton. You know how Orientals are. They like to keep a business in the family. Anyhow, Jamie and Consuelo are doing just fine. Hard workers, both of them.

They've got a baby on the way. Guess I'm going to have to give them a raise." He picked up Marian's glass. "How about a refill?"

"Maybe just a splash."

The air had cooled, and the stones gave off a dusty scent. Doves murmured mournfully among the pear trees. In the distance a quail called its three-note remark.

"It's so peaceful here," Marian sighed as Owen handed her the glass. "The Berkshires are pleasant, but the summers are so short. There's something about California. . ." She paused. "Something about the way the air feels that's different from anywhere else . . ."

Owen studied her face. "You could come back," he said softly.

She shook her head. "No . . . I can't."

He sipped his drink and stared at the garden.

"But thank you for saying that," she said.

"I meant it, Marian."

"I know. But I think it's about time we got the whole thing resolved, don't you? It's been almost three years. It's silly to keep putting this off."

"Putting what off?"

Her eyes were dark. "I've filed for divorce, Owen," she said.

"On what grounds?"

"Incompatibility." Her voice was soft, but firm.

"After twenty years?" he scoffed in indignation.

Her eyes searched his face. "Do you intend to contest it?"

"You've met someone and you want to get remarried? Is that it?" Old anger flared, ancient, territorial.

She shook her head.

He drew a deep breath and clutched the arms of the chair. "I'm sorry," he said slowly. "I don't reckon I'll contest it if that's what you want."

"I'm not asking for any settlement."

"You're not?" He stared at her in surprise.

"There's nothing here that I want, and I certainly don't intend to take your money," she said.

"I ought to give you something to live on. After all—"

"I'm doing just fine on my own, but I do want to be sure that the children are provided for." Her tone was brisk.

"I damn well intend to provide for the children."

"Julian too?"

The muscles in his jaw tightened once more. "We'll work something out."

They studied each other in the rose-colored light. Marian was the first to avert her eyes. "I've set up a meeting with Harvey on Monday. Is that okay with you?"

"I'll give Danny a call," Owen said grimly.

She gave a little sigh. "I hope this can all be very civilized, Owen. I'd like for us to be friends. That's important to me."

"I guess I can manage that," Owen said, covering his pain with rough irony, "if you can."

The following Tuesday, Kate drove her mother into Sacramento to catch the plane. "It's too bad," Marian was saying, "that Julian had to go to Palm Springs for the weekend. I was so disappointed. I can't believe he couldn't change his plans and at least meet me in San Francisco for dinner."

"He said it was business."

"It's been three years. You'd think he could take a couple of hours off to see his mother." Irritably, Marian lit a cigarette.

"Mom?"

"What, sweetheart?"

"Did you know that Julian's queer?"

"Good heavens, Kate," Marian said with a forced laugh, "do you have any idea what that means?"

"Of course I do. Homosexual."

"Honey, you really shouldn't say such things."

Kate stared ahead at the road. "It's true, Mom. I thought you probably knew."

"What on earth makes you say a thing like that?" Marian demanded. "You really shouldn't—"

"But it's *true*," Kate repeated.

"Did he tell you so?"

"He didn't have to."

"Well, honey, maybe you misunderstood. Things aren't always what they seem."

Kate gave her mother a troubled glance. "You don't know Julian anymore. Not the way I do."

Guilt surged up like bile in Marian's throat, and she covered her eyes with her hand. After a few minutes, she said, "You're sure?"

"Yes."

She tried hard to suppress the panic that threatened. Was it something she had done? Or not done? "Does Owen know?" she asked.

"Are you kidding?"

Marian once more pressed her fingers against her eyelids and fought for composure. "Poor Julian," she whispered.

Kate glanced at her. "Why?"

"What?" Marian said, looking up.

"Why 'poor Julian'?"

"Oh, honey," Marian said in a flat voice, "you don't know how mean the world can be." After a moment she added, "I suppose I should never have left."

"You think that would have changed anything?" Kate asked incredulously.

"I suppose not." Marian stared out the window at the flat brown fields. Heat waves rose and quivered above the stubble, and a line of clouds sat brooding on the horizon. Despite the heat, she shivered. After a moment she asked, "Is he doing all right?"

"Well," Kate said, "he's got a really nice apartment, and I guess he's making pretty good money. He's been buying antiques, and he goes out a lot to the symphony and stuff." She looked at her mother. "I know he wanted to see you, Mom, but I think—well, maybe he's a little self-conscious about everything, you know?"

Marian nodded. A great weight had settled over her, pinning her down, making it hard to breathe. Maybe she had known all along. There must have been signals. Maybe she had just refused to see them. Would it have made any difference if she had? To reassure herself, she reached out and ran her fingers through her daughter's red-gold hair.

"I'm so glad he trusts you," she said."Please, darling, keep an eye on him, will you, and let me know how he's getting along?"

"I will."

Sometimes it happens quite suddenly that we realize we haven't really been seeing a person that we thought we knew quite well, and Marian felt this way now looking at the young woman who sat beside her. Behind the guileless confidence there was a quiet strength that came as a surprise, though why it should was not altogether clear. Marian smiled and said, "He's lucky to have you for a sister."

They were both silent for several minutes. The blue line of the Coast Range wavered in the distance, the undulating edge of the great Central Valley. The empty vastness of the valley matched the emptiness Marian felt within her heart.

"Mom?"

"Yes, sweetheart?"

Kate's smooth forehead was creased with a frown. "When people fall in love, does it stay like that forever? I mean, does it always feel that strong or does it sort of go . . . up and down?"

"I suppose it's sort of like the tide," Marian said. "It rises and ebbs. It can't always stay the same. Why do you ask?"

Kate's frown deepened. "Oh, I don't know. Last year it all seemed so clear to me, about Tommy and me. And then he went to Oregon, and I went to Berkeley and . . ." She fell silent for several minutes, then she said, "You know, Mom, I wrote him every day the first two months, but lately it just seems like . . . well, it's just not the same."

"Does he still write to you?"

"All the time. I feel really bad about not writing back, but I can't think of what to say." She gave Marian a quizzical look. "Do you think that means I don't really love him?"

"No," Marian replied. "I could tell from your letters how much you care for Tommy. But you and he are still so young. Frankly, I think it's better for you to be apart for a while. That way you can have some time to consider your commitment to each other. Just give yourself some time."

At the terminal gate, Kate gave Marian a hug, and her eyes filled up with tears.

"Darling, what's wrong?" Marian asked. "Why are you crying?"

"I promised myself I wouldn't," Kate gulped, pulling away. "I'm sorry."

"What is it, sweetheart?"

"I just never thought you and Daddy would split up."

Stricken, Marian put her arm around her daughter's narrow shoulders. "Sweetheart, if there was any way to make this easier for you, I would. I feel like such a shit. I really do."

Kate looked up, and her tear-streaked face crumpled into a crooked smile. "Oh, Mom," she said, "I love you."

# CHAPTER

# 37

## San Francisco, California
## October 1961

A persistent knocking woke Julian at eleven a.m. He started to sit up, then collapsed back with a groan. The room came into fuzzy focus as did the events of the previous evening. He'd spent it with an aging, overweight executive with cold, moist hands, wrinkled skin, and a penchant for dirty language. It had taken awhile, even after a bottle of wine and a substantial hit of dope, before Julian could dispel the memory of those clammy hands and get to sleep.

But, it was over, and two fifty-dollar bills lay on the kitchen counter. Fuck last evening. He smiled at the irony. As the knocking continued, Julian struggled up, threw on his robe, and dragged himself to the door.

Kate stood outside, a bag of groceries in her arms. "Hi," she said. "I had errands to do, so I thought I'd drop by and bring you a few things. You look lousy," she added, walking past him into the room.

Julian carefully navigated to the sofa and collapsed with a sigh. "I think I've got the flu," he said, pressing his hand to his head dramatically.

"Did you take your temperature?"

"Shit," he mumbled, closing his eyes, "you sound like Mom."

She began unpacking the groceries. "I haven't seen you in awhile. I thought you were going to call me."

"Haven't had time," he murmured, wishing that his head could be removed and sent out for repairs.

"Stuart keeping you busy?"

"Who?"

"Stuart. You know, the guy I met here?"

"I don't know any Stuart."

Kate frowned at him. "Jeeze, Julian. You introduced me to him last time I was here."

He thought for a minute, then remembered. "Oh, you must mean Brett."

She closed the cupboard and stood looking at him. "I thought you said his name was Stuart."

"Brett. Stuart. What's the difference," he mumbled, rubbing his eyes. Why couldn't she leave him alone?

"Hey," she said, placing a firm hand on his shoulder, "are you okay?"

Julian's stomach was clenching into a knot, and his neck was beginning to ache. He snuffled and grabbed a Kleenex. He needed a hit, but what was he going to do with Kate? Then he remembered that he needed to visit Larry and replenish his supplies. "Shit," he groaned.

"What's wrong? Did you have a fight?" she asked.

"No, we did not have a god-damned fight," he cried, glaring at her through the intense pain between his eyes.

She chewed at her lower lip and studied him.

"Christ," he moaned, "this is ridiculous." His head was roaring. He felt like a beetle trapped under a glass—frantic, scrambling.

"I don't understand," she said. "I thought he was your friend."

Julian laughed sharply. "He's not a friend, he's a client."

"A client?" Kate gave him a bewildered look.

"Yes, goddammit, a client. He stops by on his way home from work for a blowjob. He pays me for it. So see, he's not a friend. Our relationship is strictly professional."

He began to laugh uncontrollably, giggling, hiccuping. His eyes began to water, and he dug at them with his fist.

"And I'll tell you something else, baby sister," he continued, "I don't have the flu either. I'm strung out because I haven't had a hit of dope for going on twelve hours. I used up the last of my supply last night after doing a trick with a clammy old faggot from Des Moines.

You see that money on the counter? That's my funny money for the day. Buys me another brief vacation from my problems—if I can walk far enough to purchase the ticket."

He tried to focus on her face, but it wavered and blurred. He knew she was staring at him, though, staring and staring with wide, disbelieving eyes.

"So you can leave now," he shouted. "Go on. Get the hell out of here! Go call Dad and tell him he was right about me all along. I really am a lousy, no-good fag. And while you're at it, you can tell him I'm a junkie, too. That should really make him proud!"

He had intended sarcasm, but his voice was shaking. When she continued to simply stand there and stare at him, he clasped his hands to his face and burst into tears. Christ, how could he have said that to her, his little sister? Now she would hate him. She *should* hate him. He had wanted to hurt her, to drive her away. But what if she went? Then there was nobody. *Nobody.*

He heard footsteps and half-rose, intending to stop her. But she was still there, standing at the window, her back to him. He sank down. Tears continued to squeeze from his eyelids and run down his cheeks, and he swatted at them as though they were insects. Was she just going to stand there all day, her shoulders hunched, hands knotted behind her back? He sucked in his breath with a shuddering sob. She turned slowly and looked at him. He couldn't meet her gaze.

"How long, Julian?" she said.

"What?" he managed to croak.

"How long have you been doing drugs?"

He tried to think, but everything was fuzzy, out of focus, hopelessly jumbled together. "Maybe a year. Maybe longer. I don't know."

"You should see a doctor," Kate said.

This struck him as grotesquely funny, and he gave a choked laugh. "Oh sure. That's just what I should do. Maybe he could give me an aspirin or something. Look," he continued, trying desperately to pull himself together, "the only kind of doctor I could use would be one who'd write me a prescription for junk so I wouldn't have to blow creeps to pay for my habit."

"You've got to stop."

He swallowed hard, trying to appease a wave of nausea. "I don't think I can."

"Why not?"

"You think I haven't tried?" he shouted. "You don't know what it's like. I thought I could handle it, but . . ."

The room was very quiet. Kate walked to the kitchen and began putting away the rest of the groceries. He followed her with his eyes. "Want some coffee?" she asked.

"All right," he mumbled, then sat staring out the window as she heated the water. Fog swirled. Thoughts wandered. See a doctor. Sure. That was a good one. There wasn't a doctor in the world who could provide a cure. There wasn't anything anybody could do. It was useless to try. God, he was tired. So tired.

She put the cup of coffee down in front of him. "What can I do to help?"

For the space of several breaths he sat looking at her sweet, sad face, then he lowered his eyes, pulled the robe more tightly around him and said, "Just don't stop coming to see me."

Seated at his usual table at an exclusive private club on Taylor Street, Alan Townsend was just remarking to his good friend Robert Ashford that the blanquette de veau was a shade too salty when he paused mid-sentence and stared intently at the doorway.

"My dear," Robert chided, "what on earth are you gawking at?"

"Robert," Alan said, "who is that with Edwin?"

Robert glanced toward the door. "I've never seen him before," he said. "But no doubt if you asked, Edwin would say the lad's another cousin from Minneapolis. Amazing, isn't it, how many cousins dear Edwin has?"

"I wonder," Alan murmured, his eyes still fastened on Julian's impeccable profile, "just how much this cousin cost him for the evening."

"What a scandalous thing to say," laughed Robert.

"Not that I'm questioning his taste."

Robert turned around for another look, then said, "Nice-looking boy. I suppose someone with Edwin's money can afford to indulge their fantasies, but I do think it's rather vulgar to show him off that way."

"I wish," said Alan, "that I was vulgar enough to trot over there and demand an introduction."

"Really, my dear, you'd be asking for trouble," Robert scoffed. "Edwin's taste may be excellent, but his sources leave a lot to be desired. A pretty package can disguise tawdry goods."

"You sound just like my father," Alan noted, "and I stopped listening to him thirty years ago."

For the next hour, Alan tried in vain to think of some discreet way to get an introduction, but he was unable to elicit so much as a glance from Edwin's companion. Indeed, the young man seemed engrossed in what Alan decided must be a murderously boring conversation. Disgruntled, he finally allowed Robert to coax him away.

Once outside, his head began to clear as the fog-laden air buffeted him with briny, invigorating waves. The whole episode seemed immature and silly.

"Sorry," Alan said. "I'm a bit beside myself this evening, I'm afraid." He was at once annoyed by his own apology and felt Robert looking at him with an air of incredulity.

"No matter," Robert said. "You know how jealous dear Edwin is."

They didn't speak for several minutes and, when they did, it was about other things. But that night and every night thereafter for a week, Alan met with Edwin's companion in his dreams.

The following Sunday, Alan was leaving the Hall of Science in Golden Gate Park, having just presented a paper on Etruscan statuary to the Society of Architectural Historians, when he caught sight of the young man he'd seen in the club in the midst of a milling crowd near the entrance to the Steinhart Aquarium.

The sight of that perfect face and shining flaxen hair sent an unnerving jolt of electricity through him. Brushing aside his two companions who were chattering on about the virtues of Roman baths, he pushed his way through the crowd, realizing just in time the folly of rushing up and presenting himself without a proper introduction. Chastened, he followed the young man into the cool, dim interior of the Aquarium.

Alan stopped at the counter to buy a guidebook and pretended to read it. The young man was slowly making his way along the corridor. In the muted light from the tanks, the youth's hair took on a silver cast that Alan found irresistibly beautiful. He stopped at the dolphin tank and leaned against the rail, resting his chin on his hands and watching the creatures with a distant, melancholy gaze.

Summoning his courage, Alan stopped next to him, pulled the guidebook from his pocket, and began to study it. In the half-light of the Aquarium, the pages of the book seemed made of thin sheets of turquoise. After several minutes, Alan glanced toward the lad and said, "Beautiful, aren't they?"

The young man turned. His eyes, Alan noticed, were the color of lapis. That simple fact gave him a rush of happiness.

"Yes," he said. "Very beautiful."

Alan looked down at the book as if it might contain a script that he could read. "It says here," he continued, "that dolphins communicate with extremely complex sounds that might almost be called a language." He looked up again. "Do you think it's a real language?"

"Yes, but far too subtle for us to understand."

Alan was rarely at a loss for words, but speechless, he stood there looking hopelessly into those lapis eyes. The young man looked back with the patient expression of someone who has asked a difficult question and is waiting to get a reply.

"Well, yes," Alan said at length. "I see what you mean. If it is a language, it must be quite different from our own."

"Entirely different."

"Most likely," Alan said inanely.

The lad turned, and for a moment, it seemed that he would walk away. Alan, who had never in his life succumbed to desperation, involuntarily cried out, "Wait."

"Yes?"

"By the way, my name is Alan Townsend."

"Julian McPhalan."

"Didn't I see you—" The sudden look of anxiety that clouded the boy's face deflected his question "—in here last Sunday?"

The fear dissolved, replaced by a smile so beautiful that Alan stared in admiration. "Could be. I usually come here on Sunday. It's my day off."

"Oh, a working man then, and where do you work?"

Julian shrugged. "The Blue Fox. But that's just temporary."

"You have another . . . calling?"

The eyes were guileless. "I'm a writer."

"Ah." Alan nodded. "Fiction?"

"Poetry."

"A noble ambition."

Another heart-melting smile. "I know I'll never be able to make a living at it, but it's what I like to do more than anything."

Alan studied the perfectly formed young face. A white-ground vase came to mind. Fifth century. Sepia lines describing the features of a marvelous Apollo. "What do you write about?" he asked.

"The sea. Him." Julian nodded toward the tank where the dolphin floated upward in a glitter of bubbles, broke the surface, then dove again. "About the tragedy of his life."

"You find him tragic?"

"Don't you?"

Alan sucked in his breath. "Perhaps those walls do not a prison make."

"Oh, he's caged all right," said Julian. A series of mournful, high-pitched bleats echoed in the hall, followed by a staccato of clicks and whistles.

"Eerie, isn't it?" said Alan, turning to look at the sinuous grey shadow.

"Not nearly as frightening as the guys who put him in there," said Julian. Once more he turned and started to walk away.

"Wait," Alan said quickly. "I was just on my way to the Tea Garden for a quick cup. Care to join me?" When Julian didn't reply, he added, "I'd like to hear more about your writing." The boy's eyes narrowed, surveying him critically. Alan smiled his most ingratiating smile and said, "Come on, what do you say?"

Julian shrugged. "Okay."

They sat down at a small table next to a waterfall. An early fog had arrived, and the sun had become a white jade disk that cast a muted, silvery light over the eucalyptus and juniper. The tourists had gone elsewhere, and the garden was nearly deserted.

A pretty Japanese girl, not more than twelve or thirteen, took their order and brought them a pot of tea, two stoneware cups, and a saucer with two fortune cookies. "How long have you lived in the City?" Alan asked, keeping his tone purposefully casual.

"Not long," said Julian.

"Where are you from?" Alan asked.

"Auburn," Julian said. "I hated it."

"I've never been there. Why did you hate it?"

"A nothing town. A desert. No art or music."

"You like music? What kind of music?"

"Symphony. Opera. Chamber music. Some jazz."

"Do you play?" asked Alan.

Julian's face closed a little, and he paused. "I used to. I wanted..."

"Yes?" Alan prompted.

Another tight smile. "I studied violin and piano. At one time I hoped to become a professional musician."

"What stopped you?"

Julian held up his left hand. It looked perfectly normal to Alan, who arched one questioning eyebrow and waited. "Had a little accident," said Julian. "I fell off a tractor and got my hand mangled in the disk. It looks okay, but there's no feeling in the last two fingers. Put a bit of a crimp in my technique."

"Ah." Alan sat back and sipped his tea.

"No big loss. But my mom was disappointed."

"She wanted you to be a musician?"

"She wanted me to be *something*," Julian replied with a sharp little laugh.

Alan smiled sympathetically. "But I thought you were a writer. That's something, isn't it?"

A flush of color rose in Julian's cheeks. "I said I was trying to *learn*. I've got a ways to go."

"I'd enjoy seeing some of your work."

"Why?"

Alan laughed self-consciously. "I've been known to help worthy young artists and writers from time to time. A modest sort of philanthropy." He hesitated, surprised by his own nervousness, then added, "I was intrigued by what you said about the dolphin. Do you often write about the sea?"

Julian poured himself another cup of tea and took a sip before answering. "I've always loved the sea. When I was growing up, I used to keep aquariums. They were all over my room."

"Filled with fish?" Alan asked.

"Fish, seahorses." Julian smiled. "There I was, stuck in Auburn, a hundred miles from the coast and my room looked like a set for Captain Nemo's parlor."

"Complete with red-velvet curtains and brocade wallpaper?" asked Alan with a hint of mild sarcasm.

Julian grinned. "I didn't go quite that far." He paused for a moment, then said, "I was trying to remake my world, restructure it to fit my expectations."

"I've done something similar," Alan mused, "coming here to San Francisco, starting over . . ."

"You're not from here?"

"Not originally, but I've lived here for nearly fifteen years. It's become very much home to me."

The fog was settling lower over the garden. Beyond the gate, the tops of the eucalyptus trees were obscured by the swirling mist, and the air smelled fresh and invigorating.

"Well," Alan said, "shall we see what the future holds?" He picked up the saucer of fortune cookies and held it out to Julian.

Julian smiled and took one. They both broke open the crisp shells.

"You first," said Alan.

Julian peered at the tiny ribbon of paper. *"Beware of tall, well-dressed men with grey eyes."*

"What?" Alan said in shocked amusement.

Julian laughed. "Actually, it says, *You will soon make great strides in your chosen profession.*" He glanced at Alan, his eyes twinkling. "Maybe I can get a job in a cookie factory writing fortunes. Now let's hear yours."

Alan read, *Disregard all previous communications.*

"That's an odd one," Julian said.

"Decidedly inscrutable," Alan agreed. Then he chuckled. "Actually, I've never liked a single fortune that I got from a cookie."

Julian's smile was guarded. "What time is it?" he asked suddenly.

Alan checked the Cartier on his wrist. "Half-past three. Why?"

Julian scraped his chair back on the rough stones of the terrace and stood up. "I didn't know it was so late," he said. "Got to go."

"Must you?" Alan said, rising urgently to his feet. The small cloud of happiness that had descended on him rapidly evaporated, replaced by the chill reality of the fog.   "I thought we might . . . have dinner together."

Julian pushed his hands into the pockets of his windbreaker and stood looking at Alan with an indecipherable expression. "Maybe another time." He started to walk away.

"Wait a minute. Where can I reach you?" Alan called after him.

Julian turned and seemed to waver for a moment, then he took a scrap of paper from his pocket and scribbled a number on it with the stub of a pencil. "I'm usually there before noon," he said brusquely, handing it to Alan.

"Do you like to sail?" Alan asked. "I have a boat. Since you're so fond of the sea . . ."

There was a flicker of interest in Julian's eyes. "Maybe," he said.

"I'll give you a call." As he watched Julian disappear through the tall wooden gates, Alan thought, I must be mad, chasing after some cheap little hustler, even if he does have a face like a Botticelli angel.

But that was reason talking.

# CHAPTER

# 38

"It's your age," Robert commented dryly. "I went through something similar myself a few years back."

"I can't imagine you losing your head over a whore," Alan muttered.

"Well, he wasn't exactly a hooker," sniffed Robert, "just freelancing around the club a bit, but he was a great- looking boy. Exceptionally talented in the boudoir."

"So what happened?" Alan asked with vague interest.

Robert shrugged. "We had a good time together for a couple of months, but he was rather a silly little piece. I was bored to death inside a year. Sent him off to Majorca with an acquaintance of mine from Oxford, and never heard from him again. Nothing like a little familiarity to breed some sensible contempt. I thought you'd learned that with your friend from New Orleans."

A frown creased Alan's high forehead. "Gary? Oh come now, Robert, Gary wasn't a bit like Julian."

Robert peered over his spectacles. "No? He certainly had nice manners, and he looked fabulous in evening clothes."

"A puffball," Alan scoffed. "All surface gloss. Underneath he was a vapid little gigolo."

"Well, wouldn't surprise me if within six months you were saying the same about young Julian," chuckled Robert. "After all, you've only spent a couple of hours with the lad. He's playing hard to get, and don't you love it. Why don't you just take him out sailing and get on with it? I'm sure he'd think of a hundred delicious ways to thank you."

Having spoken, Robert returned to his copy of *Architectural Digest,* leaving Alan to brood over his Remy Martin.

The sun shimmered in the little troughs between the waves and turned the sails a dazzling white. Julian shaded his eyes and looked across the bay. Bright orange against the dark blue sea, the twin towers of the Golden Gate reared skyward like upraised arms. A ridge of fog lay sleeping beyond the headlands.

Despite the breeze, the early October sun was hot, and Julian stripped off his shirt, leaned back against the rail and closed his eyes. If only I could go on like this forever, he thought, feeling the spray on my face, listening to the gulls. He sank down and rested his head against the polished wood. The sun covered him like a blanket.

He woke with a start to find Alan smiling down at him. "Have a good nap?"

"Where are we?" Julian asked dazedly.

"I just put in at Angel Bay," said Alan. "I thought we might go ashore. Have you been here before?"

Julian shook his head and grabbed awkwardly for his shirt, but a sudden gust of wind whisked it from his hand and deposited it in the bay.

"Damn," Julian cried, jumping to his feet.

Alan laughed. "Don't worry about it. I have an extra you can borrow." He gave Julian an appraising glance. "You could get burned on a day like this."

Julian had folded his arms protectively across his chest. "Yes, I guess I could," he muttered as he followed Alan into the hold.

"Here we are," said Alan, taking a knit pullover from the drawer beneath the bunk. "This should be about your size."

Julian reached for the shirt, his left arm still clenched tight against his torso.

Alan eyed him curiously. "Something wrong? Did you hurt your arm? Here, let me see."

"No." Julian jumped back.

Alan looked at him in bewilderment. "Julian, I'm not trying to pressure you."

"It's not that," said Julian. He searched Alan's face, then dropped his eyes and looked down at his arm.

It seemed a thing apart from him, an unfamiliar object that had clamped itself to his chest. Slowly, he let it fall to his side. The collection of needle tracks was painfully obvious.

For a long moment, Alan stood gazing at Julian's arm. Then he handed him the shirt and disappeared up the ladder without uttering a word.

Julian sat down on the bunk and squeezed his eyes shut. The boat rocked gently on long, undulating swells. I blew it, he thought. My one chance, and what did I do? His anguish seemed to be connected to the throbbing of the sea— slow waves of pain that rose and fell with every heartbeat.

Clutching his arms against his side, he fought for breath. Goddamn he wanted a shot. He tried to calculate the time since the last one. Not time for another. Not yet. His thoughts were ricocheting wildly, unmanageable as a swarm of bees. He pressed his palms against his ears and clenched his teeth. Stop it.

The pain eased a little—drew back, still hovering over him like the shadow of some monstrous creature. He took a careful breath, let his hands fall to his sides, opened his eyes. The room swam into focus. Shivering, he pulled on the shirt and sat for a moment hugging himself. Then he got to his feet and looked up the ladder to a circle of fresh blue sky. He was terrified at the thought of Alan's reaction. His throat was dry as sand as he climbed slowly out of the hold.

Alan sat at the stern, his hand on the rudder, facing the open sea. The fog was advancing slowly toward the bay, devouring the bright blue water one bite at a time. He could feel the sting of the wind and smell the sharp tang of the approaching mist. No time to go ashore.

They would have to hurry to get back across the bay and reach the marina before the fog arrived.

He turned just in time to see Julian emerge from the hold and stop, one hand clutching the rail. Time for a decision, Alan thought. Almost simultaneously, he realized the choice had already been made.

A mixture of emotions washed over him—wild delight tempered with a bitter sense of resignation. He studied Julian's pale face, read the terror in his eyes, and felt—grateful? Why, he wondered.

It was as if an unexpected spring had suddenly arrived, thawing the tangled roots of feeling that had lain cold and dormant for as along as he could remember. For this sudden stirring of life, he was, yes, profoundly grateful.

"There's no time to go ashore," he said roughly to the boy, who stood trembling before him. "We'll have to make a run for it if we're to beat the fog. Here," Alan said, handing Julian what looked like a belt with suspenders. "Put this on. We don't want you going overboard."

Julian struggled into the contraption and Alan, who was already wearing a similar harness, clipped a rope onto the belt.

"The wind is coming up, and the waves can get rough very quickly. Just stay calm and do as I say, all right?"

Julian nodded.

Alan steered the boat away from the pier and into the open waters of the bay. Already, the distant San Francisco skyline was fading into a soft grey-white blur. As the wind increased, the boat began to rock and dip.

"We need to reduce the sail area so we can retain control," Alan said. "Take the rudder. Just hold it steady," he added, noting Julian's desperate look, "while I lower the mainsail."

After that, there was no chance for conversation during the thirty-minute race across the bay—just Alan barking orders and Julian frantically trying to follow them as the sloop slid and tilted through the choppy waves.

As they finally neared the safety of the marina, Alan gave Julian a swift, hard stare, started to say something, then changed his mind and once more turned his attention to maneuvering the rig into its berth, leaving Julian awash in recurring bouts of terror.

Still numb with anxiety, Julian followed Alan up the sidewalk that ran beside the pier. The wind had come up hard and cold, and even the sheltered cove with its line of hearty cypress trees offered little protection. Julian shivered as he hurried along the walkway toward the parking lot. He could still taste the salt from the sea spray on his lips. The deeper chill of his fear echoed the continuing slap of the wind.

Alan stopped beside his silver Jaguar and unlocked the passenger door. "Get in," he said to Julian. His voice was cool, but not harsh.

Julian hung back. "I can get a cab," he mumbled, averting his eyes from what he interpreted as an accusing stare.

"I said get in," Alan repeated, grasping Julian's arm and guiding him into the car.

The soft swoosh of the wipers was the only sound as the Jaguar climbed effortlessly up from the bay and turned south on Van Ness. Julian gazed gloomily out the window, wondering where they were headed and at the same time not really caring. Although he could feel the warm flow of air from the car's heater across his legs, he was still shivering, as much from strained emotions as from cold.

They halted at the corner of Van Ness and California, waiting as a cable car clattered across the intersection and stopped, bell clanging, on the round wooden turntable. Driver and passengers tumbled out and helped to swing the car around. Laughing and pushing, more people crowded on as the car once more lurched forward and began a sedate ascent.

Victorian gingerbread replaced the stucco facades of pastel row-houses, and Julian's attention was captured intermittently by an especially fanciful molding, by turrets and the frosty patterns of etched glass. He darted a swift glance of surprise at Alan as the Jaguar turned into a narrow drive and stopped before the most extravagant mansion on a block of genteel beauties. Without looking at him, Alan said, "Would you like to come in?"

After a moment of awed silence, Julian said, "You live here?"

"That's right," said Alan. "Would you like to come in?"

Julian swallowed hard. "I guess so."

"It's the help's day off," Alan announced, hanging his jacket on the polished walnut hall tree. He pulled open heavy, dark-oak doors revealing a spacious living room. "Why don't you make yourself comfortable. I'll get some tea."

Julian gaped at the lavish interior, the exquisite paneling, intricate ceiling details, black-veined marble fireplace. His feet seemed to sink several inches into the plush Oriental carpet. Forest-green velvet and rose brocade covered an especially fine Duncan Phyfe sofa and two Adams side chairs. Huge porcelain urns flanked the Rococo mirror above the mantel, and on a shelf above the sofa stood a handsome collection of pre-Columbian figurines. Everywhere he looked, new treasures caught his eyes—a nest of Fabergé eggs, a small Seurat landscape.

"Here," said Alan, handing him a china coffee mug, "this ought to help. Do you take sugar or cream?"

"Both," said Julian, overwhelmed by the lush surroundings and the tensions of the day.

"Have a seat," Alan said. "I'll crank up the fire. It's a bit chilly in here, don't you think?"

Julian nodded, clutching the mug to his chest.

"The English drink it like that," Alan said over his shoulder as he turned on the gas jet and poked at the small ceramic briquettes that filled the grate. "They call it Cambric tea."

"My mother used to give me this when I was sick," said Julian. The honeyed warmth began to sooth him and, for the first time in several hours, he stopped shivering.

"There now." Alan put aside the poker. "That's better." He stood for a moment with his back to Julian. Then he pulled a wing chair up next to Julian and sat down. "Now we'll talk," he said, looking directly into Julian's apprehensive eyes.

Julian looked away. "About what?"

"I want to know how you got hooked."

Julian shrugged and stared at the fire.

"I don't like junkies," said Alan.

Glancing up, Julian said, "Then I guess you don't like me."

Alan sat back and folded his arms across his chest. "The problem is, Julian, I *do* like you," he said in a low voice. "If you'll just talk about your . . . addiction, perhaps I can help."

Julian lowered his eyes again. He wanted to put his hands over his ears. "I don't want to think about it." He was surrendering to chaos once more, whirling in incoherent circles. There was only one way to calm the angry buzzing inside his skull, and Cambric tea wasn't it. He should have hailed a cab, taken a bus.

Alan was staring at him, cool grey eyes boring a path directly into his frenzied brain. "I can see that you're in no condition to discuss your problem." Alan's voice seemed to come from a great distance. "Come on, I'll take you home."

"Don't bother!" Julian jumped to his feet, and pushing open the massive front door, he bolted down the sidewalk to the street.

How he made it home he wasn't sure, but he woke twelve hours later with sunlight streaming in through the open window. For a moment, only the vivid lingering fragments of drug-induced dreams seemed real to him. Then he remembered the boat, the fog, Alan's magnificent house, his own miserable behavior. He groaned and turned over, covering his head with the pillow. Self-loathing rose like vomit in his throat. How could I, he thought bleakly.

You know why, a small, maddeningly smug voice replied. You've gotten exactly what you deserve.

"Shut up," Julian growled, sitting up, then collapsing once more amidst the tangled bedclothes. God, what a ferocious headache.

He glanced at the clock and groaned again, covering his eyes with his hands. Ten minutes 'til ten. And it was Monday. He was due at the Blue Fox in forty minutes. He hated that damned job, but he couldn't afford to lose it.

Struggling to his feet, he eyed the paraphernalia that littered the dresser top. Alan was wrong. He couldn't stop. No way. Already it was getting hard to breathe—that familiar heaviness in his chest, the nervous twitching in his legs, the runny nose. I'm sorry, he thought as he groped for the shower knob, so damned sorry.

He was getting dressed, beginning to feel only slightly better, when the phone rang.

"Julian?" For a moment he didn't recognize Sheila's voice. "Julian? Are you there?"

"Yeah. What do you want?"

"I love you, too, baby," she said with heavy sarcasm. "We got a little problem." His heart sank as she explained.

"No," he said in answer to her question. "N-o."

"He's a regular of Damien's," Sheila continued, "but Dee's out of town this week. So you'll have to fill in."

"I was supposed to be off this week," Julian argued. "And I've got lunch duty at the Fox. Can't you get someone else to do it?"

"Everyone else is busy. So you're it, Julie baby. You don't have to be there until four, so it won't interfere with your day job."

"Come on, Sheila," he snapped. "Don't make me beg."

"Won't do any good, luv. Anyway, the guy's a pussycat. You'll be in and out by teatime. Now be a good boy and do as you're told. Or should I tell Mr. Smith that you're screwing up again?"

Julian cursed under his breath.

"I heard that," Sheila chirped. "If you're going to talk dirty, save it for the clients. Take down this address. And get there on time for once."

It was five minutes to four when Julian got to the address, and the fog was closing in. The apartment overlooked Golden Gate Park—lush expanses of dark-green lawn and banks of zinnias and marigolds.

Fabian Wilson was an interior designer who, for thirty years, had made a handsome living redoing stylish apartments for San

Francisco matrons. The interior of his own flat was starkly modern. Sterile and cold.

Fabian was thin and grey, a cadaverous-looking man with patchy skin and balding scalp. Julian was far from thrilled at the prospect of the evening ahead, but Sheila was right on target. After a few minutes of obligatory conversation, Fabian took his arm and whispered, "Let me show you to our room."

As he undressed, Julian thought morosely of an endless string of emotionless encounters stretching toward the future like a row of tombstones. Lying down on the monstrous circular bed, he searched desperately for a fantasy to get him through the ordeal, and found himself able to picture only one image—Alan Townsend's cool grey eyes and angular, elegant body. As Fabian's eager mouth worked its way down his neck and shoulder, he closed his eyes and let the fantasy engulf him, and as Fabian's lips closed around his hardened cock, he barely managed to turn Alan's shouted name into an unintelligible groan.

The next morning, dreams pursued him into wakefulness— detached hands grasping at his body, garbled voices whispering in his ear, trying to run, only to find his legs mired in quicksand, struggling, crying, trying to get free. Was there any hope for salvation? "Forget it," he told himself. "Forget him." He stared grimly at the ceiling. I want out, he thought. Out of the whole rotten world.

He got to his feet and crossed the room to the dresser. As he prepared the injection with smooth precision, he paused momentarily to calculate the maximum tolerable dose. For a split second he considered exceeding the limit, then he shook his head. Not this morning. Not quite yet.

The drug flowed into him, relaxing cramped muscles, quieting the roar of confusion inside his head. With a sigh, he stretched out once more and closed his eyes. Nirvana, that's what it is, he thought drowsily. Thank god for nirvana. . . .

For a while he drifted, warm and safe, but dreams threatened once again, dark shapes hovered, jaws filled with teeth leered obscenely through the rosy mist. His eyes snapped open, and he let out a shout of terror. Something hung over the bed—a monstrous black form, a grinning skull. He rolled to his left, fell awkwardly to the floor, cowered beside the nightstand, his body drenched with sweat.

There was a chirping sound, the rustle of flapping wings. Glancing at the window, he realized a pigeon strutting on the ledge had cast its shadow on the wall. A foolish laugh escaped his throat as he crawled once more onto the bed. The laughter changed abruptly to tears, and he lay for a long time sobbing among the rumpled sheets.

He pulled himself together enough to sit up, blow his nose, and contemplate his situation. I'm sick, he admitted. I need help. His eyes fastened on the phone. His hands shook as he picked up the receiver.

"Townsend residence," a crisp, professional voice responded.

"Uh—I'd like to speak to Mr. Townsend, please."

"May I ask who's calling?"

Panic seized him and he nearly banged down the phone. "Uh . . ." he said after a long moment, "just tell him it's his, uh, sailing companion."

"One moment, please."

Julian held his breath, fighting the impulse to hang up.

"Julian?"

Alan's voice sent a rush of pleasure through Julian's aching body. "I'm sorry," he said. "I don't expect you to forgive me, but I'm calling to apologize."

There was a long silence at the other end. "Alan?" he said with alarm.

"I'm still here."

God, he had such a beautiful voice—modulated, civilized, serene, but with an undercurrent of passion. "I'm sorry," Julian repeated.

"Are you ready to talk?" Alan said.

Julian could scarcely believe his ears. Was it possible that Alan might actually give him another chance? "I—uh—if you want to," he stammered.

There was another long pause. "I'm staying in town this

weekend," said Alan in the same brusque voice. "You're welcome to come by on Sunday for an early dinner. Around six, shall we say?"

"I'll be there," Julian promised.

Carefully, he returned the receiver to its cradle. Then he put his head down on his pillow and once more burst into tears—whether from shame or from relief, he didn't know.

# CHAPTER

# 39

"I thought we'd eat out here," Alan said, ushering Julian through French doors onto a covered patio. Tubs of bright geraniums created splashes of red and pink, while rainbow-hued fuchsias trailed from hanging baskets. From a niche in the high stone wall that surrounded the garden, a Della Robbia Madonna presided graciously over a fountain decorated with dolphins and mermaids. The air was filled with a glorious fragrance—jasmine or honeysuckle, Julian guessed—and the early-evening sunlight lay like patches of gold among the ferns and boxwood.

"Sit down," Alan said. "I'll fetch the hors d'oeuvres."

Julian slid into a canvas chair, trying to temper his excitement with doses of hard-nosed logic. I'm here, he thought. One step at a time.

A hummingbird hovered among the fuchsias, probing magenta blossoms. Wings a-blur, it seemed to be standing on thin air. Julian felt, in the pit of his stomach, the same uneasy feeling of suspension. He briefly considered praying—but to whom?

"Sherry?" said Alan, appearing so suddenly beside him that Julian jumped.

"Uh—sure. Why not?" Good god, I'm stuttering like a teenager, he thought as Alan filled the glass.

Alan sat down opposite him, leaned back, crossed long legs, and took a sip of sherry. Aware that he was mimicking but unable to stop himself, Julian assumed a similar position and sipped his drink. "Mmmm," he murmured. "Very nice."

"Domecque La Ina," Alan said. "I've never understood why so many people overlook sherry as a pre-dinner drink. So much more civilized than some nasty froth mixed with hard liquor."

"I've always favored Scotch," Julian remarked.

Alan raised an eyebrow. "Not bad. But it *can* blunt the taste buds."

It was hardly a specifically sexual remark, but Julian experienced a sudden visceral glow that could not be explained by the sherry alone. He shifted his position, but the shimmer of warmth remained undiminished. Swallowing nervously, he tried unsuccessfully to meet Alan's steady gaze.

"When did you come to San Francisco?" he asked, hoping that his voice wouldn't betray his rapidly accelerating pulse.

Alan studied the rafters. "I'd just gotten back from the war. Must have been 1946."

Julian gave him a startled look. "You fought in the war?"

"Naval intelligence. Communications, codes, that sort of thing. You seem surprised."

"I guess I am. I always connect the war with—you know, John Wayne types." He laughed lamely. "Like my father."

Alan smiled. "Plato would find that amusing. Ancient Greeks used to take their lovers into battle with them." The cool grey eyes fastened themselves once more on Julian's face. "To love men was not considered unmanly in those times."

Between geranium leaves, a spider web trapped the fading sunlight and became a net of golden filigree. "Different times," Julian said.

"Weren't they, though. Yet, it was the stint in the Navy that gave me the opportunity to think about coming out. Or, at least, the impetus to leave behind a life of quiet desperation based on lies."

Julian studied the calmly handsome face. "Where were you before the war?"

"Massachusetts. Four years at Williams College. Another four at Harvard. Two years post-doc work at the School of Classical Studies in Athens. Then London for a year. I left Europe when it looked as though the Nazis might actually be getting somewhere. I ended up back in Boston, teaching a few classes at my old alma mater and dabbling in the family business."

"Which was?"

"Banking."

Julian nodded. "So how'd you end up in the Navy?"

Alan took a sip of sherry. "I'd like to tell myself that it was the noble action of a young man of high principles who went off to defend his country. But, in fact, it was an escape. I ran away."

"From what?"

Alan gave him an ironic smile. "My wife."

"Your wife," gasped Julian. "Are you serious?"

"Oh yes. That went with the territory. Like the brownstone and the summer place at Siasconset on Nantucket Island. Like the yacht and the golden retriever and the projected children, a girl, and a boy, of course, to carry on the family name. My future was very secure." His fingers had formed a steeple. He rested his chin on them and gazed absently at the fountain.

For several minutes, Julian was too shocked to say anything. Then he realized the story actually made sense. Alan was so controlled, so urbane. Out of politeness he could probably do almost anything. "What was she like?" he asked.

Alan's eyes shifted back to meet Julian's curious stare. "Pretty, charming, well-educated. And miserable. We both knew our marriage was a mistake. She thought I didn't love her, but in fact I did. In my own way. We talked about divorce, but I found the idea . . . distasteful. And the families would have been outraged. So I enlisted. I thought it would give me a few years to sort things out . . ." He lapsed once more into silence.

"But you said the war changed you," Julian prompted. "So when you got back, did you agree to the divorce?"

For a long moment, Alan remained silent, staring once more into space. Then he said, "Didn't have to. She died about three months after I came home. A suicide."

During the long silence that followed, Julian's mind spun through a myriad of conflicting thoughts and feelings—pain, empathy, grief, and a kind of bitter joy. Alan had loved someone else once. He might love again. Pulling himself together, he said, "Must have been terrible."

Alan smiled half-heartedly. "I didn't feel exactly heroic, but I did realize that I was now free to make a complete break with my past. I had already decided while I was in the service that that I wanted a new life. After Sharon's death, no one could argue with my decision to leave New England and take up residence in a totally different environment. The convenience made me feel even guiltier, of course, but not so much as to keep me from following my own instincts and heading directly for San Francisco. Well," he quickly drained the last of his sherry, "I've been here ever since." He stood up and added, "I'll go and see about dinner."

"Can I help?"

"No. Everything should be just about ready. I'll be right back."

Unnerved by the intimacy of the conversation, Julian sat gazing at the fountain, watching the stream of water arcing gracefully from a dolphin's open jaws. Alan was not the sort of man to share something like that with a casual acquaintance, Julian thought.

Alan reappeared with two bowls of bouillabaisse on a tray along with a fresh baguette, a lightly dressed green salad, and a bottle of chilled white wine.

The dinner conversation was much lighter—literature, sailing, and the California wine industry. By the time Alan brought fresh raspberry sorbet and homemade madeleine's for desert, Julian was feeling quite relaxed. "Let's take our coffee in the parlor," Alan suggested. "It's getting rather cool out here."

Hands behind his back, Julian was studying a Degas pastel of two elegantly posed dancers when Alan came in with the coffee and two snifters of cognac on a silver tray. He set the tray on the marble coffee table and made a ritual of pouring, fussing over the cream and sugar, offering chocolate truffles. "Have a seat," Alan said, waving his hand toward the Victorian sofa. "A toast," he said, handing Julian a snifter and taking the other for himself. "To the future."

The unwavering eyes and gently ironic smile made Julian's heart lurch in his chest. Raising his snifter, he echoed, "To the future."

Alan took a swallow of cognac, sat the snifter down on the table, and settled into a leather wing chair. "Now, then," he said, "shall we discuss the future?"

Julian shifted uncomfortably, despite the plush cushions of the sofa. "What about it?"

"Tell me about Larry Flagstaad," Alan said.

Julian frowned. "How do you know about him?"

"My dear," Alan said, sighing, "I know a great deal about what goes on in this fair city. So how on earth did you get yourself mixed up with Flagstaad?"

Julian looked down. "Larry's been a big help to me."

"I can imagine what sort of help he's been," scoffed Alan.

"No, really," Julian protested. "He took care of me when I first moved here. I owe him."

Alan picked up his cognac and swirled it angrily. "What do you mean, you owe him?"

Julian could feel the panic beginning to build once more and quickly forced it aside. He was not going to fall apart again. Was *not*.

"Well?" said Alan.

"I *do* owe him," Julian muttered. "He's done me a lot of favors."

Alan stared at him incredulously. "You really believe that, don't you?"

Julian began to squirm beneath Alan's gaze. "I was flat broke when I first got here. I had nowhere to go, no job, no money. Larry took care of me."

Alan raised his eyebrows. "Oh, he took care of you all right."

"It's not Larry's fault."

"What I'd like to know," said Alan, "is where you get the money to pay for your habit."

Julian's jaw jutted forward. "I work for it."

"Doing what?"

"I told you. I work at the Blue Fox."

Alan swirled his cognac and took a sip, his eyes never leaving Julian's face. "Come on," he said with quiet vehemence, "you don't get that kind of money busing dishes at the Blue Fox."

Julian shrugged and looked away.

"Where does the money come from?" Alan pressed.

"I already told you," Julian said, fumbling in his shirt pocket for his cigarettes.

"Don't lie to me, Julian."

"Take a guess," said Julian sarcastically. "You said you know what goes on in this city."

"I want to hear it from you."

Julian took a moment lighting his cigarette, trying to get his emotions under control. He blew out an angry stream of smoke and glared at Alan through narrowed eyes. "I run errands for Larry. I deliver packages. I entertain his friends."

"In other words," Alan said, "you deal drugs and prostitute yourself."

Unable to maintain any semblance of composure, Julian jumped to his feet and cried, "It's none of your goddamned business."

Alan rose and faced him. "I'm making it my business."

"I've had enough of your patronizing crap!" Julian shouted. "Just be glad I haven't asked you to pay me for my time."

Alan smacked Julian across the cheekbone, sending him sprawling back onto the sofa. In the next instant, hands closed like vices on Julian's shoulders, and he found himself looking directly into Alan's furious eyes. "Don't *ever* say anything like that to me again," Alan said. The hands released him abruptly, snapping his head back against the velvet pillows.

Terrified, Julian lay immobilized, hardly daring to breathe. Waves of electric heat flashed over him, ending inexplicably in icy chills. Alan towered above him, his face contorted by what Julian realized was a look of terrible sadness.

"I'm in love with you, Julian," he said.

It was the last thing Julian had expected to hear. He felt the blood drain from his head as he stared up in total disbelief. He throat began to ache, and Alan's face blurred into soft-focus. "What?" Julian whispered as he pushed himself slowly up on his elbows.

Alan sat down beside him on the sofa and rested his hand on Julian's shoulder. "I love you," he repeated gently. "I want to help you."

Julian turned away and lowered his eyes. "You'd just be wasting your time."

Alan's hand grasped Julian's shoulder more firmly. "You're wrong, Julian. There's a lot I can do if you'll only let me."

Julian pulled away and got unsteadily to his feet. "You don't understand," he choked. His one coherent thought was that he should run somewhere and hide, burrow deep into a cave and disappear, escape at any cost from the expectations he was certain he could never hope to fulfill.

Alan's arm stopped him. "I *do* understand," he said. "Listen to me, will you? Sharon was an addict. That's what killed her. She'd been taking drugs for years and after I got back from the war she . . . she took an overdose one Sunday night and died the next day." For a moment there was silence, then Alan added, "Don't end up like that, Julian."

Julian wavered, struggling to sort out the conflicting thoughts that tumbled through his brain. If only—if only— "No," he cried, trying to break away from Alan's grasp. "I can't."

Alan spun him around and fixed him with his cool grey eyes. "Yes, you *can*." For an instant longer, Julian clung to the last thread of resistance. Then he buried his face in Alan's shoulder and surrendered to wrenching sobs.

"Shhh," Alan murmured, stroking his hair. "You can move in with me. I'll get help for you. I want you here with me, Julian."

"But what about Larry?" Julian sobbed, desperation giving way to sudden icy fear. "What about . . . Mr. Smith?"

"Let me worry about that," Alan said.

# CHAPTER

# 40

## Berkeley, California
## October 1961

"Come over for dinner Friday," Kate said. "I'm staying at a friend's apartment while she's out of town, so I can actually cook something for you."

"Can't," Julian told her. "I'm busy."

"Please. I haven't seen you for weeks. Besides, I'm tired of eating alone."

Julian laughed self-consciously. "Well, if you're sure it's no trouble, Roo. I'll come to the rescue."

She fixed his favorite dinner—grilled lamb and artichokes and a bottle of zinfandel. And for dessert there were strawberries and baklava and tiny cups of rich Greek coffee. She had covered the table with a pink cloth and found two enormous roses to provide a centerpiece. She could smell the roses as she watched Julian pick at the remaining crumbs of baklava.

"Was it okay?" she asked.

"Super."

"Really?"

"Absolutely."

She made a face and got up to clear the table.

"Let me help," he said.

"Sit down. This is your party. Next time you can treat me."

He sprawled on the sofa, while she put the kitchen in order. Dave Brubeck's *Take Five* played softly.

"You're looking better," Kate said, collapsing into an overstuffed chair and tossing the dishcloth aside. "Been getting a little sun?"

He grinned and leaned back, hands behind his head. "I've met this man," he said.

"You look like you've swallowed a canary."

He laughed, blushing. "Something like that."

"So tell me about him."

Julian straightened up and leaned forward eagerly. "He's incredible, Roo. He has a fabulous art collection, and he's written books on history and archeology, and he travels all over the world giving lectures and . . ."

"Slow down," protested Kate, laughing. "God, Pooh, he sounds fantastic. Does he have a name?"

"Alan. Alan Townsend. Also, he has a sailboat. We go sailing every weekend."

"Must have a bundle."

"I guess so. He's got a wonderful house on California Street. One of those Victorian beauties with a turret and a Tiffany window. I mean, Jesus, Roo, it's unbelievable."

Kate gave her brother a hard look. "So what's your connection with him, Julian?"

A flush spread across his cheeks. "He's not like the others," he said. "He's not a . . . *client,* if that's what you mean."

"How'd you meet him?"

"I was at the Aquarium watching the dolphins. He was standing next to me, and we started talking. It was so easy to talk to him, you know? We went to the Tea Garden and he wanted to know about my writing and . . ." He spread his hands helplessly. "See? Every time I start talking about him, I just babble like an idiot."

"Are you in love with him?" Kate asked.

Julian twisted the edge of a sofa cushion. "I don't know," he said. "I don't know what I feel. I admire him. His clothes, his house, everything. It scares me. I keep thinking it's all a dream, and I'll wake up and he'll disappear." He grimaced. "I don't know what he sees in me. I've made such a mess of my life . . ." He pulled furiously at the edge of the cushion.

"Does he know you're an addict?"

Julian looked at her. "He knows. He wants me to go into a private hospital in Marin County and go through their rehab program."

"Can you afford that?"

"No. But that's the crazy part, Roo. He's offered to pay for everything. I don't understand. He . . ." Julian gave Kate an afflicted look. "He says he loves me."

Kate nodded. "Do it, Julian," she said.

## San Francisco, California

"How about another cognac?" Robert enquired solicitously, pausing next to the ornate eighteenth-century armoire that served as his bar. Alan sat, legs crossed, on the sofa, staring absently at one of the Indian miniatures that adorned the white walls. "Alan?"

"Sorry. What did you say?"

"Would you like another?"

"Yes, of course.

Robert poured a splash into Alan's empty snifter and seated himself across from his friend. "All right. Tell me about it."

"I'm sorry. I must seem entirely preoccupied."

"Entirely."

Alan took a drink. "I'm having trouble keeping a clear head these days."

"You may as well give me the whole story."

"And now you're grinning like an unabashed voyeur."

Robert laughed. "And you, my dear, are being infuriatingly evasive."

"I'm embarrassed," Alan sighed, taking another sip of cognac.

"Why?"

"I should have more sense. Christ, Robert, you'd think I'd know better than to get myself involved with some . . ." The sentence remained unfinished amidst the strains of the Mozart's *Flute and*

*Harp Concerto* playing softly on the stereo. "I've always been so prudent," Alan finished. "So careful to avoid a scandal."

"You've been extremely discreet," Robert agreed, "unlike some people I know."

"Such as Edwin and his little coterie? Three drinks and he turns into a raving queen. It's really quite disgusting."

"I hear he's furious at you for stealing away his favorite plaything," said Robert, a smug look on his cherubic face. "Apparently he made quite a scene at Joseph's party the other evening."

"How very like him," Alan scoffed. "I'm always expecting him to show up in pillbox and pantyhose."

"So tell me," Robert said, "how is our Tadzio faring these days?"

Alan shook his head. "We shall see."

"Go on," Robert prompted.

"He's decided to go through the rehab program. I expect it to be a nightmare, but the boy has a lot of courage." A smile softened the firm lines of his mouth.

"Well, if you're intent on squandering your money on the lad, it's heartening to see some potential return on your investment."

"I didn't ask for sarcasm," Alan admonished. "You did inquire, after all."

"So I did. Do go on."

"And he's decided he wants to go to college," Alan continued. "He's planning to go to night school to finish his high-school requirements. He's been studying constantly. It's really quite impressive."

"That can't leave a lot of time for recreation," Robert commented.

Alan's eyes wandered to the seventeenth-century Mughal miniature that hung next to the fireplace—a portrait of three princes riding across the countryside. "You know," he said, "I feel like a sultan that's been given the exquisite gift of some rare creature not quite of this world. I'm almost afraid to lay a finger on my treasure for fear it will shatter. Or turn to stone."

Robert's eyebrows arched. "My dear," he murmured, "you *are* in trouble."

"Admittedly," said Alan.

"So what do you intend to do, continue to support the dear lad in a manner in which he is no doubt rapidly becoming accustomed?"

"I guess so. At least for now."

"I don't envy you."

"I'm not surprised," said Alan, his eyes once more straying to the Mughal miniature. "But do you know, Robert, it's been at least thirty years since I've felt this alive? It has occurred to me that I've been living in a comfortable vacuum, insulating myself from every unpleasantness, taking absolutely no risks. I was becoming an artifact in my own collection. This whole episode has been vastly intriguing to me. I feel so invigorated. So full of *joie de vivre*." He gave Robert a sideways glance. "How's that for a pathetic admission?"

Robert took off his glasses and carefully wiped the lenses with a linen handkerchief. "Perhaps fated is more like it. The whole business does, you must admit, have a certain . . . inevitability about it."

"That has crossed my mind."

Robert replaced his spectacles and smiled at his friend. "Well, my dear," he said, "perhaps the gods will be kind."

"The gods, dear Robert," Alan answered, "belong to another age."

### Marin County, California

Had he realized in advance just what he would experience, Julian might never have agreed to let Alan drive him across the Golden Gate Bridge and into the cool, fog-shrouded hills of Marin County to the private clinic that lay nestled in a grove of eucalyptus trees. But we protect ourselves from future uncertainty by refusing to think about it, so it wasn't until Alan's Jaguar had disappeared among the redwoods and rhododendrons that Julian felt the beginning of a profound and paralyzing fear.

His throat was dry, and his hands shook as he unpacked the small suitcase of belongings that he was allowed to bring with him. He put on one side of the bed a snapshot of himself and Alan standing on the prow of Alan's sailboat, and on the other a photo of his mother holding Kate and Alex in her lap.

He sat down slowly on the bed, picked up the copy of *The Odes of Pindar* Alan had given to him the previous evening and, opening it, read,

> *There is one race of men, one race of gods;*
> *both have breath of life from a single mother.*
>
> *But sundered power holds us divided, so that the*
> *one is nothing, while for the other the brazen sky is*
> *established their sure citadel forever.*
>
> *Yet we have some likeness in great intelligence, or*
> *strength, to the immortals, though we know not what*
> *the day will bring, what course after nightfall*
> *destiny has written that we must run to the end.*

The words swam before his eyes. He glanced around the room. Everything was in motion, undulating slowly, as though the world had turned to water that rose and fell like brightly colored waves. Gulping air like a beached fish, he dug his fingers into the mattress, but the unnerving liquidity continued.

They had let him keep his clothes—there were no hospital gowns, no institutional uniforms—but they had taken his belt and tie, and the reason for that was suddenly very clear to him. He jumped up and hurried across the room to the window. A wrought-iron grill covered the glass. The window could be cranked open for fresh air, but the grill was securely locked.

He swallowed and stared through the bars at the flagstone courtyard three stories below. No escape there. Cursing, he pulled the curtains across the glass, blocking out the coral glow of the sunset. Let me out, he thought wildly. I can't go through with this.

Whimpering, he paced from window to door and back again, a thousand disconnected thoughts racing through his mind—Marian's studio at Mockingbird, huge canvases covered with splotches of raw colors describing a chaos he couldn't understand. What are they about? he had asked her. About anger, she replied. Was she angry with him for falling off the tractor? Angry about his hand? He had failed her, and she had gone away to punish him. *You're never going to amount to anything,* Owen shouted at him. *You're a worthless, lazy bum.*

What had he done wrong? Why did everybody hate him?

He remembered when he was twelve, he'd spent the night in the juvenile detention center. He'd been caught stealing hubcaps with two other boys. An older boy had come up to him in the hall outside the bathroom, had nudged him against the wall, pretending to tell him something while he slid his hand inside Julian's shirt, worked it downward past the waistband of his jeans. He could recall so distinctly the sudden electric excitement that he felt, the warm rush of desire.

A guard had interrupted, knocking the older boy aside, grabbing Julian by the scruff of the neck. *Perverted little creeps,* the guard had bawled. *Fucking fairy perverts.* Julian was terrified that someone would tell Owen, but nothing was ever said about the incident. Julian forgot neither the pleasure, nor the guilt. He was wrong again. His ideas were wrong, his hopes were wrong, his feelings were wrong, his sensations wrong. Betrayed by mind and body, he wondered what could go wrong next.

Then came the accident. The tractor tilting, the harrow blades slashing. You're lucky you didn't lose that hand, the doctor had said. The hand was saved, but Julian had lost his mother. She would never love him again, never look at him again with that special glow of pride as he played her favorite Mozart sonata, never again tell him, *Your talent is special, sweetheart. You're going to do wonderful things.*

He'd tried to talk to her after the accident, tried to tell her how he felt. She had tried to listen, to help, to sympathize. But a gulf had opened between them, and it seemed to Julian that she spent more and more time with Alex. He couldn't help noticing that when Alex played, Marian's face took on that same glow of delight that was once reserved for him. Two years later she was gone.

What a crazy summer, that last summer he'd spent at Mockingbird. The fights with Owen, the trip to LA to see Ray, and the interlude with Jared Marley. It had started out so beautifully, a special bond that Julian nurtured with growing delight. Someone thought he was all right, that he was smart, creative, talented. Those sessions after class, the talks, the books borrowed and lent, the Saturday afternoons spent working together on the student literary magazine.

But he had been unprepared for the physical demands, for the hurried, brief encounters, the furtiveness. It shouldn't be so shameful. It wasn't wrong, was it? Perhaps it was. Owen certainly thought so. Mother probably did too. Only Kate had ever tried to understand. Only Kate. . . .

He lay down on the bed and curled into a fetal ball, pressing his thighs together, trying to stop the shivering. Get some sleep, he told himself, but his head felt as if it might explode at any minute, and the muscles of his back ached with tension. Only Kate. She was the only one who'd ever tried to understand.

But, no, that wasn't true anymore. His eyes blinked open as the thought came to him. Now there was Alan. Despite the shivering, the ache of his muscles, he managed to smile. Yes, now there was Alan. He squeezed his eyes shut and tried to picture Alan's face, the cool grey eyes, the high forehead, the sweep of silver hair.

Last night had been the best night of his life. The feel of Alan's arms around him, the gentle sureness of his hands, the warmth of their entwined bodies. If only Alan were here. With Alan beside him, Julian felt he could withstand anything.

But Alan's book was here. Julian bolted up-right, searched wildly for the book, found it on the floor beside the bed.

*Though we know not what the day will bring, what course after nightfall . . .*

That was it! The book would be the link, the symbol for Alan's presence, the talisman that would let him run the course full to the end. "I'm going to do it," he murmured, pressing his face against the smooth red-leather binding. "I promise you Alan, I'm going to see this through."

But it was far worse than he had anticipated. For what felt like an eternity, he lay shivering, soaked with sweat, his stomach twisted into lumps of pain, every tissue in his body screaming in torment. He was dismayed by the humiliation of the flesh, the degrading victory of matter over mind. Between recurring bouts of gut-wrenching nausea and uncontrollable shivering, he clutched the book of poems in his shaking hands and read through watering eyes,

> *Heavy was the assault of Achilles*
> *when he came down from his chariot and with the*
> *edge of the angry sword struck down the child*
> *of the shining Dawn. All this is a way the men*
> *before me discovered long ago, but I follow it also,*
> *carefully.*
> *When the ship is laboring, always the wave that rolls*
> *Nearest her forefoot, they say,*
> *brings terror beyond aught to all men's*
> *hearts. But I gladly have taken on my back*
> *a twofold burden*
> *and comes a messenger . . .*

"Please, Alan," Julian prayed silently. "Let me do this for you. Let me be worthy . . ."

He screamed and threw the book across the room as a knife-blade of pure agony sank into his stomach and tore through his entrails. It was alive, that pain, a demon that was burning its way into his very soul. "Stop it!" he screamed. "Stop it stop it stop it. Somebody make it stop. Please make it stop!"

This was insane, hopeless. He couldn't bear another minute of this agony. Alan's fault. His idea. "Damn you, Alan. How could you do this to me? You bastard. I hate you. I hate you, Dad. I hate you, Dad." Hands grappled to hold him, and he punched out wildly. "Hate you, Dad."

His head throbbed, and he realized he had been bashing it against the wall. His face was covered with blood, hot and sticky and revolting. *I hate my father*, he thought with sudden clarity. Weak, legs melting, he let the two orderlies lead him to the bed.

"Water," he whispered, but no amount of water could assuage that unholy thirst.

Nurses came and went, white shadows bent over him, cool cloths covered his forehead, muted voices murmured to him that all was well, that everything was fine. *Yes*, he thought, *but I hate my father. What do I do about that?*

He slid out of the bed and crawled across the room. It had to be here. Okay, there it was. His fingers grasped the slim volume. Shivering, he pressed the book to his chest. After a while he fell asleep.

"How are you feeling?" Alan's voice sounded thin and far away over the phone.

"Better." After three weeks, the worst did seem to be over.

"They say I can come see you on Sunday," Alan said. "Would you like that?"

"I look awful," replied Julian, glancing in the mirror to confirm his words. His own pale face stared back at him, the cheeks hollow, the eyes edged with shadows.

Alan chuckled. "It's not a spa, Julian. You're not there for a beauty treatment."

Julian grinned sheepishly. "Really? I've been having the time of my life."

"I'll bet," Alan replied without rancor. "Seriously, Julian, are you all right? Are they treating you well?"

"As well as I deserve."

"How's the therapy going?"

Julian took a deep breath. "Well, I'm in a group session this week. We all sit around and tell each other about our rotten childhoods. I guess it's doing some good. Misery does love company, after all."

"Can I bring you anything? Books? Magazines?"

Julian sighed. "I'd kill for a glass of champagne, but I guess that's off-limits."

"I won't have you trading one vice for another," Alan scolded, but his voice was warm.

"Then just bring yourself," said Julian.

"I'll see you on Sunday."

"Until Sunday," Julian echoed. He hung up the phone and sat for several minutes staring out at the garden. Sunlight drifted through the redwoods, casting slanted beams of golden light among the clusters of magenta rhododendrons. The grass was the color of emeralds.

He was intensely aware of every nuance of sensation—the rhythm of his heartbeat, the rise and fall of his breathing, the scent of damp leaves and pine needles that drifted in through the open window. He realized with quiet gratitude how long it had been since he had felt this way. Smiling a little, he shook his head, then picked up the book and read:

> *Alkimadas, you have been true*
> *to the splendor of your race. Twice, my child, at the*
> *precinct of Kronian Zeus, only a random draw*
> *despoiled you and Polytimidas of Olympian garlands.*
> *Melesias I would liken to a dolphin*
> *in his speed through the sea's water,*
> *a man to guide the strength in a boy's hands.*

# CHAPTER

# 41

## San Francisco, California
## November 1961

From the top of Russian Hill the view was superb. Spread below like a flat blue cloth, the harbor was dotted with sailboats and wreathed with tufts of fog. The Bay Bridge stretched its arms toward Yerba Buena, while Coit Tower stood guard over the docks of the Embarcadero.

Carl got out of Jerry McClosky's VW Beetle and stood for a moment looking down Leavenworth Street toward the bay.

"It's the brown-shingled place on the left," Jerry said, extricating himself from the tiny car. "If you think the view's nice out here, wait 'til you see it from inside."

Jerry McClosky was a musician's agent. Upon arriving back from Europe, Carl had contacted him at the urging of one of the Conservatory professors. Almost at once, Jerry had come up with two offers for guest appearances, and put Carl in touch with a group of young musicians who were forming a chamber orchestra.

Later that month, Carl led the new ensemble in their first performance at a music festival in Carmel. At his hotel after the concert, he found a message from Jerry waiting for him. Would Carl be interested in staying in San Francisco as a visiting assistant conductor of the San Francisco Philharmonic? Would he ever.

Back in the City, Carl decided that at last he could afford to look for more desirable living quarters, and once again it was Jerry who came up with the solution. Another client of his, a bass player, was moving to Chicago, and his apartment would be available.

Carl's footsteps echoed on the bare wood floor. The ceiling rose twenty feet above a single spacious room, two large windows framed spectacular views of the bridges and the bay, a circular staircase led to a sleeping loft, and everywhere stark white walls set off the mellow tones of the woodwork and the polished hardwood floors.

"What do you think?" Jerry asked. "Big enough to accommodate that piano you've been wanting?"

"Plenty big."

"Solly loved it. Hated to give it up."

"I can't imagine he'll find anything like this in Chicago," said Carl.

"Chicago's okay, but it's not San Francisco," Jerry laughed.

"What's over here?"

"Kitchen and bath. And there's a patio out back."

Between the adjacent houses, a beam of sunlight slanted down, filling the patio with a warm, golden glow. "I like it, Jerry," Carl said, trying hard not to appear too excited.

Jerry grinned. "Kinda thought you might."

Carl accepted Jerry's invitation to celebrate over dinner. The restaurant was small and cozy, with white tablecloths and sturdy bentwood chairs.

"Fabulous pâté," Carl noted.

"The owner's special recipe."

"You know the owner?"

"An old friend from New York."

Carl laughed. "I can't get over it. All of you New Yorkers heading West and I've been itching to go East for the longest time."

"Why is that, Carl?"

"Obvious, isn't it? More opportunities. Better orchestras. The West is still a cultural boondock. I want to be where the action is."

"San Francisco's not a bad place to begin a career," said Jerry.

"Maybe not, but it's a far cry from the great orchestras of Europe and the East Coast."

"And which orchestras do you consider best?"

"Chicago, Cleveland, and Philadelphia in this country. In Europe, Berlin and, of course, Vienna." Carl paused and thought a moment. "I'd say that New York, Boston, and Paris would come next. And maybe London." He returned to his assault on the pâté.

Jerry smiled. "So, what did you do in Europe this past summer? Besides romancing the delectable Mrs. Chambers."

Carl took a drink of wine. "Mostly I dragged poor Lilly from one music festival to the next—Rome, Vienna, Amsterdam, Salzburg. It was wonderful. I met a lot of people. That's another reason I'd like to be on the East Coast. There's more opportunity for contact with the European music community."

"So you're ready to head East?"

"Don't get me wrong, Jerry," Carl said quickly. "I'm delighted that you got me the position here, but I don't intend to limit myself."

"My thinking exactly," agreed Jerry. "You know, Carl, a career in this business can be a very tenuous thing. Choices are crucial and timing is all-important. You're off to a fine start. Don't let your impatience get the better of you."

Carl laughed. "I see you've been assessing my flaws."

"I have to get to know your weaknesses if I'm going to help you play to your strengths," Jerry replied with a grin.

Carl lifted his glass. "To your good judgment, Jerry."

Jerry nodded. "And to your very considerable talent."

## Berkeley, California

Kate sat at the desk in the dorm room that she shared with Christy Malacchi and stared out the window at the sage- green eucalyptus trees. She'd put aside her French II text book and the thick volume of *History of the Ancient World* and opened her journal to the most recent entry,

*November 7, 1961*

*Dear Great-grandfather,"* she read, *"It's been a busy week. I went to a harpsichord concert with Chris*

*last night. It was great. Bach, Scarlotti, Corelli—all*
*wonderful. This afternoon there was a lecture on*
*'The Role of the Chorus in Greek Tragedy.' Tomorrow,*
*Chris and Donna and I are going to the City to hear*
*Seiji Ozawa conduct Mahler's Symphony No. 5. More*
*and more, I feel myself drawn toward music. I don't*
*know why. Maybe it's something Mom said about*
*trying to find out who you really are. So, who am I?*

Outside the window, students pedaled past on bikes, their backpacks
filled with the novels of J.D. Salinger, treatises on *The Way of Zen,* and
the essays of Carl Jung. Edmund Teller had lectured that afternoon
on the benefits of atomic energy, and Joan Baez sang folksongs on
the lawn by Sather Gate. Kate watched for several minutes as the
knots of students wound their way among the hibiscus bushes and
centennial firs.

The world was changing. There was an intense excitement in
the air. People looked different, more exotic. Boys wore their hair
longer. Girls wore their skirts shorter. English style was everywhere
apparent. London was the city of the sixties.

London. Kate sighed. For years, she'd hardly been aware of
the world outside the gates of Mockingbird. Now, she wanted to go
*everywhere,* experience everything. She picked up a pen.

*November 14, 1961*

*Dear Great-grandfather,*

*Christy and I were talking last night about what*
*a person can be satisfied with—how can so many*
*people be satisfied with so little? I thought I could be*
*content with a place, a home, a marriage, a family.*
*Now I'm not so sure. What is it that makes some*
*people want so much more?*

*I feel as though I'm on a one-way street, that a year ago I could have married Tommy and stayed at Mockingbird and been content with that, but I didn't do that and now there'll never be a way to go back. But being here, finding out so many new things, meeting so many new people, I now realize that I don't know who I am or what I can do. I want to try, Great-grandfather, I want to see what's possible. Maybe I can't be a concert pianist like Alex or a poet like Julian or an artist like Mom, but maybe I can do something worthwhile, make some sort of contribution. I don't want to regret my life. I'll never have a better chance to strike out in a new direction and see where it will lead . . ."*

"Hi." Christy breezed into the room and tossed her books down on the batik-patterned bedspread that she and Kate had created in an attempt to personalize the institutional beige rabbit-warren that they inhabited. Chris pulled off her raincoat and sprawled on the bed. "I'm exhausted."

"Rough class?"

"I don't see how I'll ever survive calculus," Christy groaned. "My brain's totally fried." She pulled up on her elbows and gave Kate a grin. "Maybe I just wasn't cut out for academic life."

Kate sighed and turned back to the window. "I wish I knew what it is that I'm cut out for."

"I thought you'd decided on music history?"

"I really do find it fascinating—those gorgeous nineteenth-century composers, the beautiful music they wrote, the romantic things they did. Chopin, Liszt, George Sand, Delacroix. What a wonderful, romantic era."

"Yeah," Chris said with a wry smile, "all that tuberculosis, those folks dying of syphilis . . ."

"Oh, Chris," Kate cried, "do you have to be so . . . morbid?"

"Just being realistic." She flopped over onto her stomach, cupping her face in her hands. "It wasn't all champagne and violets, you know."

"I know," Kate conceded, "it's just that everything was so . . . *passionate* then, and now it seems like it's all so . . . mundane."

"Speaking of romantic," Chris said, sitting up, "you got another letter from Tommy." She shuffled through her books. "It was in the box downstairs." She tossed the envelope to Kate, who sat staring at the familiar, careful script

"Aren't you going to open it?"

Kate set the envelope down on the desk. "Damn it," she muttered. "I don't know what to do about Tommy."

"Marry him?" Chris suggested.

Kate shook her head sadly. "I used to think that was exactly what I wanted to do. We had it all planned. I was going to finish school and he was going to finish school and then we would get a place of our own, a place like Mockingbird. Only . . ."

"Only what?"

"Only there isn't any other place like Mockingbird," Kate said. "And I don't know if that's really what I want to do anymore. I just . . . there are so many other things I want to do. I want to travel. I want to go to Europe. I want . . . I don't know, I want to do *something*."

Chris lay back down and hugged her pillow. "That's what keeps me at it," she said. "I hate being chained to a book night and day, but I sure don't want to end up like my sister—living in some crummy tract house, taking care of a couple of screaming kids with a husband who sits around watching football and drinking beer. Jesus, what a drag. Gina's put on twenty pounds and looks like an old hag. Boy, if that's what marriage does for you, count me out."

"I'm so confused," sighed Kate. "I don't know what I want anymore."

Christy glanced at her watch. "Wow. It's almost six. We'd better get to the dining hall. You ready?"

"I'm coming," Kate said, hopping up and grabbing her sweater from the back of the chair. She followed Christy out of the room, leaving Tommy's letter unopened on the desk.

# CHAPTER

# 42

## Boston, Massachusetts
## November 1961

Marian hugged her coat around her as she hurried along the sidewalk. The wind was bitterly cold, even for Boston. Its chilling fingers found every tiny crevice between coat and flesh, and she was shivering uncontrollably as she ducked into the foyer of the Beacon Hill Gallery. She stood in the entryway, rubbing her hands together, stomping her numb feet, and staring through the door into the floodlit gallery beyond.

Her first one-man show had been up for close to a month, but she still felt an odd sense of astonishment whenever she walked into the gallery and found her own work on the walls. Thirty-five drawings and paintings—portraits of her children, her friends, her parents. Works so personal, so autobiographical, that she felt that she herself had been stripped naked and hung on the walls for all to see.

She had almost backed out of having the show at the last minute, but the gallery owner had been so distressed that Marian had, grudgingly, agreed to go through with the exhibition. And here it was, her own history looking back at her from the pristine white walls, a documentary of her life presented in vibrant colors, dramatically lit to expose every nuance of gesture and expression.

"Ghosts . . ." she muttered, blowing on her freezing fingers. "That's what I told Carl, didn't I? I said I painted ghosts, and here they are—a whole god-damned gallery full of them."

"Marian, darling!" Claudia Aimes, the gallery's owner, hurried toward her with open arms. "How good to see you. But, my dear, you must be chilled to the bone. It's freezing out there today."

"It is, indeed," Marian agreed, "but I had to drop Alex off at the Conservatory, so I thought I'd stop by and see how things were going."

"Here, let me take your coat," Claudia said. "Come on back to the office. I just brewed a fresh pot of coffee."

Gratefully, Marian followed the art dealer through the gallery and into the crowded office. Paintings and prints lined the walls and cluttered the floor. Ceramic vases and pieces of metal sculpture covered the shelves and desk.

"Sit down," Claudia said, clearing a pile of drawings off the seat of a leather chair. "Do you want cream or sugar?"

"Just black."

Claudia was a striking figure—tall and lean, with red-brown hair pulled back in a tight chignon. She was always beautifully dressed—silk blouses, tweed suits, unusual pieces of jewelry. Marian felt shabby by comparison in her pea jacket, baggy wool slacks, and scuffed boots.

"Thanks," she said as she took the cup of coffee from Claudia's well-manicured hand.

The dealer sat down behind the desk and sipped coffee from a porcelain cup. "How have you been, dear?" she asked.

"Okay," Marian replied. The strong, hot coffee tasted wonderful.

"Getting any work done?" Claudia asked.

"I've started a new series of still lifes. I'd like to do some figures in interiors, but I want to work out some compositional problems first. But," she took a quick sip of coffee, "it's been pretty hectic what with pre-Christmas rush at the frame shop and Alex getting ready for a recital." She hesitated for a moment, then asked, "Anything sell yet?"

Claudia shook her head. "I'm afraid not."

Marian tried not to look disappointed, but her heart sank. The show had cost a fortune to prepare, despite the discount she got from the frame shop where she worked. She'd wanted everything to look perfect for the show and hadn't skimped on using good materials.

She'd hoped to make back at least part of her expenses. "That's too bad," she said.

"I've done my best, but my clients are reluctant to put their money into something that's so . . . different. Your work just doesn't look like anyone else's. It's so personal. Of course," she added quickly, "that's why I love it. But, it's just not the sort of thing that these clients are used to. It's funny," she sighed, "it took me forever to get them to accept abstract work, and now it's the only thing they'll buy."

Marian managed a smile. "Well," she said, "at least now nobody can say that I've never had a one-man show."

"That's right," exclaimed Claudia. "And you did get a few nice reviews. It certainly won't hurt your career."

Marian nodded. "I appreciate everything you've done for me."

Claudia leaned forward and put her cup down on the desk. "Listen, dear, I wish I could have sold everything in the show. Your work's exceptional, but I think it's just too unusual for this town. Boston's a conservative city. New ideas are slow to catch on. Frankly, I think you'd do much better in New York."

"I agree," exclaimed Marian, "but I haven't been able to get anywhere with that bunch."

"It's a tough nut to crack," agreed Claudia. "Still, it's just a question of connecting with the right dealer. I sent some of your slides around to my contacts in Manhattan, but didn't get any nibbles."

"I thought Jon Fisher might take me on," sighed Marian. "He seemed to like my work. But he said I'd have to move to Manhattan. With no money and Alex still in school, I'm just not in a position to do that right now."

"He's an excellent dealer," Claudia said, tapping her lacquered nails on the desk's smooth top, "and he's got a wonderful stable of talent. He could probably do something for you." She laughed shortly. "More than I can, goodness knows."

Marian studied the perfectly made-up face, the chic hairdo, the expensive earrings. In a way, she envied Claudia and was angry that those who traded in art seemed to be faring so much better than those who created it.

Still, she liked the woman. What was it one New York dealer had told her? "I'm the butcher, and the artist is my meat." At least with Claudia she didn't feel like a slab of bacon. "I know you've done what you can," Marian said, "and I am grateful for your help."

Claudia smiled. "More coffee?"

Marian looked at her empty cup. "No, I . . . I really should get going." She stood up and held out her hand. "Thanks, Claudia."

"Keep working, darling," Claudia said, gripping Marian's outstretched hand. "Things are bound to turn around for you eventually."

"What happens when the show's over?" Marian asked as they walked toward the door.

"Well," Claudia said, "I'll be happy to keep a few things here on consignment. I can't store too many though." She laughed and gestured toward her office. "You can see what a mess of stuff I have on hand."

Marian nodded grimly. "I'll make arrangements to pick them up the first part of next week."

"Tuesday would be good," said Claudia. "Just give me a call and let me know when to expect you."

Well, thought Marian with faint amusement as she stepped out into the cold and headed down the street, you've created a crowd of ghosts, and now you'll have to live with them.

She pictured herself as an old woman, tunneling her way through a studio piled high with stacks of unsold canvases. What the hell, she thought with bitter satisfaction, they're better company than a lot of people I can think of.

---

## San Francisco, California

Seated at a marble-topped table in the bar at the Fairmont Hotel, Carl checked his watch and stared at the wallpaper. "Lillian, my darling," he grumbled under his breath, "you are very beautiful, very sexy, very rich, very shallow, and right now," he checked, his watch again, "very late."

He toyed with his glass of chardonnay, twirling it in small, mean circles. Five minutes, he thought. Five minutes and then I'm going to order dinner and you, dear Lilly, can go without or eat alone.

For at least two full minutes, he continued to sit tapping his fingers, then he motioned to the waiter. "If my table's ready, I'd like to be seated. Apparently my companion has been detained."

"Very good, sir." The waiter bowed. "I'll see to it at once." Carl downed the last of his wine.

"Darling." He heard Lillian's voice and looked up in time to see her gliding through the doorway, her sable stole askew round her shoulder. "I am sooo sorry to keep you waiting, precious."

"I have rehearsal at eight-thirty," he reminded her curtly, "so we'll have to cut dinner short. I wish you hadn't begged to come here if you weren't planning to be on time."

"Oh, Carly," she pouted, "don't lecture me. Marcus made me go with him to a perfectly dreadful cocktail party up on Twin Peaks. You should be glad I got here at all."

"Ah. Madame has arrived just in time," the waiter beamed. "Your table is ready."

Lillian staggered slightly as she turned to follow the waiter. "Are you okay?" Carl whispered, guiding her toward the dining room.

"Of course. It's my damned shoes. The toes are too pointed."

Carl eased her into her chair.

"Waiter," she called, "don't run off. I'd like a vodka martini, please. With an onion."

Carl sat down and regarded her glumly. "You really ought to lay off that stuff."

"Well, well," she laughed, brushing the stole from her shoulder, "just look who's giving me orders. If it isn't the Boy Wonder himself."

"It doesn't take a genius to see that you don't need another drink."

"I told you not to lecture me."

"It's not improving your disposition. Or your conversation," he said.

"You didn't seem worried about making conversation last summer," she hissed, "just about making it. In Europe you couldn't get enough of me. Now I barely see you at all. You haven't called me in a week even though I told you Marcus was out of town."

"Be reasonable, will you? I had a performance to get ready for. I should be at rehearsal right now, but I wanted to see you so I—"

"Oh," Lillian exclaimed, "am I supposed to be impressed that the great maestro deigned to give me an audience?"

"Can't you understand that I have other commitments? I can't just waltz in to keep you amused every time you snap your fingers."

"Oh, you and your damned music," she snarled. "I don't want to hear about your stupid commitments. I just want you to be around when I want you."

Carl leaned back and gave her a long, appraising look. "Then I suggest, Mrs. Chambers," he said, "that you find yourself a lover who's as vacuous as you are. I don't have the time to play your kind of game." He got to his feet, carefully pushed the chair up to the table, and turned toward the door.

"Where do you think you're going?" Lillian cried.

Carl wheeled around and gave her an exasperated look. "I'm going home, Lillian. I'm going to take a bath, have a roast beef sandwich, and go to rehearsal."

In the archway between the dining room and bar he accosted the waiter. "No martinis," he said. "Take her a bowl of onion soup and a cup of coffee." He fished two twenties from his pocket and handed them to the waiter. "Then get a taxi to take her home."

"Yes, Monsieur Fitzgerald," the waiter called after him as Carl strode briskly into the cavernous Fairmont Lobby. "I will try."

# CHAPTER

# 43

## San Francisco, California
## December 1961

"Come on, Roo," Julian pleaded. "It'll be fun. You haven't been anywhere for weeks, and it's going to be such a special party."

"But I wouldn't know what to say to all those fancy people," Kate protested. "You know what a klutz I am."

"You're *not* a klutz. Besides, it's a coming-home party for me as well as a reception for the Friends of the Symphony."

"But, I don't have anything to wear."

"Alan invited you personally," Julian persisted. "Please? It would mean a lot to me."

"Dammit, Julian," she groaned. "All right, I'll be there."

"Seven-thirty on the twentieth, okay?"

"Okay."

On the night of the party, she arrived at Alan Townsend's mansion a few minutes late, dressed in a rather plain blue gown, her one pair of high-heeled shoes, and no jewelry. Timidly, she knocked on the carved wood door.

"May I take your cape, Madame?" the butler asked, deftly swirling it from her shoulders before she could respond. "This way, please. The guests are in the library."

"Katie!" Julian came toward her, champagne glass in hand. "You *did* come. I was afraid you'd changed your mind."

"Gosh," she said, gazing at him in admiration. "You look super. I've never seen you in a tux."

"And you are lovely," he exclaimed, kissing her cheek. "Come on, I want you to meet Alan. Do you want some champagne?"

The house was even grander than she had imagined—priceless oriental carpets, crystal chandeliers, marble busts, drawings by Degas, Poussin, David, Constable landscapes, jade horses prancing across a Louis XVI table. A live string quartet played works by Dvorak. Who were these people who were her brother's friends?

She immediately liked Alan Townsend's candid eyes and quiet smile. On the phone he had been so formal, but now he quickly put her at ease and escorted her on a brief tour of the downstairs rooms, pointing out a painting here, an antique there, telling her amusing anecdotes of how various pieces had come into his possession. "So there you have it," he said as they headed back to the library, "part of it at least."

"It's fantastic," Kate said. "Like a museum, only better."

"An eclectic collection, but it suits me," Alan said with a smile.

"Thanks for showing me around."

"My pleasure. Julian's fortunate to have such a charming sister." The grey eyes grew serious. "And such a supportive one. He's been though a rough time."

"I know. I really appreciate everything you've done for him."

Alan smiled. "He's very special to me. Now, can I get you anything? Some more champagne?"

"No, thank you. Please don't let me keep you from your other guests."

A number of latecomers had arrived, and Kate scanned the crowd looking for Julian. Her gaze landed instead on an incredibly good-looking dark-haired man who was standing next to the fireplace, one hand resting on the mantel. There was a presence about him that at once captured her attention. He was deep in conversation with an attractive grey-haired woman who was hanging on his every word and nodding in agreement. He seemed to radiate a charismatic aura that was irresistible. I wonder who he is? Kate thought.

"Having fun?" Julian was suddenly beside her.

"Who is *that?*" she asked.

He followed her gaze. "Over by the fireplace? Oh, that's Carl Fitzgerald. You've heard of him, haven't you?"

"The conductor?" Kate gave a little squeak of delight. "Is that really *him?*"

"You want to meet him? Come on, I'll get Alan to introduce you." Kate hung back. "I wouldn't know what to say. Besides, he's busy. I wouldn't want to interrupt."

Julian laughed. "I'm sure he wouldn't mind. He's got quite a reputation with the ladies, and you're certainly the prettiest young lady in the room."

"Oh, Julian," Kate said, blushing, "don't tease me."

"Who's teasing? Oh, by the way, have you met Maury Sheldon and his wife? Of course you haven't. Let me introduce you to them. They have the most fab collection of Impressionist paintings."

A half-dozen introductions and three glasses of champagne later, Julian was involved in a discussion with a balding, overweight journalist, and Kate, left to her own devices, made unobtrusive forays around the edges of the crowd, trying not to feel too painfully out of place among the glittering company.

The quartet was playing Mozart now, a festive, sprightly piece that she didn't recognize. She nibbled a chocolate truffle, sipped champagne, and noticed that the small gold and crystal clock on the mantel announced that it was almost nine-thirty. "I'd better go," she told her brother, catching him alone for a moment.

"So soon?" Julian exclaimed. "But the party's barely begun."

"It's a long drive back to Berkeley," Kate reminded him, "and I'm supposed to be in the dorm by eleven."

He gave her hair an affectionate little tug. "You've never liked parties very much, have you, Roo?"

"I just never know what to say to people. All that glib chatter and clever small talk. A game I never learned to play."

"Sorry you came?"

"Not at all." She squeezed his hand. "It's great to see you looking so good, Pooh. And Mr. Townsend seems awfully nice."

"I'm just so damned lucky that I met him."

She kissed his cheek. "Take care of yourself, and call me when you can."

She was on her way into the foyer when she literally collided with Carl Fitzgerald, sending half a glass of champagne down the front of his shirt. "Oh my God," she cried, grabbing a napkin and dabbing at the spot. "I'm sorry. I didn't see you. Oh, I am so sorry!"

He laughed and took the napkin from her. "No harm done," he said, giving her an appraising look that made her face go hot. "There is one problem, though."

"What?" she asked, gazing at him wide-eyed.

He gave her a dazzling smile. "It seems we're both out of champagne. May I get you a fresh glass?"

"Oh, I, no, I mean thank you. I was just leaving. I... I really have to go."

"Don't rush off on my account, Miss..." He raised a questioning eyebrow.

"McPhalan. Mary Katherine McPhalan. Kate."

"And I am Carl Fitzgerald." He held out his hand.

"Oh, yes sir, I know," she said. "I mean, everybody knows who you are."

"Not everybody," he said with a laugh. "Not *yet* anyway. Well," he prompted, "don't you shake hands?"

Blushing more deeply, she extended her hand. To her astonishment, he swept it to his lips. "I haven't seen you here before," he said, taking her arm and steering her back into the living room. "Are you new in San Francisco?"

"Not exactly," she said. "I mean, not to San Francisco, but I've never been to Mr. Townsend's home before. I'm Julian's sister," she added.

Carl nodded. "Ah. And what do you do, Miss McPhalan?"

"I go to school."

"Where?"

"Berkeley."

"What do you study?"

"Music history. That is, I'm a music-history major." Dammit, she thought, stop stammering.

"What period interests you most?"

"The nineteenth century," she said quickly. "Especially piano literature. Especially Chopin."

"A fascinating composer," Carl said with an encouraging smile.

"Oh, I love his work," she exclaimed. "What I'd really like to do is to analyze every one of his compositions and see exactly where they fit in his life. I want to know all there is to know about each of them—what he was doing when he wrote them, where he was, who he was with. Like the *Preludes,* for example. Clearly they were influenced by Bach, yet they're so different. Some of them are almost like fragments, and the way they're paired, major and relative minor? Bach would never do that. Someday, I'd love to write something about Chopin. More than just a biography—a really complete analysis of his life and work."

She stopped, embarrassed, but Carl was looking at her with such tender attentiveness that the breath caught in her throat. "I'm sorry," she faltered. "I didn't mean to rave on. I'm sure you must want to get back to your friends."

"Actually, your enthusiasm is quite refreshing," he said.

She stared at him. His eyes, she thought, were absolutely gorgeous. Deep brown shot through with golden flecks. "I really should go," she said weakly, starting once more toward the door.

"Well, Miss McPhalan," he said, "I do hope we meet again. Perhaps next time you won't have to rush off so quickly, and we can continue the conversation."

His words sent a chill of excitement racing down her spine. She tried to speak, but words wouldn't come, so she merely nodded and backed away, unable to free herself from his eyes.

Carl's companion for the evening, a pretty brunette who was assistant development director for the symphony, came through the arched doorway from the living room and took his arm. "Who was that girl you were talking to?" she asked.

"Kate McPhalan," said Carl, watching Kate as she stood at the front door bidding her host goodnight. He liked the way she moved, aware of her body without seeming self-conscious. He wondered if she was a dancer. She had a dancer's build—slender, high waist, long legs, and that hair—a red-gold cascade that fell to below her waist.

"Kind of a plain little thing," sniffed the brunette. "Except for the hair."

"I found her wonderfully unspoiled," Carl said. "And unpretentious."

"A veritable Giselle, no doubt," laughed the development director. "Come along, darling, you can dally with the peasants another time. Right now I want you to say hello to Winifred Cohen. She's been dying to meet you."

# 44

## Berkeley, California
## January 1962

Kate returned to Berkeley from Christmas vacation a day early, and set to work on a research paper for her symphonic-literature class. After spending half a day at the library, she discovered that a manuscript she needed was in the San Francisco Music Conservatory collection.

"How about interlibrary loan?" the librarian suggested.

"That's okay," Kate said. "I'm going over to the City anyway. I'll stop by the Conservatory while I'm there."

After lunching with Julian at Coe's Auberge, she spent the afternoon in the Conservatory library. Surprised to find that it was nearly six o'clock, she hurried from the reading room. But as she started down the stairs, Carl Fitzgerald appeared at the foot of the stairwell. Kate froze, one arm thrust incongruously into the sleeve of her coat.

"Well, hello, Miss McPhalan," Carl said, grinning up at her. "What are you doing here?"

As though on cue, a trumpet began to blare in the practice studio next to the stairs and Kate's response was lost in a shriek of brass.

"What?" Carl said, laughing as she came down the stairs to meet him.

"I said, 'How nice to see you.'"

"Where are you rushing off to this time?" he asked, helping her into her coat.

"Thanks. Home."

"Where's home?"

"Berkeley, remember?"

"Ah, yes. Music history. Nineteenth century, right?"
Dressed in casual slacks and a beige pullover sweater, he seemed much less intimidating than he had in evening clothes. In fact, he looked quite young. Kate smiled, pleased that he remembered. "Right."

"How about a cup of coffee," he offered.

Her heart began to pound at an alarming rate. "Well, I guess I could spare a few minutes."

"How 'bout the Cliff House?"

"Oh yes," she said, "I've always loved the Cliff House."

He gave her a boyish grin. "Me too. There's just one small problem."

"What's that?"

"No car. So I guess we'll have to take the trolley."

"I have a car," she offered quickly.

"An independent woman," he said.

She absolutely loved his eyes, which right now were twinkling with merriment, teasing her with a flirtatious glance. "Don't you drive?" she asked as they stepped through the door into the crisp, San Francisco evening.

"I never got a license."

"Really?" Kate gave him a wondering look. How on earth could anybody grow up in California and not get a driver's license? "How... weird."

Carl burst out laughing, tossing back thick, dark hair with a little jerk of his head. She absolutely loved his laugh. And his hair. "I've been called a lot of things," he said, "but I've never yet been accused of being weird."

Kate felt her face grow warm. "I only meant that it was . . . well, a little odd."

"Not for a city kid like me. I leave the driving to the transit authority."

———ooo◦❁◦ooo———

Fog covered the hills like a fleece coat and the ocean's muted roar could be heard inside the Cliff House's cozy, fire-lit dining room. Kate warmed her hands on the sides of the coffee mug and studied Carl's face as he talked.

"After that my grandfather took me to the university twice a week so I could talk to other students and have a chance to study different scores." He tilted the chair back on its hind legs like a rearing horse. Kate wondered how he managed to keep the chair at such an acute angle without falling. "So you see," he continued, "I no doubt owe my entire career to my grandfather's stubbornness."

The chair bucked forward with a jerk. Carl neatly deposited his cup on the table without spilling a drop. "But that's enough about me. Tell me how you happened to get so interested in Chopin."

"My Grandpa Philip was a musician of sorts."

"What sort of sorts?"

"A violinist."

"Oh?" Carl was studying her again with a peculiar intensity that she found unnerving. And delightful. "Tell me about him."

"There's not a lot to tell. He was an amateur musician, but he loved music. He stayed with us for awhile when I was growing up."

Carl rested his chin on his hands, his eyes devouring her face. "Go on."

"He lived in Boston until Grandma Charlotte died," Kate remembered. "Then he tried to live with us at Mockingbird, but he missed the city so much he decided to go home."

Carl tilted his head. "Mockingbird? What's Mockingbird?"

"Our ranch. It's up in the foothills on the American River near Auburn. It's where I grew up."

"Sounds great, but not for Grandpa?"

"He really missed Boston. He was a Unitarian minister, but he also tuned pianos and gave lessons, and he played the organ in movie theaters before the films had sound-tracks."

"Wow. That's cool."

"By the time he lived with us, his arthritis had gotten so bad that he couldn't play. It used to break my heart. He spent most of his time rearranging the compositions he'd written over the years."

"A composer too?"

"Waltzes, marches, that sort of thing."

"I hope you kept some of his music," Carl said.

She started to reply, but stopped as her eyes met his. There was a sadness there that puzzled her. He reached across the table and took her hand, ran his fingers across the lightly freckled skin, the short-clipped nails, the firm strong wrists. "You have good hands," he said.

"I do?"

"Yes."

He was silent for a long moment and then said abruptly, "I'd better go."

Startled, she blurted, "Why?"

"I have an appointment to get to," he said, the strange sadness still lingering in his eyes.

As she drove toward Russian Hill, he was very quiet. Neon lights dazzled the damp pavement with flickering swatches of color. She stole an occasional look at him, searching for something to say, but his silence was impenetrable.

"Turn right at the next corner," he said. "You can pull over any place along here."

She parked the car against the curb. "Well, good-night, Carl." She turned toward him. "I certainly enjoyed . . ." Her voice died before the longing in his eyes.

He leaned forward and kissed her very gently on the mouth. Her heart was beating wildly, and her throat was dry as sand.

He gathered his coat around him and started to get out of the car, then turned back to her and said, "I'd like to call you. May I?"

"Yes, of course," she managed to say.

"How do I get your number?"

"I live in Richardson Hall. They'll know how to reach me."

He looked at her for a long moment. Then he nodded almost curtly. "Good night, Miss McPhalan."

In the rearview mirror, she saw him still standing beside the curb, looking at her as she drove away.

## Eugene, Oregon

Tommy Ashida lay on his back and studied the cracks in the ceiling of his room in the men's dormitory at the University of Oregon. Sometimes the lines looked like calligraphic inscriptions, sometimes like roadways drawn on a map, sometimes like abstract sketches of animals. Today they were the bare branches of trees against a winter sky.

He turned his head and looked out the window. It was the same—black scratches of bare limbs against a pearl-grey ground. From the next room came Elvis's voice crooning, "Don't be cruel to a heart that's true. I don't want no other love . . ."

"Damn it," Tommy muttered, sitting up and glowering at the photograph that sat on the bedside table, "why don't you write?"

Kate's smiling face looked back at him like a broken promise. "You're not the only girl in the world, you know," he told the photograph. He thought about the girl who sat next to him in design class. Maybe he should ask her out. He tried to recall what she looked like. He remembered blond hair. Long. Or was it shoulder-length? And blue eyes. Maybe green.

"The hell with it." He picked up a sneaker and flung it across the room. The shoe made a satisfying thump against the wall. Elvis's voice broke off, and a moment later a bearded face peered through the half-open door.

"Hey, man, is the music bothering you? I can like turn it down if you're trying to study."

"It wasn't the music, Greg," Tommy said.

Greg's head bobbed up and down like a cork. "Hey, I can dig it. You wanna talk?"

"What's there to talk about?"

"Well, stay cool," Greg advised. He started to close the door, then paused. "Hey, Tommy, you got those drawings ready for Anderson's class?"

"They're on the desk," Tommy replied without enthusiasm.

"Mind if I take a look?"

"Help yourself."

Greg bent over the drawing board. "You sure do nice work," he commented, rubbing his nose thoughtfully. "You're going to pull another A for sure."

"I suppose."

"Hey, man, you okay?" Greg asked. "You been real freaked out ever since you got back from Christmas vacation. You and your lady have a fight?"

"What lady?"

Oblivious to the sarcasm, Greg pointed to Kate's picture. "You know, her."

Tommy studied the photograph. "Not a fight. Not exactly," he said. "It's just not like it used to be. She's . . . changed. I only got to see her for a day. Her old man still hates my guts."

"Maybe you ought to call her," Greg suggested. "Let her know how you feel."

Tommy thought for a moment. "You know, that's not a bad idea. Can I use your phone?"

"Go ahead. I'll just wait here."

"Sure you don't mind?"

"Naw, I can dig it."

"Thanks, Greg." Tommy reached the doorway in two steps.

———∘∘∘❧∘∘∘———

## Berkeley, California

Kate dashed into her dorm room to find her roommate sprawled on the batik-covered bed. "Well?" Kate asked hopefully.

Christy sat up and shook her head. "Sorry."

With a groan, Kate sank into a chair. Tossing her notebook onto the floor, she slowly unbuttoned her raincoat. "I should never have expected him to call," she muttered. "I mean, he's so much older and everything. Oh dammit, Chris. I wish I'd never met him."

Christy closed the copy of *Catcher in the Rye* and hugged her knees to her chest. "What's he like?"

"I already told you."

"Tell me again."

Kate stared glumly out the window at the grey swirls of fog. "He's fabulous," she whispered. "I've never met anybody like him. It's not just that he's sophisticated and good-looking and worldly and talented and—"

"Stop," Chris gasped, flopping back on the bed and hugging her pillow. "I can't stand it."

"But he's also . . . I don't know. There was something wistful about him. Almost sad." Kate gave her roommate a soulful look. "Does that make any sense? I can't imagine he could actually be sad. He must have thousands of beautiful women following him around, throwing themselves at him. How could he be sad?"

Chris sat up. "Maybe he feels like he had to put on a show for all those fancy socialite types. Maybe he'd just like to be himself."

"It would be kind of hard, wouldn't it? Being a celebrity, I mean. Everybody always fawning around you. It would be like constantly playing a role." She shuddered. "What a drag."

Chris rested her chin on her hands. "I'll bet he is kinda lonely. He's not really all that old, is he?"

"He seemed a lot older when I met him at Mr. Townsend's. But the other night he didn't seem nearly as unapproachable. He was almost . . . human."

"Of course he's *human*," laughed Chris. "Even fabulous, sexy, handsome, talented geniuses are human, Katie."

"I know," Kate said sheepishly. "I only meant . . . I guess I thought of him as being in a totally different world. Completely out of reach." She sighed. "Well, I guess I was right, wasn't I? He hasn't called, has he?"

"No," Chris admitted. "He hasn't called."

At that moment, Marsha Lindsey, whose room was down the hall, burst through the door, a huge grin on her face. "Telephone." she announced, beaming at Kate. "A man."

"Ohmygod," Kate whispered.

"Get going," Chris cried. "Hurry!"

Ten minutes later, a glum-faced Kate returned to her room. "Well?" Chris prompted.

Kate took off her sweater and threw it on the chair. "Tommy."

The girls sank down on the floor and for several minutes were lost in mournful contemplation.

"I know," Chris said. "Why not interview Carl for that paper on Liszt that you're writing?"

Kate hesitated. "He's probably busy. I'd be bothering him."

"Well, don't just sit here feeling sorry for yourself."

Kate stood up. "You're right. After all, I'm busy too. I'm going to the library."

## Eugene, Oregon

Greg sat down on the bed and looked around the sparsely furnished room—one narrow cot, one wooden desk with a large drawing board on top, drafting equipment laid out precisely to the side, one slightly wobbly, varnished nightstand next to the bed. On the stand was a photo of Kate, a tarnished brass lamp, a water glass with a single red rosebud and an anthology of haiku poems.

Greg picked up the book and opened it to a page marked with a slip of paper. "Today only, walking in the spring," he read, "And then no more." He looked up as the door opened. "Wasn't she there?" he asked.

"She was there." Tommy slumped down next to his friend. "It's hard to talk on the phone."

"Yeah. Like, technology is very impersonal."

"Yeah."

Greg got to his feet. "Well, buddy, gotta get off my buns and get to work on the drawings for old rabbit-ears's class tomorrow. Catch ya later."

"Thanks for letting me use your phone," Tommy said.

"Anytime, hey."

Tommy stared at Kate's smiling photograph. "You might just as well be in another galaxy," he said.

---

## Berkeley, California

Kate left the library reading room after nine and headed back to the dorm. Mist shrouded the hills, obscuring the lights of the City, turning the eucalyptus trees into towering silver ghosts. Head down, she trudged along the path, thinking of another foggy evening in San Francisco, the sound of the waves crashing against the rocks below the Cliff House, the neon patterns on the streets, the look in Carl's eyes that moment before he kissed her.

If that was all there was, then why did it happen, she wondered. What's the purpose of all this pain, these terrible, complicated feelings? God, I really thought he liked me. He was so wonderful, and now I'll never be able to forget him . . . .

She thought of Tommy, and guilt stung her like drops of acid. How could I do this to him, she thought with dismay. But now I can't stop thinking about Carl and . . . Dammit! Life is so weird. I just don't understand *anything* anymore.

Angrily, she stomped up the steps of the dorm. In the foyer, Karen Brewster looked up from behind the switchboard.

"Hi," she said. "There was a message for you. Some guy named Fitzgerald called. He said he'd call back at ten.

Hey," she called after Kate. "It's only nine-thirty, girl. What's the rush?"

# CHAPTER

# 45

## San Francisco, California
## January 1962

Carl insisted on sending a cab to pick her up. The evening was dazzlingly clear. From the window of Carl's apartment she could see all the way across the bay to the campanile on the Berkeley campus. I was there, she thought, and now I'm here. And this is a different world.

"May I take your coat?" Carl said.

"Sure. Thanks." She had decided on a simple black wool dress that left her neck and shoulders daringly bare, and she felt a little rush of warmth as Carl's eyes appraised her.

"The view's beautiful," she said, meaning the panorama outside the window.

"Indeed," he concurred, his eyes lingering on her shoulders. She could feel the color rising in her cheeks. "What can I get you to drink?" Carl asked.

"Anything. Whatever you have."

"I have quite a variety. Any favorites?"

"You choose something." She felt utterly incapable of making a decision.

Carl cocked his head to the side and appraised her with narrowed eyes. "I think," he said, "that you should have Lillet."

"Lillet?"

"A French aperitif. Golden, spicy, and guaranteed delicious."

"Sounds wonderful."

When he came back with their drinks, she was admiring the small collection of Chinese porcelains that were displayed in the

Biedermeier breakfront. "They're beautiful," she said, taking the little goblet of golden wine from his hand. "They must be very old."

"Not that old. Not in Chinese terms anyway. They're Qing Dynasty," he said.

She decided that she would have to take a course in Oriental art and find out about Qing dynasty porcelains. "How did you get interested in Oriental ceramics?" she asked.

He was wearing a dark suit and a white shirt with the collar open and was so damned gorgeous that once again she was feeling hopelessly intimidated.

He didn't answer at once but stood there studying her. Then he said, "I was planning to take you out somewhere sensational for dinner, but would you mind if we had something here instead?"

She wondered if he was disappointed with the way she looked. He seemed to read her mind. "You're so incredibly lovely. If I take you out and show you off, everyone will stare and whisper. By tomorrow morning there'll be rumors all over town. Would you be angry if I was selfish and kept you all to myself this evening?"

"Actually," said Kate, "would you be angry with me if I took off my shoes? I just bought them this afternoon and my feet are killing me."

Carl burst out laughing, and Kate immediately joined in. He stripped off his jacket and kicked off his loafers. Saluting her with his glass of wine he cried, "To comfort."

"Amen," Kate echoed.

"Let's go see what we can find in the kitchen."

They cooked pasta with a mushroom sauce and enjoyed every bite. She told him about her paper on Liszt and he told her about his studies in ethnomusicology. They discovered that they shared a passion for Vivaldi, Stendhal, fog, gardenias, broiled salmon, and blackberry cobbler.

Next, they went through Carl's record collection and played two of his Miles Davis' albums, then discovered that they had been to half a dozen of the same jazz concerts at the Senator Hotel in Sacramento. How, they wondered, could they have missed seeing each other?

Kate was astonished when Carl looked at his watch and announced that it was almost midnight. According to the dorm rules, she had to be in her room by eleven. But since she was already late, she enthusiastically agreed when Carl said, "Say, why don't we go past the Jazz Workshop and see what the MJQ is up to? They ought to be just about hitting their stride."

North Beach was aglow with lights and traffic. Silver Mercedes alongside battered VW vans inched through the crush of pedestrians. Italian motor-scooters ignored the signs and invaded the sidewalks, sending people in tuxedos and evening gowns scattering, along with beatniks dressed in black berets and fishnet stockings and tourists garbed in flowered shirts and walking shorts, looking like displaced refugees from Hawaii.

The club was crowded, filled with smoke and music. Kate hesitated when she saw the little sign: "No One Under 21 Allowed", but Carl laughed and said, "Don't worry about it. I know the owner."

She was so excited to be sitting there, sipping white wine, watching eyes swivel toward them as people recognized Carl and whispered their discovery to one another, staring openly at Kate. "You see," Carl said above the moan of the sax, "I told you we'd start a minor scandal."

"If I was over twenty-one, would it be a major scandal?" Kate asked, then mentally kicked herself for making such an inane remark. But Carl collapsed across the table in a fit of laughter as though she had said something irresistibly funny.

The trumpet-player joined them for a drink. The owner ordered champagne. It was past two when they finally made their way out into the still-crowded streets. Carl hailed a cab, opened the door for her and bowed. "*Enchanté, mademoiselle.*"

"Where to?" the driver said.

Carl looked down at Kate. "I'd love to take you home with me," he said, "but I have a feeling that might get both of us in trouble."

"I'm afraid you're right," she replied. "The Dorm Mother might send the Morality Police."

"Berkeley," he told the driver.

When she walked into her room at quarter of four, Chris sat up in bed and cried, "Jesus, Kate, where have you been? You're in all kinds of trouble!"

"Oh?" said Kate serenely.

"The Dorm Mother wants to see you. You're going to be campused for the next six months."

"Who cares?" said Kate.

## February 1962

Over the next three weeks, Kate found every excuse to go to San Francisco. She spent hours in the Music Conservatory library, and by the third time Carl Fitzgerald just *happened* to be there too, she decided it really wasn't a coincidence.

There was a small Italian bakery near the Conservatory where they began to go for coffee and a pastry after they had finished work. For hours they sat and talked about art and music and books and films, shared stories of light and darkness. Became friends.

They held hands as they walked back to the parking lot, and he would kiss her goodbye before she headed east across the bridge. Three weeks seemed like an eternity. Time had become unpredictable. When they were together, it seemed to fly past. When she was alone, the hours crept by in a gray haze. Such delicious torture.

It was the kind of early February day that could only happen in San Francisco, and Golden Gate Park was swarming with activity. Families sprawled on blankets, children raced in noisy circles, kites dipped and fluttered, fingers dangled in ponds, babies tottered through the daisies, shoes and sweaters were left behind where they had fallen, lying in the grass like discarded snake-skins.

Carl wore an anguished expression as Kate searched for a parking place along the crowded curb. "Maybe over by the windmill," she suggested. "It's not quite so warm close to the beach."

"And it seemed like such a good day for a picnic," Carl lamented. "Trouble is, everyone else thought so too."

"Wait." Carl's face brightened. "Let's try Sutro Park. Unless you know of a good cemetery."

"Cemetery?"

"Best place in the world for picnics. Excellent free reading material. And the local population is unusually well-behaved."

"I vote for the park," said Kate. "Where is it?"

"Sutro Park? Haven't you been there? It's just across from the Cliff House."

She gave him a coy look. "How fitting."

"Perfect for our three-week anniversary," he agreed.

Calla lilies lined the walks, and red and gold nasturtiums covered the hillsides. An elderly couple sat reading the Sunday paper, and at the far end of the park two small boys struggled to hoist their kite into the breeze. Otherwise the place was deserted. Carl opened the wine, while Kate pulled a loaf of bread from the wicker basket.

"Ummm," Carl sighed, lounging on the blanket. "These strawberries remind me of Vivaldi."

Kate giggled. "I've never heard it put that way before."

Carl shaded his eyes and squinted up at her. "The bread," he continued, "is Beethoven—hearty and substantial. And the grapes are Bach, of course. You can line them up and address them one at a time."

"And the wine?"

"Ah. The wine is Mahler—all depth and passion. And you, dearest angel," he grasped her wrist and pulled her gently down beside him, "you are the music of the spheres which only poets and saints can hear."

"So are you a saint or a poet?" she teased.

"When I'm with you, I'm both." His eyes held hers. "I love you, Kate," he said.

She stared at him, astonished.

He stared back. "What's wrong?"

She pressed her fingers to her mouth, trying to muffle a gasp.

He sat up. "What's the matter?"

"I . . . I don't know what . . . what you're doing," she managed to say.

"Doing? What do you mean?"

"Why . . . why are you bothering with me?"

He looked stunned. "Bothering with you?"

She tried to control her emotions, but felt totally overwhelmed. "I mean, we're just not . . . that is, you're you and I'm me and . . ."

"I think that means we're us?" he said hopefully.

"No. I mean yes, of course it does, but I've just got to know why you're doing this."

He looked so completely baffled that she had to laugh.

"What exactly is it that I'm doing?" he said.

"Do you just take girls out and give them a whirl and then toss them back where they came from," she blurted, "because if you do, I've got to know because—"

"Is that what you think?"

"I don't know what to think." she wailed. "I've never met anybody like you. You're incredible, and I'm just a student, and I . . . I love you so much I can't stand it, but I figured I was crazy to think that you . . . oh damn!"

He gathered her in his arms. "Hey," he begged. "Come on. I didn't mean to upset you."

She took a long, shaky breath. He hugged her and shook his head. "I'm as mystified as you are."

She blinked up at him. "You are?"

"This wasn't exactly in my plans. I've got so many goals. Getting involved with someone just isn't . . . logical. Always before I've had some . . . reason. I guess I always thought it was a game. You know, a challenge." He seemed suddenly shy and self-conscious. Then he moved back from her a little, gazing at her. "But I'm tired of playing games, Kate."

"Really?"

"Really." His fingers brushed through her hair. "You are so sweet, so smart and charming. I adored you the minute I saw you that night at Alan's party. You were . . . different from anyone I'd ever met. You were honest. You don't know how much that means to me." He gave her a strange little smile. "I trust you, and for me, that's very, very special." He bent and kissed her cheek.

"Oh, Carl," she cried and threw her arms around his neck. His lips met hers, and a delicious rush of warmth engulfed her, as though her blood had turned to honey and every inch of her flesh was filled with an almost unbearable sweetness. She pressed against him and whispered against his neck, "Carl, let's go home."

He sat back and held her at arm's length. "Are you sure?"

She nodded.

"You're amazing," he said.

She looked away. "But first, I should tell you something."

"What?"

She took a quick breath. "I'm not a virgin."

"That's all right," he replied gravely. "Neither am I."

"But that's different, isn't it?" she exclaimed. "I mean, I thought, I . . . I just didn't want you to be—disappointed."

Again he put his arms around her and held her close. "My dear, sweet Kate," he said, "there is nothing about you that disappoints me. Whatever happened in the past is over. For both of us. Our future has just begun."

Shafts of golden light slanted across the bed, and outside the window bamboo wind chimes played their muted song. Carl sat on the bed and watched her as she unbuttoned her blouse and tossed it aside.

"Come here," he said. She went to him and stood before him as he undid the waistband of her slacks. His hands brushed against her thighs as he slid the slacks over her hips, and she shivered and closed her eyes. "Sweet," he murmured, his breath warm on her bare stomach, "so sweet."

His hands moved over her, loosening her bra, slipping off her panties. Gently, he pulled her down beside him on the bed. She gazed at him dreamily, distantly aware of every moment of every heartbeat, every sound and scent, the soft sound of the wind chimes, the whisper of the breeze that flowed in through the open window. He began to kiss her hair, her eyelids, the curve of her neck. "I've wanted you so much," he whispered, "but I was afraid. Afraid."

"But why?" she asked, clinging to him, holding him close.

"I don't know." There was a desperation in his voice that melted her completely.

"Whatever it is," she heard herself say, "it doesn't matter."

Her breasts tingled as his tongue circled her nipples. His lips traced a path across her belly and she stirred. "Carl?" she murmured, "what . . ."

"Shhh," he whispered. "Trust me."

She felt his breath on her inner thigh, his tongue caressing her, provoking sensations she had never dreamed existed. Her fingers buried themselves in the coolness of his hair, and she moaned in wonder at the unexpectedly exquisite pleasure. She was drowning, and she didn't care— waves rising fast, faster. "Carl," she gasped, "please darling, please . . ."

She felt his weight on top of her, his hardness pushing deep within her, carrying her with him through the roar of waves that crested ever higher until they broke, spilled over the edge of the world, and ebbed into a luminous silence.

She lay still for a long time, eyes closed, floating somewhere between sleep and wakening. It seemed that time had stretched itself into a soft cocoon, and she was drifting through it, safe and warm and languorous. Carl lay beside her, his head against her shoulder. She could feel his cool hair against her cheek, and her hand rose slowly to touch the soft, dark strands. He stirred and opened his eyes and smiled at her.

"Carl?"

"Hmmm?"

"What did you mean when you said you were afraid?"

He sat up slowly and turned away from her. She waited, troubled by his silence. The room was growing dark as the twilight sky deepened, and the breeze that wafted through the open window had grown damp. She shivered violently.

He glanced around. "Cold?"

When she nodded, he gently pulled the quilt around them and put his arms around her.

"You haven't answered me," she said in a small voice.

"I know." He kissed her hair and hugged her. "I almost didn't call you."

"Why?"

"I didn't know if I was . . . ready."

Her heart began to pound. "Ready for what?"

He moved away and lay on his back, hands beneath his head, and stared up at the ceiling. "I've been involved with several women over the past few years, and they've all been dear to me, but I knew right away that you were . . . different. You're just not like the others, and—" He turned his head to look at her and touched her cheek. "I just didn't know if I was ready to . . ."

"To what?"

"To make a commitment."

"What kind of commitment?"

"I never considered sharing a future with any of them." He studied her for a minute, then sat up and switched on the light next to the bed. "Hey," he said, "are you hungry?"

She giggled. "Famished."

Grinning, he scrambled to his feet and held out his hand. "Me, too. Let's get dressed and walk down to the Wharf and get one of those shrimp cocktails, what do you say?"

"Can we get two?" she asked, jumping up.

"We'll get a dozen if you like. I'll buy you all the shrimp on the Wharf. All the shrimp in San Francisco."

# CHAPTER

# 46

## Sacramento, California
## March 1962

Jorge Morales sat on the patio, an open copy of *Newsweek* resting on his knees. Robins hopped and chirped on the lawn. Beyond a brick wall, the neighbor's almond tree was covered with white flowers.

Distracted from his reading by a butterfly, Jorge watched idly as it fluttered among the blossoms. With a sigh he looked back down at the magazine. The melancholy eyes of a small, dark-skinned child stared back at him. "*Madre,*" he grumbled, tossing the magazine aside, "I do what I can. Isn't that enough?"

"I've brought you some tea." His wife Rose emerged from the kitchen and sat a tray down next to him.

"Thank you, paloma."

She sat down on the step. "It's so pleasant out here in the garden."

"Yes. Very pleasant."

She caught his tone and glanced at him. "What's the matter, darling?"

"Nothing."

"You're brooding, aren't you? Is it about what that reporter said at the reception yesterday?"

Jorge winced at the memory. They had gone to see Carl conduct the Sacramento Symphony. What a thrill to see his son striding out onto the stage, to hear the roar of applause. Such pride had welled up in his heart. But after the concert, they had gone to a reception where the local music critic had turned to Jorge and said, "You must be very proud of your step-son, Mr. Morales."

"Always he cuts me out, Rosita," Jorge said, picking up the cup of tea. "He never lets me be a part of his life. Can a son disinherit his father? If he could, I believe Carl would do that."

"It was just a mistake," Rose protested. "I don't think Carl—"

"My presence causes him embarrassment," Jorge interrupted, shaking his head. "Next time I will stay home."

"Darling, don't say that. He doesn't mean to hurt you."

"Rosita, for years I tried to win acceptance from your papa, and never was I able to change his mind," said Jorge softly. "In his eyes I was always detestable. I could forgive him his anger because I know it was because he loved you and wanted first your happiness."

She rested her hand on his knee. "My happiness is you, Jorge."

"And mine is you, paloma," he said. "But your Papa never understood that, did he? And now when I see in Carl's eyes that same terrible disgust . . . I am sorry, Rosita, I feel such pain."

"Papa was wrong about you, Jorge. And so is Carl," she said.

"I wasn't much of a father."

"Wasn't your fault."

"No? All those years, I was never there."

"But you were working, and then the war came and—"

"Either absent or an invalid. Some father. But it's not just me, Rosita. That I could understand. But to reject his heritage?" He shook his head. "Sometimes Carl truly doesn't believe that I *am* his father." Jorge stared at the garden. "He even said so once. He was only nine or ten—just after we moved to California, remember? He stood in the kitchen in our house on V Street, and he shouted that I was not his father. Do you remember that, Rosita?"

"That was a dreadful thing to say. But he was so despondent that first year after Papa died."

"I know. But I am full of hurt that he has made such a wall between us. I don't know how to help him take it down."

"He's still young," Rose said, reaching for her husband's hand. "There's still a lot of time for him to change his mind."

A smile flickered over Jorge's face. "Ah, but he was splendid yesterday, wasn't he? Did you see the way he walked out on that stage? Did you hear how they applauded him?"

"Yes."

"I wish I knew more about his music," Jorge said. "I listen and I try to understand, but I know I miss so much. This is part of my hurt, Rosita. I have nothing that I can give him except my love. And that he does not want."

Rose turned her head to hide the hurt, but Jorge saw it anyway.

"*Madre*, what a fool I am to sit here feeling sorry for myself. Forgive me, paloma."

"Hey, Dad." Silvio bounded toward them across the lawn. "You want to play catch?"

"Sure," Jorge said. "Get your bat. We go down to the park and I pitch to you, okay?"

"Super."

Jorge got stiffly to his feet and rested his hand on Rose's hair. "You are my angel."

She smiled up at him. "Still?"

"*Siempre*. Always."

She watched him hobble across the lawn. If only—she thought, then pushed the thought aside. Regrets would change nothing. Time might change a lot.

"What a pretty house," Kate exclaimed. "So nice of your parents to ask me to come for dinner."

Carl's jaw was set at the stubborn angle that she had, in their seven weeks together, already learned to associate with his darker moods. Once again, she wondered why he was so sensitive about his family.

She had thought perhaps they were poor and that he was ashamed of them, but the charming white-brick house before her appeared anything but impoverished. She gave Carl a troubled look as they started up the walk, but he smiled tightly and took her hand. "A necessary ritual," he commented.

"Carlo! Carlo!" Allison, Carl's little sister, dashed out of the house, and Carl scooped her up. Skinny arms and legs flailed as Carl swung her around and set her giggling on the lawn. "More," she demanded, holding up her arms. He picked her up again, and she nestled against him, eyeing Kate curiously. "Is that your girlfriend?"

"This is Kate McPhalan," he said. "And this, Katie, my love, is Allison Elena."

"Hi," Kate offered.

Ali studied her for a moment, then twisted away and grabbed Carl's hair with both her hands. "Are you going to marry her?" she asked with a pout.

"You never know."

"Well, then," sighed Ali, "I'll try to be nice to her."

"I knew I could count on you," Carl said, setting her down.

"My big brother's great, don't you think?" Ali said to Kate.

"I certainly do."

"Do you think he's a genius?"

"I've heard people say so."

"I think," Ali stated, "that he's every bit as good as Leo Bernstein."

"That's Leonard Bernstein," Carl corrected.

"I know, but all that hair makes him look like a lion, so I call him Leo."

Kate and Carl laughed.

"Come on," Ali said, taking Kate's hand, "I'm sure you'll want to meet the rest of the family."

The dinner was delicious. Both Rose and Jorge were relaxed and charming, and even Carl seemed to become less moody as the evening progressed.

"What beautiful china," Kate said, running her fingers along the edge of the white and gold porcelain.

"My great-grandmother brought it with her when she left Ireland in 1850," Rose explained. "Then my mother hauled it along when she moved to Arizona just before World War I. You might say it's covered a lot of territory. Carl's Grandma Eleanor loved it and used it all the time, but I'll admit, with three kids around the house, I save it for special occasions."

"I'm not going to have any china," Ali announced.

"What will you eat on?" asked Kate.

"Plastic plates and chopsticks. That way there's nothing to break."

"Very sensible."

"Of course, I'm not going to get married," Ali continued.

"No?"

"It's old-fashioned. I'm going to have my own house, and no one can come in unless I say so. I'll send out invitations to exciting men when I feel like having an affair."

"Ali," Rose scolded, "what a way to talk. What will Kate think?"

"You couldn't get anybody to have an affair with you," Silvio offered. "You're too skinny and ugly."

Ali stuck out her tongue at him. "At least I'm not a blubber-lump like you."

"Skinny-minnie, skinny-minnie," taunted Silvio.

"Stop that," Rose cried. "Behave yourselves."

"Come on, Sil," Carl offered. "Why don't we go up to your room? You can show me that science project you're working on."

"And Allison is going to help me with the dishes," Jorge said, getting to his feet.

"Can I help?" Kate started to get up.

"I wouldn't hear of it. You and Rosita have a chat—woman to woman, eh? Come on, Ali."

"I'm a woman too," Ali protested.

"But you are a *little* woman still. And besides, I need your help."

Rose shook her head, smiling. "It's the bane of Silvio's existence that he has a little sister who's always tagging after him. It was different when Carl was home. He was always the peacemaker."

"Maybe he learned it from his father," Kate noted.

"Jorge and Carl are alike in so many ways."

Kate caught the sadness in Rose's voice and hesitated, then said,

"I suppose it's none of my business, Rose, but why does Carl use the name Fitzgerald?"

Rose put down her cup and gave Kate a small, sad smile. "It's a long story. You see, when Jorge and I were first married, we were very poor. He was working in a cannery in Tucson, and I hadn't even finished high school. A couple of months before Carl was born, Jorge was offered a job working on an oil rig in Texas. He hated to go, but the money was good and my parents had room for me and the baby, so we decided that he should take the job. We thought we'd be able to save enough to buy a little place of our own in a year or so.

Then the war came, and Jorge enlisted in the Marines and went off to the South Pacific. It was two years before he came home, and when he did, he spent most of that first year in the V.A. hospital in Oakland. I ended up splitting my time between Tucson and California while my parents took care of Carl. He was almost six by that time. He didn't even remember his father."

"He talks a lot about his grandfather," Kate said. "I guess they were very close."

"Dad adored Carl," Rose said. "Especially when he discovered how talented he was. He gave him lessons, encouraged him. And Carl idolized his grandfather. They spent all their time together." Rose shook her head. "Unfortunately, Dad never approved of my marriage. He had many fine qualities, but he also had his prejudices."

Kate nodded. "My dad's like that."

"Prejudice is such a dreadful thing. I always thought that with time Dad would see what a wonderful man Jorge was. But I was wrong. And I never thought about the fact that Carl and his father had been pushed worlds apart. I knew that it was good in terms of the music. Dad took Carl to concerts, introduced him to musicians. It's easy to look back and say, 'How could I let this happen?' But at the time . . ." She paused and gave a little sigh.

"Jorge had been in California before he shipped out, and he loved it, so after he got out of the hospital, we decided to move to Sacramento. At first, we stayed with his cousin and tried to save up some money. Anyway, it all changed when Carl was nine. His grandparents were killed in an auto accident, and we decided to sell their house and use the money to buy a little cafe. That was the beginning of Casa Morales."

Rose picked up her cup and toyed with it. "But poor Carl. His whole world had collapsed. There he was, living in a strange house in a new town with parents he barely knew. He was desperately unhappy. Jorge tried to help him, to break down the barrier that had grown up between them, but it was as though Carl blamed him for what had happened." She fell silent.

"Thank you, Rose," said Kate, "for telling me."

Rose smiled. "Well, families all have their problems, don't they?"

Later, as Kate and Carl prepared to leave, Jorge turned to Kate and said, "You must be taking good care of him. He looks very happy."

"I'm trying."

"You know," said Jorge, "you remind me of Rose when she was your age."

"Do I?"

"She is a woman of much grace, my Rosita. She has a mantle of courage about her. You have this, too. Like a light about your face."

"Thank you," Kate said, blushing.

"Ready?" Carl put his arm around Kate's shoulder. She looked up at him and noticed that his eyes were exactly the same color as his father's.

"Ali. Silvio," Rose was calling. "Carl's leaving. Come say goodbye."

Ali came running and jumped into Carl's arms. "Bye, big brother."

"Bye, little sister."

"When can I come and visit you?"

"Soon."

"Promise?"

"Of course."

"Will you take me to one of your concerts?" she demanded, hugging him.

"I'd be honored."

Ali held out her arms to Kate. "I'll hug you too, please."

Kate gave the child a tight squeeze. "You're my big sister now," Ali said. "I'm adopting you."

"Why, thank you," Kate said as everyone laughed.

"That makes you an official member of the family," Rose told her.

"Adios," Jorge called after them. As Kate eased the car away from the curb, she looked back in the rear view mirror and waved to him.

# CHAPTER

# 47

## Near Sonoma, California
## April 1962

The next day Kate drove along a highway northwest of Sonoma. The fields alongside the road were filled with a springtime bounty of yellow daisies and deep-blue lupine. Forests of redwoods stood like the pillars of some great cathedral, their topmost branches holding up the sky.

"Your mother's a wonderful cook," Kate was saying. "That chocolate cake was delicious. My mom never cared much for cooking, but our housekeeper used to bake the most marvelous goodies for us. She was Japanese, but she made the best peach pie in the world." I'm talking too much, she thought uneasily, and Carl's so quiet.

"Let's get some lunch," he said. "All of this food talk is making me hungry."

"But we're out in the middle of nowhere," Kate protested.

"I remember a little cafe at a vineyard somewhere near here. Let's stop in the next town and get directions. Maybe we can find it."

They stopped at a gas station in the village of Forrestville and got directions to the Russian River Winery.

Then drove through apple orchards, sage-green leaves rippling in the breeze. "We must be getting close." Carl sat up straighter. "There's the sign. Turn left."

The car bucked to a stop, and Kate turned into a gravel driveway. Vineyards lined the road, new fruit already visible hanging in thick clusters between the emerald leaves. "Oh," Kate exclaimed as a charming old stone structure nestled beneath giant oak trees came into view, "how pretty."

"I thought you might like it," Carl said with a grin.

A plump blond girl wearing a blue-and-white apron led them to a table beneath an arbor of wisteria. Kate studied the menu. When she glanced up, she found Carl watching her with somber eyes. "Aren't you going to order?" she asked.

"I know what I want. The poached salmon is terrific."

She closed the menu. "Me too then."

Lunch was delicious, but Kate could scarcely eat. She was painfully aware of Carl's eyes constantly upon her. "Is something wrong?" she finally asked. "You keep staring at me."

He didn't answer for a minute, and when he did his face was very solemn. "We've had a wonderful time these past two months," he said. "But I think we need to talk about the future."

Her stomach knotted. Here it comes, she thought. He's going to dump me.

He reached across the table and took her hand. "I believe I have a great career ahead of me, but it won't be easy," he said. "I have a very strong commitment to my work. I think you know that. The music comes first, before anything else. I'd be misleading you if I told you otherwise."

"I understand," she said in a small voice.

"I don't expect to have a conventional life," he continued earnestly. "I think you can understand that too."

She nodded.

He paused for a moment, staring at her and biting his lower lip. "I want to be fair, Kate. I care for you very much, and I don't want to give you any false expectations. What I'm trying to say, not very well I'm afraid, is . . . Well, I just . . . I don't know quite how to say this." His hands tightened around hers.

"I know what you're going to say."

"You do?" He looked relieved. "Well, then will you?"

She blinked. "Will I what?"

"Marry me?" he said weakly.

"Marry you?" She snatched her hands from his, knocking over

her coffee cup. Half its contents splashed into her lap, and the rest flooded the remnants of her dinner. "Oh God!" she wailed.

A waitress rushed forward with a towel. Carl mopped with a napkin. Kate daubed at her dress, not knowing whether to laugh or cry and doing some of each. When the frenzy subsided, they looked at each other across the soggy table.

"You didn't answer me," he said. "Perhaps you forgot the question?"

She pressed both hands to her face. "Oh God, you're serious, aren't you?"

"Of course I'm serious."

"Oh, yes," she breathed. "I'd love to marry you, Carl Fitzgerald."

## Eugene, Oregon

Over spring break, Tommy had moved to a small apartment two blocks away from the UO campus. Today, he had volunteered to clean up his landlady's overgrown garden, and Mrs. Johnson was delighted. "Such a nice Oriental boy," she told her neighbor across the street. "So quiet and polite. They bring up their children so well, those Orientals. You'd think we Americans could do the same."

Panda, Mrs. Johnson's black-and-white cat, inspected Tommy's efforts, blinking down at him from the tool house window ledge, distracted occasionally by the gold and black butterflies that circled among the apple blossoms. When one butterfly strayed too close, Panda twisted into the air and made a grab for the fluttering wings. Having missed, the cat sat down and began to bathe. Tommy sat back on his heels and laughed. "I saw that," he chided. "Can't admit you blew it, can you?"

The cat answered with a blink and a mew.

"Tommy?" Mrs. Johnson eased her plump bulk gingerly down the back steps. "Oh my." She paused to look around. "This looks so much better."

"Thank you, Mrs. Johnson."

"Here." She pulled an envelope from her apron pocket. "This came for you in the morning mail."

Tommy's heart skipped a beat when he saw the return address. "Thanks, Mrs. Johnson!" he exclaimed.

Her eyes twinkled. "I thought you might want to see it right away." She glanced around again. "Well, keep up the good work."

"Yes, Ma'am." Tommy set the letter down and wiped his hands on his jeans, smiling when he noticed that the stamp was upside down. Dear, sweet, funny Kate. He tore open the envelope, pulled out the letter and read:

*Dearest Tommy,*

*This is a really difficult letter for me to write. So many things have happened the last four months that I don't know where to begin.*

He scanned the two pages with mounting desperation. *Please write and tell me that you understand. With every loving wish, Kate.*

Tommy read the letter a second time. Then, with great care, he folded the piece of paper, put it back in the envelope, and sat holding it in his lap.

He looked around the garden. The sky was still blue. Sunlight still sparkled on the grass. A blue jay lit on a branch and hopped back and forth, screeching raucously. A few pink petals floated downward and settled on the lawn.

Everything looked the same, yet it was as if each particle had been emptied of its contents, sucked dry and left as a husk that had only the appearance of reality. The substance had disappeared. There was no light, no color, and no sound. The world had become a ghost of itself.

After a long time, Tommy got to his feet, walked up the steps to the back door, and quietly entered the house.

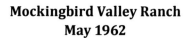

## Mockingbird Valley Ranch
### May 1962

"Living together," Owen roared. "What the hell do you mean you're living together?"

Kate's chin tilted defiantly. "Exactly what I said. Carl asked me to move in with him, and I said yes."

Owen's face had turned crimson. "Well you can just move right out. I'm not going to have my daughter living in sin with some . . . some half-breed musician."

"Daddy, he's a symphony conductor!" Kate cried. "He's a . . . a *celebrity*. How *dare* you call him a half-breed!"

"First a Jap and now a wetback," Owen growled. "Where the hell is your sense of propriety?"

"You narrow-minded bigot. You have no right to talk about Carl that way!"

"I am *not* a bigot," Owen retorted. "I don't know how you can say that, Mary Katherine. Look at the way I took care of the Ashidas all those years, giving them a job when nobody else would hire them. And look what I've done for Jaime and Consuelo. Why, if it weren't for me, they'd still be over in Davis picking tomatoes."

Kate glared at her father. "How liberal of you," she sneered. "You don't mind letting minorities slave for you, just so long as they don't start getting the idea that they're real people, right, Dad?"

Owen sucked in his breath.

Kate stood her ground, hands on hips.

"You just don't understand about these things, Mary Katherine," he said. "There's good reason not to go mixing blood, begetting mongrels. You don't see horses breeding with cattle, do you?"

"Oh God," she cried, "of all the demented—"

"All right, all right." Owen grimaced and rubbed his nose. "Just simmer down."

"I'm sorry I asked Carl to come here," Kate said. "I'm sorry I asked him to meet you at all. Obviously, it's beyond your capabilities to be civil!" Folding her arms, she turned away and stood, chin up, staring out the window.

Owen sighed audibly.

Kate whirled around. "And don't you dare say anything to Carl about Mexicans. I should never have told you about his family."

"I suppose he's Catholic."

"If he is, he hasn't mentioned it to me. We're going to write our own ceremony and be married in the garden. With or without your permission."

"You may be almost twenty, young lady, but I'm still the boss around here, so don't you go telling—" He halted as Consuelo appeared at the door.

"Telephone, Mr. McPhalan. A Mr. Wheatland calling from Los Angeles."

"We'll continue this discussion later," Owen growled over his shoulder as he stomped away. Kate collapsed on the sofa.

"He only wants you to be happy," Consuelo said.

"But Carl is what makes me happy. Why can't he see that?"

"Fathers are all the same. Never is there a man good enough for their daughter."

"But I can't bear for him to talk about Carl that way." Kate grabbed a sofa cushion and crushed it to her.

"Just give him time to get used to the idea. He'll come around."

Kate blinked. "Consuelo, what time is it?"

"Three-thirty."

"*Three-thirty*? I've got to take a bath and wash my hair!" Tossing the cushion aside, Kate jumped to her feet.

Consuelo looked after her. "Goodness yes," she said shaking her head, "only two hours until Jamie goes to pick up your young man at the station. Only two hours to make yourself beautiful."

A basket of bread in one hand and a plate of ripe tomatoes in the other, Kate peeked through the screen door at the two figures seated on the terrace. They had been in that same position for over an hour, face to face across the patio table, poised as intently as two chess players. "I wish I could hear what they're saying," Kate said.

Consuelo looked amused. "I don't think they're doing much talking."

"They were talking a lot at first. About baseball, of all things." Kate shook her head in wonder. "I had no idea that Carl knew so much about baseball."

"Well," said Consuelo, glancing out the door, "it looks to me like right now they've gotten down to a serious drinking match. Your father's been pouring bourbon, and I haven't seen your young man turn down a drink yet."

Kate groaned. "Men are so weird. Why do they have to turn everything into a competition?"

"It's just their way."

"Trying to drink each other under the table," Kate muttered, "of all the silly, pointless . . ." She put the food down on the table and threw up her hands in exasperation. "I'd better go and tell them dinner's ready before they both pass out." Crossing the sunny patio, she paused beside the table and said, "Dinner's ready. Are you two ready to come in?"

Carl looked up at her with a lazy smile, his face slightly flushed, tie loosened. "Sure," he said, taking hold of her hand. He got up a bit unsteadily. "After you, sir," he said, giving Owen a formal nod.

Owen got to his feet and picked up his highball glass. Without blinking, he gulped the rest of the drink and put the glass down hard on the table.

Carl, his eyes intent on Owen's face, picked up his own glass.

"Salud," he said, and raising his glass, he downed the rest of the bourbon in a single gulp.

Owen pursed his lips. "Let's eat."

Kate followed them both into the house, shaking her head.

Owen opened a bottle of red wine and made a ceremony of pouring each of them a glass. Despite Kate's anxiety, the dinner conversation was mellow. The salad plates came and went, and Consuelo brought in a steaming earthenware bowl of her excellent rabbit stew. "More wine, my boy?" Owen asked jovially.

"Of course," said Carl.

Owen stood up and reached across the table to pour the wine, but nothing came from the bottle. His eyes narrowed in dismay.

Carl cleared his throat. "It might be easier, sir," he said, "if you first removed the cork."

Owen looked at Carl, then at the cork that was still in the neck of the bottle and began to laugh.

Kate also began to giggle, and Carl, though he tried not to, soon joined in. Owen sat back down and wiped his eyes with his napkin. "Good point, my boy," he managed to say between fits of laughter.

After dinner, as the hills turned purple in the distance and the cool mist rose from the canyon, they took a walk around the ranch, Owen pointing out the various buildings, answering Carl's questions about the fruit-growing operation with obvious enthusiasm. Later, there was coffee beside the fire and some of Consuelo's wonderful orange and almond cake.

"Well," said Owen with a yawn, "I reckon it's about time for me to turn in."

"Sounds good to me," said Carl as he got to his feet. "Sir," he held out his hand to Owen, "it's been a delightful evening. I'm looking forward to seeing some more of the ranch tomorrow."

"We're proud of our little spread," Owen beamed as he gave Carl's hand a shake. "Nice to have you with us, my boy."

"Goodnight, darling," Kate said, kissing Carl's cheek. "Consuelo will show you to your room. Your bag is already there."

"Then I'll see you both in the morning," Carl said, smiling his most dazzling smile.

When Carl was half-way down the hall, Kate turned eagerly to her father. "So, what do you think?"

Owen rubbed his chin. "Well, he seems fairly sensible."

"Yes?"

"Seems to have pretty good prospects."

"Yes?"

"Holds his liquor pretty well."

"Yes?"

"I suppose you could have done worse."

Kate tried to go to sleep, but she was too excited. After an hour, she got up, opened her bedroom door, threw a blanket around her shoulders, and stepped out into the courtyard.

"Hello," came a soft voice.

"Carl?" she whispered. "Is that you?"

He was sitting beneath the oak tree, shirt open, feet bare. Joey, the German shepherd, lay beside him, resting his great wolfish head on his paws. "I couldn't sleep," Carl said.

She sat down beside him. "Me neither." Together they looked up at the star-splashed sky. Joey whined a muted greeting. His tail thumped softly against the tiles.

"It's so quiet here," Carl said.

"It's always beautiful at night."

"It must have been a great place to grow up."

"The best."

He rested his head against the trunk and looked up into the branches. "What a beautiful tree."

"It's really two trees," she told him, "an oak and a fig. Daddy calls them the Old Man and His Lady."

"How'd they grow like that, all twined together?"

"Nobody knows. Dad says Great-grandpa planted them. They're

like the guardians of the house." She leaned against him and rested her head on his shoulder.

Carl drew her close and kissed her, slipping his hand beneath the blanket to stroke her bare shoulder. "Say," he whispered, "do you suppose maybe we could go to your room and look at some etchings or something?"

She giggled. "No etchings, but there might be a few watercolors up there."

"Maybe we shouldn't," he said, raising his eyebrows. "Now that I've met him, I really wouldn't want to duke it out with your dad."

"He already knows that I'm living with you. I don't expect he thinks we have separate bedrooms."

"Well—" said Carl.

"Come on," she said. Joey followed them into the house and curled up on his rug inside the kitchen door. Carl and Kate carefully made their way up the stairs.

She lay down on the bed and watched him as he unbuttoned his shirt and started to slip it off. His smile was soft. Then he glanced at the dresser and the smile froze on his lips.

Kate sat up. "What is it?"

He was staring at a photograph of Marian. "Who is that?"

She looked at the photograph. "My mother."

Carl spun around. "Your mother?" His face had gone white.

"Yes," she said. "What's the matter? You look like you've seen a ghost."

He looked again at the photograph. "What's her name?"

"Marian."

"You didn't tell me you—" He swallowed hard.

"That I had a mother?"

He stared mutely at the photo.

"Carl, what on earth is the matter?" Kate got up and started to take his arm, but he pulled away.

"Nothing."

"I told you that Mom and Dad were separated. She and my sister live in Boston."

"Oh," he said in a small voice.

"What is it, darling? What's wrong?"

"Nothing. She . . . she reminds me of someone, that's all."

Kate looked at the photo. "Oh?"

Carl swallowed. "She's quite . . . beautiful."

"Yes, she is." Kate took his hand. "Come on," she said softly. "I believe we were interrupted."

He sat down on the edge of the bed, but responded only half-heartedly to her kiss. "Are you all right?" she asked.

"I don't know. I feel sort of light-headed. Maybe it was the wine."

"Or the bourbon," she offered. "You're not ill, are you?"

"I don't think so."

"You're really pale."

"Maybe I'm just tired." He looked contrite. "Would you be angry if I went back to my room?"

"This was your idea, remember?" she said with a pout.

"I'm suddenly so damn tired."

"Fine," she snapped. "And I've just developed a dreadful headache."

He reached for her hand, but this time she pulled away. "I'm sorry," he repeated.

"She must have been somebody very special," said Kate angrily.

"Who?"

"Whoever it was my mother reminded you of."

Carl was silent for a minute, then said, "Yes, she was."

"Just leave," cried Kate. "You can go to bed with your memories."

She turned her back to him, and after a minute the door opened, then closed. Hugging the pillow tight, she cried herself to sleep.

His touch awakened her. The moon cast a silver curtain across the bed. She sat up and threw her arms around him. "I'm sorry."

"Don't say a thing," he whispered. "I love you. Only you."

She tried to say, "I love you too," but his mouth covered hers. Shaken by the urgency of his desire, she clung to him in the darkness.

At length they slept. When she woke he was gone. He left a note telling her that he had gotten a ride to town with Jamie, that he loved her, that urgent business had come up in San Francisco, and that he would call her very soon. Puzzled, she sat down on the bed and stared at the photograph of her mother.

# CHAPTER

# 48

## Boston, Massachusetts

"Marian?"

"Who is this?" The voice sounded familiar, but she couldn't quite place it.

"It's Carl."

Marian sat down on the edge of the bed. "Carl?" There was silence. "Carl?"

"God," he said. "I don't know where to start."

"What's wrong? Are you in trouble?"

"You might say that."

"Where are you?"

"Here. Home. San Francisco."

"I haven't heard a word from you in almost a year," she said. "I was wondering how you were."

"I'm in love."

Marian smiled. "I thought it might be something like that. Congratulations."

"You don't understand."

"It can't be all that bad. What's the problem?"

"I've met the most wonderful woman, and I adore her, and we're going to be married, and oh God, Marian, she's your *daughter*."

Marian blinked. "My daughter?"

"Kate."

"Kate?"

"Yes, Kate!"

She was speechless for a moment, then slowly she said, "How on earth did you meet her?"

"We were at a party in San Francisco. And then the next day she was at the Conservatory and then—oh I can't explain it all. But hasn't she told you about me?"

"In her last letter, she told me she was seeing someone, but she didn't give me any details. Just that she'd met someone special, but she didn't know where it was leading. I was going to call her. When did all of this happen?"

"Recently. The last couple of weeks."

"I see."

"I had no idea she was your daughter."

She laughed self-consciously. "I'm sure you didn't."

"I don't know what to do."

"What is there to do?" she said, trying to maintain her composure.

"Does she know about you and me? No, I mean, obviously she doesn't, but what should we do? I mean, should we tell her that we— Jesus, Marian. Tell me what to do."

"Do whatever you like."

"When I saw your photograph in her room . . ." There was another long pause. "I'm frightened, Marian. I don't want to lose her."

"What makes you think you'd lose her?"

"But what can I tell her?" His voice was desperate. "I mean, I can't just say, 'Look, Kate, your mom and I were lovers,' can I?"

"You could."

"What do you think she'd do?"

Marian picked up a pencil and began to tap it on the side table. "I don't know. She might find it amusing. But then, perhaps she wouldn't see it that way. I really don't know, Carl."

"I can't take a chance. She mustn't ever know."

"I think that's a mistake," Marian said. "It's never good to keep a secret like that. Maybe I should talk to her, try to explain—"

"But she doesn't have to know! Don't you see? I was afraid that she'd already talked to you. Why should we upset her over something that happened years ago?"

There was considerable sadness in Marian's smile. "Yes," she said, "years ago."

"I didn't mean—"

"I know you didn't. Listen, if that's what you really want, then I won't tell her. It's up to you, Carl. I don't want to cause you any trouble."

"What about Alex?"

Marian frowned. "I'll talk to Alex."

"Thank you." His relief was palpable.

"But please think about it and call me back if you change your mind."

"I'm sorry. This has me so confused. It was dreadful of me to call you. I just . . . I feel like a fool."

"Of course you had to call me," she said soothingly. "I'm glad that you did. We need to work this out somehow."

"The world is such a strange place, isn't it, Marian?"

"Yes, it is."

"You know, I was right about one thing, though."

"What?"

"I said that I'd see you again, remember?"

She gave a little chuckle. "Well, I can't think of anyone I'd rather have for a son-in-law."

"There is," he said, "something about this that I'll never figure out."

After she'd hung up, Marian sat for a long time staring at the portrait of Carl that hung on her bedroom wall. Somewhere in some very deep place inside she felt a sense of dread spreading like liquid ice. She squeezed her eyes shut and took a deep, shaky breath. Then she got up and made her way down stairs. "Alex?" she called. "Honey, I have to talk to you."

## San Francisco, California
## July 1962

Jerry McClosky hefted his considerable bulk forward on the sofa and took a drink of Chablis, eyeing Carl over the rim of his glass. "So tell me," he said in his booming voice, "how did it go in Edinburgh?"

Carl spun around on the piano stool. "Okay."

Jerry laughed. "You don't have to be so modest, Carl. I heard that you were the hit of the entire festival."

Carl looked pleased and said nothing.

"So, was I right?" Jerry continued.

"Yes, you were right. The climate for contemporary music is much more favorable in Europe. Of course, it didn't hurt that they had decided on a Russian theme for the festival." Carl shrugged. "But I should have listened to you about Atlanta."

"Hmpf," Jerry grunted. "Next time, take my advice."

Kate made her way past the Steinway and set a plate of stuffed mushrooms down on the coffee table. "Careful, Jerry. They're hot."

"Ummm." Jerry took a bite. "Delicious." He wiped his mouth and winked at Kate. "Now, then," he said, "let me tell you about something else that's come up. I got a call last night from Venice. They're pulling together the last of the program for the festival next April." He paused and mopped his forehead with the crumpled napkin. "They heard about the Shostakovich you did in Edinburgh and wondered if you'd be interested in doing something similar in Venice."

"Venice?" Carl exclaimed. "Of course I'd be interested."

"I thought you'd feel that way. Here's what I have in mind. The LA orchestra's scheduled to appear, but their new music director has some prior commitment and can't be in Venice that week. Since you've worked with LA recently, I've suggested that you fill in as guest conductor."

"What's the program?" Carl asked eagerly.

"They planned to do the Stravinsky *Symphony in Three Movements*, and I'm not sure what else."

"The Stravinsky will be fine." Carl looked thoughtful. "I'd like to do some Bartok. Maybe the *Concerto for Orchestra*. Or, no, what about the *Second Piano Concerto*? Could we line up a soloist, Jerry?"

"If you're going to do Bartok, I'll tell you who I'd like to get," Jerry replied, sitting forward. "Stefan Molnar."

Carl's eyes widened. "Do you think he'd do it on such short notice?"

"He's just cancelled a tour in South America, some flack over the contract, so he might be available. It wouldn't hurt to ask. Besides, he likes doing Bartok. He *is* Hungarian, after all."

"I thought he was Czech," Kate said.

"Mother Czech, father Hungarian," Jerry said. "He left Prague in '48 and moved to Geneva. Seems his father was a great supporter of the anti-Russian forces. He turned up dead a few weeks after Stefan and his mother and brother got out. All very traumatic for a fourteen-year-old kid."

"I would think so," said Carl.

"Have either of you met Molnar?" Jerry asked.

"I haven't," Kate said, "but I have some of his recordings."

"He was at Tanglewood the summer I was there," said Carl, "but I barely met him. I've seen him perform a couple of times. What's he like to work with?"

"Oh," laughed Jerry, "he has a reputation—moody, difficult, temperamental. I think he enjoys the image, but you don't play a concert schedule like his year in and year out if you're not extremely disciplined. He keeps his professional commitments, whatever his personal problems may be."

"He looks like Manolete," said Kate.

"Who's that?" Jerry asked, popping another mushroom into his mouth.

"Jesus, Jerry," Kate chided, "The bullfighter. You know, *Death in the Afternoon*?"

"Unpardonable barbarism. I'm a member of the SPCA."

"Haven't you ever read Hemingway?"

"Who?" Jerry asked, then laughed and ducked as Kate pelted him with her napkin.

"If you children don't mind," Carl said, raising an eyebrow, "I'd like to get back to business. So when are you going to call Molnar?"

Jerry held up his hands. "Take it easy, will you? I'll give Rube a call next week."

While Kate was busy in the kitchen putting the finishing touches on dinner, Jerry finished his Chablis and said to Carl, "By the way, I've been meaning to ask you about your selective-service status."

Something in his tone made Carl look up from the review of the Edinburgh Festival that he was reading. "Selective service? Gosh, I don't know. I had a student deferment. I haven't really thought about it. Why?"

"How long has it been since you heard from your draft board?"

Carl shrugged. "I don't know. Quite awhile."

Jerry tugged at his tie. "You're what, twenty-four?"

"Twenty-three."

"Ever go in for a physical?"

"Once, about five years ago. I filled out a bunch of papers, they sent me a 2-S card, and that's the last I heard from them."

"Well," said Jerry, "let's just keep it that way." He sat forward and poured himself another glass of wine. "After all, we can't have you conducting the Army Band, now can we?"

"I certainly hope not," Carl said.

"Don't worry about it," Jerry said. "Salud." He smiled as he hoisted his glass.

# CHAPTER

# 49

## San Francisco, California
## August 1962

Julian hopped off the cable car at the corner of Hyde and California and looked up the street at the house he had begun to think of as home. The fog that usually swept in through the Golden Gate to keep the city cool still lay far out to sea, and afternoon temperatures had climbed well into the eighties.

He took off his sport coat and slung it over his shoulder. The scent of roses was pungent as he opened the gate and bolted up the front steps. Remembering with a flash of irritation that he'd forgotten his key, he rang the bell and waited impatiently. Reade Wilkes, Alan's butler, greeted Julian with his usual mild civilities.

"Where's Alan?" Julian asked, tossing his coat on the hall tree.

"In the study." Wilkes watched as Julian peered into the oval mirror to straighten his tie. "Will you and Mr. Townsend be dining at home this evening?"

"I don't think so. Alan said something about going to the opera."

"Very good, sir."

"Julian? Back so soon?"

Julian spun around at the sound of Alan's voice. "I got in! I just talked to the dean and they're letting me in on provisional status starting in January. Isn't that fantastic?" he cried as he bounded up the stairs.

"Congratulations. I knew you could do it."

"Not by myself. I owe everything to you, Alan."

"I provided some encouragement, but you did the hard part." Alan gestured toward his study. "Come in and tell me all about it."

Julian perched on the window seat. "The dean had read a few of the poems I sent him. He said I was very talented."

"I'm not surprised. I've been telling you how good they are."

"I know, but I didn't think anyone else would think so."

"Doubting my critical ability, are you?" Alan said with a laugh.

"Of course not. But, it was nice to hear it from someone who has no . . . vested interest."

"Ummm. Well, wonderful that you'll be starting college in January."

"I applied for a loan," Julian said. "And I might be able to get a job in the bookstore. Then I can start paying you back what I owe you."

"You don't owe me a thing."

"Yes, I do. You've been fantastic. There's no way I could ever repay you, but I want to try." Julian tilted his head back and smiled. "For the first time in my life I feel like I'm really getting somewhere. You know, like there's hope."

He was quiet for a moment, then added, "All the time I was growing up, I kept trying to make Dad proud of me, but I never could. I wanted so much to do things right. I wanted . . ." Julian looked out the window. The sheer white curtains cast soft shadows across his face. He looked at Alan and said, "Doesn't it ever bother you? Doesn't it ever make you angry or sad or frightened that people hate you just for being who you are?"

Alan leaned against the mahogany desk and crossed his arms. "Of course it does. But I can't let the fear and misunderstanding of narrow-minded bigots determine who and what I am."

"It hurts," Julian said. "It hurts me to realize that everything I want, everything I *am* is wrong, suspect. *Criminal*, for God's sake. I'm a criminal just by being who I am."

Alan smiled sadly. "Two thousand years ago, you would have been a prize," he said. "A young man such as you—handsome, intelligent, of good family. Kings would have vied for the honor of your company."

"What happened?" Julian asked.

Alan shrugged. "It's our fate to be born into this crass and narrow time. That's why I moved to San Francisco. I can live better here than I ever could have in Brookline. You know," he smiled, "they say that San Francisco is a prostitute with a heart of gold. She's been so naughty herself that she's very slow to censure others. I think you'll find that here you can live your life the way you choose. But," his look was gentle, "that doesn't mean that your father will ever accept it."

"I wish you were my father," Julian said.

"Oh, Lord," Alan said with a laugh. "Please don't make this any more complicated than it already is."

Very suddenly, Julian stood up, took Alan in his arms and kissed him on the mouth. Then he looked up at the older man and said, "I'll never forget what you've done for me."

As Alan ran his fingers through Julian's flaxen hair, he replied, "I'm the one who's received so much."

"Have you?"

"These last twelve months have been the happiest I can remember," Alan said. "You've brought me to life again, Julian. Taken me out of the mausoleum that I'd built for myself and taught me to see the sunshine. And for that I'm very, very grateful."

## Stockton, California
## November, 1962

Ben Ashida, Tommy's cousin, sank into a wicker porch chair and patted his stomach. "Boy, I'm stuffed," he said. "Thanksgiving's my favorite holiday."

"Mine too," agreed Tommy. From inside the house he could hear his cousins giggling and shouting as Uncle Fred amused them with his magic tricks. David, Willie, and Francis were still at the dining table discussing farm price-supports. Connie, Pearl, and the older girls were busy clearing away the remains of the Thanksgiving feast.

"So how's school going, cousin?" Tommy asked, settling himself in the porch swing.

"Pretty good," said Ben. "I got three A's this semester. All I gotta do is write a paper for my history class, and I've got it made."

"Decided about college yet?"

"I'm gonna apply at San Jose and San Francisco State. Mom wants me to go to UOP like Freddie, so I can live at home, but," Ben grinned and drummed on the arm of the chair, "I'm ready to get out of Stockton."

Tommy laughed. "You mean you don't want to be a farmer?"

"Shit no. I've spent all the time I want to picking tomatoes and pulling weeds. I got other plans."

"Like what?"

"I want to be a journalist. News coverage, stuff like that. I like being where the action is."

"Sounds good."

"Hey." Ben leaned forward, "Mom said you almost got drafted after that missile crisis thing last month. What happened?"

"I got called up for a physical." Tommy paused and then said, "See, a few years ago I registered as a C.O., and apparently the draft board didn't like that. They've been making life rough for me ever since."

"So what's your classification?"

"They finally gave me a student deferment. That's what I should have settled for all along."

"I hope I can get a 2-S," Ben mused.

"Shouldn't be a problem. It seems like they're mostly taking older guys who aren't in school."

"Freddie had to go in for a physical last year, but he got a 4-F because of his asthma. You know, I think he was disappointed. I think he actually wanted to go."

"A lot of the guys at school are talking about joining up," Tommy said. "Especially since the missile crisis."

"Mom was really upset. So was Connie."

"Was she? She didn't say anything to me, but of course she's like that."

"She and Mom talked about it quite a bit. Of course, Pop and

Uncle David were all gung-ho," Ben sighed. "Ready to go out and give the Commies hell. To hear them you'd have thought the Reds had taken San Francisco and were marching on Denver."

"Out to prove they're good Americans, I guess. It was rough back in the forties being treated like spies just because we were Japanese."

Ben looked thoughtful. "You were in one of those camps, weren't you?"

Tommy's face darkened. "I was born in one. Tule Lake."

"Remember anything about it?"

"Not much. I was only three when we were released. I've tried to talk to Dad about it, but he just gets mad."

"Francis is like that," Ben nodded. "He was ten when the family went to Manzanar. And Mary was eight. She told me that before they went, Francis got beat up really bad by a bunch of the neighborhood kids, and then some kind of vigilante group came around one night and busted up the store. Broke all the windows and tried to set fire to the place. Scared the hell out of everybody. I guess that's when your folks took off for Sacramento and ended up at Tule Lake instead of Manzanar."

"I read some clips from an old newspaper. It seems that Tule Lake was the worst of the bunch."

"How come?"

Tommy frowned. "They put the trouble-makers there, the ones who refused to sign a loyalty oath. They wouldn't swear total allegiance to the U.S. 'cause they were scared they'd be deported to Japan and left without any country. They called them the no-noes because they didn't want to join up to fight the Japanese army."

"Jeeze." Ben shook his head. "Talk about a double-bind."

"Right. I guess that's why I should have known better than to file as a C.O. It was stupid."

"Any time I try to ask my dad, he won't tell me anything. It's like they're embarrassed or something."

Tommy snorted. "It's the government that should be embarrassed. Liberty and justice for all, like hell."

Ben chewed at his thumbnail. "Tommy, if you do get drafted, will you go?"

Tommy thought for a moment. "I don't know."

"Do you think you could kill somebody? I mean, just blow them away because they were supposed to be the enemy?"

"Maybe, if I thought they really *were* the enemy." He hunched forward and pressed his fingertips together. "But I don't see the Indochina thing that way. I don't think we have any business being there. I might . . . go to Canada."

Ben nodded slowly. "That's sorta the way I feel. But I'd like to know what's really going on. That's why I want to go into journalism."

They both fell silent. From somewhere a radio played softly. "Puff the Magic Dragon, lived by the sea . . ." "Hey," Ben said after a minute, "you ever hear from your girlfriend? That redheaded politician's daughter—what was her name?"

"Kate." After a minute he added, "She's getting married next month."

"No shit? Who's she marrying?"

"Some big-shot symphony conductor. It was in the San Francisco paper."

"Sorry."

"Well, that's the way it goes."

"I saw her dad was re-elected to the State Assembly." Ben eyed Tommy uneasily and searched for something to say, but came up blank. Finally, he got to his feet. "Want to catch the last of the Lions' game?"

"No. That's okay."

Ben stood there awkwardly for a moment, then retreated into the house. Tommy stared at the pyracantha bushes. They looked so festive, covered with clumps of scarlet berries. Could it have been almost eight months since Kate's letter? The anguish seemed so fresh. It had the sharpness of a recent wound. "It's going to be this way forever," he told himself with a twinge of panic. "Get used to it."

---

∘∘◦❉◦∘∘

## Eugene, Oregon

"Kyoto?" Tommy stared at Professor Winston in surprise. "Sounds terrific, but I couldn't afford it."

"Don't be so sure. There are scholarships available, and you have the grades. At least think about it. The application deadline isn't until February."

"Thanks, Dr. Winston. I will."

As Tommy walked across campus toward the bookstore, a small bud of hope uncurled itself in his heart. What if there was some reason for the collapse of his dreams? Some larger picture that he hadn't been able to see? When one door closes, another opens, his mother had often said. Could Dr. Winston have given Tommy a key? The more he pondered the idea, the more excited he became. He made a U-turn and headed for the International Studies Office.

"Do you have a brochure on UO's international summer program in Japan?" he asked the receptionist.

Taking the brochure she handed him to one of the study tables, he opened it and read:

> The Kyoto five-week summer program in architecture and landscape architecture employs a unique experiential process that involves learning in the landscape of Kyoto and its surrounding areas. Students visit numerous places that enrich and enlighten the classroom experience and empower students to pursue their intellectual interests on a daily basis. Located on the central part of the main island of Honshu, Kyoto, once the capital of Japan and home to the Japanese Emperor and Imperial Court for about 1,100 years, is renowned as the repository of the traditional arts, culture, world-famous temples and gardens and traditional works of art.

Fascinated, he devoured the brochure. The next day, he visited professor Winston and picked up an application.

# CHAPTER

# 50

## Mockingbird Valley Ranch
## December 1962

"I've never seen the ranch look more beautiful," Marian exclaimed as the car started up the long, winding drive between the rows of pear trees. The orchards were lush from the winter rains, vetch already spreading swaths of violet down the slopes, wild mustard rampant between the grapevines.

"Wait until you see the yard, Mrs. McPhalan," Jamie said. "We've worked for days to make it pretty for the wedding."

Marian smiled. Mrs. McPhalan. She had almost forgotten that such a person had ever existed.

"Look, Mummy," cried Alex as they neared the courtyard gate, "there's Kate"

"Remember," Marian whispered, "not a word about Carl. You promised."

"I won't tell on you."

What a weekend this is going to be, thought Marian helplessly as she climbed out of the car.

"Mom," Kate cried, running to embrace her mother. "I'm so glad that you could come. And Alex, it's been forever. How beautiful you are. Lord, isn't it a gorgeous day? I just knew it would be perfect. Come on." She grabbed a suitcase from Jamie's hands and started toward the house. "I can't wait for you to meet Carl."

Marian followed Kate into the courtyard and stood looking around. The patio had been transformed into a garden. Baskets of fuchsias and geraniums hung from every rafter along the wide veranda, and enormous vases of gladiolus and pink and white carnations filled the air with a spicy fragrance.

"I told Jamie to put your bags in the guest room," Kate announced. "Everyone's out in back. Carl's parents just arrived. They'll be staying for the weekend, too. Is Aunt Gwen going to get here in time for the wedding tomorrow?"

"She's planning on it," Marian replied as she followed Kate through the house and out into the rose garden.

The grape arbor, empty of leaves, had been transformed into a floating island of white and yellow blossoms, as though spring had miraculously arrived in time for Christmas. Carl stood beneath the blossoming canopy, talking to Owen, Rose, and Jorge.

"Hello, Marian," Owen said, stepping forward to greet her. He kissed her dutifully on the cheek. "You're looking well."

"Thank you," she replied, feeling overwhelmed. "Ummm, congratulations on your re-election."

"Thank you. This is Jorge Morales and his wife, Rose," continued Owen. Marian smiled mechanically and shook extended hands. "And I'll let Kate introduce the bridegroom."

Marian looked directly at Carl for the first time. He hadn't changed as much as she'd expected. His hair was a trifle longer, his features more defined, his smile a bit more dazzling. She flinched when he touched her hand and wondered if her own smile looked as forced as it felt.

"I've heard so much about you," he said.

Marian muttered a reply and looked away.

"And this must be Alex," he continued.

Marian glanced uneasily at Alex. For an awful moment, she was certain that the girl planned to shatter the fragile structure of their deceit, but though her eyes narrowed with undisguised contempt, her mouth curved in a superior smile. "How nice to meet you, Carl," she said. "I'm delighted that my sister is marrying a musician. It should make for interesting family reunions."

Kate grasped Carl's arm in a proprietary gesture. "Not just a musician, but a wonderful conductor as well."

"Yes, I know," said Alex.

Carl gave her a peculiar stare, then turned to Marian and said, "Kate tells me that you're an artist, Marian. May I call you Marian?"

"Yes, of course," she said a little breathlessly.

"I'd love to hear about your work," he said.

The feeling of déjà vu was more than she could bear. "I'd be happy to tell you all about it sometime," she said, "but we just got off the plane and I'd like to freshen up a bit." She took hold of Alex's hand. "Will you excuse us?"

"I'll show you to your room," Kate said. "Isn't he incredible?" she bubbled, as they walked toward the house. "Aren't I the luckiest woman in all the world?"

The rehearsal dinner was served on the patio—grilled ranch squab and fresh tortillas, platters of avocados and spiced oranges, artichokes with lemon butter, plates of sliced tomatoes with fresh basil.

"Just look at this food." Marian exclaimed. She had recovered from her case of nerves and was determined to make it through the weekend.

"And you should see what Consuelo and her friends have in store for us tomorrow," Kate said.

"Since this was to be a small family wedding," Marian laughed, "don't you think you should have had a small family feast?"

"Feasts must be outrageously munificent," Kate declared.

"We agreed to pull out all the stops," Owen added. "Don't know how long it'll be until I have another daughter getting married." Laughing, he winked at Alex.

"Don't hold your breath," said Alex. "I have my career to consider. That comes first."

"Sounds just like your mother," Owen noted, avoiding Marian's look.

After dinner, the party drifted into the house as the sun's warmth faded and the air cooled rapidly. Marian stayed behind, settling herself on the edge of the fountain, watching the water splash against the moss-covered stones. It had been right to come, she decided. Her absence would have been harder to explain than her obvious nervousness. The irony of the situation made her smile.

"Marian?"

She looked up into Carl's coffee-colored eyes. For a moment her heart lurched. Then she felt a sense of calm, a genuine fondness without a trace of guilt. "Hello, Carl," she said.

"Mind if I join you?"

She patted the stone bench beside her. "Not at all."

He was silent for several moments, then turned and said, "It really is good to see you. I hope you feel the same."

"I wasn't sure at first," she admitted. "It was very strange after all this time."

He laughed uneasily. "I kept hoping I wouldn't do or say the wrong thing. Alex really had me unnerved there for a minute."

"I'd feel better without the subterfuge," Marian said with a sigh, "but it *is* good to see you again."

"I've missed you," he said. "I think that more than anything I've missed our conversations. I always loved talking with you."

"Well," said Marian, "I think that's a pretty good basis for a friendship."

"I'd like for us to be friends."

"That's fine with me." They smiled at each other in the fading light.

"I think this is going to work out after all," said Carl.

"Hey, you two," Kate called from the doorway. "Come on in. It's getting cold out there. We've built a big fire and talked Alex into playing some Christmas carols."

Carl got up and held out his hand. "Madame?"

"Just one thing," she said as they started toward the house.

"What?"

"Whatever you do, don't start calling me Mom."

They were both laughing as they walked through the doorway into the living room.

Julian sat for a long time looking up the driveway toward the adobe house that once had been his home. He studied the weathered wooden sign that marked the boundary of his father's domain. *Mockingbird Valley Ranch.* He remembered the summer that David Ashida had carved that sign and the ceremony with which it had been planted at the entrance to the property. Memories piled up like thunderheads. He gunned his new BMW R69S motorcycle, an early Christmas present from Alan, to banish the memories before they could overwhelm him.

"Could I see your invitation, sir?" Consuelo asked him at the gate.

"I'm Julian," he told the woman. "Kate's brother."

"Oh, excuse me, sir. Please come in. The guests are in the rose garden."

"Is my mother here?" he asked.

"She got in yesterday. I believe she's in the guest suite. Shall I tell her that you're here?"

"I'll tell her myself." His throat was dry. The house smelled of orange peel and candle wax, just as he remembered it. In the hallway the light was very dim. He hesitated, then knocked lightly on the door. It opened almost at once.

"Hello, Mother," he said. "Merry Christmas."

Her eyes flooded with tears as she embraced him. He clung to her, fighting the impulse to dissolve into tears himself.

"I'm sorry," she said, stepping back and holding him by the shoulders. "It's been a rather emotional day."

"Mothers are supposed to cry at weddings," he told her huskily.

"How well you look, Julian. It's so good to see you. Alex, look who's here."

Julian stared at his sister. "Alex?"

She wore a pale blue velvet gown trimmed with white lace. Her long blond hair was swept up on her head and tiny pearl earrings glistened in her ears.

"Julian," she cried as she ran to hug him, "Isn't this fun?"

Allison Morales skipped down the hall holding the long white dress above her skinny knees. "Katie, look at my dress," she cried as she burst into Kate's room and spun around several times. "Isn't it divine?"

"Just the thing," Kate exclaimed. "You'll be the prettiest flower girl in California."

"You're not dressed," Ali cried in alarm. "You're not going to marry my brother in a bathrobe, are you?"

"It's still an hour before the ceremony."

"Are you ready?" Alex rushed into the bedroom. "I guess not," she added, frowning.

"Why is everybody so hysterical?" Kate said in dismay. "I've been dressing myself for twenty years. Certainly I can manage today."

"Let me see your shoes," Alex said. "Mama said you had them dyed to match your dress."

"How's the bride doing?" Gwen's beaming face appeared at the door.

Kate rushed to embrace her. "Oh, Aunt Gwen, I'm so glad you got here."

"I spent thirty minutes on a damned runway at O'Hare waiting for the snow plows, so I missed my connection in San Francisco. But here I am." She stepped back and surveyed her grandniece. "You are so lovely, darling. I wish you every happiness."

The three generations of women assisted the bride, fastening and fussing and adjusting the satin and lace. "The veil was Great-grandmother Maude's," Kate said.

"Beautiful," Gwen sighed. "Where are you spending your honeymoon?"

Kate laughed and Alex rolled her eyes.

"No honeymoon for me," Kate said. "Carl has a major concert coming up in two weeks, and he's very deep in rehearsal." When Gwen tutted and shook her head, Kate grinned. "Besides, we'll be living in San Francisco. What could possibly be better than that?"

Carl and Kate had written most of the short ceremony that united them as husband and wife. Drawn largely from the writings of Lao Tzu and Saint Francis, the service was performed by a local minister in the courtyard next to the fountain. The entwined branches of the oak and fig provided the illusion of a domed cathedral.

Everyone remembered their lines. Ali tossed out her bucket of rose petals with enthusiasm. Gwen and Consuelo cried while Rose and Marian stood dry-eyed and beaming. Julian did his best to remain invisible. The best-man, Silvio, and maid of honor, Christy, looked on with approval, and four members of the San Francisco Chamber Orchestra played splendidly.

After the ceremony the wedding party trailed across the lawn and clustered around the arbor where the tiered cake stood in splendid isolation on its snowy damask cloth. Piles of presents teetered amid the flowers. Pastel ribbons shivered in the afternoon air. Champagne flowed, glasses tinkled, the cake was cut, strains of Mozart blended with the laughs and cries as the gifts were revealed from the depths of their pink and silver wrappings.

"I'm going to go change now," Kate told her father. "Carl and I want to get back to the City before dark."

Owen hugged her and kissed her on the cheek, his face flushed from the champagne. "I hope you're happy, baby," he said expansively. "I hope it's everything you wanted it to be."

He watched his daughter sweep off toward the house, dragging the lacy train behind her with superb nonchalance.

"We're almost out of champagne," Jamie informed him. "Should I get some more from the kitchen?"

"I'll get it," Owen said. "You make sure everybody's got enough cake." The kitchen was dim, and Owen didn't notice the young man who waited in the shadows.

"Dad?"

Owen turned from the refrigerator. When he saw his son, his face darkened. "What do you want?"

"I thought we ought to talk," ventured Julian.

"What about?"

"Dad, it's been three years since I left home. I thought maybe—"

"Look, Julian," Owen said, "your sister invited you here. I really could care less."

"I don't know what Kate's told you, but—"

Owen brought his fist down on the counter. "She's told me enough." The look on his face made Julian step backward. "Oh yes," Owen said, his voice beginning to shake, "I know what you've become."

"I've had problems, Dad. But that's all past. I've started a new life—"

"I guess you're living pretty well these days as some rich fag's whore."

Suitcase in hand, Kate heard the angry voices and paused outside the kitchen door. "I can't be more than I am," she heard Julian say. "But that's never been good enough for you, has it?"

"You disgust me, Julian," Owen growled.

"No matter what I've done, I've never measured up. Do you know how hard I've tried to please you?"

"You're a dirty, goddamned fag."

Julian gave a strangled laugh. "You never tried to understand. I didn't ask you to love me. Acceptance. That's all I ever wanted. Okay, I'm a dirty, goddamned fag, but I'm still your son. Doesn't that mean *anything* to you?"

Kate opened the door just in time to see Owen's fist connect with Julian's jaw. "Daddy," she cried. "Don't!"

Julian crumpled against the wall, pressing his hand to his chin. Blood seeped through his fingers and spattered the tile floor. Kate tried to run to him, but Owen grabbed her arm, his fingers like a vise around her wrist. "Get out," he hissed at Julian. "Get out and never come back."

"Julian!" Kate shouted as her brother stumbled toward the door.

Julian steadied himself against the doorframe and looked back. "It's all right, Roo" he heard himself say calmly. "It's his house. I'll see you back in the City."

Eyes, were they his, looked at the tall figure next to the counter. "Goodbye, Father," he said.

Then he was outside. His legs were walking across the courtyard, hands opening the gate. Stars, like huge accusing eyes, stared down at him. He kicked the motorcycle into life. His legs were weak and he wanted to lie down, but some unknown force was holding him, moving his arms and legs, pushing against his back.

A man with a long beard was standing in front of him, holding a paper, reading aloud in a sonorous sing-song voice: "I saw the best minds of my generation destroyed by madness, starving hysterical naked, dragging themselves through the negro streets at dawn looking for an angry fix—" Julian smiled grimly. He knew where he was going. He gunned the cycle and skidded down the drive.

# 51

## Mockingbird Valley Ranch

"How could you?" Kate wailed.

Owen sat down heavily on the stool next to the counter. He spread his hands and stared at them. "I didn't mean to hit him. I got so angry." He looked at Kate. "I'm sorry, sugar."

Kate glared at him through her tears. "You don't know what you've done."

"There you are," Marian came through the doorway, "Aren't you about ready to—" She stopped and glanced from face to face. "What happened?"

Kate spun around to face her mother. "Ask him."

"I got into a little argument with Julian," Owen muttered.

"Little argument?" Kate cried. "You beat him up, that's what you did."

"What?" Marian gasped.

Owen held up his hands. "That's not true. He'll be okay."

"He won't be okay." Kate started for the door. "I've got to go after him."

"You can't go running off," Marian cried. "It's your wedding night. What about Carl?"

"He'll come with me. We've got to go back to the City anyway."

"Darling, listen to me," Marian said. "I'll go and look for Julian. You can't spend your wedding night running around the—"

"I'm the only one who knows where to look for him!"

Owen got to his feet. "Maybe I should go with you."

"Forget it," Kate said, giving him a scathing look. "You'd only make things worse."

"Kate? Ready to leave?" Carl's smiling face appeared at the door. Kate rushed to him, and Carl gathered her in his arms. "What's the matter, luv?"

"Daddy and Julian. He—they—Oh, Carl, I should never have invited him to come."

Carl looked past her and met Marian's eyes. "What's going on?"

"Owen lost his temper and took a swing at Julian," Marian explained.

"We've got to find him!" Kate sobbed.

"All right," Carl said soothingly. "Now dry your eyes. Let's just go on as if nothing's wrong, okay?" He kissed her forehead. "Get your things. I'll help you."

"I'm sorry, Carl," Owen said stiffly as Marian ushered Kate toward the bathroom. "I didn't mean to mess things up."

"I know you didn't, sir."

"Look," Owen said, "I don't know what Kate told you about her brother—"

"I know about Julian."

"Well, hell, then you can understand why I'm so damned upset."

Carl rested his hand on Owen's shoulder. "I'll do whatever I can to help."

"Thank you, son. I appreciate that." Owen managed a wry smile. "Will you do me a favor?"

"Of course,"

"When you find Julian, will you give me a call?"

"Sure."

Owen held out his hand. "Carl, I'm not much good at telling people how I feel, but I'm damned glad to have you in the family."

"Thank you," Carl said giving Owen's outstretched hand a firm shake, "I'll take good care of Kate."

"I know you will, son."

---

"I look awful." Kate wailed, staring into the mirror.

"No, you don't." Marian adjusted the collar of Kate's pink wool suit.

"My eyes are bright red."

"Well," said Marian, a lump rising in her throat, "Everyone cries at weddings."

Kate turned to hug her. "Oh, Mom, how did this happen?"

Kate and Carl dashed across the courtyard through a hail of rice. At the gate, Marian grasped Carl's arm. "Thank you," she whispered.

He bent and kissed her cheek. "Everything's under control." He gazed at her for a moment. "Goodbye, Marian."

## San Francisco, California

The fog had arrived at sunset, obliterating the hills, turning the buildings to ghosts. Kate drove slowly through the darkened streets. "I don't know where to look," she said, stopping the car in front of a Chinese cafe. The blue neon sign blinked on and off, advertising chop suey and egg rolls. "I was hoping he'd be at Alan's, but Wilkes said he hadn't seen him."

"Where's Alan?" asked Carl.

"Paris. Giving a paper at a conference."

"Where else could Julian have gone?"

Kate thought for a minute and said, "I have a very sick feeling I know exactly where he went."

"Where?"

"His old buddy Larry Flagstaad."

Carl grimaced. "Do you know where this Flagstaad character lives?"

"No idea."

"Maybe if we drive around we'll spot Julian's bike."

"I don't know what else we can do."

They drove in circles through the narrow streets—up to Coit Tower, back down to Columbus Avenue. Perplexed, Kate parked the car across from Washington Square. A little Christmas tree squatted in the center of the park. Someone was playing "God Rest Ye Merry Gentlemen" on a guitar while discordant voices sang a dubious accompaniment.

Suddenly she saw him. He was sitting on the steps of the church, half-submerged in shadows. "There he is!" She jumped from the car.

"Do you want me to come with you?"

"No. Wait here." She raced across the park. "Julian?"

He looked up. "Well, hello, Roo," he said lazily. "Merry Christmas."

She stared at him. "You didn't, did you?"

"Didn't what?"

"Get high. Shoot up."

"What if I did?" he replied. "It's Christmas, isn't it? Everyone deserves a little holiday cheer." He patted the stone step. "Sit down. Might as well enjoy the evening, what's left of it."

"You idiot," she groaned, sinking down beside him.

"Now is that any way to talk on Christmas?" he scolded. "You should be nice to your big brother. Hell, somebody should be." He let his head flop back against the pillar. "Oh Christ," he mumbled. "What are you doing here? It's your wedding night."

She jumped to her feet. "Get up."

"Why?"

"I'm taking you home with me. I'm going to stay with you every minute until Alan gets back from Europe. You're not going to do this, Julian."

"Oh, really?"

"Really."

Again that strange, tired laugh. "You're crazy, Roo. You know that? Carl would be just delighted if you dragged me home with you tonight."

"We'll work it out."

He let out his breath in a long, slow sigh. "I'll be all right."

"I can't leave you alone. You'll mess everything up."

"That's for me to decide, isn't it?"

"No."

He studied her tiredly, then lowered his eyes. "Yes, it is."

"Julian, listen to me—"

"It's okay." He waved his hand dismissively. "I just needed a little something to get me through the evening."

"And what about tomorrow, Julian?"

"Tomorrow?" His gaze was vacant. "What do I care about tomorrow?"

"Please come with me."

"Nope, I'm celebrating. I'll celebrate in my own small way, if you don't mind. And you, dear sister, go back to your husband and celebrate your own good fortune." He propped himself up on his elbows and blinked at her. "See? I'm up. Very up." He giggled.

"I can't leave you like this."

"Sure, you can. Just walk away."

"Let me take you home with me," she pleaded. "You can leave first thing in the morning if you want to, but please don't stay out here all night."

"Don't be silly. I'll go on back to Alan's in a little while. I have my key." He patted his pocket proudly. "See? I'll be fine."

"You'll be all alone. You'll get depressed. You'll—"

"No, no. I'm fine. This is just a momentary lapse. Just a one-night stand, so to speak." He giggled again. His eyes were glassy in the reflected light. "You believe me, don't you?"

"I want to believe you."

"Well," his head fell back on the step, "that'll do." With great concentration he hauled himself upright. "Go on now. Go home to your husband. I've got enough problems without getting blamed for more."

"I'm not blaming you."

"Good. Now go home."

She took his hand. It was ice-cold. "You're sure you'll go to Alan's?"

"I promise. Go on. Don't worry about me."

"I always worry about you, Julian," she muttered, "for all the good it does."

## Sacramento, California

"I wish you'd let my office arrange for your flight back to Boston," Owen was saying. "This airport stinks."

"I didn't come out here to accept charity from you," Marian said primly. "I managed to get here on my own. I'll manage to get home."

"You're a damned stubborn woman, Marian," Owen told her.

"So you always said."

In the harsh glare of the coffee shop's fluorescent light, he studied her unhappily. "Are you sure you have enough for Alex's schooling?"

"We're doing just fine. But we do need to discuss her college plans."

"Where does she want to go?"

Marian sighed. "She's determined to go to the Cleveland Institute of Music."

"Cleveland? What the hell for? I figured she'd stay in Boston or maybe go to New York. Why Cleveland?"

"She's utterly infatuated with a pianist named Stefan Molnar. He teaches at the Cleveland Institute, and she won't consider studying with anyone else."

Owen frowned. "Is this guy any good?"

"One of the best. I can't fault her judgment. It's just that I'm concerned about her attitude. I'd hate for her to get in over her head."

"Well," Owen noted, "maybe she'll change her mind."

"Maybe."

They were silent for a moment. Engines droned in the distance. "That must be my flight," Marian said. "I'd better go find Alex."

"Wait a minute."

"What is it?"

Owen cleared his throat. "I've been thinking about Julian."

"Oh?" She appraised him with narrowed eyes.

"I guess I've been sort of unfair."

"That's an understatement."

He gave her a somber look. "Doesn't it bother you?"

"It only bothers me because I know there are people like you who refuse to accept it."

"You make it sound like it's no big deal."

"And you're making far too much out of something that's really none of your business."

"It is *too* my business. First of all, it's unnatural. Perverted. Secondly, Julian could get into all kinds of trouble running around with people like that."

"That didn't seem to bother you when you kicked him out of the house."

"I didn't kick him out. He decided to leave."

"All right," she sighed. "I'm not going to argue with you."

"And thirdly, it's my business because it's a potential embarrassment. A man in my position, in the public eye—"

"Oh, so that's it," Marian snapped. "You're afraid Julian might hurt you politically? Well, Mr. Assemblyman, that's really inconvenient, isn't it?"

He squirmed beneath her look. "Be reasonable, Marian. Danny thinks I should take a crack at a Senate seat in '64. It'll be an uphill battle, and I sure as hell don't need any scandals. Bad enough that I—" He stopped.

"That you're divorced?"

"Doesn't exactly help my political chances."

Marian folded her arms. "Looks as though Julian and I have caused you a lot of trouble."

"I didn't mean that."

"Just what did you mean?"

He had seen a storm rise in her eyes before. "Forget it. That wasn't what I wanted to talk about."

"What then?"

He drew in his breath. "I've been thinking I really have been . . .

unfair to Julian. Whatever sort of . . . proclivities he has, I went too far the other night. I want to apologize to him. Katie's furious with me, and I hate that. I thought if I wrote to Julian, told him I was sorry . . ." He glanced at Marian. "What do you think? Sound like a stupid idea to you?"

Marian studied him for a moment, then reached out and gently patted his hand. "Owen," she said, "I think that's one of the best ideas you've had in a long time."

# CHAPTER

# 52

## San Francisco, California
## December 1962

On a foggy late-December evening ten days after the wedding, Kate was curled up in bed reading George Sand's *Winter in Majorca* when she heard a knock on the door. The apartment was dark, and beyond the window the lights of the city were barely visible in the fog. She flipped on the porch light and peered out.

"Julian," she cried. "What a surprise." When he came in, she saw his face and added, "Jeeze, Pooh. You look terrible."

He closed the door behind him. "Anybody else here?"

"Carl's at rehearsal. What's the matter?" She started to turn on the light, but he grabbed her hand.

"No. No lights."

"What's going on?"

"Could I have a drink?"

She closed her eyes tight, then opened them. "You're strung out again, aren't you? Damn it, Julian."

"Please," he said. "Could you get me a drink?"

"All right." She brought a snifter of brandy. He took it in a single gulp.

"What's wrong?" she repeated.

He sank down on the sofa. "I need some money."

"What for?"

"I can't tell you."

"Tell me."

"I've got to leave town for a few days. I'll pay you back as soon as I can."

She switched on the small lamp beside the sofa. He flinched and looked away. "What do you want money for?"

"I can't tell you."

"Then I can't help."

He turned back with a look of desperation. "Don't say that, Kate. I haven't got anybody else I can go to."

"Look, Julian," she said, "I've always helped you any way I could. But I'm not going to give you money for drugs."

"It's not for drugs!"

"Then what?"

He lowered his head. She could see the muscles in his jaw working. "I've got to leave town. I just need a hundred bucks." He looked up at her. "Seventy-five. Anything."

"Not unless you tell me what's going on."

He lowered his head once more. "I'm in real trouble."

"What kind?"

"We got into this stupid argument . . ."

"Who?" For one wild moment she thought he meant Owen.

"Alan. I didn't think he'd be back from Europe until Thursday, but he came home today and—" His hands were shaking visibly. "He found out."

"About the drugs?"

He nodded.

"Did he kick you out?"

"No. Oh God, if only . . ." His eyes were stricken. "He found a stash I'd hidden in a drawer. He was furious, and he started down the stairs yelling at me and then he slipped and fell and . . ." The words strangled in his throat.

The image blazed before him—the crumpled figure at the base of the stairs. He remembered asking Alan if he was all right. Did he want a doctor? Alan's eyes were open and dazed, blood trickling slowly from his mouth. There was a lot of blood.

Then Julian was leaning over the body, searching frantically for a heartbeat, crying to Alan to please be all right, please. And Alan's eyes, vacant and staring.

"He's dead," Julian said to Kate.

"Did you call a doctor? Did you take him to the hospital?"

"Jesus," he cried, "you're not listening to me. I told you, he's dead!" He hunched forward, hugging himself, rocking back and forth. "What am I going to do?"

"When did this happen?"

"Earlier this evening. Right after he got home."

"And you didn't call an ambulance or anything?"

"He was already dead. There was no heartbeat. No pulse."

"I can't believe you didn't call an ambulance."

"I had to get away. Don't you understand? They'll think I did it."

"What do you mean?"

"The police."

"Why?"

"They'd ask me questions. There'd be an investigation."

"You can't run away. Everybody knew you lived with Alan. If you take off the police *will* think you did it."

"They'll think so anyway."

"But it was an accident."

"Yes, but—"

"You'll have a chance to prove it."

"Will you think about what you're saying?" he shouted. "I'm a fag and a junkie. You think they'd listen to me?"

"But you can't run away." Kate cried. "Where would you go?"

"Somewhere. Anywhere."

"But if you get caught, you—"

"I'll never get caught. I'll kill myself first."

Kate's hand covered her mouth. "Oh God, Julian, listen to me. Was anybody else at home? Did anyone see you?"

"No. Nobody was there."

"Please let me call our attorney," she begged. "He can help you—"

"No!" Julian scrambled to his feet. "They'll send me to jail. Do you know what they'd do to me in jail? Do you have any idea?"

"They wouldn't put you in jail. You haven't done anything."

"How do you know they wouldn't?" he shouted. "How can you be sure?"

She searched for an answer and found none. "Let me call our attorney."

"I won't go to prison. Not ever." He ran to the door.

"Julian," Kate cried, "Where are you going?"

"I've got to get away!" He wrenched the door open, tearing the chain from the wall. Kate plunged after him and grabbed his arm, but he flung her aside.

"Julian!" she screamed after him.

"I'll be right home," Carl said. "Stay put until I get there . . . No, I'll get a cab. Just stay there."

When he strode onto the stage, the members of the orchestra turned to look at him. "I'm afraid we're going to have to cut this rehearsal short," he told them. "There's been a family emergency."

Kate met him at the door. "Any word?" he asked.

She shook her head. "I'm scared, Carl. I don't know what to do."

Carl took off his coat. "I think we'd better stay right here. He'll come back when he's cooled down."

"Should we call the police?"

"No." He checked his watch. "Damn. It's too late to call Doug this evening. First thing tomorrow, we'll get some legal advice." Carl took Kate's hand and led her to the sofa. "Try to relax. I'll get you some tea."

"He was terrified. I've never seen him like that."

"He's got a hell of a problem."

"Do you think the police would actually charge him with something?"

"I don't know, Kate. If they found evidence of drugs—"

"Oh, God. I hadn't thought of that." She buried her face in her hands. "Poor Pooh," she said, her voice trembling, "Why does everything turn out so badly for you?"

Carl put his arm around her. "Julian's been in scrapes before and always managed to land on his feet. We'll get Doug working on it first thing tomorrow."

They were still sitting on the sofa an hour later when the doorbell rang. "That's him," Carl exclaimed. But his hand froze on the doorknob when he saw two policemen waiting on the porch.

Kate jumped to her feet. "Who is it, Carl?"

"The police."

"Oh my God!

Carl opened the door.

"Mr. Fitzgerald?"

"Yes."

"I'm Lieutenant MacRay, San Francisco PD, and this is Sergeant Blake." He held up his identification. "Is your wife at home?"

"Why?"

"We need to talk to her about her brother."

# CHAPTER

# 53

### San Francisco, California

Outside the morgue the mist was thick as cream, and a small blue light cast an eerie haze over the alley. "If you'll follow me please, Mrs. Fitzgerald," the officer said.

The scent of formaldehyde made her gag. "We need a positive ID," the policeman said. "We just need to know if he's your brother. Then you can leave." He lifted the corner of the sheet.

Julian's face was the color of pale blue porcelain. Against the wax-like skin, his hair looked like silver straw.

"Mrs. Fitzgerald," the policeman said, "is this your brother?"

Kate's eyes didn't move from the unearthly face. This is it, she thought. This is what it all comes down to. "Yes," she managed to say.

"Would you like to sit down?" the policeman said. "Could I get you a drink of water?" He tried to take her arm.

She pulled away. The dryness in her throat would hardly let the words pass. "How did it happen?"

"One of our patrolmen spotted him trying to break into a car down on the Embarcadero. They ordered him to stop, but he ran and they went after him. He pulled something out from under his coat. The patrolman thought it was a gun and fired a warning shot. The bullet ricocheted and struck him in the chest. We're certain it was an accident, but there'll be an investigation. I can promise you that."

"He didn't have a gun," Kate said. "I know he didn't have a gun."

"No. He'd taken out his wallet. God knows why. Maybe to get rid of his identification. I don't know."

She nodded. After a minute, she said, "Could I be alone with him please?"

She didn't hear an answer but she heard the door open and close. Gently, she pushed the sheet down to his waist. His shoulders and chest were smooth as a child's. The wound was not large—a small dark crater ringed with a purple bruise. She pulled the sheet up and smoothed it as though she was putting him to bed. "Where are you, Pooh?" she whispered. "Where have you gone?"

The body on the table seemed like a plastic replica. "Julian?" she said. "Why don't you answer me? Julian? Julian!" Her own scream seemed to come from miles away.

Arms grasped her and pulled her toward the door. She struggled wildly, hearing her own voice shouting, "Let me go! Julian, where are you?"

Then she was in the dim-lit corridor and Carl was holding her and the tears finally came like a great tide, bursting over her, sweeping her away.

---

## Fair Oaks, California

The phone was ringing and ringing. Why didn't someone answer it? With an incoherent groan, Dan Papadakis, Owen McPhalan's attorney and campaign manager, clawed through the bedclothes and grabbed the phone. "Yeah?"

"Danny," Owen's voice was thin and brittle. "We need to talk."

Dan sat up and looked at the clock. "Jesus, Owen, it's three a.m. Can't it wait 'til morning?"

"No, it can't."

Dan blinked and rubbed his forehead. "Okay, Mac, what is it?" As Owen explained about the accident at Alan Townsend's mansion and its aftermath, Dan felt suspended. Was he dreaming? Desperately, he tried to piece together a plan. It would take all his skill to avert the disaster of a political scandal. He'd have to pull a lot of strings.

"So that's the story," Owen finished. "I thought you ought to know. I wasn't . . . sure what I should do."

Dan clutched the phone, thinking hard.

"Danny?"

"I'm here. Just stunned, that's all. Give me a minute." After a long pause, he inhaled and said, "All right. I'm heading right over to Mockingbird. Don't talk to anyone. We need to figure this out."

"What is it, Danny?" Helen mumbled sleepily. "What's wrong?"

"I need to talk to Owen about something. Go back to sleep. I won't be long."

She sat up and stared at him. "In the middle of the night?"

Dan pulled on his trousers and grabbed a coat from the hanger. "I said go to sleep, Helen. Don't worry about it."

Three hours later, he left Owen sitting in the ranch kitchen. At the door, he turned and looked at the figure slumped at the breakfast table. "We can work this out, partner," he said with as much conviction as he could summon. "Just remember, 'No comment' is the mantra. I'll take care of everything else. No leaks, understood?"

Owen nodded, sipped coffee, stared at the tabletop.

"Okay. I'll see you downtown around noon and we'll put out a statement. Just try to relax. And . . ." he hesitated for a moment, "I'm sorry about Julian."

Owen didn't reply.

---

## Mockingbird Valley Ranch
## January 1963

Owen got out of bed and stood for a long time looking out the window at the grey January dawn. Usually, he felt a little glow of satisfaction when he studied the familiar landscape of his ranch. But today, there was no glow. Not in the sky, which was slate grey. Not in the orchard, which was filled with rows of leafless trees deep in their winter hibernation. And certainly not in his heart. Today, he would bury his son.

He pulled a cigarette from the pack on the dresser, flicked his lighter, sucked in the smoke, then let it out in a long stream. His eyes burned from the smoke. Or from unshed tears.

He turned away from the window and went into the bathroom to take a piss and wash his face. Back in the bedroom, he dressed—-jeans, a flannel shirt, no need to dress up yet. The funeral wasn't scheduled until noon. He sat down to pull on his boots.

From downstairs, he could hear the soft murmur of voices and the dull banging of pots and pans. Consuelo would be fixing breakfast. God knows, there was a house full of company.

Marian and Alex had arrived the night before. Kate and Carl had driven up from the City in time for dinner. Everyone else would be coming around eleven—Christy Malacchi and her parents, Jorge and Rose with their children, Silvio and Allison, Dan and Helen. Connie Ashida had called and asked if it was all right for her to attend. She would bring Tommy if that was okay. David would not be joining them. Yes, of course, Owen had said. It was like the wedding party, only in reverse. Like a black and white photograph, or a negative. The happy gathering turned inside out. A grieving party.

Owen got heavily to his feet and made his way down the stairs. Might as well get the day underway.

Marian couldn't bring her self to get dressed and go downstairs. Not yet. She clutched her bathrobe around her and sat huddled miserably on the chair next to the bed. She hadn't slept well, and she felt numb and empty, her thoughts buzzing here and there like disoriented gnats.

She had just been here, in this very room, four weeks ago, so full of joy and gratitude that things had turned out so well for everyone. Julian and Kate had both found love, she and Carl had averted a potential disaster, even Alex seemed determined to behave.

And now this. How could everything have suddenly gone so wrong? What could she have done differently?

Alex came in with a cup of coffee in her hand. "Here," she said, thrusting it at Marian. "Everybody's downstairs. Maybe you should get dressed."

"I want to take a shower first," Marian said, taking the coffee mug.

"Well," Alex said as she headed for the door, "don't take too long. I'm hungry."

Marian took a gulp of coffee. "Tell them to go ahead without me," she called after her daughter. "I don't need any breakfast."

Owen, Carl, and Kate were gathered around the kitchen table reading *The Auburn Journal* newspaper. Carl watched his new wife as she read the obituary that appeared on page three. She was biting her lip and her eyes were misty, but she was holding up pretty well, he thought.

It had been a rough couple of weeks. Not exactly what he had envisioned for the beginning of their life together as husband and wife. Kate was totally engrossed with Julian's death—grieving, giving way to bouts of crying, then notifying people, making arrangements for the funeral. She hadn't even sent any thank you cards for the wedding gifts yet. Not that he blamed her. But he had to admit to feeling a little neglected.

He hadn't known Julian well, but he seemed bright and interesting. Carl knew too many artists and musicians to be concerned about sexual preferences. It was talent that mattered, not who you went to bed with.

Owen was unusually quiet—sipping his coffee and staring woodenly at the sports page, his mind obviously elsewhere. Joe, the ranch dog, lay at his feet. Usually, Joe stayed on his mat by the kitchen door, but with animal intuition he seemed to feel Owen's anguish and refused to leave his side.

Alex breezed down the stairs and pulled up a chair next to Kate. From across the table, she gave Carl a contemptuous look, then smiled to herself and looked away. Nasty little brat, he thought. At fifteen, she was provocatively attractive with long blond hair, luminous blue eyes, and a pouty, sensuous mouth. Why didn't she have pimples or something, he wondered. Did she have to look so perfect? He glared down at the entertainment section and tried unsuccessfully to ignore her.

Consuelo brought breakfast to the table—corn muffins and ham, a platter of oranges sprinkled with pomegranate seeds. Carl and Alex dug in while Kate and Owen picked at their food.

# CHAPTER

# 54

At eleven-thirty, the cars began pulling into the yard. Owen and Kate went out to greet the guests, and a sort of informal receiving line formed in the courtyard. It was still cold, but the rain had held off. Marian and Alex joined Kate and Owen while Carl stood back a little. It was not his brother, after all.

Soon the company had gathered, the hearse and the minister arrived—the same Episcopal priest who had presided over Carl and Kate's wedding—and the knot of mourners followed the hearse up the drive to the top of the bluff.

Julian would be buried in the family plot at the base of the bluff overlooking the river, but Kate had decided to have the service at the top. No one would want to scramble down the steep path that led to the flood plain.

There was a single, huge old oak tree at the summit and everyone came together under its sheltering branches. Owen, Carl, Silvio, and Dan took the casket from the back of the hearse and carried it to the little platform that Jaime and Owen had built beneath the oak tree. Bouquets of flowers—white roses and chrysanthemums, potted paper-whites, wreaths of eucalyptus—surrounded the platform.

As the minister began to read from the prayer book, Jorge Morales looked around the crowd. He knew most of the mourners—they had just been to Carl and Kate's wedding. He wondered, though, about the Japanese couple standing at the back of the group. The woman looked too old to be the boy's spouse—probably his mother, Jorge guessed. They both seemed a bit awkward and ill at ease. Jorge vaguely recalled that Owen had once employed a Japanese foreman at Mockingbird. Perhaps they were part of that family.

He glanced at Owen who was standing next to the casket like an honor guard—stoic and steely eyed. Silvio was standing next to him, and Jorge couldn't stop thinking, my God, what if it was Silvio? How could I bear it? Silvio, with his handsome face and his earnest, thoughtful expression. If I lost him . . . Jorge thought, but couldn't finish the sentence.

Instead, he looked at Carl, who was standing next to Kate. He had his arm around her shoulders and she was leaning against him. A little flicker of happiness lit up his thoughts. He's a good man, my Carlos. He will take care of her. I only wish that . . . Once again he stopped before completing the thought. Maybe someday . . .

Jorge looked once more at the casket. Well, at least, he thought, Julian's finally come home.

Tommy Ashida held his mother's hand as he watched the ceremony. He had insisted on coming to the funeral even though his family had been evicted from Mockingbird Ranch three years before. He asked David to come with them, but his father, still smarting from the humiliation of being forced to leave his position as foreman, gruffly refused to accompany his wife and son. So they had driven up from Stockton by themselves.

Tommy had taken a few extra days of vacation from his classes at the University of Oregon. He would leave right after the ceremony to go back to Eugene. Connie planned to drop him off at the Sacramento airport before she returned to Stockton.

When Connie had asked Tommy why he was so keen to go to Julian's funeral, he had told her, "He was always nice to me." And it was true. Julian and Tommy hadn't been especially close—Julian was such a loner and preferred to spend his time hiking along the river or riding his motorcycle. But he had been courteous to Tommy and his family. He had never called them "Japs" or made rude comments about them as some people did. And he had taught Tommy quite a bit about seahorses and angelfish and the other curious inhabitants of Julian's numerous aquariums. Julian was a nice guy, Tommy thought.

It was painful to see Kate and her new husband, Carl. Tommy was awed by Carl's good looks and his easy charm. No wonder she had chosen him over a poor Japanese college student. He'd never *really* been good enough for her. He should have known that from the start. But he had dreamed that he could overcome all of the problems, the obstacles. Didn't they say, "Love conquers all?" Well, apparently "they" were wrong.

Anyway, he had made a new plan. He would go to Japan. He would find his own destiny. He would discover his ancestral heritage. That very morning, before they left Stockton, Connie had handed him a little white silk bundle tied with a golden cord. "What's this?" he asked.

"It belonged to your grandfather, Frank Yoshinobu," Connie said. "He wanted you to have it someday. I think that that day has arrived."

He had untied the cord and opened the rectangle of silk. Emblazoned in the center was a beautiful Japanese design of three flower petals done in gold thread. He gazed at the design, then gave his mother a questioning look. She just smiled.

Now, he reached into his pocket and felt the little bundle. It was a key of some kind. And someday he would discover what it unlocked.

Kate had cried herself out. Somewhere about ten days after Julian's death, she had run out of tears. And so now, she stood listening quietly as the minister read the Service for the Dead.

She had collected some of Julian's favorite poems and psalms to supplement the service, beginning with the mysterious and unsettling twenty-second psalm: "My God, my God, why have you forsaken me?/Why are you so far from saving me, from the words of my groaning?/O my God, I cry by day, but you do not answer/And by night, but I find no rest."

She then added several verses from Baudelaire's *Les Fleurs du Mal*: "In vain I sought to trace and fit/Space in its mid and final stance,/I know not under what hot glance/My wings are crumbling bit by bit./The love of beauty sealed my doom./Charred, I have not been granted this:/To give my name to the abyss/That is to serve me as a tomb."

But she finished the service with the triumphant 121st Psalm: "I will lift up mine eyes unto the hills, from whence cometh my help. . . ."

Kate lifted her eyes to look at the granite summits of the Sierra, but they were hidden behind a veil of mist. Silent. Obscured. They offered no help. There were only the low grey clouds and the distant hiss of the river and the cold breeze sifting down from the snowfields.

The river was running high. She could feel its distant danger. The river in flood could happen all at once. You went to bed one night and the river's song was mellow and soft but come morning there was a new song in the air. A song with a violent pulse and a raging lyric. It called you to come and look and dared you to defy it. And you could see the current flowing like a great tide. You knew that there were boulders beneath the surface, and that if you fell into that opaque water you would surely die. For the river was dark, and wild, and howling like a beast. And you were afraid.

She shook her head to disperse the sudden terror. Four men from the funeral home were preparing to carry the casket to its final resting place in the family plot half-way down the bluff. The grave was already dug.

She shivered and Carl put a protective arm around her. She let him lead her back down the dirt road to the ranch house. Inside there would be a fire in the hearth, some food and wine, perhaps some happy stories to exchange. But her heart was heavy with loss.

Kate had asked Alex to play some of Julian's favorite pieces, ones that he had loved and played before the accident that left him unable to continue his music studies. So, as Marian sat gazing into the fire, the calmly poignant notes of Chopin's *Nocturne in B-flat minor* drifted from the Steinway. People gathered around to listen.

Owen came out of the kitchen with two glasses of wine and handed one to Marian. "You looked like you needed this," he said.

She glanced up at him. "Good guess," she said. The wine was white and cold. Maybe it would help dull the pain.

Owen sat down next to her. For awhile they were both silent, lost in their own thoughts, half-listening to the bittersweet sound of the Nocturnes. Then Marian stirred and said, "I was wondering if you ever sent that letter to Julian. You know, the one you were thinking about writing just before I left from Kate's wedding?"

Owen took a drink. "I sent it."

"Good."

He looked at her, then back at the fire. "I don't know how everything ended up like this."

"I know."

"Sometimes I wish we could just . . . start over."

"Do you think it would turn out differently?"

"I reckon not," he said. "We'd still all be the same people with the same flaws and the same problems. Maybe it was just . . . meant to be like this."

"Life teaches tough lessons," said Marian. "Especially to people as stubborn and selfish as we are."

Owen took another drink. "God," he said, "I wish I'd listened to him more. Not pushed him so hard. Tried to understand him."

"We both have our regrets," Marian said, "for all the good they do."

The crowd thinned as the afternoon wore on. Kate was talking to Jorge and Rose, trying to maintain a brave face, when she saw

Tommy and Connie standing beside the door, getting ready to leave. On a sudden impulse, she crossed the room and smiled at them. Connie smiled back and took her hand. "I'm so very sorry about your brother," she said softly.

"Thank you," Kate said. "It was good of you to come." She turned to Tommy. "You too. Thank you."

He nodded. She tried to read his expression, but it was as impenetrable as the shrouded mountains. For a moment their eyes met, then he turned and took his mother's arm and opened the door.

"Tommy?"

He stopped and turned toward her.

She didn't really know what to say, so she said, "Good luck."

He looked at her for a long moment, then he said, "*Sayonara*, Kate."

She didn't know that *sayonara* meant, "Goodbye, perhaps forever."

## End Book One

# PLAYLIST FOR AMERICAN RIVER: TRIBUTARIES

The following musical compositions are mentioned in this book:

Chapter 6
Mozart, Symphony #41 in C Major, K. 551, "Jupiter"
Bach, *Cantata,* No. 80
Beethoven, Symphony No. 9 in D Minor, Op. 125

Chapter 7
Paul Anka, "I'm Just a Lonely Boy"
Ricky Nelson, "It's Late"
Frankie Avalon, "Venus"

Chapter 9
Beethoven, Piano Sonata No. 4 in E Flat Major, Op.7
Liszt, Piano Sonata in B Minor, S.178

Chapter 10
Mozart, String Quartet in B Flat Major, "Hunt"
Mahler, Symphony No. 2 in C Minor,*Resurrection*

Chapter 16
Haydn, Symphony No. 104 in D Major, "London"

Chapter 18
Tchaikovsky, Violin Concerto in D Major, Op. 35
Mendelssohn, Violin Concerto in E Minor, Op. 64
Brahms, Violin Concerto in D Major, Op. 77
Vivaldi,*The Four Seasons*

Chapter 19
Johnny Mathis, "The Twelfth of Never"

Chapter 23
Rachmaninoff, Piano Concerto No. 2 in C Minor, Op. 18

Chapter 27
Elvis Presley, "It's Now or Never"

Chapter 29
Brahms, Symphony No. 2 in D Major, Op.73,
Liszt Piano Concerto No.1 in E Flat Major, S.124
Mussorgsky, *Pictures at an Exhibition*

Chapter 31
Strauss, Blue Danube Waltz, (Montovani version)
Stan Kenton, *Cuban Fire*

Chapter 33
Beethoven, Piano Concerto No. 1, Op. 15
Liszt, Rhapsody No. 2 in C Sharp Minor, S. 244
Bach, *The Italian Concerto*, BWV 971

Chapter 35
Mozart, *The Magic Flute*, K 620

Chapter 41
Mahler, Symphony No. 5

Chapter 43
Chopin, The Preludes

Chapter 44
Elvis Presley, "Don't be Cruel"

Chapter 48
Bartok, Piano Concerto No. 2
Stravinsky, *Symphony in Three Movements*

Chapter 49
Leonard Lipton and Peter Yarrow, "Puff, the Magic Dragon"

Chapter 54
Chopin, Nocturne in B Flat Minor, Op. 9, No. 1

CPSIA information can be obtained
at www.ICGtesting.com
Printed in the USA
FFOW03n1620080717
37536FF